H

"Brilliant characters...a stunning portrait of the terrorist mind...one frightening and believable tale...psychological depth that drives the genre to a new level."

-*Bookends*

"An international techno-thriller...a cast of intriguing characters, males *and* females... Non-stop action...the outcome a stunning turnaround. The stuff that blockbuster films are made of. Neary's first novel is a smash."

-*West Coast Lifestyle*

"Lifted from today's headlines...etched in splendid prose. Once the freight train begins to roll, you won't be able to put it down."

-*ebookadvisor*

Brian Neary

Hawk

bneary.com
Los Angeles
CA

ISBN 978-0-615-29194-9
WGAw 1337870

Manufactured in the United States of America

bneary.com
Los Angeles
CA

For Karen Angelina

Acknowledgments

Of the many thank-yous owed, these are but a few. To my first editor Michael LaRocca for your keen eye. To my anonymous friends at CIA for your advice, patience and input. To Robert Little for your Special Forces expertise. To Dr. Fred Magee, High Energy Laser Laboratory, Hughes Aircraft Co. and to R. Barry Johnson, Chairman of the Lens Design Group ISOE, thank you both for your brilliance and you patience. To Kenneth R. Timmerman and Vali Nasr for your penetrating work on the Middle East. To Richard Haass for your contributions on U.S. foreign policy. To Joshua Cooper Ramo for your stunning treatise on modern thought. And to Fareed Zakaria for your global perspective. To Jerry McBrearty, Tony Milch and Alice Jawetz for your vigor and guidance. To Neil Portnow, Ron Anton, Artie Mogul and Jeremy Railton for your support through the years. To Quincy Jones, Paul McCartney and Hank Waring for your encouragement. To John Belushi for his stubborn will and brief friendship. To Mike O'Neil for telling me to do this. To Dan Horgan for his sweet rememberings. And to my family for their years of unbelievable support.

Hawk

PROLOGUE

2004 – Minnesota, U.S.A.

10:30 a.m. Typical Duluth weather. Cold as hell. Fingers of fog creeping up West 1st Street. Somewhere high above Lake Superior, ghostly, echoing in the mist, an eerie sound of the 60s. The sweet melodic voice, the prophetic warning: "I think it's time we stop children, what's that sound, ever-body look what's goin' down..."

Down along the icy I-35, a beat-up old red Explorer, windows open wide, CD player cranked high, rattling along atop the deadly black ice. Oblivious to the danger, the driver, Quentin Hawk, was busy singing some out-of-tune harmony with the Buffalo Springfield. He wasn't into Old School, but his policeman father had just sent him an oldies CD for his 37th birthday, and he was dutifully following the old man's scribbled admonition. "Rap's for crap, Boyo. Stick this in that pile of junk you drive and turn it up. This is real music."

Joseph Quentin Hawk was on his way home from a little game of hoops with his buds. He drained the last bit of yellow from a bottle of Gatorade, did a half-genuflect at the 2nd Street stop sign, and hung a quick right into the lot at Parkland Pharmacy. Stopping in the handicapped zone, he jumped down from his truck and left the motor running.

Only take a minute.

Pushing through the automatic door, Quent jogged to the freezer and thumped a frosty yellow bottle out of its tray. Before the refrigerator door had re-sealed itself, he was standing at the front register, gulping down the cool sweetness.

With his free hand, he ripped a wrinkled fiver out of his gym shorts and slapped it down in front of the young purple-haired checker.

She looked up into his compelling green eyes. A coy smile blossomed on her freckled face. The silver spikes sticking out of her lower lip flashed in the neon overheads.

"Anything else I can get for you, sir? Anything at all?" she cooed.

Sexual in-your-end-ohs. 6th grade humor from Quent's little sister, Mary Kate, when she noticed her girlfriends making eyes at her handsome older brother. At the time, both of them were still kids in grammar school. But the phenomenon had continued non-stop, right into his adulthood.

Over the years, Mary Kate had witnessed a ton of startled women caught doe-like in the lure of big brother's notorious green orbs.

To his credit, Quent remained honestly oblivious to his own appeal, which only served to make him all the more appealing.

"HELP! Somebody! Help me!" A woman's terrified scream ripped through the silence of the Pharmacy, ruining Miss Purple Hair's big moment.

Quent had already spun around and was running toward the source.

"Hel..." The sharp *crack* of breaking glass cut the woman's second scream in half.

Quent reached the last aisle of the store, looked around the end cap of ready-to-wear eye glasses and froze. The prescription girl was slumped over the pharmacy counter, her head flattened in a pool of her own blood. A huge man in a triple X muscle shirt was staring down at her. His neck was wider than his head; his bulging arms heavily veined and tattooed.

The giant oaf was hopping back and forth from one foot to the other as if the floor were on fire, his bloated calves jiggling like fat brown balloons. A foamy white smear of saliva bubbled on his lips.

Howling like a wounded bull, he screamed down at the girl's unconscious form, "Euw supid bitch gurk!"

His upper torso began twitching spasmodically. His face contorted. His lips flexed in and out as if he were trying to form a sentence. But no sound came.

His body began another cycle of violent twitching. His frustration stamped across his contorted face. Then suddenly, he stopped moving. His shoulders slumped. His eyes glazed and the big face froze. He stared into space as if his system had crashed.

Three seconds passed. Then he snapped back to life as if nothing had happened and spun away from the counter, awkwardly lurching down the aisle toward the pharmacist's window.

Quentin leapt over the counter and caught the injured girl just as she was sliding off the blood soaked counter. Her eyes fluttered open. He could see she was slipping into shock.

Then came another fearsome howl, "Gob-lin. Goblin. You hab lis?"

An elderly white-haired pharmacist cowered behind the little window. Raw panic in his eyes.

The *animal* screams were growing more intense. "You hab lis. I know. Gib heow to mee. Now. I'll uck euw up geud..."

The old man forced his lips into a tremulous smile. "Certainly sir, now if you could repeat..."

A massive hand shot over the glass and grabbed him by the throat. The end of the sentence died in his windpipe. He lunged sideways, coughing and squirming, trying to pull himself away.

No use. The giant's other hand caught hold of his tie and jerked him off his feet like a weightless rag doll. The old man's head made a dull thud as it broke through the glass partition.

The big hands lifted him high into the air and shook him violently. The garbled scream now pitched into a furious whine. "Gob-lin. You hab. I wunt it! Gib me neow. I sweaaa I kill euw."

Quentin Hawk was hunched behind the counter packing Kleenex into the gash on the girl's head.

"Syringes, where?"

Her eyes opened wide, unblinking. Unresponsive. He pulled her head close.

"Syringes! Where do you keep the syringes?"

She raised a shaking hand and pointed. He crawled toward a stack of cardboard file boxes and looked back at her. She nodded.

He pulled out the bottom drawer and grabbed the largest needle he could find. Snatching two vials of liquid off a shelf, he jammed them into his pocket and raced back to the girl. He pressed her hand firmly against the darkening wad of Kleenex in the wound. "Hang on. I'll get help"

Quent hurdled the counter and ran to his left.

The giant weightlifter was holding the old man's limp body high above his head, slamming him against the "Prescriptions" sign.

"GATOR," shouted Quent, calling the big man by his professional name. "Hey Gator Man!"

The oversized head whipped around in Quent's direction, one hand still holding the druggist off the ground. He strained to see who'd called him by name, his eyes blinking the sweat away. "Whah?!" he bellowed.

"I'm a doctor," said Quent. "Sports medicine. Dude, you've been stacking. Synthol, Dianabol prob'ly. I can fix it. Let me get this into your arm. Now!"

Quent held up the syringe and the two vials of liquid and moved in closer. "Nubain! Like oxymorphone. Stop the pain. Guaranteed, man. Two minutes. You need it. Let me give it to you, dude."

Immediate recognition from the big man. He'd already ingested a pharmacy full of enhancement drugs. He knew their names as well as he knew his own. He knew their antidotes as well.

Gator Jennings, professional Pride Fighter, dropped the pharmacist on the floor like a flimsy T-shirt and lumbered toward Quent, his eyes jiggling in their sockets.

He stopped awkwardly in front of Quent. And like some huge obedient child, he knelt down on one knee, pushed up the sleeve of his sweatshirt and stuck out his huge right arm. It looked like a giant, bloated, purple-veined sausage.

Quentin took a step in closer. He raised one of the vials to eye level, examining the liquid, ready to insert the syringe. Then, without warning, he slammed downward violently, plunging the long hypodermic needle directly into the center of the monster's right bicep.

The pain was instant, intense, and debilitating. Gator Jennings screamed in pain and grabbed at the syringe with his left hand. Quentin reached to his right, caught the top of a red fire extinguisher, and swung it as hard as he could into the left temple of the giant head. Gator crumpled to the ground, face up.

Quentin dropped to the floor and slammed both of his legs across Gator's throat. He grabbed the big left arm and levered it backward across his own knees, hoping to set the hold before his opponent regained consciousness. Quentin leaned back to get maximum leverage and pushed down hard on the massive arm. Gator came to – screaming, the pain causing him a moment of articulate clarity.

"Stop. Enuf. I give. I give. Stop!"

"Move and I'll break it," shouted Quent. He released the pressure – but only slightly.

Behind him, there was a rush of commotion: metal hitting the ground; stamping of feet; the squawk of a radio.

Something hard jammed into the back of Quent's left ear. "Let him go asshole!" said a male voice. "Parkland Policc. It's over. You're a bad ass, okay? Took the big man down. But it's over. Let him go. Now!"

The barrel of the cop's revolver jammed repeatedly into the skin behind Quent's ear. "You hear me, asshole?" yelled the cop. "Let him go. Now!"

"He's a juicehead," shouted Quent. "It's roid rage. You better cuff him before I let him go."

"Who the hell are you? Doctor Seuss?" A second policeman un-holstered his weapon.

"CIA. I'm with the god damn CIA. Agent Quentin Hawk. My badge's out in the car."

"Yeah. And I'm the Easter Bunny. Put your arms behind your head jerkwad and step over here. Slow."

CIA Satellite Office, Duluth Minnesota

Agent Joseph Quentin Hawk entered the Fremont Building on West 34th Street, shoved his I.D. card into the slot at the back of Elevator 3, and rode up to the penthouse level. Dark oak panels spanned the length of the reception area. In the center of the polished wood, the familiar blue and gold insignia, the name deeply etched in two-dimensional letters:

Central Intelligence Agency
Charles Fontina, District Director

A dark-haired, middle-aged woman looked up from behind the marble counter and smiled. "Good morning, Agent Hawk."

"Morning Diane, I hear Chucky Cheese wants to see me."

"The Director is waiting for you. He's in a bit of a mood. I wouldn't let him hear you call him that."

"You mean I'm on the shit list again? Gee, what a surprise," Hawk smirked. "Thanks for the warning, Di." He walked to the chief's door, knocked firmly and entered.

At 5'5," 145 pounds, Director Charles Fontina was a small man...*with an even smaller brain.* One of several colorful descriptions offered by Agent Hawk when dining with his buddies at the Oktoberfest Bar and Grille. To say that Hawk and his boss didn't exactly get along was an immediate cause of laughter among field agents at the CIA's Duluth office.

Chucky Cheese was crouched behind his massive brown desk, holding an incident report in front of his 59-year-old face. His opening words came from behind the report.

"You picked a fight in the back of a Rite Aid drug store out in Parkland? Is that right, Agent Hawk?"

"I'm sure, sir, after you've have time to read my report, you'll see that's not what happened." Quent had chosen to begin with an appeasement approach.

As usual, it wasn't going to work for him. Director Fontina's response came back heavy with condescension. "Where was your weapon when all this happened?"

"The guy's a Pride Fighter, sir. Name's Gator Jennings. 6'7," weighs in about 340. I've seen him fight. When I got there, he was in the middle of steroid rage. Strangling the pharmacist; holding the guy's ass about three feet off the ground." Quent demonstrated with his hands. "My gun wouldn't have done me any good, sir."

"Yeah. We all know you're a tough guy, Hawk. *Tai pong*...or some crap like that."

"*Muay Thai*, sir, it's a form of mixed martial..."

Fontina cut him off. "I don't give a shit, Hawk. An agent is never to be without his piece in public. "Where the hell was yours?"

"I was on my way home from the gym, sir. Little intra-agency half court game. We play every Tuesday. Ya see, I was still wearing my shorts, so I left my gun..."

Hawk could see he was wasting his breath. So, he reverted to form. "Not trying to brag, sir, but there isn't enough room in my jock strap for me and my gun at the same time. You know what I'm sayin'? Besides, it keeps falling out in the middle of my jump shot."

Director Fontina's face colored slightly. His teeth clamped down hard several times before he responded. "Agent Hawk, while you're serving out your two-week suspension from duty without pay for that last insubordination, you might consider this. The U.S. Government has a strict code of behavior for its law enforcement agents. You took an oath to uphold that code when you joined. We of the Central Intelligence Agency are just that, an intelligence gathering organization. We're not a gang of street fighters."

Before Quent could respond, Fontina held up his hand for silence. "This is not the first time you've received a suspension for 'acting in a manner unbefitting an agent in the service of his government.' You're skating on thin ice."

"So, what was I was supposed to do, sir? Just walk away and let this juicehead kill the druggist? Maybe a couple of women and kids too?"

"Fist fights are for the local police. Next time you see some domestic violence, call the cops, and butt the hell out! Is that clear? And stay out of Parkland. We don't go there. It's not our kind of area."

Director Fontina slammed the incident report into the out box at the top of his desk, a look of disgust on his ferret face. "Leave your badge with my assistant on your way out, Hawk. Now get out of my office."

Part I

1

What is a good man but a bad man's teacher?
Lao Tzu

8: 30 P.M. - Malibu Colony, California

California's stunning Malibu coastline has dissolved into a necklace of blinking amber jewels. Five thousand moneyed beach dwellers, cocktails in hand, settle into the second half of Monday Night Football.

By the end of the fourth quarter, the night has cooled, the sand has turned black and most of the gentry has lost interest and shuffled off to bed. Blissful sleep from Topanga to Trancas.

While the coasters dream, others toil to keep them safe.

The Facility – Malibu, California

Three miles up the south canyon of Leo Carrillo State Park, tucked away from prying eyes, 85 brainiacs are beginning the second shift of the day in a top secret industrial unit known as The Facility.

The Army's premier laser laboratory is perched atop a eucalyptus knoll, veiled by outcroppings of angled strata and wave-cut terraces. The Army Corps of engineers blended the little slate-colored buildings into the rock formations of the canyon so skillfully that the complex stands invisible amongst the natural vegetation. The only sign of motion is the occasional circle of the blue heron floating gently above it all.

But deep within The Facility the motion is constant, the energy palpable. Overhead cranes straining in their trellised tracks; heavy machinery slamming steel into steel; lasers whining, cutting molten holes through reinforced Lutetium, yet no sounds escape the double sealed doors.

There is no map, no public access road. The Facility has no address.

No one knows it's there.

Bent over a massive table of blueprints, Facility co-founders Doctor Lukas Towne, Head of the U.S. Military's Department of Laser Research, and his partner, Doctor Cynthia Teller, Head of Ocular Surgery for the US Navy, were focused on a production problem.

Cynthia's frustration is showing. "The Super Hornet does Mach 1.7. The lens disintegrated at 1.3 Gs. Can't we get the wizards at Leica to make one that's more stable?"

"Right after I sing 'Dock of the Bay' on the Ed Sullivan show."

Old guy consciousness. Cynthia's name for Luke's dated references. "I'm serious, Luke. You know how far behind we are."

"Yeah, too far to worry about it now."

Together, the pair is entrenched in the most important venture in their Facility's 12-year history. The top secret weapons project is called The Mind's Eye Laser System. Equal parts ocular science and laser technology, it's funded by one of the largest research grants in U.S. history, a $300 million infusion from the combined coffers of the Departments of Defense and Commerce.

The revolutionary Mind's Eye System has been six years in development and will cost the government another hundred million before it becomes operable.

"Excuse me, Doc." Luke's assistant suddenly poked his head into the room."

"Make mine half pepperoni half meatball," said Luke. "Cyn, how 'bout you?"

"I have Defense Secretary Morton Ramsey on the line for you, sir."

Cynthia Teller checked her watch; it was 1:45 in the morning. "This can't be good."

Together, she and Luke began madly pushing blueprints aside, eventually locating the Polycom phone at the bottom of the pile. Luke set the phone in the middle of the table, pressed the 'conference' button and raised his voice slightly. "This is Doctor Towne. Doctor Teller is here with me, sir. How are you?"

"Very well, thank you. So tell me doctors, how's the project coming?"

The two scientists exchanged a nervous look. They were one month away from third stage financing. The receipt of capital hinged upon their making a successful product demonstration in front of a combined board of Pentagon bigwigs and members of the Joint Chiefs. Lens stability was just the latest of several problems holding them back. They were seriously behind schedule.

Cynthia Teller signaled that she'd field the question. "Well sir, since you've reached us at one in the morning, Mr. Secretary, you're aware we're working double shifts. I'd venture to say that you've been through enough of these situations to sense that double shifts are not a very good indication of timeliness."

Luke grinned. His partner's surprising audacity was such an incongruity. Cynthia Teller was 42, a petite 5'3" with classical Nordic features and feminine bearing – a very attractive woman.

The Defense Secretary's answer was surprisingly positive. "Doctor Teller, let me assure you I appreciate your directness. Hearing the truth is always preferable to the load of bear crap I get from most folks."

Defense Secretary Ramsey was a former senator from Georgia, and a public darling known for his folksy colloquialisms and down-home demeanor. Insiders on the Hill saw him differently. There was a savage vindictiveness that lay coiled beneath each folksy turn of phrase. They had nicknamed him 'the Cobra.' Anyone incurring Ramsey's disfavor would be struck suddenly. And the bite was often politically fatal.

True to form, the Defense Secretary had first ladled a bit of honey, but now it was time to get to his real purpose. "Actually, I'm calling about something else. It's a personal matter. And the person in question here is the President of the United States himself." Ramsey paused dramatically, implying maximum gravitas. "You are aware that our administration has taken quite a beating for... shall we say... our failure to exact retribution for the 9/11 attack. The President's position in the polls has fallen steadily, and along with it, so has our dominance in the eyes of the rest of the world. In my opinion, most of Europe is a bunch of teat-sucking freeloaders. A pack of meat hogs who never gave a crap about us in the first place."

Ramsey emitted a grunt of distain before continuing. "Here's the point. What we need is a turn-around. Something to reestablish the U.S. Military as the power player in this little game of who's got the button. We need to kick some ass. You with me so far?"

"Yes sir," said Cynthia, shooting a grimace at Luke. *Where the hell is he going with this?*

"Let me put it to you directly, Doctor Towne. The President needs a confidence builder. A public event. A boost to win reelection. And he's asked me to bring you to Washington to cook something up."

There was a moment of confused silence. Finally, Luke Towne responded. "I'm sorry Mr. Secretary, I'm not sure I understand the request."

"Well let's make it plain then. You're the guy we put in charge of Laser Guidance. The guy who made Schwarzkopf look like a genius. The guy who delivered the bombs. On television, in front of the world. Smart bomb videos. Line 'em up and shoot 'em down. Bang bang.

"Well, the President wants you to do the same god damn thing for him. Ya get it? And he needs it now, before he loses any more ground. Just so you know, the President asked me to ask you for your help; he didn't order it. But I'm ordering it. You getting the gist here? To be clear, all prior assignments are to be put on hold. All previous Pentagon orders are temporally rescinded. Tomorrow morning, 0500, the Eagle will be gassed up, sittin' on the runway at Santa Monica waiting for you. We'll see you in D.C. tomorrow afternoon. Have a good flight."

End of phone call.

When Luke disconnected the speaker phone, Cynthia Teller began shouting. "Three hundred sixteen million in research crapped on so they can win a goddamn popularity contest! This is outrageous. We're so far behind now, if you're not here we'll never gonna deliver on time. They'll cut off the funding. No question. This is insane. Why don't we just frickin' resign now. Save ourselves a lot of embarrassment."

Doctor Teller was the U.S. Navy's Chief of Ocular Surgery and Advanced Research. She was one of the Military's most vital assets, half of the Mind's Eye project's driving force and an irreplaceable member of The Facility's team.

"Easy now," chided Luke Towne, unflappable as always, "We've still got time on the meter. They just want some kind of fancy firecracker to show off with. I'll think of something. Take us about a day and a half."

Luke and Cynthia had been through many wars together. They were an inseparable team, far more than just friends. She summoned her most persuasive tone. "You're wrong, Lukas. I can see it coming. They've already got something in mind. It'll take you away permanently. We can't let that happen. We're too close."

"Naw, it's just a bureaucratic hiccup. I'll go up there, drop a few five-syllable words and be back here in two days."

"This is no hiccup, Luke. I'm telling you, once you get there, they're going to suddenly remember who you are, and they'll never let go of you. Your research days will be over."

It was raining as Cynthia pulled onto the tarmac of Santa Monica Airport's Runway One. The big gray/green Strike Eagle, its engines whining, stood in the darkness like a menacing harpy, waiting to take Luke to Washington. Because of Luke's position as Head of the U.S. Military's Department of Laser Research, a dual seat F-15E was held on permanent standby for his use. It was stationed in Fresno, California as part of the 144th Fighter Wing.

Cynthia's insides were boiling but she said nothing. The Secretary of Defense himself had given the orders, and in point of fact, the man virtually signed their checks.

Luke brought no luggage with him. *No one needs luggage for a day-and-a-half.* Leaning back into the car, he gave Cynthia a brotherly peck on the cheek. "Not to worry, Cap'm. I'll see you on Monday."

2

Washington D.C.

The President of the United States, Thomas Rundle Crowley, had tried everything in his power to halt his decline in popularity. In the aftermath of the murderous attacks of 9/11, the nation was still mired in a contagion of fear and vulnerability. Though it had occurred three years earlier, there was still an intense communal need for retribution. *Someone should be held responsible.*

In an attempt to reverse his fall from favor, President Crowley decided to do something about it. On December 26th 2004, bolstered by the recommendations of the 911 Commission, the President ordered "a sweeping overhaul of the intelligence community." His decree mandated the mutual sharing of resources and a total realignment of authority under a new (presidentially appointed) national intelligence director. A more united effort from the CIA, FBI, NSA and the other dinosaurs of law enforcement might breathe new life into the system, enhance communication, and promote better national security.

The plan was an internal disaster.

To the 15 powerful agencies of the U.S. Intelligence gathering community, the idea of 'sharing' information was unthinkable; a transgression of traditional boundaries. Surrendering their authority to a Presidential appointee was perceived as a direct threat to their very existence.

Instead of bringing his intelligence forces together as brothers in a communal spirit of renewed energy, the President's order set them against each other in a bitter struggle for territorial dominance.

It was war at the core.

Smelling blood in the water, the media sharks swarmed in and succeeded in making things worse. The National Review labeled the Crowley plan a "sublime miscalculation...revealing an acute ignorance of human nature...a giant albatross." The Washington Post, in their now famous editorial, called it "...a fresh coat of appeasement on the ass-end of the same old wooden horse."

Crowley's ratings plunged.

The Oval Office – Washington D.C.

January 6th 2005 brought a frigid rain to Washington. The lights in the Oval Office came on at 5 a.m., an hour earlier than usual. On President Crowley's mahogany desk, a Time magazine lay open, its editorial page marked with angry red lines.

The President handed the Time magazine to his secretary, Carolyn Leahey. "Would you read this out loud for me, Carolyn? Sometimes I get a different perspective when the words come out of someone's else's mouth."

"Certainly, Mr. President."

She read the title, "A Time for Truth," then looked up for his approval. At his nod, she began. "'Three years ago, the city of New York was boldly and brutally victimized. And not by a sophisticated technology stolen from a superpower; but rather, by a rag-tail band of unsophisticated, uneducated foreigners – easily recognizable by their beards, their language and their intentions. Wasn't NSA supposed to be listening? Scanning the signals? Telling our leaders whom to look out for? Wasn't it the job of our Pentagon protectors to pick them out of the crowd, detain them, and protect us from their malice? And what of the CIA? Wasn't it their job to warn us of impending threats to our public safety?

"'To the Intelligence community and to the administration whose job it is to direct them, the American people find you guilty of inconceivable oversight. You have failed to protect us. You have failed to execute the very duties for which you were appointed. In a word, our Ship of State has foundered.'"

There was a moment of uncomfortable silence in the Oval Office. Carolyn Leahey averted her eyes. "I'm sorry sir," she said, then waited for him to speak.

"Thank you, Carolyn. That's all for now."

Thomas 'Run' Crowley had already fired two teams of spin doctors. And his approval rating continued to plummet. Something had to be done.

A week after the Time magazine article, against the advice of counsel, Crowley fired his Chief of Staff and brought in a rookie: a Cornel lawyer, young and brash like so many in his profession, a whiz kid with an answer for everything.

"Mr. President, what we need here is a public victory."

"Meaning..." said the President.

"Meaning...the Intelligence community dropped the ball on 9/11. It's obvious. The media knows it. The public knows it. So...we force the Intel bastards to fix it. Take responsibility for their mistakes. Make some arrests. Nullify a threat. Deliver something big, something highly visible. A show of strength. That's what the public needs. Fireworks. A reason to believe again. The key to reelection; some good old American fireworks."

Alone in his office, the President scanned the afternoon tallies; three points lower in the poles. *Sure as hell nothing else is working.* Crowley punched the direct line to his Secretary of Defense, Morton Ramsey.

"Yes, Mr. President."

"Morton, I need you to get a hold of that scientist."

"Sir?"

"You know...what's his name, the smart bomb guy."

"You mean Doctor Luke Towne, sir? Runs The Facility?"

"Yeah, that's the one. Tell him I need some fireworks. And let's get him up here pronto."

6:40 a.m. Twenty minutes to go. Crowley thumped his watch and checked it against the Franklin antique ticking next to the book case. For the second time he went to the bathroom and washed his hands. He splashed water on his face and stared into his own tired eyes. He was pale. The famous iron jaw had ceased to protrude. *This one had better work.*

At 7 a.m., Dr. Towne was shown into the Oval Office.

Developing the President's new strategy would demand the full-time services of Luke Towne, his partner Cynthia Teller and the entire 85-man staff at The Facility. Luke's 'day-and-a-half" would stretch into six months. Cynthia Teller's fears would be confirmed. Their 10 year, $300 million project would get dumped into the Presidential waste basket.

All in the name of fireworks. And for President Crowley, the fireworks would succeed dramatically. His ratings would soar.

Right before his political machinations set off one of the worst potential disasters since Hiroshima...

3

Duluth, Minnesota

Quentin Hawk skidded to a stop and stepped out of his battered red Explorer. He stood at the curb surveying the situation, a smirk on his face. Fifteen inches of snow had fallen since he'd left his house for his morning workout. It was *colder than crap,* and he'd forgotten to bring his jacket. It was obvious he was going to have to dig his way back in.

"Nice. Really nice," he cracked, his breath blowing little parentheses of steam around his words.

He jerked the snow shovel out of the back of his truck bed and began throwing snow over his left shoulder. Quent was big and athletic. His movements were smooth and efficient. As usual, his temper was not so smooth. Three minutes into the process, the shovel hit a buried rock. His left hand slipped off the handle and knifed into the rusty shovel blade. Raising his bloody hand in front of his face, he looked into the gash and saw his first two knucklebones laid bare.

"Son of a bitch!" He flung the shovel over his shoulder and began the awkward climb through the hip-deep snow toward his house.

Once on the front porch he saw it immediately; a long blue envelope stuck to the center of his door, its familiar blue, white and gold emblem glinting in the morning light: *Central Intelligence Agency, U.S. Government.*

"Perfect," he quipped.

Quent had always had an authority problem. He loved working for the CIA. He just hated the people that ran it. He was perpetually expecting to be fired.

This is probably it.

He snatched it off the door and clomped into his house, heading for the kitchen sink. There he dumped a stream of Betadine over his open knuckles and wrapped his hand in a Cabo Wabo T-shirt which he'd been using as a dish towel. With a kitchen knife, he stirred some hot water into a bowl of instant oatmeal and sat down at his Formica dinette set. Carefully wiping the knife blade on the inside of his pant leg, he used it to pry open the bad news.

Effective immediately. You are hereby permanently transferred to the Los Angeles division. Code 15.

Code 15 was an order of highest priority which translated as, 'Take your weapon and the clothes on your back and leave at once.' It was signed by Chief Charles Fontina; Chucky Cheese.

Arrogant moron. Shit-for-brains. Inbred idiot, stupid f...

When he'd run out of superlatives, Quent resumed stirring his oatmeal.

No explanation. Just pack your gear and move west.

"Damn," he said, grunting through a mouthful of lumpy goo, "Looks like I still got this freakin' job. For a minute there I thought it was my lucky day."

Pacific Palisades, California

A very long cab ride from LAX to the far end of Sunset Boulevard left a puzzled Agent Quentin Hawk standing in front of a condo complex known as 'The Royal Hawaiian Gardens.' The name (spelled 'Hawiian') was chiseled into a piece of driftwood hanging above a group of parking spaces designed to look like thatched huts.

"Welcome, Mr. Hawk," said the gray-haired gentleman with the manicured fingernails. "Your unit is on the ground floor, end of the path to your right. Got one of the best views in the building. Glad to have you with us, sir." Squinting out from underneath a white Banana Republic sun visor, the manager looked to be in his mid sixties. He was so tan Quent figured his name had to end in a vowel.

Best in the building? Me? Right.

"So, how come the name's spelled wrong?" asked Quent, starting out on the wrong foot already.

"Won't matter when you seen the view, pal. It' good luck,"

"How's that?"

"You're in for a run of good luck, man. Happens every time a new tenant mentions the wrong spelling. Never fails. Somebody gets rich or pregnant. So we left it that way. You know what I mean? For good luck."

"Right. Well, thank you, I could use some."

The Plumeria, named for the Hawaiian Lei flower (frangipani) was a deluxe one-bedroom end unit. Agent Hawk walked into the kitchen, amazed to see a fruit basket waiting for him on the pink and gray coriander countertop. And there, right next to the grapefruits and oranges and avocados, was a lease agreement with <u>his</u> name printed neatly across the top. The lease term? Twelve months.

Gotta be a mistake.

The little card attached to the fruit basket had a Hula girl painted on the front; it read "Aloha from Hawaiian Gardens."

In the ensuing months, it would matter little that not one single Hawaiian plant, flower or tropical tree could be found anywhere on the property called Hawaiian Gardens.

What did matter to Quent was that his new condo was hanging off the edge of a rock cliff overlooking the cerulean blue sea of the Pacific Coast. It had an unobstructed, window-to-window view of the surf crashing down 24/7. Any time he wanted, he could pull open one of the sliding glass doors and get a snoot-full of salty West Coast air. The Malibu pier was visible, eight miles up the road.

A one year lease!

It appeared that Agent Joseph Quentin Hawk, 15 years a foot soldier in the Duluth Agency, was stepping on to a whole new playing field. No sludgy Minnesota Astroturf. *Real grass, dude!*

This was California, man! Chicks, suntan oil, roller skaters in bikinis, the beach, Hollywood, bitchin' cars. And the weather! California weather was like nothing he'd ever experienced back in Duluth.

He stepped outside on the balcony and drew in a deep breath. Warm air. *Unbelievable.* He rolled his jet-lagged body into the new, white-rope hammock that was strung up in the south corner of Plumeria's view terrace.

Two more breaths and Agent Quentin Hawk was snoring quietly, deep in a dream, the hammock rocking gently with the rise and fall of his chest.

It was 1987. He was back in seventh grade; Mary Star of the Sea Grammar School. An unfortunate dream.

Little Quent was seated on the wooden bench outside the principal's office. This was not his first experience with Sister Mary Agnes. But unlike his former encounters for fighting or farting or throwing spit balls, this one was unique.

His class had been given an English assignment: *Write an essay on one of the Eight Beatitudes.* Quent had chosen Beatitude #3, '*Blessed are the meek in spirit, for they shall inherit the earth.*'

Being of Irish/Italian stock, he already knew if you acted 'meek,' you were being a pussy. Meek meant you'd get your ass kicked, and that was certainly never going to happen to anyone with the family name of 'Hawk.'

Quent rode his bike over to Mary Shurtle's house to ask for help. Sixteen-year-old Mary, herself a former graduate of Mary Star of the Sea, was considered 'too wild' by the nuns and had been expelled several times for smoking. She had been a babysitter for Quent's younger sister until the day Mary and Quent were caught in the Hawks' garage, making out in the back seat of Joe Senior's Pontiac.

Together, the two conspirators scratched out the following little verses for Quent to hand in:

A bad deal

The Earth doesn't glow like it used to
They've stolen the blue from her skies
Her mountains are bald, worn and wasted
The light's gone out of her eyes

Her hair is dyed black and skuzzy
Her breasts so flabby they sag
Who but the meek and the stupid
Would want such a dried up old hag?

J. Quentin Hawk 1978

The 'hag' poem earned Quent an 'F' and an invitation to the Principal's office.

As he awaited his fate on the worn wooden bench outside Sister Mary Agnes's office, he prayed to his favorite deities; the Blessed Mother, God, Saint Rose of Lima, Padre Pio; "If you'll just get me out of this one, I promise...."

"In here, Mr. Hawk," cracked the shrill voice of 'Big Aggie' herself. Sister Agnes was an overweight woman with a voice like Hitler and the jowls of a Saint Bernard. With a triumphant sweep of her meaty arm, she slapped Quent's confiscated binder down on her desk. Expelling a breath so foul it could melt soap, she roared, "And what do we have here, Mr. Hawk?"

Quent's knees trembled; fear gurgled in his stomach; but rebellion raged behind his intelligent green eyes. "Looks a lot like you got my binder there, Sister Agnes," he answered, barely able to stifle his own giggle.

"That answer will cost you an additional week in detention, young man," bellowed the incensed nun. "You know quite well it's this filthy poem of yours we're discussing here."

'Big Aggie' was a one-woman tribunal. Her face was coiffed in pure white gauze. Her infallible girth was layered in reams of coarse black wool. She crackled of brimstone. The scent of starched piety trailed behind her as she hurried down the halls interpreting the will of God, spewing guilt, imposing conformity of thought, word and deed. Handing out detention slips.

Big Aggie was all-knowing. It was obvious because she taught science and math and nobody understood any of that stuff.

When Quent tried to explain to her that the version of the poem found in his binder was just a rough draft and not intended for submission, her upper lip curled in disgust. Her words came thundering up from under her rigid white wimple. Her silver crucifix bounced on her chest. "Mr. Hawk," she boomed, "dirty thoughts are just as reprehensible as the sinful acts they precede."

On his way home to receive the wrath of his father, young Joseph Quentin decided that 'they'd all let him down.' And if he were ever to believe in God or the saints again, it would certainly not be the Catholic ones.

That summer, as if to formally cement his break with Catholicism, 13-year-old J. Quentin Hawk met the beautiful Carmen de Lorena.

Joseph Quentin Hawk, the youngest son, had grown up on the south side of Duluth in a family so Catholic that his mother was a daily communicant; so Irish that his three brothers and one sister were named for the Saints on whose feast day each was born; and so Italian that his godmother started putting wine in his baby bottle when he was two.

The Hawk boys were known for loyalty to family and friends. Four brothers so tough their reputation as fighters extended beyond their borough. The name Hawk garnered respect and a great deal of fear amongst the toughs of Duluth's Delaney District.

Joseph, like his brothers before him, began showing signs of athletic brilliance by age 12. But unlike his older brothers (who grew up to be nice looking fellows), by age 12 young Joseph had already developed into a handsome, Irish/Italian package of girl-candy – from his powerful young physique, to his thick wavy hair, to his piercing green eyes.

Joseph lost his virginity at the tender age of 13 to Carmen de Lorena, a beautiful 22-year-old Puerto Rican prostitute. Carmen was believed to be the personal property of one Vinnie Colombano, a big-time Mafioso from Queens. Carmen's luscious body was the subject of many a barroom fantasy. Understandably, she was considered off-limits to everyone.

Carmen Lorena paid $50 to 13-year-old Joseph Hawk for the pleasure of being his first lay. She paid for the pleasure for two reasons: first, she thought of little Quent as a gorgeous piece of fresh, home-grown salami (Ba Boom!); and second, she knew from that day forward, no one would ever dare to 'mess with Carmen' as she would forever be under the loyal protection of the Hawk boys – a promise as potent as any 'Muerta.'

In his senior year at Ohio State, Quentin Hawk stood 6'4," weighed 242 pounds, ran a 4½ 50 and could bench 350 pounds. He was the first all league wrestler ever to be drafted by the Minnesota Vikings. He went in the third round as a tight end, and banked a fat signing bonus the day after he graduated.

That summer, he took his bonus and flew out to California where he spent three months on the beach getting tan, and getting ready to play pro ball.

It was at State Beach in Santa Monica that Quent met the famous Brazilian Jiu-Jitsu champion Royce Gracie. After losing to Quent in a game of two-man volley ball, Royce challenged him to a one round wrestling match. Unaware of Royce's prominence, Quent, a two time NCAA collegiate champion himself, extended his hand and smiled confidently.

"Sure you want to do this? I kinda outweigh you."

At 6'1" Royce Gracie was three inches shorter than Quent; and at a mere 176 pounds, he was three weight classes below Quent's 242 pounds.

"Always liked a challenge," answered the genial Brazilian, a 6th degree black belt at 18, and the owner of the most submission victories in the history of the MMA (Mixed Martial Arts).

"Alright. How 'bout we have a go right now. Right here in the shallow water," said Quent.

The match lasted 23 seconds - Quent submitting to Gracie's triangle leg choke, a move that few in the States had ever seen. And a style that was banned from college wrestling.

Royce then revealed his true identity to the stunned Quentin Hawk and the two men formed a lasting friendship. At Royce's invitation, Quent spent the rest of the Summer as a part time pupil - studying the new style of grappling and ground fighting – taking his licks directly from the master.

When he wasn't being throttled on the mat by his new friend, Quent got into surfing and, as with most athletic endeavors, he became proficient almost immediately. One day riding the shore break at Topanga, he stepped on some coral in the shallow water and tweaked his knee. It hurt from time to time but then somehow just disappeared in the warmth of the sun.

At the end of summer, he flew back to Minnesota and showed up at camp on a Friday. He was tan and already in great shape from paddling, lifting and running on the beach. He sailed through his physical, picked up a playbook and went home to study.

Monday morning there was a thin envelope taped to his locker door. His knee had been pronounced irreparable by the highest priced orthopedists that Viking money could buy, and management had decided to cut their losses. He'd been released.

Impossible. Unbelievable. Eight years of high school and college ball and not one game missed due to injury. Hawk was put together with heavy gauge wire.

Quentin Hawk, famed collegiate athlete, would never become a pro. No more game-saving receptions, no rings, no glory.

No shit.

For most young horses, this would have been devastating. For Hawk it was tough, but not terminal. It was back to the world of ordinary humans.

Only J. Quentin had never been ordinary.

Almost immediately he applied for a position with the CIA. If he couldn't catch balls in the NFL, he could certainly catch crooks for the CIA. It made perfect sense to the Hawk.

He was eagerly accepted by the Agency. And so began 15 years of service and an unprecedented record of arrests and convictions. However, the record was equally notable for another reason – his repeated, undaunted, and unrelenting conflicts with authority.

On the positive side, Quent was blessed with ferocious powers of concentration. He was meticulous, hard working and intuitive. His *Hawkish* determination was admired by fellow agents who would always volunteer to serve with him on any assignment. On the not-so-positive side, he was pigheaded and uncompromising. He hated being told what to do. Hawk was a problem. And his disregard for Agency procedure was routinely condemned by his superiors.

After concluding an investigation of an illegal arms consortium, Quentin was summoned to Chief Charles Fontina's office. As usual, the chief was not happy with the way things had been done. "Let me make it very clear for you, Agent Hawk. Your attitude, your methods and your manners are not appropriate to this Agency! I've never seen an investigation in which so many procedures were abrogated and so much was done wrong."

Quent answered with typical arrogance. "Musta got some of the shit right, sir. Perps got life, didn't they?"

"Dismissed. And Agent Hawk, I'm warning you, one more insubordinate word, and you're on review without pay. Are we clear?"

"As a bell, sir," answered Quent with a broad smile, having elevated smiling to an insubordinate art form.

Agent Quentin Hawk had not advanced as expected. Chief Fontina had summarized the situation perfectly; it was a matter of attitude, methods and manners. His arrests always held up in court, but he just couldn't act like a company man.

What made it more difficult was that he had no intention of ever acting like a company man. Quentin Hawk could be charming, respectful and socially adept when he chose to be. But when it came to his superiors, he never chose to be.

Certain members of his family would speculate that his problems with authority were environmental, originating way back in 1836, when the French Sisters of St. Joseph arrived in Mississippi at the little village of Carondelet.

To these (recovering Catholics) Big Aggie and her posse of wimple wearing moralizers were really just the tip of a gigantic, 2000-year-old, highly structured, theological poison dart.

Quentin himself, on the other hand, believed the problem was genetic. When asked by admirers why he wasn't further along after 15 years, he would shrug his extremely wide shoulders and answer, "A pretty smart police captain once told me, 'If you're not willing to put your feet in the stirrups, they won't let you drive the team.'"

The pretty good policeman was Captain Joseph Hawk Senior; 35 years on the beat, a minor legend himself on the Duluth-Superior force. Joe Hawk Senior (a Golden Gloves champ) was a hard-nosed Irish cop who raised his sons to stand tall and fight for what they believed in. On his first day in uniform, Hawk Senior had taken offense to a remark made by his watch commander and knocked the surprised lieutenant through his own office window.

Like father like son.

Except Hawk Senior was much better than Quent at navigating the politics of law enforcement, reaching the position of captain in just five years, a position he still held.

Hawk Senior's true opinion was left unspoken, until one Friday night after a Notre Dame victory and several pints of Guinness, when his wife, Winnie, asked how Quentin was doing.

"It's a shame, Win," he said. "Quentin's an idealist. A true cop's cop. An independent thinker. He's gonna get royally screwed by all the political asswipes that run most everything in this country."

Hawk Senior went on to explain that the sudden trip out to sunny California wasn't a promotion. It was some fat bureaucrat's clever method of sweeping son Quentin under the rug. His stubborn but talented young son was going to end up writing tickets under a pier somewhere.

Old man Hawk didn't know from mixed metaphors, but there was nothing mixed about what was happening to Quent. His career in the CIA was going down for the count.

4

The Facility – Malibu, California

As usual, Doctor Cynthia Teller was correct. Once Luke Towne got to Washington, his CV was resurrected and the Pentagon suddenly 'remembered who he was.' Very quickly he was put in charge of developing and executing the entire White House 'public confidence' strategy.

Together, she and Luke went over the White House request in great detail. She was repeatedly stunned by their obvious desperation. The President's advisors insisted on an impossible complexity of goals: to reverse the President's position in the polls; to restore the American public's confidence in their country; and to reestablish Europe's perception of America as a world power.

It would take Luke and Cynthia and their team of technicians five arduous months to formulate the plan, vet the participants, and deliver the technology. An additional month would be required to install the laser hardware.

Newbie White House Chief of Staff, Mike Yost, demonstrating his copious lack of experience, gave Secretary of Defense Morton Ramsey the job of 'expediting the process.' Ramsey, whose only skill was spinning Georgia homilies, demonstrated a lack of understanding so divisive that he alone added a full three weeks to the process. President Crowley would later remark privately, "Ah yes, Mort Ramsey. The man's ignorance is only surpassed by his inability to make a decision."

The Pentagon, Arlington VA, Ring A

June 10th, the second Thursday of the month. Time for Secretary of Defense Ramsey to 'expedite;' to bring the next echelon of governmental management up to speed. For the briefing, a senior group of D.C. cognoscenti was convened in the Pentagon's counterterrorism boardroom.

The Special Intelligence Committee (so named by Secretary Ramsey) was about to receive a full security update on the President's new strategy. Among them were the Vice Chairman of the Joint Chiefs, the Under Secretary of Defense (Acquisition, Technology and Logistics), the President's national security advisor, the heads of both the CIA and NSA, the President's Chief of Staff, the Chairmen of the Senate Select Committee on Intelligence, both majority and minority heads, plus several senior military advisors.

Sitting at his antique desk in the outermost ring of the Pentagon, Defense Secretary Morton Ramsey reviewed his notes one last time. Ramsey, an antique himself at 68, and one of the more egocentric members of the President's cabinet, shook his head in admiration. The document was one of the most well-planned proposals he had ever seen.

On the surface it was a brilliant piece of political strategy. On a covert level, it was a masterful and sophisticated work of counterterrorism as well. Its author, Doctor Lukas Towne, had created something extraordinary. But even more impressive than the document itself was the dossier of the man who had created it.

The list of Doctor Lukas Towne's accomplishments was stunning. Before becoming the Army's preeminent authority on laser defense systems, Doctor Lukas Towne had spent two decades in the Military. The man had been a colonel in the U.S. Rangers, retiring as the second most decorated officer in the history of U.S. Special Forces. His awards of merit were literally too numerous to mention. Secretary Ramsey ordered his speechwriter to list some of them in the margin, in case, during his speech, he might need to 'punch things up a bit.'

Penciled in the margin of Ramsey's speech were a few of Colonel Lukas Towne's citations: Master Parachutist Wings; Ranger Tab; Special Forces Tab; Legion of Merit; five Bronze Stars (two for valor, three for service and achievement); Purple Heart; two Air Medals; and two Meritorious Service Medals.

At the bottom of the second page, his assistant had drawn an arrow pointing to the following note: "Last year, for his work with Cambodian and Vietnamese refugees, Colonel Lukas Towne received a Letter of Commendation from President Crowley himself."

Ramsey took one final look, snapped his black leather folder shut and headed down the hallway toward the Pentagon's counterterrorism boardroom.

The nation's Defense Secretary was dressed in a dark green gabardine suit, button down chambray shirt and maroon rep tie. Sartorially frozen in the 60s, he smelled of English Leather; his salt and pepper hair gleamed with Pantene conditioner. His Nunn Busch shell-cordovan wing tips were so new, the bottoms were still slippery.

Pentagon Counterterrorism Boardroom- Ring A

The nation's bombastic Defense *diva* strode boldly into the dimly lighted boardroom and pulled the door closed behind himself. He waited for the double security mechanism to seal itself, then moved directly to the podium.

Surprisingly, he dispensed with his customary acknowledgments and folksy wit, and launched directly into his speech. *Gonna smack these long nose Harvard bastards right in the middle of their pedigrees.*

"Gentlemen, I am keenly aware that the liberal press holds all of you responsible for your failure to protect our citizens from the attacks of 9/11."

The men sitting at the long table were stunned by the Secretary's blatant accusation.

"I am also aware that the 9/11 Commission itself agrees with the media. The cable channels and the internet are rife with amateur nut bags accusing all of us in the Intelligence community of treasonous misconduct. And that slimy bunch of international freeloaders who call themselves our allies, they think we should all be replaced."

He could feel the emotional uplift in his audience. *This was not the way meetings on counterterrorism customarily began.*

Ramsey leaned into them, his face jutting forward. "Let me assure you, gentlemen, I do not intend to let this continue. We, the soldiers and statesmen gathered together at this table, represent the most dominant military force in history, the foremost intelligence gathering organizations in the world. Without us, this country would not even be here!"

His voice dropped, his delivery a touch more personal. "The sad truth, my friends, is that this country has lost its confidence. The world thinks we're a bunch of 4-H club girl scouts. Our own citizens are scared. Most of them think we've already become a second-rate power."

Ramsey's teeth clamped in anger as he spat out the next line. "That's another one of the defeatist labels we can thank the goddamn son-of-a-bitch liberal press for."

Ramsey picked up the first page of his speech and slapped it down on the podium – damning it to the past. "Something needs to be done, gentlemen. And it's going to be done right now.

"Several months ago, our President asked the members of the Intelligence community to do something about this situation. To share their resources, to unite as brothers and send a message to all potential terrorists who might think that

America has gone soft. To quote the President's exact words, 'We need a show of force.' A goddamn show of force!

"Well here it is. As you already know, next month in Paris France, there's an important international event, the Paris International Conference on Technology. It's been planned with utmost care in the hope of bringing our divergent world a little closer together.

"As it happens, most of the world's scientific community will be attending the event; more than 80 nations. Well, six months ago, due to his exemplary work in laser optics, our premier laser scientist, Doctor Lukas Towne, was honored with an invitation to deliver the commencement speech."

The Defense Secretary paused dramatically, then raised his finger in the air, a wry smile on his face. "But gentlemen, there are a few things about our Doctor Towne that most of the outside world may not be aware of. Our Doctor Towne is not just any scientist. He's one of <u>us!</u> By that I mean, he's Army. A 20-year man. A rather famous one at that. Doctor Towne used to have a different title. It was Colonel Luke Towne, Head of U.S. Special Forces. As it happens, Colonel Towne is the second most decorated soldier in the history of U.S. Special Forces. He ran tech ops for us in Nam. And he's tougher than gator gut. (True to form, Ramsey couldn't resist a little Georgia hominy.)

"As our premier laser scientist, the doctor runs our U.S. Military's weapons guidance program. Doctor Towne's design of the so-called Smart bomb is commonly accepted as the signature weapon of modern warfare.

"One final note; during his career as the Army's Head of Special Forces, the men under his command nicknamed him 'the Pit Bull;' hence, from this point on, I am codenaming this operation 'the Pit Bull Strategy.'"

Ramsey waited for the implication to register, then finished with typical bravado. "The President and I are sending the Pit Bull over to Paris to take a bite outta some Frog ass and any other son of a bitch principality that thinks they're going to get away with harboring or financing terrorists. We're going to put on a little show of our own. A show that no one's ever going to forget. Here's how it's gonna go!"

For the next 15 minutes, the Secretary of Defense detailed the plan to "...reestablish the U.S as the most respected and most feared military organization in the world." In part, it would involve the unveiling of a devastating new anti-terrorist weapon developed by the pugnacious Colonel Towne. The total package would have international impact. The American public would "...sleep easier knowing that the Pentagon and their President were attending to their national security."

"The rag heads will go scurrying back into the holes they crawled out of. And America will return to the impenetrable bastion of freedom we've always been."

The Defense Secretary finished his briefing with a moniker of reinforcement. "And gentlemen, mark my use of the word. I said impenetrable and that's exactly what I mean."

5

1973 – The Sabra Refugee Camp, Beirut, Lebanon

In 1973, Mahmood Aziz, a 15-year-old Palestinian child of the Sabra ghetto, proposed marriage to the love of his life. Six months later his 14-year-old wife, Adara (Virgin), delivered two healthy and beautiful twin boys, Ahmad and Farad.

Possessing no education, but skilled with his hands, 15-year-old Mahmood went door to door through the tangled streets of Sabra offering to repair small appliances. By working 12-hour days, seven days a week, he was able to put meager rations on the blanket which served as the family table.

Each day was a struggle. Each night was torn by the fears of his wife and the tears of his children. The home of their grandparents had been bulldozed by Israeli soldiers. *The Israeli soldiers might come again in the dark and kill us.*

By the time his boys had grown to nine years of age, Mahmood had exhausted his body and was no longer able to provide adequate food for his family. In desperation, he stowed himself in the back of a produce truck, held a pocketknife to the driver's throat, and forced the terrified Egyptian driver to pull over in a darkened alley.

Out of the shadows came the twins, Farad and Ahmad, led by their mother, Adara. They carried only the clothes on their backs.

With Adara and the twins safely concealed under boxes of bananas and oranges, and further shielded by tall water cans of wild orchids and peonies, Mahmood Aziz and his family were driven past the Israeli camp guards, through the gates of the Sabra Refugee Camp, and into the city; undetected.

When the driver reached the heart of central Beirut, Mahmood closed his knife and left his last 150 Piastres on the passenger seat.

And the Aziz family disappeared into the alleys of Beirut.

After a frantic week on the streets, they took refuge in the Old Ras Hotel, an abandoned pile of crumbling bricks and rubble. During the Six Day War of 1967, Israeli bombs had reduced the once proud structure to a scatter of debris. The Lebanese police ignored the place. Aware that migrants and criminals had laid claim to the rubble, as long as no one in the surrounding neighborhood complained, 'what matter.'

For the Aziz family, the relative safety of Room 2C, high off the street on the second floor, was a bountiful fortune like none other in their short lives. Although the room had no running water and no window glass, it was warm at night, and it still had its two original beds, a luxury that no one in the Aziz family had ever experienced.

Rejuvenated with hope, Mahmood resumed his work as a handyman. Almost immediately he was recruited by a local Hizb'allah ("the party of Allah") official to help rebuild Lebanese homes which were constantly being destroyed by Israeli incursion. Because of his love for his own children, Mahmood was eventually assigned to work on damaged school-yards and classrooms, always a high priority in Hizb'allah's restoration efforts.

Mahmood's twin boys flourished. By age nine, they were very much like American kids: curious, full of energy, and hooked on Lebanon's version of rock and roll music. Little Farad had a beautiful singing voice (sounding like an angel by his father's telling) and Ahmad had a knack for keeping rhythm.

Although rock music was strictly forbidden by their family's Islamic faith, the boys decided to start a band anyway – in secret. Farad and Ahmad set out to interview their friends as potential bass and guitar players. As no one had real instruments, the finalists were chosen on the basis of their ability to play air guitar in front of a portable radio. To conduct the band's first rehearsal, the boys would have to sneak out of the Old Ras Hotel while their parents were asleep.

For the twins, sneaking out of the hotel at midnight was a regular event. One had simply to climb out on the fragile fire escape, grab on to the awning of the building across the alley, and swing down on to the patio of their friend Hakim's house. Hakim had been selected as the band's keyboard man.

It was 10 p.m. on July 7, 1982, a Monday night, when Farad and Ahmad swung across the alley and dropped silently down on to Hakim's tiny patio.

"Damn," said Ahmad.

"Forgot your drum, didn't you man?"

"Be right back." Ahmad swung back across the gap with the agility of a lemur and returned to the fire escape in an instant with his drum. The drum was actually a large hat box stolen from the back of a dress store on Hamra Street. The purple feathers printed on its sides had given the band its name, 'Purple.'

Ahmad tossed the drum across to Farad.

It was the hat box that saved Farad's hands from incineration. The explosion was ghastly. An Israeli tank shell slaughtered the eight Syrian resistance fighters who were hiding in Room 3C. The violence of the blast was so horrific it injured 40 people in adjacent areas, 12 of them maimed permanently. It sent pieces of rebar slashing into Farad's throat. The Gaza Tribune reported 17 people killed in the attack.

Room 2C was obliterated in the process.

Farad would never see his beloved twin again, nor would he ever taste his mother's Shakshoukeh. He would never again help his father fix things. And he would never sing another note.

The Purple Band's co-founder, nine-year-old Farad Aziz, had suddenly become an orphan, left alone on the mean streets of Beirut to fend for himself.

2005 – Beirut, Lebanon. 4 a.m. – 31 Years Later

A giant metal crane peered down from the corner of Riad Al Soth Square, a prehistoric bird frozen in time, hovering over the abandoned bones of Beirut Hospital's West Wing. Financial problems had ended its planned renovation and the deserted structure had become a community eyesore: mounds of gravel, rotted lumber, and twisted rebar left to rust in the damp night air. The once vital West Wing had perished, its healing powers extinguished, its hopeful voice mute.

No one saw the three men enter; no one would see them leave. Concealed by the silhouette of the massive construction crane, each man slipped through the darkness, walked up two flights of wooden stairs to the second floor, and took his place in the Oncology Ward's Operating Room B.

The little room was still connected to the hospital's auxiliary power system, but no light escaped its sealed doors. To the passerby, the west wing of Beirut Orthopedic remained a darkened appendage to the main buildings. But at 4 a.m. on the morning of June 11th, 2005, hidden deep within the skeleton, a procedure was underway. An operation of massive proportions.

Its completion would determine the precise location of 700,000 American gravesites.

Oncology Room B – Beirut Hospital

They were an unlikely trio, the three chieftains, vastly different in appearance, profession, background and bearing:

¤ Mullah Ahmed Rockmani – the idealist, a respected Shiite theologian, brilliant of intellect, a consecrated warrior of Allah, the spiritual voice and leader of *the movement.*

¤ Doctor Leon de Kennesy – the opportunist, second in command, equal in stature to the Mullah. Dr. de Kennesy was Head of Cranial Surgery at Beirut Orthopedic, a wealthy designer of micro instruments, a renowned philanthropist, a pillar of Lebanese society, the CEO and strategist of *the movement.*

¤ Farad Aziz – the soldier, a Palestinian, orphaned at 9 years old by an Israeli bomb, educated on the pockmarked streets of Beirut, suckled on hatred of the West, a dangerous psychotic, *the movement's* 31-year-old demolition savant. Farad Aziz was a late comer to the group, and from the beginning, was treated as such by the other two, more educated chieftains[1]

The three terrorists hiding in Op B were bound together by a single goal, *Velayat-e faghih*! (the Caliphate or death) Islamic domination of the world by the subjugation of all civil and political laws to a supreme religious theocracy. The Muslim governance of every human being on Earth.

The phrase had become a Jihadist battle cry in 1981 upon the assassination of Anwar el-Sadat. The captured Islamists had used their own blood to decorate their cells with the

---

1 Leon de Kennesy and Ahmed Rockmani had met as college students at Cairo University; Leon specializing in surgery, Rockmani studying comparative religions. At the time, the campus was boiling with Islamic activism but neither joined in the political activities, choosing instead to keep their passions to themselves.

Both had signed up for a class on Sayyid Qutb, the Egyptian scholar known as the father of modern fundamentalism. By a fluke of timing, both showed up for the class a day early. When no one else appeared, the two boys chided each other good-naturedly and decided to share lunch. When the call to prayer from the Aslam al-Silhdar Mosque sounded at dusk, the two were still at it.

And the partnership was formed; their secret two-man Jihad was conceived. At the time, neither boy realized the damage their youthful bond would one day unleash on the Western world.

words; and the words had become a fundamentalist battle cry. *Muslim dominance of the planet.*

Unlike their Muslim brothers, the triumvirate had created their own set of unique tactics. Since the late '70s, Muslim sects, Jihadists and Ayatollahs had been flexing their muscles, issuing public statements against the West; all of them vying for recognition, struggling to bring the cause of Allah to the public stage.

In contrast, the three men meeting in the empty Beirut hospital believed their Muslim compatriots 'talked too much and flapped their tails on the ground like impotent fish.'

Their *movement* would be invisible, cloaked in secrecy; in a word, the Jihad would remain *nameless.*

U.S. President Rundle Crowley's Pentagon experts had spent eight weeks developing their Pit Bull strategy. By comparison, the triumvirate sequestered in Op B had spent 14 years planning, funding, and training an army of Jihadist warriors – all of them eager to become martyrs for Allah. All of them sworn to the Caliphate.

Their plan was heroic in scope. Phase One would demand a massive input of cash to recruit and train a Jihadist militia. The training would be carried out in total secrecy. Islam would be the *medium*; martyrdom, the *message.*

Phase Two would require the embedding of highly trained, clandestine mercenary cells into the heartland of the U.S.

Phase Three would culminate in the triggering of simultaneous explosions; enormous, well planned, devastating blows to the underbelly of American life. Fatalities were expected to approach 700,000 with an untold number casualties. The result would dwarf the attack of 9/11.

Phase One – 1994

The initial task of building a secret Jihad had been wreathed in impossibles. The Middle Eastern economy was a financial wasteland; the founders had no money, no weapons, and no followers. Doctor Leon de Kennesy's practice was in its infancy. He had not yet begun to market the micro technology which would eventually make him a wealthy man. He convinced a family banker to *lend him $25,000 to purchase x-ray equipment for his first office.*

The Silent Jihad began with a paltry $25,000.

The money was gone in a matter of weeks. Doctor Leon was unable to fabricate any believable reasons to ask for more contributions to his fledgling practice. His fundraising efforts ground to a halt.

On the other hand, Mullah Rockmani's ascension to prominence had been almost immediate. From the start, his passionate anti-Western pronouncements had taken hold. He understood Islam's despondent youth; he spoke to their hearts, decrying their poverty, fueling their angers.

He reached out to a media-hip generation choked by their exposure to American television, taunted by visions of sexuality and Western excess. They were the offspring who had watched their parents and grandparents fall into despair, and stagnate in their own impotence.

Mullah Rockmani was a firebrand speechmaker. Short in stature, a heavy black beard, a bullet-shaped head and a bull-like stance, he literally assaulted his followers.

Standing in front of a youthful crowd, shifting his 200 pounds back and forth from one foot to the other, he would roar, "You are turning into your parents! The West is mocking your misery. America is laughing at your disgrace. They're drinking a Budweiser and watching your pathetic impotence on their big screens."

He took his message to the lowliest taverns, the poorest bazaars, rallying the illiterate, igniting their dreams, and blasting 'America's arrogant interventions.' He decreed an end to the West's 'disrespect and unholy decadence.'

The Mullah offered them hope. *Martyrdom was the redeeming weapon of the powerless.* Reward would come in the afterlife. He called them to arms with the prophetic words of his revered teacher, Sayyid Qutb, "'Brothers push ahead, for your path is soaked in blood. Do not turn your head right or left but look only up to Heaven.'"

To a culture mired in decades of poverty, drowning in despair, the Mullah's demand for a holy and redemptive Jihad rang out like the golden trumpets of deliverance.

By the end of their first year Mullah Ahmed Rockmani had developed a massive underground following.

And yet, Doctor Leon de Kennesy couldn't raise a single Piastre. Raising money in secret was impossible. No one was interested in supporting something they'd never heard of.

The wealthy wanted an explosive bang for their bucks. And by definition, the *bang* had to be public. The concept of a *silent* Jihad was beginning to feel like a non-sequitur.

Late in the Summer of 1996, a frustrated Doctor Leon de Kennesy and his spiritual compatriot, Mullah Ahmed Rockmani, sat in the shadows of Mseilha Quarry, sharing olives and wine, discussing their financial failures. Unwilling to give up his concept of secrecy, the Mullah suggested a change of plans, an idea that would change the course of their wavering Jihad. "All right then," he announced, "Why don't we give them what they want."

"What would that be, holy one?" said Leon.

"You told me yourself, Leon. The rich want some bang for their bucks. That's what you said, isn't it?"

"Yes."

"Then let's give it to them. Let's make an explosion."

In the Fall of 1996, Mullah Rockmani enlisted the services of a young bomb-making *savant*; the orphan of Beirut, Farad Aziz.

The young man was already a cult figure among Muslim youth. The wild-eyed, gravel-voiced urchin had become a symbol of Palestinian resistance, an ember of hope for the hopeless, well known for his frequent association with Hizb'allah.

The name Farad Aziz was spoken with great reverence. His talent for creating explosive devices using wristwatches, car parts, butane canisters and chicken wire had made him a legend. His homemade devices had already killed hundreds of Israelis.

It was the perfect catalyst.

Almost immediately, the Silent Jihad began receiving anonymous donations. The first benefactors were wealthy Lebanese businessmen whose children had told them tales of the great "Jew killer," Farad Aziz.

Slowly, gradually, the contributions grew larger. When the union received a silent endorsement from Hizb'allah, donations began filtering in from Iran.

By January of 1998, the coffers had billowed to just under $200,000. Leon was able to begin building a bare-bones training facility in a remote tribal region of South Waziristan. Maintaining the Mullah's penchant for secrecy, the base was given a simple, un-provocative Arabic name, *Talib* (student).

Twenty-three months later, the $200,000 plus Talib's specialized training had been successfully produced a force of 230 Jehadi fighters, all murderous fanatics, all of them conjured, trained and armed in total secrecy.

Phase One was complete.

Phase Two – 2000

Initially, Phase Two, the exporting and inserting of Jihadist sleeper cells into the American heartland, had proven to be impossible. Necessities such as driver's licenses, passports, and credible historical documentation were beyond their expertise. Freedom of movement across borders, and reliable safe houses in Europe or Canada, were financially beyond their reach.

And then, something providential occurred. At 3 a.m. on a Saturday morning, Doctor Leon de Kennesy, Chief cranial surgeon at Beirut's Orthopedic Hospital, was called in to officially pronounce the time of death on a young victim whose head had been crushed in a drunk driving accident. An unsuccessful craniotomy had failed to stop the internal bleeding in her brain and nothing more could be done.

Instead of shutting down the respirators, Doctor Leon intervened, requesting permission from the victim's parents to attempt a radical procedure never before preformed in a Middle Eastern hospital. Using a video tool of his own invention, Doctor Leon successfully located and repaired an embolism in the cerebral cortex of seven-year-old Atiya Biheiri.

Two weeks later, young Atiya was sent home from the hospital, whole and complete, snatched from the arms of death by the miracle worker – Doctor Leon de Kennesy. Her miraculous recovery established a special bond between Doctor Leon and the girl's father, Soliman Biheiri, a well-known international banker.

As if to bear witness to *the power of Allah,* Mr. Biheiri turned out to be a banker with a special clientele – a network of fundamentalist investors with a wide range of holy causes and charities.

As the head of a Saudi charity called the World Assembly of Muslim Youth (WAMY), Biheiri had a direct line to The Muslim Brotherhood which gave him access to hundreds of millions in terrorist funds. His specialty was the investment, laundering and redistribution of those funds through various international fronts, charities, banks and businesses.

Money changed everything.

When Biheiri opened his network of sources to his new friend Doctor Leon de Kennesy, the Silent Jihad became a real terrorist organization, a frightening juggernaut. The once flowering and reverent religion of Islam began to sprout an ugly growth, a newborn stalk of bloody malignance.

From 2000 through 2004, funds from The Muslim Brotherhood, plus silent contributions from sources in Iran and other nameless individuals, were laundered, invested and manipulated by Biheiri, resulting in a war chest for the Silent Jihad of just under $5 million. The money was then withdrawn from the National Iranian Bank in Dubai (NIB) by Doctor Leon and artfully used to launch Phase Two of the Silent Jihad's long range plan.

The plan stalled immediately. Every one of Talib's trained mercenaries was turned back, arrested or simply disappeared. It would take almost a year to perfect the forgeries necessary to fool the U.S. border officials. But eventually, using different ports of entry and improved documentation, the Talib mercenaries were warily transported, one by one, across American borders and into the belly of the Great Satan. The process took three years.

By September of 2003 Phase Two had successfully placed three well-trained terrorist cells deep within the borders of the United States. The initial cells were located in Minnesota, Tennessee and Texas. Each cell, called *amAtya* (family), was comprised of six members, all speaking passable English, each of them possessing varied skills, all of them ready to die for Allah. By 2005, Nebraska and California would be added bringing the total to five *amAtya* imbedded behind the lines.

Each of these Jihadist families had received 20 months of training at Talib. Six of those months were dedicated to *Americanizing* the graduates. Language, idiom, dress, customs, employable skills, these were the subjects reinforced by the staff at Talib. 'Fitting in' became an end in itself, more valuable than fighting ability or weaponry.

The primary goal of each *amAtya* was to become part of their local neighborhoods; viable cogs in the American workforce; watching television, driving trucks, eating pizza, carrying out the garbage, enjoying the weather.

Trained. Skilled. Motivated. Warriors of Allah, poised to strike. Waiting. Waiting for instructions.

No one spoke of them. No one in the American intelligence community had ever heard of them. Anonymity had been chiseled into their charter 14 years earlier by Mullah Rockmani's initial mandate, "An invisible enemy is impossible to find."

Phase Two was complete.

Phase Three – 2005

The little room in Op B still retained a faint odor from the cancer medicines left on the shelves surrounding the three chieftains. But theirs was a sickness beyond any cancer ever treated on the once vital Oncology ward. The Silent Jihad had already become an inoperable disease.

Phase Three is within reach.

Her name was Mary Schulenburg, Secretary Ramsey's second assistant. She had worked in the steno pool on the innermost ring of the Pentagon for 5 years; and she was one of Ramsey's favorites.

She was also one of Leon de Kennesy's favorites, a highly paid, technically skilled, and wonderfully creative mole.

Five hours after Morton Ramsey had finished his *Pit Bull* speech in the Pentagon's Counterterrorism Boardroom, Leon de Kennesy was in his library in Beirut, reading an exact copy of the speech.

Mary Schulenburg had proven her worth.

Oncology Room B – Beirut Hospital

Leon explained the 'fantastic intelligence coup' he had pulled off, and then proudly distributed copies of the Pit Bull speech to his partners. As they poured over each word of the coveted document, Leon unabashedly picked at non-existent specks of lint on his hand-tailored Brioni suit.

The 6'3," Doctor de Kennesy was lean and slender with dark olive skin and wavy dark hair. A pencil-thin moustache slashed across his rectangular face dividing it into two contradictory halves. From the serious top half, a prominent nose angrily asserted itself between eyes so dark they appeared rimmed in charcoal; while from the bottom half, a mouthful of perfect white teeth exuded warmth and charisma. The overall impression was a disarming mixture; simultaneous warmth and latent hostility. To his friends, Leon appeared powerful and charming; to his enemies, he was an evil two-faced, lying manipulator.

When it was clear that his two partners had finished re-reading the Pit Bull document, the sartorial Doctor Leon immediately launched into a personal evaluation of the purloined document.

"Typical," he said with a smirk. "So typical of Ramsey and his arrogance. Another show of force. That'll do it. A louder bang. Guaranteed to make all of us ignorant little rag heads run for the hills. Wouldn't you think they'd have learned something from the Vietnam debacle?"

Farad Aziz, his voice a quiet rasp, was quick to respond. "I hear President Crowley is so stupid, he still thinks they won the war in Vietnam." The beards shook with laughter. The sheer blind stubbornness of the arrogant American military establishment was a marvel that had persisted for decades.

When the laughter diminished, Mullah Rockmani spoke, and the mood turned suddenly from light to dark.

Leon and Farad waited as the Mullah took a long drink from his water glass. Carefully wiping the moisture from his heavy beard, Rockmani continued, "We have our *amAtya* in place. Martyrs to be, all of them. Years of losses trying to get them in. But we have done it. And they are there – waiting."

The Mullah looked directly at Farad. "We are so close to the ultimate success. So close. But every day we don't deliver the explosives to them, our Jihad moves closer to disaster, and complete failure.

"Remember who they are, our noble fighters. They're simple men. Men of the desert. Unsophisticated. Uneducated. We're asking them to do the impossible. To live as one with the infidel. To fit in with the most corrupt people on this earth."

The Mullah raised his hands toward heaven. "In spite of all that Allah has done for us...it can only be a matter of time. One of them is going to make a mistake. It's inevitable. Someone will get drunk or get in a fight, the neighbors will see something out of character, or whatever it might be...but something is bound to go wrong. Someone will notify the authorities and one of them will get arrested. And they'll break him in an instant. And that will be the end of it. All of it. Finished! Our years of struggle will come to nothing."

The Mullah held up his copy of the Pit Bull Strategy. "This document, this Pentagon strategy, yes, yes it's remarkable that we have it. Once again Leon, your woman...the mole, she has accomplished the impossible. But unfortunately at this moment, it's exactly what we don't need. Until we have our explosives in place, this piece of paper is irrelevant. Phase Three is all that matters. The only thing that matters. And Phase Three is about explosives! Nothing else. We cannot afford a distraction. I say again, the American scientist, this (he searched for the American word) this bull dog is completely irrelevant."

"Agreed!" said Doctor Leon, keenly aware of the right moment to back off. He pushed his large hand toward Farad Aziz, preempting any response from the young bomb maker. "Let's not waste any more time in discussion. The Pit Bull strategy, this scientist, it's all just another one of their reality shows. Is it not? Cheap fireworks and all. As you say, holy one, it's irrelevant. Let's get to the explosives."

Only then did Doctor Leon lower his hand and look toward Farad Aziz for a response. In Leon's mind, Aziz was an impetuous street rat, a dangerous psychotic. *This little punk is nothing more than a low grade mechanic. Demeaning. A danger to the movement. He's sitting across the table from a renowned brain surgeon and a most holy cleric.*

"Come on Farad," snapped Leon. "Let's have the status on the explosives?" His question was clearly not a question, it was a command.

Farad Aziz sat across from Doctor Leon, head tilted downward, a mass of unkempt black dreadlocks resting on his chest. For a moment he twisted one of the rivets on the front of his biker jacket. Farad hated this arrogant prick of a doctor. And one day he would bring him down.

The silver chain stretching from his belt to his pocket clanked against the leg of his chair as he shifted position. His head came up, a controlled anger compressing the sides of his mouth.

"It's done," he said, "Exactly as I said it would be. I've paid the Irishman. Semtex. It's Semtex. I got it from my contact in the IRA. He's absolutely guaranteed its delivery. The bricks'll be sitting on the dock in Napoli on March 1st. No sweat."

Farad shifted his eyes to the ceiling, as if Leon were some ignorant oaf. "You may not know this, *Doctor* (he spat out the word) but Napoli is the easiest port in Europe for moving contraband. The Camorra runs everything. I paid the Irishman extra. He's already taken care of them. Simple. Everyone's happy. From there, it should be the easiest port in the world to get the stuff out of and headed for Canada."

"Should be?" asked Leon, making no attempt to hide his skepticism.

"Did you hear me, Leon? When I said guaranteed, I meant guaranteed. I set it up. It's done."

"Excellent," said the Mullah, cutting short the festering animosity that was no longer a secret. The Mullah touched Farad Aziz on the forearm, a rare acknowledgment from a holy Muslim leader to one of his brethren. Attempting to achieve a moment of calm, the Mullah spoke quietly. "Farad has the explosives under control. Correct Farad?"

Farad's dark eyes were covered by the mat of black curls hanging from his forehead. He said nothing.

"Farad. So silent?" A second attempt by the Mullah to get the mercurial young bomb maker to stay focused. "Do you think we're missing something?"

Farad answered without looking up, "No, I agree with everything you said. Put on a show. Typical. It's what they always do." A moment passed, then Farad's head came up, his eyes meeting the Mullah's. "But... yes, holy one, the truth is, I think you're missing the point. Both of you."

A deep furrow knifed into Leon's large forehead. "Is it something about the explosives?"

"No it's not the explosives," croaked Farad. "It's the American scientist. And it is so relevant."

"Enlighten us then." Leon's condescension was obvious.

"All right Doctor de Kennesy, I will." Farad answered with equal condescension. "They send over the best bomb maker they've got, right? Their fancy scientist. Towne. The great laser man. Rockets through Saddam's windows. Destroyed Baghdad. And you two think it doesn't matter?

"One of their generals sticks his head out of the bunker and you think it's nothing?" Farad pointed his finger at Leon. "You work in a goddamn hospital, man. A clean room. 'Three more CCs of this. Take two of these.' This ain't a tea party. It's a goddamn war, remember!"

Farad suddenly ripped his Glock 21 pistol out and shoved the blunt muzzle into his own temple, his eyes wild. "BANG! He's dead. You understand what I'm saying? I put a big round hole in his laser brain. No more bullshit. Bang. No more bomb maker. Get it? Bang. Send one of them to hell where they all belong."

Farad lowered his pistol, his eyes boring into Leon's unresponsive face. "This ain't a board room, Leon. It ain't your fancy Cairo College either. It's real. It's the goddamn street talkin'. When your enemy falls down, you stomp his head, man. You make sure he never gets up again. It's called war. And you don't know shit about it."

Leon, ever the chameleon, knowing what was at stake, quickly changed his tone. *Perhaps this idiot will respond to a bit of bedrock dogma.*

"Farad, Farad, it would absolutely give us all great pleasure to blow the bastard's head off. Of course it would. But the goal. The real goal. When the Almighty commands us to punish the infidel, it's the Caliphate we're seeking. It's all of them. Not just one. *Velayat-e faghih!* All of them! Burning in hell's fire. A far better goal than killing one puny scientist."

Farad panned his dark eyes reverently from one face to the other; the surgeon, the holy Mullah, then back to the surgeon. How he hated Leon, the bully in the big house on the hill, the arrogant prick who treated him like a brainless donkey.

Farad pinched his own eyes tightly shut as if considering Leon's words. *After I kill the American scientist, after I've set the fuses in Satan's belly, after my name is known by 10 million sons of Allah, I'll save something special for you, Leon. Blow off your surgeon fingers one at a time. Then your feet. Then your tongue. You pig turd.*

A moment passed. Farad began nodding his head. Opening his eyes, feigning enlightenment, the words came slowly. "Yes. Of course. *Velayat-e faghih.* The infidels must die, all of them. All of them burning in hell fire. Of course I agree. Of course that is the goal set by our holy Mullah Rockmani himself."

Hooking his backpack over his shoulder, Farad stood up from the table and began moving toward the door, his stare fixed on Leon. "Well here's another worthy goal for you, mister PhD scholar. It's a quote from your beloved Sayyid Qutb, one you apparently forgot. Section two. *Milestones.* About the Americans and their lack of morality. He says it straight out. Quote! 'One of their dead leaders is worth 1000 of their live followers.' I'd say it's plain bloody clear what he meant."

His exit from the room was sudden and unexpected. In the Muslim world, the courtesy of first departure was always reserved for clerics. To bolt out of the room before the holy Mullah Rockmani was so insulting as to be a punishable act.

Mullah Rockmani and Doctor Leon remained sitting. Nothing needed to be said. The mercurial Farad Aziz was vitally important to the success of Phase Three. As the Jihad had grown, so had Farad's skill. He was now an expert with the newest detonators. Every one of the devastating explosions so carefully planned in the American heartland was solely dependent on Farad Aziz. The "rock and the hard place" were obvious.

6

Paris International Technology Convention

At 2 p.m., French President Gaston's personal limousine deposited Doctor Luke Towne at the infamous golden bridge, the $1 million swatch of architectural excess that now served as the upgraded entrance to Paris's Prince Hotel.

Doctor Luke Towne, the Pentagon's man, was 30 minutes late. Event planners had been updated that his ride through the rain and traffic from de Gaul had been unbearably slow.

Luke Towne never made public appearances. It was a complete surprise to most pundits that the Pentagon would permit their leading laser scientist to deliver the keynote address at the International Technology Convention.

As the Head of the U.S. Military's Department of Laser Research, Luke Towne was the foremost authority on laser guidance technology, and recognized as the real author of a good many of Schwarzkopf's smart bomb video success stories. In the area of advanced, experimental laser technology, as well as, the deployment of space weapons, Luke Towne was considered the *horse's mouth*.

On this, the opening day of the Convention, the Prince Hotel's magnificent, double-tiered meeting pavilion was jammed with international guests. When Dr. Towne and his attaché, Master Sergeant David Halter, entered the reception area, they were greeted with a loud burst of applause. Attendants rushed to clear a path, while a French contingent of award-winning, young science students came forward to usher the eminent American to the dais.

Once there, Luke was greeted first by France's military brass, then by several scientists, and finally by the President himself, Jean Pierre Gaston, who bestowed upon Luke the traditional buss on both cheeks.

In his formal introduction, President Gaston was kind enough to take the blame for the weather and what he called "unusually bad traffic." This drew laughter from the guests who appreciated Mr. Gaston's tongue-in-cheek remark. 'Bad traffic' was already beginning to replace 'young lovers' as the modern symbol of Parisian life.

"Ladies and gentlemen," said President Gaston, becoming serious, "We are privileged to have as our keynote speaker, a renowned and multi-talented scientist from America. Doctor Luke Towne graduated Cum Laude from the Monterey Institute of International Studies with a PhD in Optical Technology and Quantum Physics. In just over a decade, he has become the U.S. Army's preeminent authority on laser defense systems. An internationally known expert, a virtual pioneer in advanced laser technology, his contributions to current scientific thought have been revolutionary. Of necessity, most of his designs are classified as top secret or we feel he would certainly be a Nobel candidate.

"Without further delay, it is my pleasure at last to give you our most distinguished guest speaker, Doctor Luke Towne."

Luke stood and approached the podium to a barrage of spirited applause. He was a visual anomaly; 5'11¾' 200 pounds, his nose pushed slightly to one side from one too many fists, the former Special Forces Colonel (the Pit Bull) looked more like a boxer than a laser expert.

But in spite of a slight paunch at the belt line, Luke Towne was still an intimidating figure. His upper body strength was still quite evident, as was his alert commando bearing. His superior intellect was widely recognized throughout the Corps. During his second tour in Vietnam, his buddies at Camp Bu Dop had affectionately referred to him as 'the Pit Bull from Mensa.'

Twelve years since retiring from active duty, standing at the podium, Doctor Luke Towne cut a striking figure in his uniform as a colonel in the U.S. Rangers. Fifty-five years old, a touch of gray at the temples, deep-set hazel eyes, he had become a commanding intellectual presence in the scientific community.

And he still looked like the wrong guy to pick a fight with.

After acknowledging his hosts, Luke got straight to the point. "As many of you know, I am half of a scientific team. My partner, Doctor Cynthia Teller, is a surgeon and the head of the Ocular Research Department at the Eisenhower Research Hospital. Our collaboration produced the article some of you may have read in this month's Lancet Journal of Medicine."

A tremendous burst of applause interrupted Luke's speech. The Lancet article had created a whirlwind of interest throughout the scientific community and was to be the subject of his keynote address.

Luke acknowledged the applause with a polite nod, waited for silence and then continued. "Doctor Teller designed the micro lens itself; my team added the laser-assist. Together we prototyped the result as a stand-alone device. We christened it 'The Mind's Eye.'

"Six months ago, Doctor Teller implanted the Mind's Eye device in the eye of a female Indonesian orangutan. The eyesight of the Kalimantan ape most closely approximates that of a human being. Test data from that experiment is what formed the basis of the paper we published."

Luke's eyes made a quick sweep of the room. "The result of the implant was an enhancement in the animal's vision...of 92%. That's almost double its normal vision. As a result of this research, we believe that degenerative vision – the gradual loss of vision in humans due to the aging process – may be reversible."

There was a stunned silence. Luke waited a full 10 seconds for the impact of his statement to register.

After making the most of his dramatic pause, his mood changed visibly and he stepped out from behind the podium to deliver the next part of his message. "Our *Lasocular* Technology has given birth to a wide range of new and equally helpful products. In just a moment here, I'm going to show you a demonstration of how our focused laser technology can help us better protect our citizens from harm."

There was no indication that Luke's keynote address was about to undergo a major gear change. In truth, Colonel Towne's long awaited address at the Paris Convention was a feint; what in the schmata (rag) business would be called *a loss leader*. The real reason the Pentagon had sent its top laser scientist to Paris had everything to do with politics and nothing to do with medical advances.

Secretary of Defense Morton Ramsey had made the purpose quite clear, referring to Luke's potential audience as "every other son of a bitch principality that thinks they're gonna get away with harboring terrorists."

Luke and his team had written the original speech. It had been analyzed, revised and rewritten by the Pentagon. From his office at The Facility, Luke's voice transmission had been sent to Washington enumerable times, each inflection rehearsed until the experts had finally given their approval.

Nothing left to chance, no subtlety undetected.

Luke was to begin his treatise on Lasocular Technology, whet their appetite about the new laser lens, and then open the floor to a few brief questions. On cue, a scientist from Indonesia would ask a prepared question and this would be

Luke's opportunity to artfully turn to the real purpose of the presentation.

The political meat and potatoes.

Two weeks earlier, the show's line producer, Colonel Ari Shine, former head of demolition for the Mossad, had quietly checked in to the Prince Hotel with a team of specialists. Over the years, Ari and Luke had collaborated on numerous military ops, most of which were clandestine. Ari's team – four Israeli computer techs, four carpenters and six of The Facility's laser scientists – were sequestered in the hotel's basement, working round the clock in an isolated group of linked maintenance rooms (L 10 through L 16). Their combined efforts had all been in preparation for this day.

It wasn't Paris traffic or inclement weather or flight turbulence that had caused Luke to be late to the dais. It was a flawed memory chip in the primary laser cannon in room L 10 that had caused the delay. The meat and potatoes could not commence until the chip was replaced.

When Luke had landed at de Gaul, there was a cryptic message waiting on his cell from Colonel Ari Shine: "Doctor Towne, this is Chef Jean Louis. We've finished the hors d'oeuvres and refrigerated the dip. Happy to report the chips have just arrived. Party should be delayed only about 20 minutes."

Nine hundred attendees now sat 12-to-a-table in the huge rococo ballroom in rapt attention as Luke began what sounded like a description of the potential of Lasocular Technology – the term itself recently coined in his Lancet article.

He explained the conjunction of stabilized laser technology and ocular surgery and then, as if stopping to make sure everyone was on board, he asked nonchalantly, "Any questions so far?"

A scientist from France asked the first question. "Doctor Towne, we who work with laser light know that it's not a very stable medium. Atmospheric conditions, Doppler shift, all kinds of interruptions cause it to break down. How have you been able to solve the problem over distance?"

Luke paused a moment to formulate an answer that would be brief yet relevant to his colleague's knowledge base. "The signal is transported as the difference in frequency between two proton beams spatially combined at the transmitter. The frequency remains constant irrespective of the medium through which it may be traveling – fibers, free space, water, whatever."

As a postscript Luke added, “Certainly the velocity of light may decrease and the wavelength may increase a bit, but the frequency remains fairly consistent without a loss of signal integrity or fidelity. To modulate the frequencies, we used integrated piezoelectric hologram modulators plus an array of integrated surface acoustic wave transducers. We combine ‘em to shift the frequency by an amount exactly equal to the RF signal format of the information to be sent.”

There was a thoughtful silence while the scientists in the room considered the implications of the answer.

Luke took the opportunity to lighten the moment. “I'm sure these boring technicalities aren't of much interest to most of you. Doesn't anyone out there care about the orangutan?”

As the audience obliged with congenial laughter, an Indonesian scientist recognized Luke's signal and stood to ask the question they had prepared. But before he could get the words out, he was preempted by the voice of a woman.

“Professor Towne,” she called out strongly. All eyes in the audience shifted. Standing amidst the delegation from Lebanon was a woman who looked decidedly unscientific. She was fair-skinned, honey-haired and stunning. Her voice was pitched unusually low for a female, throaty and rich, but her words were crystal clear, forceful and articulate.

“Professor Towne,” she repeated, “given the proximity of the laser's power source to the brain stem, whether human or animal, how have you managed to block interference from the transmission of the brain's own electrical charges?”

It was impossible to decide which provided the biggest impact, the beauty of the questioner or the acuity of the question.

Luke walked across the stage to field her question more personally. One sentence into his answer he looked directly into the woman's amazing transparent blue/green eyes, lost his focus and forgot what he was saying.

He caught himself quickly, pulled his eyes away and turned to the audience. “As you might imagine, a good deal of our research is classified. Regrettably, the question posed by this young...scientist requires a more detailed answer than I am at liberty to give. Perhaps the published paper...in the medical journal, The Lancet...I'm only presenting a small part of it here today...perhaps the complete document in The Lancet would provide you with a satisfactory answer to your question.”

He nodded toward her, then walked to center stage and cleared his throat. "Ladies and gentlemen, there are many uses for this remarkable little lens and its attendant technology. As I've indicated, not all of them are medical. I have something else to show you. Something I feel is of equal importance. Something relevant to the use of weapons in space."

As he spoke, the curtains behind him parted to reveal a large, white-walled, three-sided room, the fourth side open to permit the audience a view. Two massive plasma screens were mounted high above the floor on either side of the stage.

"As we go along here, you'll be able to see close-ups of everything on the big flat screens, there and there," he said, indicating the large black monitors.

A buzz of excitement shot through the attendees. This was totally unexpected.

Luke walked toward the back of the set. "On the back wall there," he said, using a laser pointer, "Please notice the inverted delta triangle. At the top right corner of the triangle, you'll notice we've built a little model of a traditional American dream house. It's accurate to scale, a white, two-bedroom stucco job; picket fence, grass in the front, barbeque in the back. This kind of home has been the prototypical American dream house for the last 50 years. Millions of 'em make up our American heartland.

"At the top left corner of the triangle, across from the stucco house, is a little one-story, sand-colored house, more typical of those built for centuries throughout the Middle East and Europe."

He moved his pointer downward. "Down here, at the bottom of the triangle, we've set up this little silver pistol and aimed it at the front door of the American house."

Luke removed the pistol from its mount and held it up for the audience to see. "An air pistol, a BB gun," he announced, "Made by Daisy. It used to be every American kid's dream at Christmas to find one of these little pop guns under the tree. It works on air pressure. Packs just about enough wallop to knock a black bird off a tree limb, but not quite enough kill it."

He pumped the little gun's handle, turned and fired at a red balloon fastened high up in the corner of the back wall. Pop! His aim was accurate; the balloon popped. A couple of hesitant claps sounded from the audience.

No one was sure where this was going.

"All right," he said, snapping the gun back on to its mount. "Behind the house, you'll see we've got a bale of heavy cotton material. It'll catch the BB when it comes out the back of the house."

He walked to center stage and produced a silver PDA from his pocket. "With this cell phone I can fire the little pea shooter from way over here," he said. Then, without hesitation he pointed the PDA and pressed one of its buttons. Pop! The BB gun fired.

Its tiny pellet ripped through the center of the little house and landed in the cotton bale. There was no smoke. The house remained intact. There was no perceptible damage except for the tiny pellet hole in the front door.

"Small gun; small bullet," Luke said nonchalantly. "No real damage to speak of. At least none you can see. But there is one thing worthy of note here."

He detached the miniature house from its bearings and held it up for the audience see. "You'll notice that the exit hole in the back is slightly larger than the one made through the front . That's because, as most of you already know, a high speed projectile creates energy by pushing air in front of it, as well as by trapping particles of whatever mass it encounters on its way through a target. Result; a small hole in the front, a bigger one in the back.

"I am now going to shoot another little BB through the front door of our American dream house. But this time I'll be demonstrating a new process we've developed called Tensor Compactive Ballistics; that's TCB for short. It utilizes several of Doctor Teller's tiny ocular lenses plus some other classified components.

"Simply stated, it harnesses the expanding energy created around a projectile as it moves through space, and rapidly builds it to an explosive force many times greater than the projectile could produce by itself."

He replaced the miniature white house on its mounts, then pointed to a tiny cable dish that was mounted on a pole behind the American style house. "That little gizmo on the pole there is pointing at the Middle Eastern house. It's made to look exactly like your standard cable dish, but it isn't. Its function is to contain, expand and redirect energy. It's going to redirect the energy created by the BB when it comes out the back of the little white house. Something I'll now demonstrate."

He returned to center stage and again pointed the PDA toward the BB gun. "Remember," he said, lowering the remote for a moment, "This is still just a little BB we're shootin' here. However, I suggest this time you focus your attention on the second house, the Middle Eastern one in the upper left corner of our triangle. That's where the collected laser energy will be directed."

He raised the silver PDA and pushed its button. Pop! Once again the BB punched through the little white American house with the same effect, no perceptible damage. But ½ second later there was a violent sound like the air brakes on a massive 16-wheeler.

Pfsssssssst!

The Middle Eastern house had vaporized. There was nothing left but a tiny puff of steam. Even the posts it was mounted on had disintegrated, leaving only a spinning eddy of gray-white smoke. The Middle Eastern house had vanished.

The room went deathly silent – 900 stunned faces were frozen in shock. Luke stood immobile in front of them. Ten seconds; 15 seconds; 20 seconds; only then did a few muted whispers begin hissing across the faces.

Luke took a step forward and waited for silence. "That, ladies and gentlemen, is what the U.S. Defense Department calls TCB, takin' care of business. It's amazing what U.S. Lasocular science can do."

He waited another moment and then said warmly, "Thank you for your attention. I suggest that we wrap it up here now, and adjourn to the foyer for some of the legendary cuisine prepared by Chef Louis Carbinere. Thank you again."

Gradually and uncertainly the applause began, one group joining another until the collective response grew louder and louder. But there were many faces lined in tension; some still in shock.

As attendants opened the banquet room's doors and the scent of French cooking embraced the room, the tension lifted and the crowd began chattering and moving toward the buffet. On the way, Luke's assistant, Master Sergeant David Halter, passed him a note:

That woman's name is Kathryn. She's the personal attaché to Lebanese Ambassador Hagopian.

Almost immediately as they entered the banquet room, Sergeant Halter alerted him, "Nine o'clock. The Kathryn woman. Moving in, sir."

Luke turned nonchalantly to his left and there she was. "Kathryn," he beamed, "A pleasure to meet you. The depth of your question caught me completely off guard. Are you a scientist?" he asked, taking in the whole package.

A radiant smile. "No scientist. My father's a cranial surgeon. Brain stuff's been dinner table conversation since I was 14. Any chance I get my question answered in person?"

She hadn't let go of his hand.

"Uh, I've got to meet with some French people in about 10 minutes. I'm sorry but I don't think I could satisfy your curiosity in that short a time." *The double entendre.* He was immediately embarrassed at the implication of his words.

"How 'bout brunch, say the day after tomorrow?" she said, stifling a smile of her own.

"That would be...nice." *This is good.*

"Do you know the Doves?"

"I do." He had no idea where the "Doves" was.

"Eleven o'clock too early?"

"Eleven's good."

"See you then," she said, and disappeared into the crowd.

7

Love is the dog of hell. It will stalk you and chew your eyelids until it blinds you; then dine on your heart and leave your bones in the gutter.

Charles Bukowski

Luke Towne's keynote address was everything the Conference planners had hoped it would be. His revelation of the Mind's Eye lens and its healing potential for human eyesight had set the medical community buzzing. His brief discourse on enhanced laser stability had ignited the minds of his fellows in the scientific community.

But his demonstration of the U.S. Military's destructive laser weapons had created a tumult of outrage so widespread that all else was forgotten. By 6 p.m., the Parisian talk shows were inundated with vitriolic rant. By 8 p.m., the national newspapers had already set tomorrow's headlines in bold point, eager to run their indignation above the fold.

The Prince Hotel – Paris, France

The post conference cocktail parties were endless; more than 40 *important organizations* had invited the distinguished American scientist to stop by their suites for just a few moments of face time. It was part of the job, and one of the reasons that Luke never made public appearances.

By the time he had finished his mandatory visits, it was 2 a.m. Twelve hours of handshaking. He staggered into the penthouse elevator, happy to finally be off the political barbeque. The express car shot upward toward the 50th floor. He loosened his collar, sagged against the hand rail and shook his head at the wrinkled image in the mahogany shine.

God I look old.

He stepped off the elevator and stopped dead in his tracks. A mob of newspaper and television reporters had formed an angry clot in front of Suite 500.

"There he is!" shouted a female reporter. "How dare you threaten the world community! Who do you think you are?"

"Where the hell do you Americans think you're going with this kind of ugliness?" shouted a tall man. Then he shoved his microphone aggressively into Luke's face, waiting for the reply.

The 200-pound, former Special Forces Colonel calmly took hold of the microphone, imprisoning the reporter's fingers around it as he did. Then he gently lowered the microphone to waist level, in the process bending the reporter's hand backward at a right angle to his own forearm. The man's painful scream knifed into the atmosphere, stunning the crowd to a rapt silence.

The front-rowers began easing themselves gently backwards into the pack. Luke's expression remained sanguine. He released the pressure slightly and cleared his throat. "Ladies and gentlemen, it's been a long day and I appreciate your attention. But in answer to this gentlemen's question, I'm going directly to bed. Perhaps tomorrow would be a better time for questions."

The microphone suddenly cracked in half from the power of Luke's grip. It shattered into a mass of tiny pieces that splashed down to the marble floor. The sound of the splintered remnants hitting the hard marble reverberated off the floor and the mirrored walls. The scent of fear began to suffuse the atmosphere like a putrid leak. An uncertain silence persisted.

Luke released the reporter's hand and took a step forward. The crowd parted instantly. He passed through them, unlocked the door to Suite 500, and quietly pulled the door closed behind him.

The White House – Washington D.C.

At the White House, behind closed doors, the lights burned long into the night. The President's advisors sat in the media room, cheering each televised polemic condemning America's behavior at the Paris Convention.

The BBC news hour quoted a headline from the French newspaper, Connexion: "France's noble attempt at a peaceful sharing of world technology was brutalized by the American Imperialists." France 24, a Global news channel called American scientists "...war mongers." Le Monde Diplomatique called President Crowley the "Hitler of the 21st Century." Colonel Towne was labeled "...another Goebbels."

Big cheers in the White House Media Room were led by Chief of Staff Mike Yost, one of the plan's architects. The Pit

Bull Strategy was an overwhelming success. The international uproar was precisely what the White House had hoped for.

The more negative the responses, the more loudly they cheered.

Finally, at 10 p.m., the President joined them in the media room, greeted with boisterous applause and salvos of "Hip hip hoorays." He acknowledged their happiness with a grateful smile and thanked them for their advice and hard work. He then excused himself and went upstairs to bed, in preparation for tomorrow night's fireside chat. Next to his bed was a copy of his speech, made almost unreadable by the numerous revisions.

Anticipating the success of the Pit Bull Strategy, the President's speechwriters had spent more than 100 man hours crafting the President's retort. This time Run Crowley was going to 'hit one out of the park.' His speech was going to restore faith in the country. It was going to put the fear of devastating retaliation into any terrorist or principality that harbored thoughts of attack. And ultimately, it was going to put Run Crowley back on top of the polls where he hadn't been for months.

The President opened his fireside chat seated behind his desk, TV cameras capturing the warm reflection of crackling flames from the adjacent hearth. He began in a friendly mood by underscoring the wonderful medical advances pioneered and presented by Doctor Luke Towne at the Paris Technology Convention. With great pride, Crowley himself then introduced one more of Doctor Towne's new Lasocular techniques. "The age of glasses and contact lenses might be coming to an end."

He was referring to a revolutionary eye mapping process that might now permanently restore regular vision to a majority of people whose eyesight had simply deteriorated due to the normal aging process.

And finally, the President announced that due to Doctor Towne's Lasocular advances, America would *gift* a set of operative techniques to third world countries that would greatly reduce the heretofore prohibitive cost of eye surgery.

The camera pushed in for a close-up of the dark blue eyes and the rugged face. This was clearly a more serious President Run Crowley. His teeth clenched once accentuating the iron jaw, and he began.

"I would like to address those who find fault with America's newly enhanced protective strength. Or with our powerful military capacities. Let us not forget that it was America's superior military technology that saved all of us..." his eyes bored more directly into camera "... that rescued all of you, your children, and your grandchildren from the horrors of Hitler's terrorist attempt at world domination.

"Let us not forget that it was the willingness of the average American man on the street to leave the safety of his home and his family, to fly to an occupied and terrorized foreign country, and to fight and die for the freedom and rights of a world of strangers, most of whom didn't even speak the same language as we did.

"Must I now remind the world that it was these very same American citizens, these guiltless average men and woman, who were slaughtered by the unprovoked terrorist attacks of 9/11? Must I now remind the world that we are facing constant terrorist attempts at world domination?

"I would suggest that should America be called upon once again to protect ourselves or to rescue others from the horrors of terrorism, we intend to be prepared. And I guarantee you and your children that it will be the enhanced strength of our military technology and the same generous American men and women that will once again be there to answer the call.

"Thank you. May God bless you. May his love keep you safe, whatever your country. And may God bless America."

8

The 9th Arrondissement, France 11:30 p.m.

By tourist standards, Café Petit Blanc was a dump. Sandwiched between a loading dock and a warehouse in the 9th arrondissement, the tiny, five-windowed shack served as the commissary for the Moulin Blanc, the venerable old laundry which had been washing the blue collars of Paris for more than a century.

Paris taxis avoided the narrow industrial alleys of the 9th. It was in *terra incognita,* a traveler's no-man's-land. If you wanted a bowl of their rabbit stew and a "bière de garde," you'd have to hoof it in 12 blocks from the Grands Boulevards.

The Café Blanc was a perfect spot to hide from the press.

Her hair was pulled up in a bun. It was 11 hours after the opening of the Convention. She was in jeans, a plain cotton hoody and a pair of tortoise-shell glasses. But no attempt at looking ordinary could hide the natural radiance given her at birth. At 34, Kathryn de Kennesy was a singularly beautiful woman. And a very recognizable one; a double celebrity. Her high profile job as personal attaché to Andres Hagopian, Lebanon's U.N. Ambassador, assured her weekly coverage in the political press. But her torrid social life drew even more attention. Wherever she went, there was always a plague of Paris gossip columnists trailing behind.

The trouble had started in the sixth grade. She was first to put streaks in her hair. First to grow breasts. First to become aware she had something the older boys couldn't get enough of; and first to develop the attitude that went with the awareness.

From the age of 16, everywhere she went, people stared; men especially; so stunning a countenance, so sensual a body, they just couldn't help themselves. And neither could women. In cafés, markets, and malls, whispering behind their dark glasses and Fendi bags, the women had always stared.

But it was men who had always been the problem. Her life had been formed, shaped, and ruined by them. Just when her youthful radar for pimply-faced Persian boys had reached a measure of insight, a new breed of older, more sophisticated users had appeared.

The contenders showed up in myriad combination: athletes, the dashing Cro-Magnons; playboys, all of them narcissists; brainacks, corrupt and clumsy as teenagers; and the moguls, the one-track-mindless tycoons. At 16, Kathryn was already a highly prized jewel.

An abused sex object.

Never alone, much envied, constantly pursued.

By age 20, she had finally learned how to protect herself; how to manipulate men, how to *Do it to them before they do it to you.*

Her stunning face and voluptuous body had drawn her into the exotic world of Middle Eastern société, a sewer of male dominance and sexual perversion. Kathryn had become jet set royalty; hard edged, quick to judgment, impatient, jaded, aloof to all but the most aggressive.

Her patina of youthful curiosity had turned to the harsh veneer of experience. Too much experience. Emotional scars had begun to surface. Her mood swings were getting ugly and more frequent.

Kat de Kennesy is a predator, a man-eater. That was the word among jet setting internationals. Nevertheless, they continued to call.

Years later, a very wonderful Italian psychiatrist answered her somewhat naïve query, "Why didn't anyone ever tell me I was being such a bitch?"

His answer: "People don't criticize the beauty queen when they're trying to get her into bed."

There were, however two notable exceptions to her hatred of men: her loving father, Dave, who had died when she was a child; and her amazing stepfather, Doctor Leon de Kennesy. Blessed Leon, who had adopted her and given her everything a child could want and more. It was Uncle Leon's wealth and provenance which had launched her privileged life. The advantage, the education, the exposure to wealth. Kathryn owed it all to Leon. He was the only real man in her life, the only man she respected.

At age 22, in spite of her rare attendance at college classes, Kathryn de Kennesy earned her diploma in Middle Eastern

History from the College Lycee St. Denis. Socially it was said that her abnormally high I.Q. had pulled her through finals at St. Denis. But insiders knew that her father, renowned brain surgeon Doctor Leon de Kennesy, had been a benefactor of the College Lycee St. Denis for many years. No one on the College Board of Directors wished to lose the doctor's patronage.

On the night following Kat's wild graduation party, she got predictably drunk. Barely coherent, splayed across the back seat of her escort's Mercedes, unable to remember the number of her own apartment, she accidentally gave him the wrong address.

The next morning, on his way in to the hospital, her stepfather, Doctor Leon, found his daughter unconscious, leaning against the back door of the family home.

He carried her into her old bedroom and instructed his wife Nana to "...clean her up, feed her, and keep her locked in that room for the next three days. She is to have no calls. And no one is to speak to her, including you."

"But Leon..." protested his wife.

"No 'but Leons!' Not even you, Nana. Understood?"

On the evening of the third day, Doctor Leon came home from work at 10 p.m. and quietly let himself into Kathryn's room. He found her sitting in her bed, leaning against a huge pile of silk pillows, reading a fashion magazine. He sat down on the bed across from her and said nothing. For what seemed like an eternity, he simply stared into her eyes.

He remained silent as tears began rolling down his dark cheeks, catching in his thick beard, dripping onto his shirt. Kathryn was overwhelmed. Leon remained motionless, staring at her, tears now falling down on to the silk sheets. Then without warning, this gentle man, who in 18 years had never spoken a single harsh word to her, stood up to his full 6'3" 250 pounds, reached his massive right hand across the bed and very gently slapped her beautiful face, the physical force of the tap so slight as to be hardly even felt. The symbolic force of the blow, however, was devastating.

Then without speaking a word, he turned and walked from the room leaving the door open behind him. The next morning, at the foot of her bed, printed in her stepfather's hand, Kathryn found the name of a very famous Italian psychiatrist. Under that was a sheaf of entry forms enrolling her at The Normal École Supérieure, the Harvard of France, the renowned temple of learning which lists Sartre, Beckett and Pasteur among its graduates.

On that day, Kathryn de Kennesy's 22-year-old world came to a screeching halt. And something new began – or so it seemed.

9

Café Petit Blanc – Paris

It was 5 a.m. The gala opening of the Paris Convention had been magnificent. As usual, she had done a spectacular job. A very tired Kathryn de Kennesy was now cloistered in a tiny back booth of La Petit Blanc Cafe. Outside the sky was dark; inside her mood was even darker. The hardest part of her job had just begun. Tension had etched dark circles into her porcelain skin. Her neck and shoulders were twisted into a painful knot.

In addition to being the personal attaché to Lebanon's U.N. Ambassador, she was also the principle translator for the Hariri government. At age 34, Kathryn de Kennesy was the Lebanese government's wunderkind; privy to their political secrets, responsible for the subtle nuance in their pronouncements, intently aware of the political games behind the games.

She held the trust of President Harrari himself. The beautiful Kathryn de Kennesy was considered the most efficient, highly intelligent and sought-after woman to ever hold a position in the male-dominated Lebanese government. They called her *inébranlable* – the unflappable one. Intense pressure was supposed to be her specialty.

At the moment, it wasn't working out that way. It was now 5:30 a.m. and the "unflappable one" was crouched in the back of a dingy old Paris bistro, the throbbing in her temples having reached timpani level. Her boss had assigned her the major share of responsibility for the International Conference on Technology. Eighty nations gathering in an atmosphere of peace and generosity to share technologies for the common good.

Then, three days before the event was to open, a delegation of 15 more Lebanese dignitaries had suddenly decided to attend the already over-booked convention. The added pressure of their pampered male egos had gotten to her. 'I'd like my room switched to one that overlooks the pool.' 'I'm allergic to shell fish.' 'I need a masseur immediately.' Demands that fell well below her job description, but demands that needed her personal touch.

And Kathryn's problems continued to mushroom. As the principal translator for the Lebanese political hierarchy, her attendance was mandatory at numerous meetings. And the meetings were constantly being reshuffled. Too many events, too many urgents, too many conflicts.

Sleep was out of the question.

She sat hunched in an ancient booth in La Petit Blanc, demolishing a legal pad with penciled revisions on her now unreadable grid of appointments. The first two Vicodin had done nothing to stop the pounding in her temples. Her tongue worked nervously back and forth behind her lips attempting to mash a third pill into submission.

She needed to get something into her stomach to help the pills kick, but the sight of the food was making her queasy. She was beginning to feel uncomfortable in her own skin. She recognized the onset of an anxiety spiral.

She gulped some water and motioned for a waiter. A crusty old rake of 70 stood up slowly from a corner table, folded his glasses, stuffed his newspaper into a back pocket and sauntered over. "Madame?"

"Could you take this all away, please?" she asked, letting out a long slow breath.

"My pleasure," he hummed. And with a flourish, he leaned over the table and began collecting the plates. Making a pretense of thoroughness, he slowly and carefully brushed the bread crumbs into his hand while allowing his eyes to hold on Kathryn's tan cleavage.

"Excuse me!" she scowled. "Do you mind!!"

Greatly pleased by her anger, the old Frenchman continued staring a moment longer before finally raising his head. Smiling unselfconsciously, he dumped the handful of crumbs down on the floor in front of her table, and crunched them beneath his shoes as he shuffled off toward the kitchen.

Kathryn's anger boiled up into her throat. "You disgusting old letch!" she roared. Then snatched up her water glass and hurled it toward the old waiter. It crashed violently into the kitchen door, exploding into a cloud of shards, narrowly missing his head.

"Pervert!" she shouted again.

She drew in several long breaths trying to calm herself. *Breathe. Breathe slowly.*

Embarrassed, she turned to see how much attention she had drawn to herself. *Nothing.* No one had even looked up.

Finally one beer-bellied trucker in a stained beret, hoisted his coffee cup and gave her a wink. Then he shoved a fork full of quiche into his mouth and went back to reading Le Journal.

This isn't Nice or Monte Carlo, you dimwit. I'm in the 9th Arrondissement. Dockworkers, truck drivers, laborers. The real French. Passion's part of the culture. The tantrums of some haughty bird? Insignificant.

Feeling stupid and embarrassed, she made the mistake of looking back toward the kitchen. There he was, peeking through the little window, a fat mocking smile on his lecherous old face. In desperation, Kathryn flipped open her laptop and began banging on the keyboard:

Cleavage, cleavage. Whaaa...I want mommy's tit back. Stupid leering idiots. Waiters. Politicians. Men – every frickin' one of 'em oughta be stuffed and mounted on the side of a barn.

She slammed down the lid of her laptop, shoved it into her Tumi bag and pushed herself further back into the booth's faded blue cushions.

She issued a quiet growl to herself. "Get a grip. You stupid twit."

Her cell phone rang. Fumbling to the bottom of her purse, she located the annoyance and snapped it open. "What is it?"

"You're obsessing, aren't you?" the male voice said calmly.

"God! Leon! I'm so sorry. I didn't mean to growl at you. I had no idea..." She glanced at her watch and only then realized what time it was.

"You haven't been to bed yet, have you honey?" The sound of his voice brought her back to her senses. Doctor Leon; steadfast, consistent, already out of bed on his way into the hospital at six in the morning, and already thinking about her.

"Well?" he prodded gently.

"Ah, well, just going over a few things, that's all."

"At six in the morning?"

She relented. "You mean because I'm over here in the 9th, hiding out in a diner, going over the schedules of the goddamn Lebanese delegation, picking at my fingernails, having a petit mal. Yes, I'd say obsessing was probably just about right."

The same calm voice, the same loving demeanor. "Yesterday you said you had all those Lebanese mucky mucks in their rooms, tucked in ready to go?"

"I did but..."

"Listen honey, I know you. Enough is enough. You've given your life to those people. You've already done more than anyone could ever possibly do. Go back to the hotel, put your adorable little bottom into a nice warm bath and relax. That's the doctor's orders!"

"I know you're right. It's time to leave. Way past time."

"Good. And ah...about that other little matter...?"

"Done," she said brightly. "Having brunch with him tomorrow at Doves."

They chatted on for a few moments and then he rang off. Leon always knew the right things to say. Always knew how to make things better. Always had the right answers. Doctor Leon, the man whose life she patterned her own after.

Thank God for Leon.

She dropped her cell phone back to the bottom of her purse. And then suddenly, magically, her shoulders dropped a notch. A kind of warming fog began seeping into her muscles. And with it came a sense of calm.

Thank you Vicodin.

Kathryn left a generous tip and slipped through the clutch of tiny blue tables out into the blustery Paris morning. A downpour was imminent. The sky was gray-black. Overhead a mass of ugly pregnant clouds was moving toward the heart of Paris. She walked six blocks south and hailed a cab for the Prince Hotel.

By 6:30 a.m., she was back in her room adjacent the suites she had reserved for the Lebanese delegation. She slid into the tub of soapy water and pulled an arm full of warm foamy bubbles up to her chin. Outside her window, the rain was falling. She tipped her head back against the neck rest, inhaled the calming fragrance of lavender and closed her eyes.

She thought once again of her stepfather. She owed everything to him. She had lost both of her natural parents while she was still in Grammar School. Uncle Leon and Aunt Nana had immediately stepped in and saved her life. They had brought her to their home in Beirut and made her their daughter. She had been reared as the treasured child of a wealthy Lebanese doctor and his brilliant artistic wife.

They raised her in a Muslim world, sent her to the finest schools. She had grown up at their dinner table, listening to his brilliance, soaking up the culture of his learned friends. Aunt Nana was a professor of art history at Beirut University and a docent at the museum of art. Little Kat was drawn to

Nana's entourage of artistic friends, Middle Eastern bohemians and non-conformists. It had been a privileged upbringing, culminating in her graduation from University with double majors and a minor in language.

Her stunning face and voluptuous body were certainly a genetic gift, but it was environment (Leon's environment) that had shaped her intellect, her global sensibilities and her religious faith. He had authored her beliefs, her politics and her Eastern view of the world.

Leon knew he could depend on his daughter. In a moment of private conversation with Mullah Rockmani, he had spoken of her allure with great pride. "You will see, Ahmed. She is fueled by the will of Allah. One day she will drive her stake deep into the heart of the problem. And if it be Allah's will, our Jihad will be the beneficiary."

Deir el Qamar – Lebanon

After disconnecting his call to Kathryn's cell phone, Leon walked out on to the terrace of his home in Deir el Qamar to watch the sunrise. He was well pleased with himself. He had always kept his fundamentalist passions safely concealed behind the heavy doors of his mansion. To all who knew him, there was no more reverent and conservative Islamist than the good doctor; Leon de Kennesy, revered surgeon, successful businessman, philanthropic donor to the causes of his beloved Lebanon.

He was a great man. He had worked hard to maintain his public image. And the privacy of such a man was sacrosanct. His private domain was off limits to the rest of the world. There would be no reason why anyone would suspect him of an illegality.

Yet one week earlier, someone had penetrated his security and hidden a tiny bug in the wireless phone now sitting on his nightstand. High in the mountains of Tal at Musa, Syria, a half track Revox tape machine had captured every nuance of the conversation. As Leon watched the sun rise over the rooftops of Southern Lebanon, someone was replaying his most intimate chat with his daughter Kathryn.

Tal at Musa, Syria

In a candle-lit corner of the tiny bedroom, lying in the arms of his young lover, he watched the tape reels turning slowly, Farad Aziz tipped his head back and closed his eyes. Nuriyah began her love making, the way he had taught her. First kissing the ugly scar on his throat, paying homage to the spoils of war; then moving down his arms toward his creative hands, the artist's hands. The source of his fame.

Farad's body began to tingle at her delicate touch. But his head was busy elsewhere.

10

Hotel Prince – Paris, France

Six thirty a.m. came suddenly to the Hotel Prince. There was a sharp knock at the door of Suite 500. An exhausted Luke Towne levered himself out of bed and pulled on the thick, monogrammed terrycloth robe reserved for the very special guests of the Hotel Prince. He padded across the deep red and gold scalloped carpet and jerked open the door. He was expecting room service, already half an hour late.

Not room service, but Dave Halter, his young assistant standing in the hallway holding two large cups of coffee and an armload of morning newspapers.

"Dave, a sight for sore eyes. Come on in."

"Thanks, Doc."

"You know I'm only inviting you in because you brought coffee."

"I knew that." Dave set the coffee on an end table.

"I called room service last night. 'Coffee and croissants at 6 a.m. Yes sir, Doctor Towne; no problem; our pleasure.' The bastards still haven't shown up. I thought this joint was supposed to be a five star."

"I think I've got your answer right here, Doc," said Dave, unfolding one of the newspapers.

A big smirk of understanding formed on Luke's face. "Ruffled some feathers did I?"

"Tar and feathers, sir. Should I read?"

Luke popped the top off the paper coffee cup, took a swig, then walked into the large closet to get dressed. He returned with one leg into his suit pants. "Shoot."

"*Le Parisien* lead headline: 'Saber-rattling Yank threatens world community with horrific new space weapon.'" The young adjutant waited for a response. There was none. "Ah, care to here more?"

Frowning into the vanity mirror, Luke completed tying his Windsor knot. "Yeah."

Dave opened a second paper. "*Agence France-Presse*: 'Renowned scientist turns Political Stooge. The term ugly American was given new meaning at the Paris International Technology Convention. What was intended to be a respectable forum for the international sharing of technological advances, was turned into a soap box for world domination by U.S. violence monger, Professor Luke Towne. This former Colonel...'"

"Enough, that's enough. Jesus. So I'm a what...a violence monger?"

"That was only the French, sir. Spain, the Germans, the Russians, they weren't quite as critical, sir."

"Not to worry, Dave, it's about what we expected."

"It is?" said Dave, surprised at his boss's nonchalance.

Luke pulled on his suit coat. "Did you get me the directions to the ...Doves? Or whatever it's called?"

"Right here, Doc," said Dave, handing over the directions.

"Wish me luck, Dave. I'm out of practice at this stuff."

The Garden of Doves – The 7th Arrondissement

Kathryn had chosen the tiny café Jardin des Colombes (the Garden of Doves), four little tables set in a sun-dappled courtyard behind the old bakery Vieux Moulin. Each table had its own umbrella of sun-yellow sailboats on a sea of Provence blue.

At the edge of the huge courtyard stood a little white lattice gazebo overflowing with fresh flowers. Luke arrived 10 minutes early, and on a whim, stepped inside and ordered a small bouquet.

"How about some white peonies and fracas?" suggested the sensuous old vendor, a gypsy-like woman, bedecked from head to toe in colorful scarves. Her eyes were bright, her smile charged with mischief. "Guaranteed to cast a spell."

"Merci, Madame." Luke stepped aside to watch as she carefully gathered the fragrant bundle. With a great flourish, the old woman set about wrapping and tying the bouquet. *Only in Paris*, thought Luke, concealing a smile; then he turned away and looked out through the lattice.

And saw her!

He couldn't believe his own reaction; he'd actually drawn in his breath. Kathryn de Kennesy's beauty was devastating. His thoughts started piling into each other like cars on a fog-bound freeway.

Like most career soldiers, Luke had had his share of women; some local, some foreign; but in the looks department, most of them had been 4s and 5s. The one notable exception was Luke's first wife, a young nurse whom he married when they were both teenagers. She was rated a 'strong 8' by all of

Luke's buddies on the base at Fort Bragg, NC, where the two met.

Again he peeked out through the ivy twined lattice. *Whoa! She's an 11. God, the color of her eyes! They're Turquoise!*

The hair on the back of Luke's neck stood up. A sudden flashback to Vietnam. A little bar where he and his buddies threw back pints of cheap beer when they got some R & R. Its owner, a toothless old Cambodian fortune teller had said, "Woman you love. She have eyes of turquoise."

It was a meaningless event in his military life, more than 20 years ago. He had forgotten it – until now. He drew in a deep breath, suppressed the memory, and walked straight out of the gazebo forgetting the flowers he'd ordered.

Kathryn de Kennesy sat at a small table, oblivious to her surroundings, sipping her coffee, studiously reading through a stack of morning newspapers. She wore a white linen suit, its jacket open to the waist with an emerald green blouse casually knotted just above a very tan bare midriff.

She looked up and saw him approaching. Her lips, a dark cinnamon color, served up a cover girl smile from the shadow of the umbrella. She stepped out into the light to greet him. The sun hit her face. The result was spectacular; her amazing turquoise eyes deepened as did the copper tone of her skin.

When he extended his hand, she gracefully slipped past it, stepped forward and placed both of her hands on his forearms. She pulled herself next to him, then turned her cheek slightly to greet him in the more intimate European fashion.

Later he would insist the move had saved his life.

As he turned his head sideways to complete the touch of cheeks, his eye caught the sudden flash of sun on steel – to the right, 70 yards across the square. He saw it clearly – a long silver tube with a black silencer screwed onto its end.

His emotions went cold! The capillaries in his brain ballooned with a rush of chemicals: casomorphin, endorphin, adrenaline. His response was immediate. Instinctive.

The clarions in his head sounded the alarm. His memory banks instantly fired.

Attack! Defend! Attack! Defend!

Time braked into stop-action – one slow frame at a time. His periphery went big screen, widening to 180. His mind flashed back to a thousand similar incidents in his military life; Vietnam, the rice paddies, the sun flashing off the barrels of the Cong 47s. He saw them again, hanging in the trees like brown monkeys, raining death down on his men.

He saw the movement as one long perception; the arc of the silver tube in the stranger's hand; the sun glinting on the silencer – coming to rest on the doorjamb; the blue Mini Cooper breaking sideways into a four wheel drift; the door swinging open, the eyes of the enemy; his tennis shoes slamming the pavement as he leapt from the car, the gun pointing as the enemy ran headlong toward them.

All of this was superimposed against the upturned cheek of Kathryn de Kennesy - the sound of water dripping in the stone fountain behind her sending little clicks of warning to Luke's brain.

Move now. Move now! Move.

Pure instinct. His fingers locked on to her forearms. His arms shot forward like pistons, thrusting her backwards out of the line of fire. The backs of her knees hit the bull-nosed edge of the fountain. The force of the contact twisted her body and dropped her into the dark water.

Simultaneously, Luke hit the ground, flattened his body and rolled to the left. *Zing!* A bullet ripped through the umbrella where their heads were a millisecond earlier.

"Stay down," he shouted. And rolled violently back to the right looking for cover. A second bullet slammed into the umbrella's aluminum pole and snapped it off with a loud crack.

The umbrella spun to the ground. *Momentary cover.* Luke sprang to his feet behind it. Head down, running as hard as he could, he raced back toward the gazebo.

It was an 8-second eternity before he dodged inside. No shots fired.

The old florist smiled, "I thought you'd be back for these," she said, extending the bouquet of peonies. But Luke was already down on his knees, peering through the lattice looking back toward the gunman.

"Get down!" he shouted, his eyes riveted, scanning the square. It was crowded with locals going about their daily chores. And for a moment, everything looked normal. Then, off to the left, 40 yards from the gazebo he saw the commotion. Two people fell to the ground; two more spun awkwardly to the left, jolted by the impact of an onrushing body.

A hooded figure emerged!

He was about 6 feet tall, dressed in a dark blue tracksuit, the hood pulled tightly around his head, running full force, holding the long-nosed hand gun at waist level.

Luke heard the *thunk* of a bullet behind him. He spun around and reached out for the flower peddler. The white peonies in her hand had already changed color, stained red. There was a jagged hole above the first tracheal cartilage where the bullet had ripped into her throat.

Too late to stop her body's forward momentum. The old woman collapsed heavily on top of him. And for a few seconds, her heart continued to pump, drenching the side of his face in sickening warmth. One final shudder and the flower lady went still.

Thump. Thump. Her dead body lurched; a second and third bullet ripping into her corpse. She was shielding him from death.

Luke pushed violently upward, launched her body into the air, and rolled out from under it. He rose to his knees, grimacing in expectation of the next bullet. For a moment, there was no sound.

Suddenly, the fat nose of the killer's gun smashed violently through the lattice. The obscene eye jerked left then right, searching.

Luke saw the hand tighten, the finger squeeze. He heard the zing of the first bullet as it whizzed past his left shoulder and slammed into something behind him.

Charging like a bull, Luke aimed his body to the left of the protruding gun muzzle. His shoulder drove straight through and into the killer's stomach. The wooden lattice blew apart and the man went down hard on his back, carrying the entire back wall of the gazebo down on top of him.

As more of the structure collapsed, a section of latticework locked around the gunman's forearm. It forced his gun arm straight up out of the rubble. As the heavy mass of lumber started to settle, it began slowly bending the arm backwards into an impossible angle. The gunman's screams built to a crescendo, like the shriek of a skill saw seized in the middle of a wet two-by-four.

As the pain worsened, so did the horrid screams.

Crack; the snapping of the ulna. *Snap;* the ugly crunch of the radius. Then an ugly staccato of small bones as each one fractured and began poking through the flesh of the arm.

Finish it! The voice in Luke's head. Years of Special Forces training: take advantage of an enemy's injury. *End it now.*

Crashing through the chest-high pile of debris, Luke moved in quickly toward his attacker. The man's right forearm was sticking straight up through the rubble like a naked flag pole – the pistol frozen in the grasp of his traumatized fingers.

Luke bent down to reach for the gun barrel. As his fingers closed around the cold steel, he heard a high pitched *creak* behind him. Wood against wood. Splintering.

The rest of the gazebo was about to collapse.

Instinct! Releasing the gun barrel, he hurled his body to the left, turning his face away, arms thrown up to protect his head. With a dramatic groan, the entire rotted wooden structure collapsed inward, launching nails and jagged struts outward in all directions. A 10" wooden shard stabbed into Luke's shoulder as he rolled on the ground.

Unaware of the pain, Luke scrambled to his feet and whirled around to face the fountain. Kathryn was there, submerged in the fountain's moat of water, peering at him over the wet stone edge.

He shouted across the square, "Run! That way!"

When he saw her safely out of the fountain, he turned away from the gazebo and began running in the opposite direction. *Too late to go for the killer. Take cover. Reassess.*

Running hard, Luke reached the safety of the square's entrance and ducked behind its stone archway. Only then did he look back toward the wreckage of the gazebo. What he saw was inconceivable; a scene from a cheap horror film.

The killer's right arm was sticking straight up from the rubble, still clutching the weapon. But as Luke watched in disbelief, the killer's other hand punched upward through the debris and began prying his own locked fingers away from the gun butt.

Screaming in pain from the effort, the man wrestled the gun away from his dead right hand and pushed it into his left.

He began firing wildly in all directions. Two young children enjoying the excitement went over backwards, blood spurting from their stomachs. The next shot slammed into the wall just six inches above Luke's head.

The son of a bitch is gonna get loose.

Running full force, arms pumping, legs churning, Luke charged blindly into the heart of the massive five-way intersection of Rue Antoine Arnauld. Lurching left then right, narrowly avoiding the crush of wheels, he set off a crescendo of screeching tires and shouted obscenities. Cars and trucks began slamming together like dominoes, reacting to the apparent crazy man zigzagging through their midst.

His 55-year-old scientist's body struggling for air, Luke stuck a violent straight-arm into the hood of a speeding green van and tried to push himself to the right. The momentum spun him off balance and knocked him to the ground, rolling like a pinball. The green van jammed its brakes and crashed under the tailgate of a pickup in front of it.

Fingers, arms and feet slapping and digging into the graveled concrete for purchase, Luke fought to stop his momentum. Finally coming to rest on his bloody hands and knees, he sucked in a huge gasp of breath. He pushed down hard he stood up again; disoriented.

Which way was I running?

Pop! Pop! Two bullets punctured a Citroën headlight to his right. He sprung wildly to the left in front of an old Renault and ducked down along the driver's side. The Renault's windshield exploded. The driver's head slammed into the steering wheel.

The sounds of multiple collisions accelerated, echoing down the narrow alleys off the intersection. A rapid fusillade of bullets sprayed across the windshields surrounding him. But Luke heard none of it! The sudden ringing in his right ear was deafening. One of the shots had nicked his temple. The impact dropped him behind the tailgate of an enormous black Hummer. Out cold, but only for an instant.

The pain stabbed him back to consciousness.

Slowly he pulled himself up by holding on to the chrome nerf bar at the back of the behemoth truck. He peered cautiously around its fender trying to get a glimpse of his assailant.

Nothing. Then he saw the blue cap 20 yards off, coming hard; the left hand extended. Bang! The Hummer's right front tire exploded. The huge vehicle lurched forward, falling to one knee like a wounded rhino.

Above the screaming pain in his right ear, Luke could hear the sound of sirens. He saw the tiny French police car cutting across the intersection. As it skidded to a halt, the door flew open and the uniformed gendarme leapt out, weapon in hand. Instantly, a bullet struck him in the pit of the stomach. He collapsed in the street vomiting blood.

Run! Harder. Blindly he ran toward a side street.

A second police car roared into the intersection and pulled in front of the first. As he ran past them, Luke shouted, "Officer down. Shooter has a hand gun. Running through traffic. Blue cap. There!"

As the French cops pulled their weapons and took up positions behind the doors of their car, Luke sprinted toward a side street, desperate for a place to hide. Gasping for breath, his head ringing, he charged into the narrow darkness and tripped on the rough cobblestones. Refusing to go down, he staggered toward a hand rail, grabbed on and righted himself. To his right was a flight of stairs. Without thinking, he hurled himself downward, taking them two at a time.

He reached the bottom of the stairs, reached out for a rusted finial and jerked himself to a halt. *Shit!* He was standing in some kind of subterranean garden, hanging plants, dripping fountains, store fronts...but there was no stairway leading out.

Move! Go! Forward!

Three paths in front of him; a little shop at the end of each one: a tailor, an art gallery, a patisserie. Luke forced his legs to move. Slipping on the wet pavers, he slammed through the closest door - the tailor shop of Marcel du Champ.

A bell clanged loudly against the door as Luke ran to the old wooden counter. His eyes swept the room: a rack of suits, a curtained dressing room, a narrow hallway leading to another door.

"Hello," he shouted; and vaulted over the counter, trying to look in all directions as he landed.

"Anybody here?"

He stood facing the tailor's rack of suits. *Maybe some* d*ifferent clothes.*

Blindly he yanked a brown linen suit off the rack and pushed through the curtain into the tiny dressing room. He tore wildly at his belt, trying at the same time to rip the tailored suit off its hanger. Dropping his pants to the floor he pulled on the first leg of the brown linen pants.

Tink!

He froze in place. Holding his breath. His heart trying to rip through his chest. Listening. It sounded like the bell, vibrating ever so gently against the door, as if someone were pushing it open very slowly.

More silence.

Then the rasp of someone's heavy breathing.

Carefully Luke pulled his one foot out of the pant leg and looked wildly around the dressing room for a weapon or a way out.

"American bastard! I know you're in there." The man's voice cut through the wall like an ugly knife blade. "You come out now. I promise I'll kill you quickly. Hear me Towne? NOW! Or I'm gonna kill you slow." The words were in English, the accent was definitely French. *Gutter French.*

There was a small window in the dressing room's back wall. Scarcely enough room for an adult to squeeze through. Still holding his breath, Luke crept toward the window and gently pushed open the shutters. The rusted hinges made a tiny squeak.

Luke froze again. Waiting. He heard the unmistakable sound of a new clip being slammed into the handle of the assassin's pistol. It was an HK 9mm. A clip of 15 shots. He'd seen it poke through the wall of the flower stand. He had his fingers on its barrel – a hundred years ago.

Move or die.

As quietly as he could he hoisted his body out over the windowsill, head first, and wormed himself through. Gingerly he lowered both feet down, feeling for a foothold on the fire escape.

Carefully he tested the platform for stability. It was old but still firm enough. He looked down. Three floors to the street; no ladder. *No way down.*

He looked up. Only a few of the fire escape's original bolts and stanchions were left intact. All were heavily caked with rust. He reached for the first rung, then stopped, his mind racing. He moved back to the little window. Poking his head into the empty dressing room he said as calmly as he could, "Hey asshole, how's that right arm feeling?"

Instantly, a slaughter of bullets ripped through the walls of the dressing room, aimed everywhere, left, right, center, high, low, and back to center again. In a rage, the killer emptied an entire clip of ammunition; only the hollow clicking of the trigger stopped the explosions.

It was an old Special Forces technique; force the enemy to respond from anger. *At least something's goin' right.* Luke was already halfway up the ladder heading towards the roof.

Each tenuous step caused the rickety frame to pull slightly outward and away from the building. His enemy would have the same problem; perhaps it would help. When he reached the fourth rung, the roof became visible: a litter of trash, empty pots and one rotting pigeon cage. His heart sank. *Another mistake. No cover. No stairs. No exit.*

He climbed up two more rungs, threw his leg over the building's edge and stepped down onto the old tar roof. *No place to hide.*

He ran to the far side of the roof and peered over the side. *Straight down. Nothing.* Retracing his steps, he slipped in behind the birdcage. Too flimsy to stop a bullet. He looked back toward the edge. The killer's head would appear any moment.

Then a desperate idea. He slipped off one of his shoes and carefully positioned it with the toe sticking out just an inch from behind one side of the birdcage. Then he raced back across the roof to the place where the ladder was connected, stretched out full-length and flattened himself against the side of the roof.

He calculated the spot where his pursuer's foot would first appear. Then moved his body forward making sure the man would have to step over him to reach the roof's surface.

In a matter of seconds he heard footsteps on the fire escape below. "You're on the roof, aren't you? Nowhere to run now, is there? You're a dead man. You know that don't you. American pig. Your fancy bombs can't do shit now." When the screaming stopped, Luke heard another clip slam into the HK's magazine.

Then the man's tone changed. It was confidence. Luke knew the signs. "Let me tell you something, my friend," the voice said quietly, "I have five brothers. They live in Iran. Five brothers." There was a moment of silence. Then he spoke again, his voice trembling with anger, each word building in volume. "You think I would let you blow up their house? You think you can play God with us, you prick. You bastard American! When I kill you, I make sure you suffer. You will suffer..."

Luke flattened himself against the lip of the roof, his face contorted, straining to block out the sound of the angry words, straining to hear the critical sound of a footstep on the first rung of the ladder. *There it is! The first one! Now the second...? There.*

Luke's eyes focused on the lip of the roof where the man's head would appear. Just about 15 inches above him. Success would depend on surprise and a bit of luck. The killer would have to place his hand on the edge of the roof. Then, throw his leg over and step down to the surface, just as Luke had done.

He jammed himself hard against the lip of the roof and waited. And waited. For some reason, the killer had stopped moving. By Luke's calculations, two more rungs and he would be at eye level with the rooftop.

The man began another barrage of vile insults, cursing and swearing, threatening to kill all Americans in the world. And in the midst of it, Luke heard him take a third step. Moving one rung higher on the latter. *That's three. One more.* Then came the fourth step!

The killer fell silent. Luke knew the man's head had reached rooftop level. He was taking his first view of the site in front of him.

The killer's eyes swept back and forth pausing at every object, examining every shadow. His words were soft. "Where are you American? Come out, so I can kill you." He rested his gun hand on the top of the ledge. An inch of its ugly silencer became visible, poking over the ledge. Only an inch; not enough to attempt a grab.

Patience.

Suddenly the killer spotted the toe of Luke's shoe, sticking out from behind the pigeon cage. Luke heard his grunt of satisfaction. "You hide like a woman. Towne. Stinking coward American. I give you some shock and awe. Some pain. That's what you need. You going to pay for what you do."

The gun arm moved slightly forward, into the space above Luke. He was taking aim. In a second, his foot would come over the edge as he climbed down onto the roof.

Now.

Luke shot both hands up and viced onto the killer's outstretched left forearm. He jerked down violently. The sudden move pulled the man's body forward and off balance. His bloody right arm flailed in the air as he tried to right himself.

Twisting back and forth, his eye suddenly caught sight of the alley four stories below him. And he panicked. Falling backwards, unable to regain his balance, he let go of the gun and grabbed on to Luke's forearm with his good hand.

At the sound of the weapon clunking to the roof, Luke stood up suddenly. A master of Taekwondo, Luke simply pushed his own arm forward slightly. The killer immediately hunched his shoulders forward in reaction, attempting to retain his balance. His eyes flashed wild in fear, realizing that his footing was now completely dependent on Luke's grip.

Luke stood rock still, emptying his own body of all tension. Time stopped. And for an instant the two stood face to face. Then, suddenly, Luke snapped his forearm downward, easily wrenching it from the killer's grasp.

Wobbling back and forth on the top rung of the ladder, the man screamed. "Help me!!!"

Another long second passed. Then Luke's right foot shot forward, and landed a savage kick to the man's sternum.

The killer' body shot backward off the ladder into space. His face froze in horror and denial. For an instant, he seemed to hang in the air. Then he was gone.

As he dropped toward the ground, the wind rushed past his body and turned him in a circular motion. The rotations increased as he hurtled toward the stone floor of the alleyway.

Luke leaned out over the edge. He saw the body strike the ground and implode. The arteries burst along both sides of the torso, spurting liquid like a ruptured melon.

In a taxicab, on the way back to the hotel, Luke calmly dictated the events of the encounter in exacting detail while all the memories were still fresh - a protocol he had followed many times in his military career. When he arrived at the hotel, he was mẹt in the lobby by his attaché, Master Sergeant David Halter. His pallor confirmed the intensity of his fears.

"God, Doc, you're Okay! What happened? The woman called and said something about a gunman! The police called. What happened?"

As they rode up together in the elevator, Luke gave a minimalist description of the events in the order they had occurred. All very low key.

As they stepped off the elevator, he handed over his Olympus 4000 digital recorder. "Here Dave. It's all in here. Plug it into the PC in the room, email a copy to the police, send one back home to our office, and one to Ramsey at Defense. Oh yeah, and while you're at it, send one to President Gaston. Be interesting to see what the French have to say about this one."

Dave took the little recorder from his boss, a strained expression on his face.

"What is it, Dave?"

Dave hesitated, "Only one person knew where the breakfast was going to be, sir. She's already called here four times."

Luke frowned as he considered the implications. "You saying it was a set up?"

"I'm just saying...ah...I'm just saying that she was the only one who knew."

Kathryn de Kennesy called the hotel several more times that afternoon and continued her calls late into the evening. She was finally put through to his room at 10 p.m. She listened in silence, finally expressing her horror when he'd reached the conclusion. Only then did she ask about the identity of the assassin.

The Paris police had faxed their report to Luke's room at seven. Luke said, "Here, I'll read it to you."

As he read the lengthy report to her, his voice remained strangely void of emotion. "'Paris police have identified the assassin as Hassan Brahman, a Syrian émigré; an activist who arrived in France from Iran just eight months earlier.

"'He apparently had no friends. He only came to the attention of the police when he was involved in a recent protest in front of the American consulate. Brahman was arrested when he threatened security guards with a tire iron.

"'He was believed to be emotionally unbalanced as a result of losing his wife and children in a mistaken American air strike in Afghanistan. In his wallet was a Lebanese news article which identified the four members of Hassan's family killed in the bombing. He had underlined words "collateral damage" several times in red ballpoint pen.'"

After a beat she asked, "Was he part of a group?"

"Apparently not. He had $2100 in his wallet. The police think the money was tied to a mugging the night before. They're fairly sure he was acting alone. No conspiracy, no one else involved. Insanity, plain and simple. A nut job. Just a product of war. I'm inclined to think they're probably right."

She was quiet on the phone. *Leon was right as usual. The American lack of sensitivity is unbelievable.* She remained still, waiting for him to speak.

"Ah, if you're not busy, how about we try it again tomorrow morning?" he asked. "Same time, same place?"

"Are you serious? You'd go back to the same place again? Where they tried to kill you."

Luke frowned. *I never used the word 'they.'* He let it go and answered her question. "As soldiers we were taught to win battles, not run from them."

She was quiet for a moment. "Well, I hate to think of myself as a battle, but...if that's how you see it. Actually I've never met a scientist who was a soldier too."

"Got a policy about soldiers, do you?"

"No policies. Got nothing against anybody. You'll just have to promise not to throw me in the water again."

"I promise."

"Okay, one more thing. Are you comfortable with Jardin des Colombes? You sure it's safe? It didn't leave a bad taste in your mouth?"

There was a moment's pause before his retort. "Miss de Kennesy, I never got a taste of anything." He heard the smile in her response.

"You're on," she replied, her voice throaty as ever.

Deir el Qamar, Lebanon

The phone rang on the ornate mahogany night stand. Doctor Leon de Kennesy's bedroom was on the second floor of his 12,000 square foot mansion, well secured behind majestic hand-forged gates in the hills above Southern Lebanon. The area is called Deir el Qamar (*Monastery of the Moon*). Only the most wealthy could afford its exotic brinks and focal prominence above the lights of the city. Deir el Qamar bespoke a lifestyle far beyond the reach of the hoi polloi.

It was 4 in the morning. Doctor Leon did not accept phone calls at 4 in the morning. The only reason he'd even heard the ring was because the maid had forgotten to turn off the machine.

It was the fifth ring. "Yes?" he scowled into the receiver.

"Ah, my good friend. Praise be to Allah." The words were in Arabic.

Leon recognized the oily voice, but refused to repeat the greeting as he was supposed to. An exact repetition of the phrase would signify that the caller was recognized and that the line was secure. But in Doctor de Kennesy's opinion, the lateness of the hour was an unacceptable intrusion, no doubt motivated by some emotional spike in the caller's medulla. Farad Aziz was psychotic. Everyone knew it. His erratic behavior and aggressive manners were tolerated for one significant reason only. His skill as 'the demolition expert' was unparalleled. And during the last five years, he had proven it repeatedly. Farad was mentally unbalanced, but he was needed.

"What is it, Farad?" Leon asked finally, keeping his voice as neutral as he could. He knew the call would be confrontational. His dealings with the man always were.

"May I speak freely, my friend?"

Leon hated being called 'my friend,' especially by someone who clearly wasn't. "Speak," was all he said in response.

"Well, I just wanted to commend you. Although the attempt at eliminating a certain laser man failed, I felt I should acknowledge the effort."

"Wrong. You son-of-a...!" Leon struggled for the words, venom boiling in his esophagus. "You know it's wrong! It's not what we agreed on! It's what you wanted to do!" He realized he was shouting now. Farad had accomplished his goal. Leon had allowed himself to be baited.

Leon set his jaw and lowered his voice. "We chose a different solution. You remember? We voted on it. Sitting in Op B. We voted! We decided to use the man, not kill him. You agreed. If we could find a way to use him, it might get us in closer. Get us inside. THEN you'd be able to use your exquisite skill set, Farad. Then you'd be able to destroy thousands of them instead of just one pig of a scientist." Leon hoped this last bit of praise would placate the lunatic. But the ploy was doomed to failure.

Farad Aziz hadn't gone to college, but he wasn't stupid; he'd grown up in the back streets of Beirut. He'd been to war. He was a man of the people. He wasn't some rich financial manipulator. And he hated Leon de Kennesy. He believed the man's lifestyle was as corrupt as the Jews and the godless Western infidels who financed them. In private conversations with Mullah Rockmani, he had campaigned against the almighty Leon, calling him 'the arrogant hawk nose,' and 'the Lebanese Jew.'

But everyone knew Leon was a financial wizard. Dr. Leon had somehow managed to turn on the money faucet. He had bought them weapons. He had paid for training in Iran and Syria. He had changed their sand-clogged dreams into a well-oiled reality. Everyone treated Leon de Kennesy with a respect that almost rivaled the most holy Mullah Ahmed Rockmani himself.

Still Farad Aziz wasn't ignorant or blind; he may not be living on top of a hill in Lebanon, but he wasn't without resources. It was his Revox tape recorder that had identified the location of Kathryn's brunch date. And it was his $2100 the Paris police found in the pocket of Hassan Brahman, the crazed Iranian assassin who had almost killed the pig scientist, Luke Towne.

11

Pacific Palisades, California

On his last afternoon before reporting in to the Federal Building, Agent Quentin Hawk went to the Hawaiian Garden's pool to swim some laps. As he was about to strip off his T-shirt, a voice behind him said, "Dude! Where'd you get that T. It's way cool."

He turned to face 27 year-old Ashley Taylor who continued into her next question. "And after you answer that, could you rub some Hawaiian Tropic on my lower back?"

"Sure," said Quent, removing the shirt, "One of my brothers is an artist. He does T-shirts. Silk screens 'em and sells 'em on line."

"Could you get one for me?" she smiled, handing him the suntan oil.

"Better if you order yourself. You know, get the right size. The web site's called 'shirthawk.com.' Lots of different ones."

"Shirt-schlock?"

"No...it's 'shirthawk.com'"

"Okay, got it," said Ashley. "Gee, your hands are strong. What's your name."

"Quentin."

"Unusual name, dude. Never heard that one."

Ashley had one more semester to complete at Malibu's Pepperdine College of Architecture, just a few miles west of the RHG. When Quent finished oiling her back, Ashley rolled over, plopped a pair of glasses down on her nose and gave his body the once over.

"You a jock or something?"

"Used to be," he said, pointing to the scar on his right knee. "You a jock?" he asked facetiously.

His attempt at humor pan-caked. "I'm an architect," she said haughtily. "I kinda like to think of myself as a plastic surgeon of style."

"You gonna change the face of Los Angeles?" he asked, thinking he'd give her an opening for some polite conversation.

"You betcha," she slurred; then ordered another Mojito from the pool boy. It was at that moment Quent noticed the three empty glasses next to her chaise.

"There are things about this city I could show you that'd blow your mind, man. Things my smart ass professors don't even begin to realize. Things the chamber of commerce duddn't put in their fancy little pamphlets. Place is turning to crap. Know what I mean? Cracks in the plaster. Serious cracks."

She slugged down her fourth drink in a single swallow and without taking a breath, carried on. "I grew up here, you know. When Westwood was still a village. Let me tell you, dude, it ain't what it used to be. In my latest term paper I put it this way." She snatched up a yellow notepad and began to read. "'Ten thousand electronic billboards are casting a five o'clock shadow on the once-upon-a-time sunny face of the City of Angeles. Santa Monica's nothing but a high-priced slum. Rows of tired bungalows from the 40s. Hiding their sagging faces behind Frank O. Gehry's ugly gray Quonsets.'" She placed the yellow pad under her chaise as carefully as if it were the Magna Carta. "Pretty good shit, huh?"

He tried to answer, but lost the race.

"And don't get me started on L.A.," she raged. "Place is history. It sucks, know what I mean. You got brain numbing gridlock on every street. You got layers a' graffiti on every frickin' overpass, street sign. Every building. Sidewalk. You got an army of meter maids in BH (Beverly Hills) tryna make the frickin' Arabs richer than they already are."

"Arabs?" said Quent.

She wasn't listening. "You got big fast food restaurants sticking out of every nook and cranny, serving a shit load of shit. Nothing but plastic eth-nik-a-see, man." (Ethnicity was a struggle) "You got big plastic boobs sticking out of every female no matter what her ethnicity." (This time it came out eth-sis-itty) "Every cashier, weather girl, waitress, meter maid. All got giant boobies! PhDs, attorneys, congresswomen, mothers. Monster cleavage – all of 'em."

She pushed her own meager breasts together for emphasis. "You got 55-year-old matrons, marching down the frozen foods aisles proudly poking out their overpriced nippies. You know what, those salt bags cost about 32 hundert. That's per nippie, man. PER NIPPIE. Real attractive. Know what I'm sayin."

"Jeeze, Ash!" Quent shouted, trying to cut off the stream of blather, "That's...quite an interesting picture." Then he looked down at this watch (which wasn't there because he'd left it in his condo) and said, "You, ah, you got me so interested, I forgot what time it was. Gotta be at an office dinner party in 20 minutes." He stood up quickly and started moving toward the parking lot. "You be here tomorrow?"

"Yeah, baby. Gotta test on Friday."

"All right. Study hard. See you tomorrow maybe. Sorry to leave so quickly."

"No prob."

Quent fled to the parking lot, heading in the opposite direction from his condo in case she was watching. Then he circled back ducking behind the big stand of orange hibiscus that rimmed the pool area.

He pulled the door to his condo closed as quietly as he could, dropped his swim trunks on the bathroom floor and turned on the shower. Stepping under the hot stream he smiled to himself. *Serious cracks in the plaster.*

Toweling off, he thought about what lay ahead. Today was a very important day; the day Agent J. Quentin Hawk was to find out why he had been suddenly transplanted from frigid Duluth to the Royal Hawaiian Gardens in sun-baked Los Angeles. It was noon, four hours before he was scheduled to meet with Chief Barbara Porter at an office located in the Federal Building at Wilshire and Sepulveda. *Four hours. Plenty of time for a nap.*

One hour later. The afternoon sun came shooting through the Plumeria's living room blinds like a branding iron, and stenciled a pattern of thin red lines across the bottom of Quent's right foot. He stirred under the Sports Illustrated magazine tented across the bridge of his nose. The rhythmic pattern of his heavy snoring continued anyway, in spite of the hot foot. The Minnesota Vikings had drafted this year's Heisman trophy winner. Quent felt that it was a mandatory read before dropping off to sleep.

Punctuality never having been one of his strengths, he was determined to begin this new relationship on the right foot; so he'd placed his cell phone close to his head and programmed its special intra-agency channel to sound the 'emergency alarm.' A feature he'd never used; never considered.

Quent was in REM heaven when the big moment came. The alarm was so loud he thought Malibu was having an earthquake. He sat bolt upright on the couch. The sudden lunge flipped the SI magazine off his face and into the half-finished bottle of Bud on the coffee table. For a long sleepy moment he watched the pungent brew pouring down on to his recently acquired Tommy Bahama area rug.

The rug had been suggested by his neighbor, Bobbi Rose, an attractive interior designer who lived in the condominium next door. Bobbi's condo was decorated with an intimidating combination of pure white, over-stuffed chairs and couches from Kreiss. There were golden accent pieces, Mayan wall sconces, pillows from India, and *all kinds of useless bullshit from unpronounceable places.* It was clear that Bobbi made a lot more money than Quent did.

Awareness suddenly dawning, Quent shot up from the couch, grabbed a rag and began madly sopping up the yellow stain from his very expensive Tommy Bahama rug. Although Bobbi had gotten him a decorator's discount, Quentin had paid more for the damned area rug than for all the combined furniture he'd ever owned, including his king-sized bed with the complimentary night stands bolted on to its sides.

"Goddamn it," he shouted, looking down at the expanding yellow spot. Then he looked at the soaking rag in his hand and realized it wasn't a rag, it was his dress shirt. His only dress shirt.

"Goddamn it," he shouted.

Quent had always shopped at JC Penney. His brothers got their Towncrafter neck-hugging T-shirts there, his parents bought their clothes there. In fact, the whole Hawk family was granted a special 5% discount by the branch manager of the JC Penney Duluth store.

Within minutes, Quent was speeding down Pacific Coast Highway, heading for the Santa Monica Mall. He'd map-quested the nearest Penney's; he was beginning to know his way around. He had one hour left to get to the meeting. And he was determined not to be late.

He swung into the parking structure. Just two levels further up, he could see the JC Penney sign glowing above its big double doors. But the parking structure was a graveyard of minivans and old people, all of them circling toward Penney's at coma speed; all of them certain to die before he'd be allowed to reach Penney's. Around and around and around the narrow structure he crept, trapped behind an aged van with a wheelchair rig welded onto its back door.

"Goddamn it."

One level over, he could see the Macy's lot, waiting for him with its 20 open parking spaces. He'd run out of time and patience. At the end of the next aisle, he made an illegal right turn against the traffic flow, mashed down on the accelerator, squealed his car around a Jaguar and nipped into an open slot near Macy's door.

Racing into the men's department, he scooped up a handful of white, long-sleeved dress shirts and ran to the nearest register. A blue-haired saleslady gave him her friendliest smile. "Anything else, sir?" she mewed. "A nice tie, or cuff links, or maybe..."

"No time. No thank you. Just the shirts."

"Would you like to get an additional 10% off by signing up for a Macy's charge today?"

"No thanks. In a hurry, just the shirts."

"I hear a bit of an accent there. I'll just bet you're not from around here, are you sir? Now let me guess, Texas?"

"YES. Texas. You're right. I'm from Texas. You're so good at this," he said, trying not to raise his voice. "But you know how us Texans are, always in a hurry. Wells to dig."

The elderly woman looked at Quent, confused. "Wells to dig?" she asked, a puzzled look on her face.

"OIL! You know, Texas. Oil wells," he said, his voice rising in frustration.

"You don't have to yell, sir," she snapped. Then she took the shirts from Quent's hand and laid them out carefully on the counter, one by one. "All righty then, let's see," she said, "The Executive by Armani, that's $90.00, and the..."

"Excuse me?" Quent interrupted. "Ninety bucks? That's like $30 a shirt, isn't it? Are you sure that's right?"

"Of course it's right, sir. It's 90 for the first shirt, the Armani Executive. That's because it's on sale. The second shirt, which isn't part of the sale, is $275. That's because it's 400 count Egyptian cotton and it's Ermenegildo Zegna's newest dress shirt."

Quent's face reddened. "Ah...here then, I'll just take the first one. Didn't mean to question your knowledge. Sorry."

"Well," she snipped, "I certainly hope not. Perhaps the next time, when you're not in such a big fat hurry, Mr. Texas, you should try JC Penney. It's down there at the end of the mall."

12

The White House

During the Pentagon's four-month development of the Pit Bull Strategy (now referred to as 'The Strategy'), numerous experts from the Intelligence community had been brought in to contribute their expertise. Each night after the day's vetting, President Rundle Crowley would climb into bed and insist on reading his notes to his wife, Virginia. Now that The Strategy had proven to be such a success, he was loath to discontinue the nightly updates. Superstition.

Fashion, interior décor, entertainment and gossip were Virginia's forte. She tolerated Rundle's 'political stuff' by interjecting an occasional 'um.'

In the middle of one of the President's musings, she suddenly felt the need to contribute. "You know Run," she said, beginning a typical non-sequitur, "I was talking with Judith Yost this morning about things. She's so proud of Mike's contribution."

"Well she should be. Best goddamn Chief of Staff I ever had. The whole Strategy thing started with his ideas. Really saved my bacon."

"Yes, well, we got to thinking, Judith and I, what would happen if one of us were kidnapped by terrorists?"

"Impossible. Never happen. Not to worry, Dear."

"But what if somebody important was kidnapped. You know, somebody like the Amazon guy, Jeff Bezos, or Tiger Woods or somebody like that? Shouldn't they have guards?"

The following morning Crowley made a call to one of his most trusted advisors, Brigadier General Orin Pierce.

"Listen, Orin, I should know the answer to this, but I don't. And I don't care to acknowledge my ignorance. Would you find out which one of our Intelligence agencies is out there protecting our VIP citizens? You know, CEOs and athletes. People that might be targets for a terrorist kidnapping?"

"I'll have your answer by this afternoon, Mr. President."

By 3 p.m., General Pierce was back on the line. "Mr. President, on that surveillance matter, I have some rather distressing news."

"Yes, Orin."

"No one is protecting prominent Americans from the threat of a terrorist kidnapping. Not one of our 15 Intel agencies has even a mention of such an assignment anywhere in their protocols."

There was an ugly pause. Finally, a stunned President said, "Any comment, Orin?"

"Unacceptable. Beyond comprehension, sir."

One hour later, the brain trust at Langley received an urgent demand from their CinC (Commander in Chief). In Crowley's mind, it was unconscionable that protective surveillance had not already been put in place - even well before the attacks of 9/11. That such a blind spot still existed was beyond comprehension. Potential disasters were still being overlooked.

The following morning in the Oval Office Crowley reviewed the CIA's hastily prepared list of prominent U.S. citizens who might be potentially at risk of a terrorist kidnap. Alone at his desk, Crowley snatched up his secure phone and was put through directly to the CIA's Director, Lawrence Shaw.

"Larry, I want this list of surveillance put into effect immediately."

"Yes sir, I'm pleased to be of service. Anything we can do to help, we're here, sir," answered the DCI brightly.

"That you hadn't already ordered this kind of surveillance, in my mind, represents a shocking omission on the part of your Agency," growled the President. "I can't imagine a more potentially damaging miscalculation than having one of our public figures kidnapped. After all the progress we've made with The Strategy, my ratings back up and climbing, the last thing I need is a goddamn kidnapping. I'm greatly disappointed with the apparent lack of thought put into this."

President Crowley and the CIA Chief Lawrence Shaw were cooperative partners. The accusation that his Agency had demonstrated a 'lack of thought' was a stunning blow to the DCI. It was also an indication that public pressure on the White House to 'turn things around' was becoming divisive even amongst friendly members of the same team.

"I'm sorry you feel that way, Mr. President. I can assure you we'll put the best minds in the Agency on it. I'm sorry for our...surveillance blunder as well."

"Well, I'm sorry too, Larry. So here's what you're going to do about it. I want a new unit formed inside the CIA. Their sole job is to take care of this surveillance issue immediately. Their activities, their names, their assignments – all of it is to remain permanently off the books. No one inside is to know the group even exists. The goddamn liberals find out we're surveilling our own people, my ass is grass. Let one kidnapping happen and the same bastards will blame me for it anyway. So do this right. Bring in someone tough you can trust to run it. You with me so far?"

"Yes sir."

"As Head of the CIA, you are to remain completely out of the loop. Whoever you choose to run the thing will report to someone I'll appoint over here at the White House. Complete deniability on both ends. Are we clear on this, Larry?"

"Absolutely, sir."

"I'll say it again. The last thing I need right now is a goddamn kidnapping in my own backyard. You and I have done some fine work together over the years. I want you to make this happen yesterday."

"Yes sir."

The President disconnected the line and left the Oval Office, slamming the door behind himself.

At 8:30 a.m. on the following Monday morning, a black Lexus limousine pulled up to the west gate of the White House. Its arrival was expected. The process of I.D. presentation and dog sniffing were completed swiftly and the long car was waved through. Behind its tinted windows sat a lone passenger, Chief Barbara Porter. She was 39 and rumored to have an I.Q. of 165. She'd been the head of CIA's Counterterrorist Operations at Langley Virginia for six years.

Over the weekend, Director of the CIA Lawrence Shaw had called her at home and given her a new job. In addition to her responsibility for Counterterrorist Operations, she was now ordered to create a new surveillance and enforcement team within the CIA. Director Shaw had referred to it as Clandestine Operations (CLOPS). He had advised her that the department's name and its identity were to remain clandestine – invisible even unto its own.

To Chief Porter, a highly respected Agency veteran, naming a department and then decreeing that the name never be used, indicated three things: *political meddling, flawed conception, and ultimate disaster.*

She had been summoned to the White House by Brigadier General Orin Pierce, the man chosen by President Crowley to be her *control.* Pierce was the obvious choice. Everyone on the Hill knew that 'dirty work' was written into the man's job description. His lair was rumored to be four floors beneath the White House. Rumored because most Washingtonians didn't know anyone who'd ever been there. And that's the way they preferred it.

The Basement – 1600 Pennsylvania Ave

No clandestine operations of any kind were ever allowed to be publicly associated with the White House. It had happened once with Richard Nixon. And it was never going to happen again.

Just like his predecessors, President Crowley understood the porous nature of the resources under his command. He also understood that often there were tasks to be accomplished that were beyond the veil of law enforcement. As a result, the President needed his own Special Team, just like his predecessors did.

And he kept them close at hand.

The President's Black Ops Team was housed in a special bunker, four stories below the White House. They called it The Basement, a name purposely designed to sound small and harmless, suggesting a dusty room, cans of dried-up house paint, and a leaky water heater.

Actually, it was an enormous catacomb of secure rooms and sophisticated equipment manned by more than 50 agents and strategists, distinguished by their lofty intellects and loftier security clearances.

The Reagan administration's spin doctors had dubbed the basement's clandestine operations "dirty tricks." The term was a brilliant ruse to deflect attention from the vigilante methods used by the agents who worked there. *What did anyone have to fear from a few harmless dirty tricks?*

The ploy had continued to work for more than 40 years. All Basement activities were permanently *off the books.* All inhabitants of the sacred cellar enjoyed transcendent legal protection, no matter which band of donkeys or elephants was currently holding the gavel.

Their general assignment was to do whatever the President wanted done. And Brigadier General Orin Pierce was the arbiter. He had held his current position for more than three decades, maintaining it through four different administrations. His covert title was Special Military Advisor to the President.

He was an arrogant son of a bitch with an I.Q. of 170. Pierce was the most feared presence in the White House, the only man permitted to enter the Oval Office without an appointment, a dubious honor that bore frightening implications for anyone who crossed him.

No one ever crossed him. His job was bulletproof. He reported to the President only; but by definition, the President was to have no knowledge of anything he did. He was a living oxymoron; a deadly convolution of power and privilege. Pierce was a tyrant who enjoyed complete autonomy inside the sanctum of the most powerful nation in the world.

He was seldom seen "above ground." He chose to remain in The Basement, slithering amongst his files and his minions. Enemies referred to him as "The Snake." Brigadier General Orin Pierce didn't seem to need friends.

As the black Lexus continued past the Presidential Rose Garden, Chief Barbara Porter, for the umpteenth time, thought about the political ramifications of her new assignment. She was aware that many of the President's congressional opponents would definitely consider the CIA's new surveillance operation an infringement of individual rights; spying on U.S. citizens without their knowledge. But then none of the President's opponents were ever supposed to hear about CLOPS.

Chief Barbara Porter was on time; but she was kept waiting an additional 15 minutes in her *control's* office. Brigadier General Orin Pierce was an important man.

When she was finally admitted, the general was standing with his back to her, pacing back and forth, speaking quietly into the phone. He was tall and too thin, his pointy face screwed into a permanent ratchet of disapproval. His head was too big for his body; it hung forward over his collar.

As she waited, Porter mused; *the man looks like a long-handled hatchet.* It was an appropriate metaphor for the General's style and bearing. The current joke among his basement staff was that "Pierce never met a man he couldn't destroy."

Chief Barbara Porter was the Head of the CIA's Counterterrorist Operations, a veteran of numerous in-house wars. She was not easily intimidated.

"Sit down," said Pierce, continuing his phone conversation, keeping his back turned to her. When he finished speaking, he took a seat behind his desk, removed his glasses, and for the first time, made eye contact with Barbara Porter. His eyebrows roped into a surprised knot. "This is a first. I don't believe I have any women working for me."

"You still don't," she said.

"Pardon me?" No one contradicted Orin Pierce.

"I said you still don't, General. I work for the CIA."

"Is it Miss or Ms?" said Pierce, about to launch into a lesson on authority.

"Chief Porter will do nicely, sir. Would you prefer that I call you Orin?"

Pierce was so stunned at this woman's audacity that for a moment he was speechless.

Chief Porter, an old hand at ceremonial dueling, seized the offensive. "As ordered by Director Shaw, I will be updating you periodically on the progress of CLOPS. With the workload you must have, General, I can't imagine that you would need to be bothered hearing the mundane details of 30 or more surveillance assignments. Unless, of course it was something relevant to national security."

Again he was speechless. She had trumped him with her opening gambit; stolen the very ideas he was about to verbalize and preempted any misguided attempts at wasting his time.

She had not insulted him. She had correctly assessed the situation. He was left with practically nothing to say. He was furious.

"I will expect written updates on my desk on a...monthly basis."

Chief Barbara Porter slid her chair backwards ever so slightly and stood up. "Absolutely, General. Anything else?"

He was forced to look upward into her face, a position of weakness. He was not about to give her the courtesy of standing. His response was infused with all the contempt he could muster. "Listen Ms. Porter, I don't buy your polite formality for one minute. It's nothing but a ruse. A thinly veiled one at that. Rest assured I will be watching you and this operation closely."

Barbara Porter stood perfectly still, looking down at Pierce. "Well Orin," she said brightly, "Please accept my compliments on your perceptiveness. And in case you hadn't noticed, men always watch women. Especially when they wear thin veils."

13

West Los Angeles, California

The Federal Building at Wilshire and Sepulveda stands tall, adjacent the VA graveyard, its windows looking north toward the Getty Museum and south toward the ghetto; the grand museum and the city of Compton; an architectural reminder of the State's obligations to the great and the small.

Strangely, the building's designer chose to hood each of the building's windows with vertical slats of aluminum. When the fog rolls in at night, the 20 floors of perpetually lighted windows radiate an eerie glow from behind their hooded eyes. West-Siders call it "The Ghost Ship."

Quentin Hawk was driving in from Pacific Palisades to the Ghost Ship. He was halfway down Sunset nearing UCLA, the crisp points of his new Armani collar laying smartly against his chest. One more right turn on Federal Avenue and he'd be there – 45 minutes ahead of schedule.

Amazing. A first. A good omen.

Until his cell phone began playing Gwen Stefani's 'Hollaback Girl' which indicated the Agency was sending him a text message. He flipped open the phone but the Westwood sun was so bright he had to pull onto a side street into the shadows of a banana leaf tree. The message read, "*Meeting changed to Venice Beach area.*" Following that was a detailed series of street names directing him to an address via the shortest route.

Bullshit. Typical CIA cloak and dagger bullshit.

Last minute changes were habitual; predictable. Back in Duluth, the Agency believed that last minute changes provided an extra measure of security. Quent couldn't believe they pulled the same crap in L.A. It was stupid. Amateur. And it pissed him off.

He made an illegal U-turn and headed straight back down Sunset Boulevard. When he reached Pacific Coast Highway, he made a left turn and headed south, knowing it would get him there eventually. Only it would twist and turn through little clusters of commerce; burger joints and boardwalks crowded with activity. Bikinis, volleyball nets, ankle tats, long legs, jut butts, and blonde hair. It definitely kicked the crap out of Duluth, which was bound to be his next assignment anyway.

He arrived 15 minutes late at the 'Venice address' which turned out not to be in Venice, but in Santa Monica. It was the Santa Monica Lumber Yard. He pulled into the rear lot, parked in one of the green zones and lowered his passenger window as instructed.

"Remain in car until contacted," the message had said, so he pushed his current favorite CD 'Match Box 20' into the slot and leaned back to wait. "Sure glad I hurried," he smirked.

Eight bars into cut one, a man in coveralls shoved an armload of two-by-fours into his passenger window headed for the back seat. Another man started attaching a roof rack to the top of his rental Pontiac.

What a cool disguise. Who'd'a thunk it? Quent loved chewing on the hand that fed him.

"Have this done for you in a few minutes, sir. Right over there, through that door. You can take care of the bill," said the one with the roof rack.

"Take care of the bill," he repeated. *Jeeze, these California agents are so clever.*

As Hawk approached the door marked Corporate Office, a guy wearing a red baseball cap, jeans and work boots stepped out from the door and smiled.

"Can I help you, sir?"

"Came here to take care of the bill," Hawk said, using the *exact wording,* just as he had been trained to do for the past 15 years.

Mr. Red Hat stepped aside. "Good to have you, sir," he said, extending his meat hook of a hand. As they shook he added, "Name's Duke Furillo. Big Gopher fan. I was there in '85, man, when you guys beat Clemson. Saw you make *the catch.* Won a hundert bucks off my buddies. Really great to have you with us. Show your I.D. to the girl inside."

"Guess that means you owe me a Gopher dog, right?" said Hawk, returning the shake. "By the way, my first name's Quentin. You can lose the sir."

"With pleasure, sir," answered Furillo with a proud smile.

Quentin entered the building and badged the darkly tanned receptionist. A door in the wall to her right buzzed and opened a crack.

"Right through that door, Agent Hawk," she said, looking him up and down like she was holding a fist full of $1s ready to stuff down his jockstrap.

Quentin Hawk was third generation Irish American. His people were Dublin farmers. Dreamers. Feet in the peat, head in the clouds. Black Irish. Quentin had thick dark hair, dark brows and devastating green eyes. Legendary green eyes. Their effect on women was always the same. Each woman knew in her heart that she was the special woman responsible for that blazing aura. And each woman longed to bask in its light.

Quent stepped through the inner door at the Santa Monica Lumber Yard to find himself on a small, wood-railed platform overlooking a massive work area. The building had once housed 10,000 square feet of lumber and looked to be about three stories tall. Quent immediately recognized the typical agency decor. They had *partitioned the crap out of it* and turned it into a bee's nest of tiny, drop-ceilinged, 400 square foot offices. *Real nice*. About the only pleasant feature was the lingering smell of sawdust.

He descended the stairs leading to an open conference area which featured a small podium, tables, chairs and a chalkboard. Five other agents were seated at separate wooden tables.

Waiting for Chief Barbara Porter.

He figured that's what they were all doing. He took a seat at the rear table. There was a tension in the air. Nobody spoke. No one had even turned around when he entered. *Probably all scared*, he thought. By Quentin's calculations, 80% of CIA agents were pussies anyway, so that would be about the right mix.

Waiting for Chief Barbara Porter.

None of the other agents could see Quent's smirk.

Nobody's got the cajones to say it out loud. Porter's probably a dyke.

A door opened behind the podium and in walked Chief Barbara Porter, dressed in a conservative black skirt, white blouse and short jacket.

Definitely no dyke.

She had an athletic face, good skin, short brown hair, an attractive smile and an okay body. She immediately began what Quentin would later describe as a 'very no bullshit speech.'

"Sit down gentlemen. My name is Chief Barbara Porter. I'm the head of a new department within the Agency called Clandestine Operations. I have personally chosen each of you to undergo high level instruction in the Agency's latest techniques relative to terrorist operations. The job brings with it the title Captain Special Operations. Assuming your test scores are good, you will each receive a 1½ category promotion plus the raise that goes with it."

Absolute mind blower. No one in the room had even imagined such an outcome was possible.

The Chief paused to let the impact of her words land soundly on the chin of each man present. She then launched a few choice body blows. "Your existence and the existence of this new department will remain a complete secret to all members of our own Agency.

"Let me repeat that so there will be no confusion. The Department of Clandestine Operations, or CLOPS, will be a cell of its own; an invisible clique within the Central Intelligence Agency. No paper trails, no names, no faces. In a way CLOPS will mirror some of our Jihadist enemies. Very hard to find. Very hard to trace.

"You might want to think about it this way. If no one is allowed to know what you're doing, then no one's coming to save you when your ass is in trouble. And I assure you gentlemen, there will be trouble."

I like this woman already.

Momentarily lost in his own fantasy, Quentin was suddenly jolted back to attention by a quote Chief Porter was attributing to the current U.S. Attorney General: "We are a nation of laws, not a nation of men."

At the mention of the man and his *asinine* quote, anger flamed in Quentin's chest, his jaws clamped down hard. His lips tightened into a straight line. From that point on, Chief Porter's words failed to reach Quentin Hawk.

She concluded by reminding them of the times of their weekly classes and the protocol expected.

"You are dismissed," she said, "with the exception of one person. Agent J. Quentin Hawk please report to my office at 4:30 this afternoon. That's 15 minutes from now."

Oh shit.

"Could you direct me to Chief Porter's office, please?" Quentin asked the receptionist.

A licentious smile appeared on the woman's overly Collagened lips. "Is your name Quentin Hawk?" Her voice was shrill; her accent, south Philly.

"How did you know that?" he asked, remaining friendly.

"I knew she'd pick the best-looking one, that's how. Nice shirt by the way. So listen, handsome, if you need any help with anything, just say my name. It's Ruthie. I'll be right here waiting if you need me."

He waited for her to give him directions to the Chief's office, but she said nothing; just stared up at him, revealing more of her cleavage as she rested her elbows on her desk.

"And the Chief's office is..." he asked again.

"Down that hallway to the left. By the way, in case you need it, my cell phone number is right there on my card."

"Thanks very much," he said, ignoring the cards and the cleavage and heading off down the hall to the left.

"Congratulations, Agent Hawk, you did very well out there," said a smiling Chief Porter as he entered her beautifully furnished office.

"I beg your pardon?"

"With Ruthie."

"You mean the Barbie out there at the counter?"

"That 'Barbie' has a Master's in criminology and a minor in forensics. The little act she gave you was a bit of a test I like to administer to certain agents whom I feel might find themselves under unusual pressure from the opposite sex."

Bitch.

Quentin stood his ground and said nothing. She stared into his eyes until she was sure he wasn't going to respond further.

"Agent Hawk, I wouldn't care to be tested in that fashion either if I were you. Please sit down. Perhaps after I explain further you might feel differently."

Quentin sat. *This should be good.*

"It appeared to me that you don't agree with our boss, the nation's head lawyer, the District Attorney of the United States?"

Hawk squinted his eyes. *I wonder where she's going with this one.* "Is that a serious question? I mean one you'd like me to answer?" he asked finally.

"Yes."

"Is it kosher if I speak freely?"

"That's exactly what I want out of this meeting, Agent Hawk. Kosher as you can possibly get."

All right, screw it. You asked for it.

"When it comes to technique in the pursuit of duty, I'm here to learn everything I can. But politics is personal. When it comes to politics, I don't give a damn what you or anybody says. And I don't have to."

"Not even the head lawman in Washington?" she asked.

"Especially not him. And since you seem to want to know, I disagree categorically with the 'head lawyer's' bullshit opinion. Because it's bullshit. We are not a nation of laws, we are a nation of men. Men built this country. Men created its laws; the laws didn't create us. As to the head lawman, I was taught the blindfold on the Statue of Justice was supposed to symbolize equanimity, not blind inbred stupidity."

Chief Porter waited in silence. As if she expected Quentin to rave on; which of course, he did.

"A nation of laws, my ass. Only a goddamn lawyer could possibly see it that way. The guy isn't even a real policeman. He never walked a beat. Never carried a piece. Never ducked a bullet. Never put his dick on the line for anything except his physical. Truth is, he's the most repugnant kind of human being known to man. A politician. Got his appointment from another cow head just like himself. A politician.

"Take a look at our congressmen and senators, the whole brood of 'em. I've never seen a more archaic, ass-kissing bunch of incompetent, out of touch, self-serving losers in my life."

Chief Barbara Porter showed no expression. When she was sure Quent's tirade had concluded, she began thumbing through a sheaf of papers on her desk. Finally, she placed her finger on a section of text and looked up. "Agent Hawk, I'm going to read you something from your file. I'm quite sure you know that reading an agent's file to him is completely forbidden by agency policy. You are aware of that, aren't you?"

"Yes, Chief Porter, I am." *Shit.*

She began reading; each section emphasized, each word clearly articulated: "Agent J. Quentin Hawk: Summary of service. Pros: a perfect record of success: 54 arrests; 54

convictions. Unanimous choice as group leader by all agents who've ever served under his command.

"Cons: A completely unorthodox and unacceptable approach to law and law enforcement. Not one positive recommend ever, from any superior in the areas of personal style, language, politics and most particularly, what is described here as 'his un-agency-like methods of operation.'

Summary: dangerous; unpredictable; Unfit for promotion.

"Agent Hawk, it is for the reasons you've just heard, that no promotions have been offered to you during your 15 years of service with this agency," Chief Porter set the paper back on her desk and closed the file.

"Before I continue, would you like to make any comment, Agent Hawk?"

"No thank you," he said, staring at his feet.

"All right then, it is precisely for the reasons I have just shared with you, that I am offering you a three category promotion from you current level. The position is Assistant Chief of Clandestine Operations."

Quentin's head rose slowly. He was certain he'd misheard.

"Congratulations, Chief Hawk." She had walked around her desk and was extending her hand. "Assuming you're game, and you pass the examinations, you will operate directly under my command. Among other duties, you will be charged with the responsibility of building this department with me and recommending each and every agent transferred in here."

Her handshake was firm. Her countenance was serious. Quentin was stunned. He let go of her hand, unsure of what to do or say. When he looked into her eyes, he could see that she was comfortable with his uncertainty. She seemed willing to wait in silence until he decided to speak.

Finally he said, "Does that mean you agreed with all that crap...ah stuff I said?"

There was a smile in her response, but he could see that she was serious about her answer. "It's not what you said, Agent Hawk, it's who you are that interests me. And I believe it's the exact kind of person I need to help me build this department."

Crap!

14

Paris, France

The second date between Doctor Luke Towne and the mysterious Kathryn de Kennesy was set for 8 a.m. at Jardin des Colombes, where, just 24 hours earlier, an assassin had tried to kill him. Luke was early; by a full 90 minutes. It wasn't his habit of punctuality that drew him to the Jardin des Colombes courtyard at 6:30 in the morning; it was his training, two tours in Vietnam and 20 years as a Special Forces legend.

He used the time to circle the area on foot, affecting the role of a casual observer, although his stroll was anything but casual. His practiced eyes took notice of every shadowed corner or ledge or façade that might provide cover for a long range sniper. He watched the people, their clothes and their actions, forming a *gestalt* of the area, a mental picture of 'normalcy.'

Later, the technique would enhance his ability to focus his attention on anything that appeared 'out of place' or unusual.

Luke knew the Paris police would be out in force, following wherever he went. He knew that his extra precautions were overkill. But thoroughness had kept him alive for 20 years of combat, so he continued to follow procedures until he was satisfied. Only then did he approach the Jardin Café.

Kathryn de Kennesy was sitting under the same umbrella waiting for him.

"Good morning," she said. As he neared the table, she stood and smiled a smile that rivaled one of his own high tech lasers.

"Good morning," he answered, dropping his eyes from her smile – almost in self defense. But her skirt was so short he became immediately fixated on her tan thighs.

God, what a pair a' legs.

"Should I call you Doctor or Colonel?" she said.

"Luke would be good," he answered, wresting his eyes back up to her face. There was no embrace this time. He simply pulled out the little wrought iron chair and sat opposite her at the table.

"Been reading about you," she said, her eyes sweeping across the pile of newspapers before her.

"So...that's the end of breakfast, right?" Luke pushed his chair back as if to go.

"I don't think so," she smiled.

"Really? Well, what do you think?" he asked, seating himself again.

"About the scientist or the soldier?"

"Both."

Their eyes locked for a beat. Such amazing turquoise eyes. She held his gaze comfortably, and somehow her little momentary stare seemed both familiar and intimate.

This is one unbelievably sexy woman.

Then suddenly the eyes changed. The sexuality seemed to dissolve; and in its place, a focused, articulate, feminine confidence.

"All right," she began, "I think two days ago, an American scientist presented us with a revolutionary advance in ocular medicine. He showed us a tool that might potentially reshape the lives of millions. It seemed the Mind's Eye lens could lead to new kinds of research that could benefit mankind in ways we haven't imagined yet.

"I also think an American colonel, representing a country victimized by one of the most savage attacks on innocent people in modern history, revealed its intentions loud and clear; to effectively strike back at all terrorist cowards no matter where they hide. And then he showed a startling demonstration of a new technology still in its infancy.

"I think your keynote address was a rare look at an injured people struggling to defend their children against a vicious and unpredictable enemy."

Luke was stunned. Truly. This speech from the lips of one of the most beautiful women he'd ever forgotten to bring flowers to.

"Too bad you don't write for one of those newspapers," he said. "I'd like to have you on my side."

"I am. I do," she answered, a very serious woman, still.

"Pardon?"

"I am on your side. And I do write for one of those newspapers. The Lebanese Daily Journal. It's part of my job. Here..." She pulled a newspaper from under the stack and placed it in front of him.

The headline: "Dual technologies from America." His eyes raced to find the article, but before he could begin reading, the serious woman across the table suddenly turned into a playful girl.

"So how'd you know my name yesterday, Doc?"

He put the paper down. There was always time for business, but never enough time for pleasure. Especially in this league. "Well," he said with a grin, "I'd like to take credit for that one, but...the truth is, my adjutant whispered your name in my ear when he saw you walk up. Guy doesn't miss much."

Before Kathryn could respond, two waiters arrived balancing armfuls of food and begin laying out a feast: pan-fried brioche and lingonberry preserves, minute steak and eggs basted, pommes frites well done, coconut yogurt with blueberries, and a double macchiato.

Luke took a long moment to savor.

"All right, so how'd you do that?" he said finally.

"What?"

"What?" he mocked, pointing at the food: "All my favorite...stuff."

She served up another radiant smile with her answer. "Got a pretty fair male assistant myself."

Luke Towne had been divorced for more than 15 years. He was rugged, successful, well-traveled, highly educated and single. In his role as Head of the U.S. Military's Department of Laser Research, he had spent more than a decade interacting with the world's leading scientists and researchers, both males and females.

He peered over his macchiato and marveled. Never in all those years had he encountered anyone as bright, well-read, interesting, interested, facile, engaging or humorous as this amazing blue/green eyed Lebanese beauty, who didn't look at all Lebanese.

They sat, knees almost touching, across the tiny table. There were occasional silences; but somehow Kathryn seemed able to make them feel like intimacies, rather than awkward gaps.

There was an intrinsic sexuality about her. She offered no flirtation, no passionate glance, no innuendo, not one indication of her sexual disposition; yet she seemed so totally comfortable in her body, so completely at ease in the moment, that she didn't have to do anything. She did nothing; but *God* it was overpoweringly sexual, alluring and inviting.

Breakfast, macchiato, conversation, wit and sensuality; their first date lasted almost three hours. For Luke, it seemed like 10 minutes. She made him feel like they had known each other since childhood.

Jardin des Colombes. The Garden of Doves. A world away. It became their place, an almost daily prequel to their love making. The perfume of the jasmine in the arbors mixed with the scent of fresh baked croissants from the Vieux Moulin – an opiate to the troubled outside world.

A week later, in the tangled sheets of an afternoon tryst at the discrete Hotel St. Claire (just across the courtyard from their meeting place), she would admit to him happily that she had insisted on breakfast because she couldn't stand to wait until lunch.

Kathryn was unlike any of the women in Luke's past. It seemed to him that all of the others had been a similar breed; drawn to his strength, his animal bearing; physical women who hung out at sports bars and slept with policemen and athletes. All of them were fueled in part with an element of conquest, ignited by the stimulation of the moment.

A few of his prior relationships had lasted beyond the two-year mark, but somehow they seemed to lack any real continuity. He recalled them as a series of disconnected incidents, mostly wild and kinetic, sustained by energy but lacking in content.

This new relationship was definitely ablaze in sexuality, but its source seemed to spring from union rather than separateness. A mutuality. It was both an emotional connection and a shared resistance to the intrusions and judgments of the world.

They were together every available minute for the two week duration of the Parisian conference. At one point, they stole away for a three-day weekend at beautiful Naoussa on the Greek Island of Paros.

Their feet bottoms were touching as they lay stretched from one end of the little white skiff to the other, each one reading, enchanted by the comfort of their silence together. After several minutes of page turning Kat held up her Oprah magazine and pointed to a pink bikini. "Luke, do you like this suit?"

He squinted over his copy of SI. "Not on her."

"Why not?"
"Too big."
"What is?"
"Her ass."
"*Her ass?*" she snapped. "Everybody can't have tiny little Malibu surfer buns you know. The average woman in the U.S. is a size 10. Did you know that?"
"Don't know any women with a size 10 ass," he lied, knowing it would get her.
"What are you saying?"
"What?"
"About my ass?"
"Nothing. I said nothing about your ass."
"Something wrong with my ass?"
"No. It's great. Your ass could launch a thousand ships."
"WHAT?" she gasped, suppressing a smile, pretending she didn't understand his Homeric reference.
He closed his magazine. "I'm saying I've never seen an ass as exciting, as magnificent, as totally devastating as your perfect little round one, dear."
"Thank you. Even though you lacked sincerity, that was the correct answer. And I'll accept it. You can go back to your *sports* now."
Both went back to their reading.
Ten minutes later Kat interrupted the silence again. "How can the U.S. possibly think they can democratize the Middle East?" she asked.
"Where'd that one come from?" he wondered out loud.
"This article on U.S. foreign policy. Ambassador Blanton says the long-term goal of this administration is to bring democracy to all the people of the Middle East. Why would you want to do that?"
"Uh...how 'bout 3000 years of non-productivity? That's about what they've got over there so far. They produce nothing. They contribute nothing. They eat sand and live in a time warp. You think that's what they want?" Luke asked with only a bit of his full rancor showing.
"Of course it's what they want, Luke," she answered, turning serious. "It's their way of life. It's all they know. It's what they believe in. That's all any of us can be expected to use as truth, isn't it? Wouldn't you agree? And while we're at it, how could any 200-year-old nation have the overbearing ego to decide the issue of governance for a culture that's 5000

years old? And what kind of an ignorant bunch of bullies would think you had the right to do such a thing??"

"Don't you think all humans deserve the right to free choice?"

She sat up straight in her end of the skiff and fixed her very beautiful eyes on his face as if sending one of his own lasers back at him. "Doctor Towne," she said calmly, "Of course you remember reading Thomas Kuhn?"

"I do, yes, *The Structure of Scientific Revolutions,*" he replied, naming the book that had made Kuhn famous. "The man coined the term Paradigm Shift, didn't he?"

"Yes he did." Then, being very careful that her tone was not condescending, she continued. "Well, then you might remember his use of the word *incommensurable.* I suggest this is a good example of it. Perhaps the real truth is that different cultures who have radically different worldviews cannot be understood by one another. It's not a question of which view is better, but rather, as Kuhn suggested, it's that sometimes different paradigms cannot be translated into one another or rationally evaluated against one another. Perhaps the real problem here is that Western and Middle Eastern worldviews are simply *incommensurable.*"

There was a moment of respectful silence from Luke's end of the boat. *This is one really smart girlie. Best to shut the hell up and enjoy the view.*

"Blondes aren't supposed to talk politics on vacation," he answered finally, acknowledging defeat by the width of his sheepish grin.

She stood up in the boat and put on a thick foreign accent. "I see. Time for beeg strong 'merican soldier man to screw some sense into stupid Lebanese chicka...?"

She stripped off her bathing suit top and dove overboard, daring him to catch her. In their mutual sharing, she had left out the part about the 200 meter freestyle – her best event in high school.

Unsuspecting Colonel Towne, assured of his own athletic prowess, dove in and gave chase. Forgetting the 20 years she had on him, he sprinted straight for her, beating the water with his strong sinewy arms until he'd made a good 40 meters out. When she wasn't in his forward field of vision, he looked behind him. There, sitting comfortably back in the boat, completely naked, head tilted back in the sun, eating an apple from the lunch she'd prepared, was his beautiful sea nymph.

Completely unexpected, so late in life, Kat de Kennesy was becoming a soul mate. An angel's whisper deep in the heart.

The two would become almost inseparable despite their work on continents that conspired to keep them apart. As often as his scientific conscience would allow, Luke would find reason to be abroad.

He was in over his head, never having dreamt that at this point in his complex and fruitful life, he would be able to feel like a kid again.

But as his youthful fantasies returned, so did his accompanying insecurities; how could a man his age hope to hold on to someone so young, and so beautiful? She was an international beauty – *a very expensive international beauty* - highly prized in a society well beyond his scope.

Perhaps he could hold her by 'being there.' At least as close as pixels would allow. To that end, he had his techs at The Facility begin constructing a high definition, closed circuit, laser teleconferencing system. The plan was to send it to Kat's home in the Beqaa Valley as a surprise present. He would mount a similar screen in his bedroom at home in Malibu. Perhaps he might at least be with her *virtually*. It was all he could think of.

15

Brigadier General Orin Pierce had been watching Kathryn de Kennesy since she first surfaced at the Paris Technology Convention. The weeks had passed without incident until the British press ran a gossip column featuring Kathryn's romance with 'America's aging hunk scientist Doctor Luke Towne.' The article was entitled 'The Scientist and the Beauty.'

Virginia Parker Crowley, America's First Lady, an ardent fan of the columns, had seen it, cut the article out of the tabloids and read it to the President at breakfast. "Do we know anything about this woman, dear?" she asked, feigning concern.

It wasn't until some days later that the President, being a forgetful husband, remembered the conversation and asked Orin Pierce to leave the de Kennesy file on his desk.

It was a simple request, made all the more simple because Pierce had ordered surveillance on the couple from the first day they met. No one had asked him to. He saw it as an essential part of his job to keep tabs on important military personnel. Anyone keeping company with a scientist of Luke Towne's import would naturally require surveillance.

Pierce leaned back in his leather desk chair, moistened his lips from the ever-present glass of tonic water and opened the file. The research was well documented, and rich in detail.

The woman's credentials are beyond question.

The adopted daughter of Doctor and Mrs. Leon de Kennesy; Kathryn's father was a prominent Lebanese physician, her mother, a professor of art history at the University of Beirut. Under the lavish patronage of the de Kennesys, Kathryn had matured from a rebellious child to a treasured daughter, to a brilliant collegian, to a beautiful and sought-after young woman.

Apparently, her drive to advance so inchoate, she continued her education and graduated from the Tyre Graduate School of Foreign Affairs with a double major, one in Middle Eastern History and a second in economics from The Normal École Supérieure.

Upon entering the work force, Kathryn's rise to political prominence was meteoric. Six months after graduate school, she moved to Awkar and became the personal attaché to

Anders Hagopian, the Lebanese Ambassador to the U.S., a position she held to this day. It was a remarkable feat for a woman.

It was her intelligence that allowed her to advance so rapidly amidst the male-dominated hierarchy of Middle Eastern affairs. But it was her stunning appearance and social skills that made her a coveted partner at the Hariri government's numerous official functions in Lebanon and throughout Western Europe. She had established her position long before that tragic day in February 2005, when Prime Minister Rafik Hariri's car exploded in a thunderous ball of flame, killing the Lebanese leader and 20 others in his administration.

His tragic death assured her permanence in the Lebanese social and political hierarchy. She had been one of the Prime Minister's favorites.

But on this night, General Orin Pierce had shifted his focus to her flesh. Kathryn de Kennesy had one of the most sensual bodies Pierce had ever seen. The woman was so striking in appearance, she drew attention to herself just by walking down the street. At 34, she was already a social phenomenon.

Too bad the woman's a fake!

The whole façade is brilliant, thought Pierce. He had seen it right from the beginning; she was too perfect. Not one freckle out of place. The perfect camouflage; hiding in plain sight; high profile; in your face; the most convincing cover of them all.

Believability. In Pierce's mind, Kathryn de Kennesy was a modern version of the Mata Hari; beautiful, brilliant, highly placed, unquestionable integrity, and way too close to the most important scientist in the U.S. Military's Defense structure.

God, the damage she could do. Subtle, insidious, high level cancer at work. Growing on the inside.

Unacceptable!

He had been working on exposing this *bitch* himself for several weeks. The problem was, the great and omniscient Pierce, second most powerful man in the White House, had found no proof that the woman was anything other than she claimed to be.

The Lebanese were fanatical about the backgrounds of their government employees. No information was ever placed in the public record. Pierce believed that in some cases (like this one) they simply didn't keep records on certain individuals. The method had a certain kind of infantile purity that impressed him; but at times like this, it drove him crazy.

Frustrated, and overworked, he had turned the file over to a hand-picked team of his finest agents. One week had passed. When no usable information was uncovered, he had launched into a tyrannical rage. The occasion was a Monday morning meeting in the conference room, a dreaded event for the special operatives who worked in Pierce's clandestine cellar.

He opened the meeting with an ultimatum. "Hear me!" he barked, "You've got two weeks. If you haven't brought me the information I need, you're gone. All of you. And your pensions are gone with you!"

He paced the length of the room, staring from face to face, the silence unbearable. "Now listen to me," he urged, switching to the quiet voice that scared the crap out of everyone who had ever known him. "Ignore the mistakes of the small brains who had this assignment before you. Forget the woman. We've been there already. Start over. Focus on her family and their relatives, and <u>their</u> relatives! Make no mistake! It's there. It's in there. She's a fake. An agent. And the man who breaks this one will earn a significant place in the ranks of this intelligence agency. An elegant place. I'll see to it myself. End of meeting."

He had burst from the conference room and marched down the hall with a kind of terrible purpose that plunged fear into the stomach of everyone in the building. *Don't get in his way. Climb inside your computer, keep your mouth shut and your door closed.*

The next two weeks passed in a flurry of investigative zeal; no one went home before 10 p.m. Every angle checked and rechecked, the competitive tension in The Basement becoming more and more ugly as the deadline for submissions drew near.

When the day of reckoning was at hand. Pierce was in his office at 6:30 a.m. to begin poring anxiously over the reports. There were 14 of them, 14 grade-one specialists, the finest minds in the intelligence community, working full-time on the same project. The most expensive and talented sleuths in the U.S. Government.

And not one *goddamn* scrap of helpful data in the bunch. Pierce was about to go ballistic.

The last report was the thinnest of them all. Ollie Jordan's name was printed neatly in the upper right hand corner. Pierce sneered at the first page – a paltry bit of information. He scanned through Ollie's account of the multiple sources he'd researched, the exact same sources everyone else had checked.

Angry at seeing the repetition, Pierce ignored the details and flipped to the conclusion. And there to his astonishment, he found the first bit of enlightenment on the de Kennesy woman to reach his desk in a month. The young agent had written, "...the only suspicious information on this woman seems to be that the first 14 years of her life are missing. I can find no birth certificate, no hospital of record, no grade school enrollment; in short, nothing."

It was such a glaring omission that Pierce couldn't believe he'd missed it himself. Every one of his high paid professionals had missed it also.

He called an immediate agency-wide meeting. The festivities began with 15 minutes of non-stop harangue at the "idiots," all of whom stared carefully at their shoes, afraid that he'd single one of them out as an example of such "rank stupidity." In situations like these, Pierce always chose someone as the responsible party. That person would suffer verbal humiliation in front of the group and often be demoted or shipped out.

This time, however, when Pierce had finished his tirade, he emitted an audible sigh of disgust and left the room without a word. The effect was devastating; even worse than if he'd fired one of them. The scapegoat had not been chosen yet. Everyone must now wait for the shoe to fall. And it always did.

Ollie Jordan hid in his office, just like the rest of them; each one praying that his phone wouldn't ring. Ten grueling minutes ticked by. Fifteen minutes. No one had dared venture into the hallway. Ollie reread his own report and set it aside, shaking his head. *Not very impressive.*

His stomach went rigid at the sound of the phone. He looked over at the bank of lights, hoping it wasn't the red one. But it was.

"My office. Now."

In a daze, Ollie marched out his door and down the hallway to meet his fate.

"Sit down Mr. Jordan." Pierce hadn't looked up when Ollie knocked and entered his office. The general just continued writing in the open file on his desk.

"Ollie, short for Ollikot. That's Nez Perce, isn't it?" asked Pierce, still focusing on his writing, still not offering the courtesy of eye contact.

"How did you know that, sir?" ask the surprised newbie.

The steely eyes now swept up and locked on Jordan's face. "I'm in the knowing business, son. I also know at Yale, you refused to drink a cup of stale beer and cigarette butts and got blackballed by the Thetas."

Ollie Jordan was rocked. There was no possible way Pierce could know this minute personal fact. It was not in any record anywhere; it was one of Jordan's best-kept secrets from college. He was greatly embarrassed by its revelation. He blushed deeply.

Pierce saw it. *Mission accomplished*, he thought. Subservience is like a magic wand. It assures obedience. *Loyalty based on fear is the fulcrum of true power* (a Pierceism*)*. Once you have them frightened, you follow it up with candy. From then on, they're yours.

The gospel according to Orin Pierce.

"Mr. Jordan, in your report on the de Kennesy woman, you saw fit to point out the obvious. That there were no birth records, no evidence of childhood and so forth."

Jordan pushed himself deeper into the uncomfortable straight-backed chair, expecting the worse. Pierce was inscrutable as ever, his face expressionless.

"Good work, young man," he said finally, playing the dramatic pause for all it was worth. "Sometimes the most important clues lie in the obvious. You were the only investigator on my staff thorough enough to consider this quite obvious, yet quite glaring omission."

Ollie Jordan sat stiffly in his chair before the great man, still afraid to react, still unsure if this were the path to heaven or the road to hell. Once again Pierce noted the discomfort, though his countenance still remained stony.

"Mr. Jordan, I am assigning you exclusively to the research and surveillance of this de Kennesy woman. You will have complete authority in the manner in which you conduct your investigation. And I emphasize, complete authority. All other staff members will report to you exclusively on this matter. And you may engage and employ any of them in your efforts; within reason. I will leave it to you to determine what is reasonable.

"At the moment, Mr. Jordan, it would appear that you're in luck. The de Kennesy woman is in Orange County, meeting with the Immigration Office in Irvine. She's registered at the Regency Hotel. I already have some men down there on surveillance. If I were you, I'd get down there myself and get up to speed.

"You may consider this a promotion, Mr. Jordan, effective immediately. In conclusion, you should know that no other employee in the history of my tenure has ever been promoted this early. You're only here 2½ months. Am I right?"

Jordan was trying to breathe calmly. "Yes sir."

"Report to Room number 70. My personal copy of the de Kennesy files and all related data is on your desk." Pierce again began printing neatly in the file before him. After a moment, he looked up, his face registering surprise that Jordan was still there. "Dismissed," he said. And then went back to his meticulous printing.

"Thank you sir." Ollie Jordan stood awkwardly and edged out the door, then walked quickly away toward his cubby hole of an office.

Pierce chuckled at the youth's conflicted response. Perfect.

Pierce was such an asshole. Everyone knew it. Everyone in the White House underground thought it. Almost everyone he'd ever dealt with in his 30 plus years of government service felt the same.

Asshole. That was the book on Orin Pierce.

But of course, that was much too simple an appraisal for such a complex and powerful magus. Beneath the surface there was much more, but no one had ever dared to look deeper. The danger was not worth the risk.

Pierce stared down at his task list. He was so busy that he'd had to put the new kid on the de Kennesy woman and hope for the best. But he still he couldn't let go of it.

He knew the woman had secrets. Sainthood was never available to people of such high profile and public purity. It just never worked out that way. In fact, the opposite was true. The best of them all had a past, a closet of deviance hidden away somewhere.

The analogy of his own profile was a case in point. Pierce's closet was cavernous. Black and horrible. He was always able to cover his excesses, to keep his own secrets walled up and hidden away from scrutiny. He did it with money. And certainly not on the salary he was paid. There were two offshore accounts, one in Guernsey and the other in the Isle of Man. The constant influx of money to his anonymous accounts had started years earlier. From endeavors that were meticulously kept – off the books.

The public Orin Pierce: a three-decade anomaly, second most powerful man in the White House, first button on the President's speed dial, was a multi-faceted, highly intelligent and greatly successful behind-the-scenes personage. The private Orin Pierce was a bipolar, sadistic, venomous and deeply disturbed pariah.

He'd had enough dissatisfaction for one day. When he pressed the green button under his desk, his driver responded immediately. The General's silver Town Car was hurriedly brought to the elevator door that serviced the basement staff. It's egress was tunneled several blocks away from the White House to permit unobserved access.

A weary and frustrated Orin Pierce would be driven to his home so he might relax and pursue more refined distractions.

Ollie Jordan, still reeling from his encounter with the Chief, had arrived at his desk to find it...gone! No desk, no chair, no ugly green file cabinet. No phone cables. Nothing. There weren't even depressions in the carpet where his desk had been. New carpet had already been laid in the empty space.

His meeting with Pierce had taken all of 16 minutes. His stomach turned over. He stood slack-jawed, turning in place, imagining that he'd entered someone else's cubbyhole by mistake. Then a ray of understanding illuminated his frightened brain. "Report to Room number 70."

A new cubbyhole.

Trying not to appear as stupid as he felt, Ollie moved off down the linoleum'd hall toward the West corridor where the seventies should be. He rounded the corner and there, a short way down on the right, stood a woman he'd never seen before. She was non-descript. Nothing particularly feminine about her except that she had longish hair and wore a dark blue dress over her stick-like figure.

She was standing in front of Room number 70.

As Ollie approached, she stepped neatly forward, looked him dead in the eyes, handed him a key and walked off in the direction from which he'd come. Not a word. Expressionless. Cold. Efficient. Gone.

There's a lesson here somewhere.

He had no clue what the lesson might be, but what he lacked in intellect, he made up in determination. *Ollie Jordan is a never-give-up, nose-to-the-grindstone kind of guy,* he thought. If there's one thing I pride myself on, it's..." Then he noticed the name on the door: 'O. Jordan' in small black Arial type. Unbelievable. He touched the letters. They were already dry.

The key let him into an 18 by 18 foot room with a wide but plain mahogany desk, a high-backed leather desk chair, two matching visitor's chairs, a waste basket and a faux window. On the desk was a thick file folder. He could see the words "Top Secret" stamped on it in bright crimson. That would mean that his security clearance had been raised along with his salary.

Agent Ollie Jordan closed the door behind him and moved to sit behind his new desk in his new office. He closed his eyes. He thought about how the other agents had ridiculed him for his observations that there was no record of grammar school attendance for Kathryn de Kennesy. "Duh," one of the senior men had responded, trying to be hip. "What do you think, Jordan, you think they had her in spy school when she was seven? Grade school doesn't count, Dumbo." They had all laughed at that one. Stupid newbie.

Ollie thumbed open the de Kennesy file. On the inside cover of the folder were the names of the two agents currently surveilling Kathryn de Kennesy. These were senior agents who'd flown to Orange County to keep tabs on the suspect. Ollie Jordan had just become their boss. And Ollie was going to make his presence felt.

When he arrived at John Wayne Airport these boys were going to be there to pick him up.

16

Royal Hawaiian Gardens, Pacific Palisades, California

Following his astounding meeting with Chief Porter, Quentin Hawk stopped off at State Beach and played two games of volleyball with a long-legged coed named Cindy, a setter on UCLA's Woman's Volleyball team. Then he jogged several miles up the beach toward Topanga. But in spite of the exercise, his adrenaline refused to slacken. On the way home, he stopped at the Fish Shanty and wolfed down two plates of swordfish with coleslaw and extra fries.

Arriving home at sundown, he opened a bottle of Pabst Blue Ribbon, stepped out on his bird-stained balcony and looked at the blue Pacific. *Beautiful!* Wrapping his tan fingers around the long neck bottle, he took a deep pull of the amber and let out a resounding burp. *A life altering transition*, he thought. *Assistant Chief of Clandestine Operations.*

With a second more resounding burp, he toasted the horizon. *Life is good.* He sat down on his beach chair, pushed back the headrest and instantly fell asleep.

At 6:00 in the morning, when the seagulls arrived to add further decoration to his furniture, Quent was still out on his balcony fast asleep. He was dreaming about women. Not one woman in particular, but rather, parts of women – the physical parts: thighs, ankles, napes, stomachs, waists...when a thumping sound interrupted his reverie. *The sound of the headboard from the condo above. The two of them never let up.*

For a while he listened. Any second she was going to moan, "It's gonna happen, it's gonna happen, oh baby, it's gonna happen." He waited. And waited. The thumping continued. Maybe this time it just wasn't gonna happen.

As the cobwebs began to clear, the thumping turned into pounding. It was then he realized it wasn't headboard heaven from upstairs, it was the front door. His own front door. Some idiot was pounding at his front door at 6:00 in the morning.

Six feet four, 220 pounds of very athletic, recently promoted agency muscle, clad in boxer shorts, jerked open the door. "You know what time it is, bud?" Quentin growled.

"Got your free copy of the LA Times here, sir," answered a kid of about 17. "You get it free for the first month, then...."

"Stop," ordered Hawk. "I don't want any!"

When Hawk attempted to close the door, the kid stuck out his foot. Hawk's eyes fired wide in disbelief. "Am I mistaken, or did you just put your foot in my door, kid?"

"It'd really help me out, you know, earn my way to college."

"I've never seen your ass before. Why would I wanna help you out?"

"Ah...because, you know, earn my way to college."

"You're not gonna live to see college, dipshit! Get your damn foot out 'a the door. Now!"

The kid pulled back his Nike'd foot and backed away. "What a dickhead," he said loudly as he hurried down the path toward the street. Agent Hawk took a deep breath for control and closed the door. He was just about to pull up the covers when...

Bang bang bang -- more pounding on his front door.

"Holy shit hook!"

Hawk snatched up his badge from the coffee table and walked back to the door. He jerked it open again and jammed the shield into the face of whomever it was this time.

There were two seconds of silence.

"That fake badge supposed to scare me or something, dickhead?" *Again with the dickhead.* Only this time the words came from a husky, bald, tattooed adult of about 250 pounds. Quent figured him for a machinist because his hands were permanently stained with oil; "clean dirt," as Hawk's Irish uncles called it. Behind the machinist stood the paperboy, delighted with this turn of events.

"I'm obliged by law to tell you that this badge is real. That I am a duly appointed officer of the law and..." But just as Hawk was speaking the word "officer," his years of street experience alerted him to the probability that this idiot was preparing to launch a right-handed roundhouse KO punch to his jaw.

So Hawk casually turned away toward the inside of his apartment, as if to set down his badge; then suddenly and unpredictably, lunged backward launching his own violent mule kick toward the man's mid section. The force of Hawk's kick actually moved his own body three feet backwards toward his swinging assailant, which added additional force to the tremendous impact to the man's body. It was, however, just a few inches off target. To quote Hawk's own description, which he included in his written report, "Got him right in the nards."

The burly machinist went down on the concrete with a sickening thud. The roundhouse punch he was in the process of throwing whizzed by Quent's chin and landed flush on the nose of the 17-year-old paperboy as he rushed in to land a few licks of his own on the "dickhead."

Right before taking one to the chin, the kid had shouted "Kick his ass, dad."

Knocked out by his old man. Perfect.

There were now two bodies on the ground. The younger one was squirting blood from his nose like a busted sprinkler.

Yawning, Quent cuffed the bigger one, hand to ankle; went in to get his cell phone and returned to the porch to make the call. He took a bitter swig from last night's Pabst and dialed the Malibu Police Station to request assistance. Next he dialed in to Ruthie to make sure he had enough time to eat before his class at the Yard in Santa Monica.

Waiting for the switchboard to put him through, he looked down at the two 'jerkwads' on the ground. Emptying his beer down on the paperboy's head, he offered some advice. "Here, kid. When you get to college, this'll help you out. Drink lots of it."

Forty-two minutes before the start of class in Santa Monica. Quent was headed south on Sunset, hopping to get some breakfast at his favorite new eatery, Mort's Deli. He checked his watch again. Thirty-eight minutes to go. A moment of truth. *Punctuality, or French toast? The new Assistant Chief Quentin Hawk or the old screw-up from Duluth?*

The tires squealed as Hawk cut across two lanes making a right turn on to Swarthmore Avenue. Nothing in Duluth could match the French toast at Mort's.

Santa Monica Lumber Yard

Quent pulled into the Yard, 20 minutes late. His beeper went off. The read out said it was Barbara Porter. He hit the talk button immediately. "Quentin Hawk."

"Chief Hawk, Could you stop by my office when you get in please?"

"Sure can, Chief."

"Good," she said. "See you then." And clicked off.

20 minutes late. Screwed for sure.

"Nice to see you again, Agent Hawk," said Ruthie. The Chief's assistant still looked just as tan, but the Philly accent was gone. Her voice was thick, rich and articulate. "Sorry to do that to you yesterday, but orders are orders."

"Understood. No problem."

The automatic door opened and Ruthie nodded him toward it. He entered the Chief's office to find her typing very intently. Without looking up she said, "Have a seat please, I'll be right with you."

Chief Porter was wearing washed out jeans and a plain white, long-sleeved man's shirt. Her hair was up and Quentin thought she looked pretty damn fine. When she finished typing and turned toward him, he saw that the top two buttons of her shirt had inadvertently come undone from the pressure of her breasts.

Damn. He forced his eyes upward and focused directly on her hair.

"Something wrong, Agent Hawk?" she asked.

"No, Chief," he lied. Then realized he couldn't keep looking at her hair for the rest of the meeting. "Ah, actually, I hope you'll pardon me Chief, but I think some buttons came undone on your shirt there, and..." Her hand moved smartly to her shirt front and redid the two offending buttons.

"Thank you Agent Hawk, you're a gentleman. And it's appreciated."

"No problem." The intimacy of the moment made him uncomfortable.

She ran her finger along some type on her desk and then looked up. "Now, Assistant Chief Hawk, tell me, should I place any significance on the fact that your first official act outside of this office was to beat up a paperboy and his father?"

He blanched. "I never touched the kid! It was his father who swung..."

Barbara Porter had already raised her hands in the air – laughing. "Relax...just a little good natured shit, that's all."

This stopped him cold. His female boss. *Good-natured shit?*

"First of all, you're an Assistant Chief, okay? You don't owe me any explanations unless I sincerely ask you for one. And I'll make it very clear when I do. Otherwise, I will always assume you have good reasons for your actions. And hopefully they don't need justifying to me or anyone else."

Quentin took in a very deep breath. "Thank you Chief. I appreciate that...very much."

"Well, it seems to me, you don't close 55 out of 55 cases because you're stupid." She tilted her head to the side as if to add "now do you?"

She continued, "You filed your police report with Malibu PD in a timely fashion; your description of the incident was concise. Everything was done perfectly by the book, exactly according to the way you've been trained; cxactly the way a regular CIA agent should do his job."

The lights went on in Quentin's head. *A regular CIA agent.* She saw it in his face.

"Something...?" she prompted.

"I'm not a regular agent anymore. As of yesterday."

"Precisely. I have no suggestions as to how you might have handled the situation differently this morning. I would also say, however, that a more serious attitude about your public image might be in order. The less your name appears in any public record from this point on, the better." Her eyebrows raised, silently questioning his understanding.

"Clandestine ops," he answered.

"Exactly. For the last six years, I've been running a significant portion of the Agency's Counterinsurgency Operations in all its iterations. Suddenly, a new category has been added. We have been...*handed* some additional responsibilities. Someone at State has given it a catchy name, CLOPS for *Clandestine Operations.* Here's what it means."

She handed him the Langley one sheet outlining their expectations for the CLOPS Offensive, and continued her explanation. "We're ordered to provide immediate covert surveillance of selected private citizens. The stated purpose of which is to preempt possible terrorist kidnapping."

Quent scanned the page, then read a portion out loud. "'...surveilling prominent American scientists, businessmen, or individuals important to our economy.'"

He squinted at Chief Porter. "Important to our economy? Every freaking citizen that might be important to our economy? Oh yeah! That's a great idea. How 'bout Britney Spears and Alicia Keys? Why not P Diddy? He's making a shitload. That has to be way important to the economy. For sure. You know what I'm saying?"

Barbara Porter remained silent, a tolerant smirk on her face. "You finished?" she asked finally.

"Done," he answered with a smile.

"I can assure you that my boss, Lawrence Shaw was not consulted on this one. My guess is, he was told. Langley is simply following suit because they have no choice."

She let him consider the implications for a moment. Then withdrew a second sheet from the file and handed it across the table. Her tone was laced with frustration. "We've just received the list of so called 'important citizens.' Here's a postscript; apparently, *someone* in high office is of the opinion that we've already botched our first assignment."

"But we haven't even started yet."

She issued a very unfeminine 'grunt' and continued. "During the Tech Conference in Paris, someone tried to kill one of our scientists. We don't know if it was a terrorist group or just some nut bag; but I guess in some way it proves the validity of what we're trying to do here with CLOPS. It also proves just how far behind we are.

"The target was a scientist, Doctor Luke Towne. Head of the Military's Laser Research Department; the man that invented smart-bomb technology. He and his partner, a Doctor Cynthia Teller, run a top secret installation out in Malibu. It's called The Facility.

"To put it bluntly, even though we just got the 'protect' list, we should have already been on top of this one."

She bit down on a section of doughnut and chewed angrily. "I'm afraid you're gonna have to initiate the surveillance on these two immediately. Pick a couple of your best agents and create some kind of temporary protocol, because Langley hasn't sent us the official one yet. Improvise, make it up as you go, whatever; but obviously we need to get on it before something worse happens."

"You said there was an attempt on this scientist's life? What happened?"

Chief Porter laughed. "Apparently they picked the wrong guy to mess with. It seems Doctor Luke Towne, the scientist, isn't just a scientist. He was also a colonel in the Special Forces. Nicknamed the Pit Bull. We've been able to keep it out of the papers, but his attacker's skull was crushed when Doctor Towne threw him off the roof of a four-story building."

Quent smiled. "Sounds like we could use him here."

"True."

Quent took the files from her hand. "Thanks Chief, I'll start with Towne and Teller and keep you posted."

"Good. All right one last thing," she said. "And it's off the record, not to leave this room. Yes?"

"Okay."

"I picked you for this job because you're the only experienced agent who could possibly hope to sell this load of rubbish to a group of experienced agents. I'm truly sorry to put you in this position. On the other hand, I know you're the one to get it done. And that's why I'm giving you the ball. The difference here is, this time you'll be pitching instead of catching."

It was hard to fault this woman. She had actually studied his illustrious athletic career. *Amazing.*

She was content to wait, watching the realizations playing across his face, hoping she'd chosen the right man. When she saw him gently shaking his head in acknowledgment, she added, "You've got four days to interview our CLOPS candidates. Pick the best 30 and give them their surveillance assignments. On Monday, I'll congratulate them, swear them in, and then I'm going to turn them over to you. They're going to be your guys, so you might work up something to say ahead of time."

Quentin stood up. "Thanks Chief. Could I make copies of the one sheet for the guys?"

"Just ask Ruthie to get 'em for you."

As Quentin reached the door, Chief Barbara called out, "You know the French toast isn't the only good thing they serve at Mort's. The Huevos Rancheros is unbelievable."

17

It stuck in his head. Ruined his focus. Sitting at his kitchen table in the Plumeria, fighting with himself over the words for the speech, Quent crumpled another version and lobbed it into the waste basket. The way she'd said it. "...a more serious attitude about your public image might be in order." "...the Huevos Rancheros at Mort's is unbelievable."

Cold.

He'd always hated criticism. From the time he was in grammar school, even the most harmless remark, unintended, helpful, whatever...all of them struck hard inside him like flint on stone.

Grow up. Why can't you act like everyone else? School isn't a joke. Why can't you just show up on time. Why do you insist on being different? Those weren't the exact words, but that's what his bosses and teachers and coaches had been saying since he was a kid.

He'd been at it since four in the afternoon. Trying to write the damn speech. Unable to silence Porter's voice. Caught between resistance and realization.

At four in the morning, there were still no usable words on the paper. He gave up and went to bed.

On Thursday morning, Quent began conducting intensive personal interviews with each of the prospective agents on Chief Porter's pre-qualified list. It continued through the weekend, non-stop. Early on Monday morning, he handed in his list to the Chief for review.

She scanned the names rapidly, uncapped her pen and signed off. "I notice that all of the people you've selected are men, except for Angie Dumont. She's only got two years service and most of that was behind a desk. I'm curious, did she have some special qualifications?" As an afterthought she added, "She just kinda sticks out from the rest."

"You noticed the great body, too," said Hawk.

Chief Porter's face remained passive. "You're testing me aren't you Agent Hawk?"

"You mean like the time you tested me with Ruthie and the New Jersey accent thing? No Chief. I wouldn't think of it."

Porter remained silent, waiting for his explanation, commanding herself not to be charmed by Hawk's faux insubordination.

"Well," he said, "Dumont didn't originally apply for a desk job. Some dipshit bureau chief probably took one look at her and figured she was too pretty to get her hands dirty. But the truth is, she's a gifted athlete. Runs in her family. Her uncle Charlie was the first man to clear 7' in the high jump. My dad was at the Coliseum in L.A. when he did it. Anyway, one of my guys turned out to need rotator cuff surgery, so Dumont got the nod."

Quent checked his watch. "I'm sorry Chief, I've only got three minutes before I have to make my speech." His discomfort was obvious.

"Good luck, agent Hawk. They're a fine group. And I know they all think highly of you."

Quent had changed the location of the meeting from the main conference area to one of the smallest classrooms. An attempt at intimacy; hoping to create a locker room feel, something he was most comfortable with.

The classroom desks were arranged in an informal semi-circle. Without speaking, Quentin began by simply passing around the agency's one sheet – the Langley document explaining the general purpose of their new assignment as CLOPS agents. After giving his boys time to scan the document, he stood before them, looking down at their concerned expressions. He held the one sheet up for all to see.

"What an unbelievable load of mind-boggling, political horseshit this is."

A great explosion of laughter rocked the room. There was a mass feeling of release. It appeared that Quentin was still one of them.

Time to throw 'em the fast ball.

"I'd like to read you something from the transcript of yesterday's Meet the Press. Senator DeSalvo was asked about the failure of our Intelligence community to prevent the attacks of 9/11." Quent looked up, "This is a direct quote from

DeSalvo, 'Mistakes were made...the CIA is a dysfunctional organization...a rogue organization. It has to be cleared out." [1]

He stared down at his audience. "Did everyone hear that clearly?"

In the classroom next door, Chief Porter's eyebrows slammed into little arcs of surprised excitement. She moved her chair in closer to the blackboard.

"Incompetents. A collection of has-beens. That, gentlemen, is the public perception of the Central Intelligence Agency.

"I'm not making this shit up. The press is all over this DeSalvo story. And the White House isn't saying a word. You know what that means? That means it was us! The inefficient CIA, ancient dinosaur, failed to stop Bin Laden's planes from taking down the Twin Towers. Our mistake. Totally our fault. This ain't no soap opera, boys, this is for real. Senator DeSalvo and a bunch of politicians went on a fishing trip and hauled in a big fat tuna!"

He pointed his finger at them. "YOU.

He held up the Langley one-sheet. "Now they're telling us we gotta arrest the bad guys before they've done a goddamn thing. Everybody knows it's against the law to do it that way.

"I'm not the paranoid type, but what's that sound like to you? Time to retire the old bulls? Send 'em out to pasture? Get rid of the dead wood? Why else would senator Assbite be saying this kinda stuff on Meet the Press? The Pentagon's expanding their territory. What used to be ours at CIA – isn't. You don't have to be a rocket scientist to get it. It's simple."

He waved the one-sheet at them again. "What this little pile of bullshit really says is, 'No terrorists. No job.' We don't deliver, we're history."

Quent walked from behind the desk and sat on its front edge – closer to his audience. *Time for the changeup.*

"You're all here for a reason. You got special skills. CLOPS agents are going to be the best prepared interdiction force in the world. We're here to get six months of intense training."

He paused a moment before delivering the bad news. "But as of Monday, the State Department has changed all that. They've instructed Chief Porter to cancel all the training and put us into the field immediately."

There was a jolt of adrenaline in the room.

"Now I pretty much know every one of you guys...and girl, Angie. I picked you myself. So this *brilliant assignment* requires us to do the impossible. So...fine. We'll o the impossible. I been at this a few years and I can't think of a better bunch of people to do it with."

Quentin had them in the palm of his hand.

Chief Barbara Porter let herself out of an adjacent classroom. She had been sitting in the teacher's chair, close to the blackboard, able to hear every nuance in Quentin's speech. *Knute Rockne rides again. Talk about a born leader.*

Back in Quentin's *locker room* the agents listened attentively as he explained the group structure he'd worked out for the CLOPS strike force. He had divided them into four sub units: explosives; audio; SWAT; and research. Each unit was to remain on call 24/7 waiting for their assignments.

He ended the meeting with a challenge. "I graduated from Duluth Catholic High in '76. Our class motto was some bullshit like, 'There are no strangers in the world, just friends we haven't met yet.' So, 25 years later a bunch of strangers stole into New York City and murdered 3000 of us while we were asleep."

He pointed at his men. "Well, listen up. Nobody sleeps on my friggin' watch."

18

Lumber Yard – CLOPS Headquarters – Santa Monica

At the end of Quentin's "No one sleeps on my friggin' watch" speech, he informed his team that they would receive their surveillance assignments promptly. He dismissed them and made his way back toward his temporary office – a special cubicle distinguished by a tall plastic fichus plant and a single louvered window.

Stacks of files were amassed in little heaps all over the floor of his cubicle. He adroitly maneuvered his way through the maze and sat down before his computer. He entered a security code and was admitted to the central computer system, located at *the big house* (Quent-speak for Langley, VA).

From an intra-agency search engine he requested specifics on the U.S. Army's high security Laser Research Laboratory located on the California coastline. In seconds he was presented with an in-depth report on The Facility.

He scrolled through a partial list of employees, their resumes, fingerprints and photos. The next sub file included pictures of the place – a small group of gray/green buildings, neatly camouflaged in the hills near Malibu Canyon.

The Facility was the personal domain of its scientist/founders, Doctor Cynthia Teller (U.S. Navy) and Doctor Luke Towne (U.S. Army ret.), both of them under the direct supervision of the Pentagon.

Although Agent Hawk was keenly aware of the festering schism amongst CIA, Pentagon, NSA and the rest of the intelligence community, he was completely unprepared for the blatant animosity he was about to experience as he attempted to contact the first name on his list, Doctor Cynthia Teller.

"Doctor Teller's office," snapped a young female voice. "This is Marta. What can I do for you?"

"This is Assistant Chief Quentin Hawk with the Central Intelligence Agency. I would like to schedule an appointment with Doctor Teller please."

"Uh huh. That was CIA you said?"

"Yes."

"Well Mr. Lock, I'm afraid the doctor won't be taking any meetings with anyone for the next few months. She's working on a high priority government project. Could someone else help you?"

"I'm afraid not," said Quent, "this is a matter of urgent CIA business involving Doctor Teller personally, and I'm afraid I'll have to insist on the doctor's presence."

"You can't order me around, Mr. Glock? You don't even know me. And for your information, we work for the Pentagon. We don't take orders from anyone else."

"Miss Parker," he said, looking at her picture and rolling the dice, "I'm with the CIA. I know what you ate for breakfast this morning. I know where you live. I know who you think you're having an exclusive sexual relationship with. I know everything about you. At the moment, you've got on so much eyeliner you look like a raccoon! Now do what I tell you! Get that blob of stringy black hair out of your eyes and write this down."

Marta Parker's head snapped around, looking for the man who knew what she looked like. Frightened, she pulled her unkempt black hair away from her sooty eyes. "Where are you? How do you know about my... relationship?"

"Stop looking around Marta and write this down very clearly. I'm only going to repeat it once. My name is Agent Quentin Hawk, H...A...W...K. I'm with the Central Intelligence Agency. If your boss does not make herself available to me within 10 days from today, I will arrest both of you for obstruction of a Federal order. Is that clear?"

"Ye...yes sir." Then silence.

"Are you writing?"

"Yes sir. The Central Intelligence Agency."

"In a moment, you will automatically be provided with a contact number at CIA headquarters. You will call that number within the next two hours, ascertain that it is in fact the Central Intelligence Agency. Then you will confirm a time and place for the meeting between Agent Quentin Hawk and Doctor Cynthia Teller. Is that clear."

"Yes sir."

Quent punched a two-digit combination into his handset and hung up. When Marta Parker returned the call she would be automatically transferred to an agency switchboard set up at the CLOPS Yard in Santa Monica. A recorded voice would give her the actual number of CIA Headquarters in Virginia plus directions on how to enter a specific code number. She would then be given detailed instructions on setting up a meeting between the specific participants identified as 'Doctor Cynthia Teller and Assistant Chief Quentin Hawk.'

The system of telephone connections was nothing more than a blind, set up by CLOPS to accomplish a dual purpose; to verify their authority while simultaneously preserving their anonymity. The callers would know that they had actually reached the CIA, but the existence of CLOPS and the nature of their operations would be isolated from the rest of the Agency.

Within two hours, Miss Parker had confirmed her boss's availability 10 days hence, respectfully requesting that it be held at a Malibu restaurant near The Facility, thus enabling Doctor Teller to "maximize her very heavy work schedule."

The Healthy Sandwich – Malibu, California

Punctuality had never been one of Quentin Hawk's strong suits back in Duluth; but since he would now be demanding timeliness from the agents under his supervision, it seemed only right to change his ways. Although he denied Barbara Porter's role in this decision, he had decided to alter his standard M.O. 'for the sake of his men.' As a result of this new behavior, he was fast developing a low tolerance for people who were late.

He was sitting in a pink leatherette booth at the Healthy Sandwich, a 'lunch boutique' in Malibu. He was waiting for Doctor Cynthia Teller. She had picked the place herself; it was in a commercial park supposedly a short distance from her office at The Facility. She had mentioned her own tight schedule and asked that he be on time. He had arrived early. It was now 2:15 p.m. and she was late.

The place was crowded, overflowing with Malibu businessmen, all drinking wheat grass smoothies and talking three-picture deals. Twenty-five big shots, one aspiring actress in an adjacent booth, blabbing into her cell phone, and one pissed off out–of-place CIA agent.

Apparently the Navy's Head of Ocular Surgery was as flakey as everyone else in L.A. The woman had been given his private cell phone number; his cell phone wasn't ringing and

Quent was not happy.

He entered some notes in his Blackberry and watched the door. She was now 20 minutes late. Enough! He angrily dialed Doctor Teller's own private number. She answered immediately, "This is Doctor Teller."

"Doctor Teller, this is Chief Quentin Hawk of the CIA, your 2 p.m. appointment. Perhaps you forgot?" He didn't care if she could hear the displeasure in his voice.

"No," she said.

"No what?"

"No I didn't forget. I keep my appointments Mr. Hawk."

"Well I've been waiting in this granola joint you picked since five minutes to 2, Doctor."

"So have I," she said with emphasis on the I.

And as she spoke the words, Quentin's eyes met the eyes of the aspiring actress in the adjacent booth. He saw her lips moving as she spoke the words "So have I" into her cell phone.

...Oh shit it's her.

They closed their cell phones at exactly the same time. She was still looking at him, a blank expression on her face. Her booth was five steps away from his. But it felt like five awkward miles in slow motion as *big Chief Quent* and his red face lumbered out of his booth and stepped across to hers.

He tried to compose himself before speaking, but he felt like *such an asshole* that he couldn't think of what to say. Before uttering a word he actually scratched the top of his head *like a monkey* and then heard himself say, "Ah... I thought you were an actress."

Doctor Teller looked up into those legendary Irish eyes. She saw his touching, childlike embarrassment; she also couldn't help noticing that all that sensitivity was packaged into the muscled, 6'4" body of a beautifully toned athlete.

The smile she then bestowed on Quentin seemed to forgive his every transgression since the first grade. But then her smile disappeared like cash on the *come out*, and the first words she spoke were anything but warm. "Please sit down Mr. Hawk and let's get on with it. What's this about?"

He wanted to tell her that mistaking her for an actress had sounded like a compliment, but it wasn't. Quent thought all actresses were posers. Total morons who played 'let's pretend' for a living and should be denied the right to vote on anything except hair care products. But instead he slid into the booth across from her and 'got on with it.'

"I appreciate your taking the time to see me," he said. "I know the office must have sounded vague when you asked them what this meeting was for. I apologize for all the mystery. I hate the whole 'boogie man in the trees' thing; it's just the Agency's idea of high security. Everything's handled on a need to know basis."

"Understood Mr. Hawk. I've been in the U.S. Military 20 years. I get it."

Looks like an actress, sounds like an MP.

"All right then, let's get to it," he said, responding to her abrupt manner. "The Agency has developed a list of the country's most valuable human assets; scientists, doctors, businessmen, the ones most likely to be targeted by terrorists. You and Doctor Towne are both on the list as potentials for kidnap and ransom.

"From now on you'll have our round-the-clock protection. All I need from you is to approve two of my agents with security passes into The Facility. I've instructed them to stay out of your way. Their job is to remain in the background and provide unobtrusive surveillance."

Her face torqued into a state of horror, as if Quent's words were as repulsive as vomit. "First off, Mr. Hawk, there's no way in hell I would allow an agent from the CIA or anyone else not connected with my team into The Facility. This is the most intensely secretive, highly guarded Army installation in the Western United States. I hope you're not suggesting the Military can't take care of its own?"

Before he could respond, she rushed on. "Secondly, I currently hold an active rank as Captain in the U.S. Navy. The Facility and everything we do here is funded by the Pentagon. If we needed protection, which I don't believe we do, who do you think I'd call? The U.S. Navy, or a bunch of suits, hiding in the trees, fingering their laptops?"

Bitch!

Quent, mindful of Chief Porter's gentle admonitions, responded with as much graciousness as he could muster. "Please, Captain Teller, I'm sure the security at your Facility is second to none. I didn't mean to suggest otherwise. But what about on your way in to work, when you're out shopping, or on your way home? Do you or the colonel have round-the-clock protection for yourselves?"

"Protection? If you'd ever met Luke Towne, Mr. Hawk, you'd know he's hardly the kind of guy who needs protecting.

And I'm capable of taking care of myself, thank you very much. I think the whole thing's a complete waste of resources."

Quent pressed on, maintaining his composure. "Well, Doctor Teller, as the director of this Facility, you certainly have more experience in the area of resource commitment than I do." Doing his best to give *the bitch* her due. "However, on orders from the President, the Office of Homeland Security and the Secretary of Defense, I've been assured that certain of our country's most valuable scientists are probable targets. As you and the Colonel have come under my purview, I only wanted to alert you about the upcoming surveillance and save you any fears or embarrassment."

"Why CIA? Doctor Towne and I are both local. That's supposed to be the FBI's job in the first place. Isn't it?"

"Because of the international origin of most terrorist organizations, the Agency has been given jurisdiction even though the people we hope to protect are within our borders. The Fibbies aren't real happy about it, but that's the way it is."

Hawk then stood up abruptly, slid out of the booth and extended his hand. "And now," he said, "if you'll excuse me Doctor, I know you need to get back to work."

When she extended her hand, he held on to it and added, "Left my computer running. Hid it under the palm trees so the Pelicans couldn't crap on it. "

As she watched him walk away, Cynthia Teller remained thoroughly calm, her expression passive. But the jolt of *whatever it was* that shot through her body at the touch of his hand was making her uncomfortable.

That was....strange, and...strange.

19

Beirut, Lebanon

In spite of the constant supervision and intense scrutiny of Leon de Kennesy and Mullah Rockmani, Phase 3 of the Silent Jihad was failing. The task of smuggling explosives across American borders had been riddled with impossibles. Every single attempt had been thwarted, each effort turning into a more costly failure than its predecessor. There were myriad pitfalls; highly paid contacts suddenly turned unreliable; explosives sniffed out and confiscated. Mistakes had been made, hundreds and hundreds of mistakes.

In the end, every one of their Talib-trained Level 3 soldiers attempting to bring explosives into enemy territory had been arrested. In Leon de Kennesy's mind, low level martyrs were plentiful, easy to come by and easy to lose. But highly skilled martyrs were very hard to come by, very costly to train, and too valuable to lose in such great numbers.

In desperation, Doctor Leon decided on a change of strategy. Instead of continuing to spend their financial resources on smuggled explosives, only to have them confiscated, or worse, to discover they had magically disappeared, Leon decided to try something new. Modern Military strategists call it an "effects based" approach. A deviation from the traditional tenants of warfare. Something indirect. Something off target.

Perhaps a little new technology might accomplish something my soldiers can't.

After weeks of detailed research, Leon purchased a system of computers on the black market. The system he acquired was unique. Its massive hard drives were laden with exotic software that mirrored the spidering techniques used by NSA.

Leon was told that the equipment had been stolen from a high security U.S. Military installation in Pensacola. When several weeks later, an article appeared in the New York Times confirming a major theft of computer technology from Fort Myers, Leon knew his new black market source was trustworthy. He promptly hired the man at an enormous salary to maintain the equipment and teach others how to use it.

Ten months passed. Leon had said nothing to his partners about his computer scheme. And then, at one of the triumvirate's meetings in Op B, he was forced to reveal his new strategy. It began with an announcement by the bomb maker.

For a change, Farad had arrived early, eager to tell them about a reconnaissance coup he'd 'pulled off.' When it was time for Farad to speak, he announced, "My brothers, I've located two FIM-92 portable Stinger surface-to-air missiles. At the moment a German guy is holding them for me. Guy's defected from the EADA. Anyway, all he wants $79,000 each."

Farad addressed Leon with as much deference as he could feign. "All I need is the check from you, Leon, and they're ours. But I got to do this fast or we'll lose 'em."

When Leon explained that there was no money left to buy Stingers because it had been spent on technology, the two men had almost come to blows.

"Computers!" raged Farad. "How can I kill anyone with a goddamn computer? Stingers kill aircraft. Computers don't do shit. All they can do is keep records."

"Precisely, you illiterate..." Leon shouted, then stopped himself in mid sentence. *There's a better way to deal with this idiot.*

Leon began again. "I apologize, Farad. I haven't explained how these computers will help you accomplish your job. I understand your concern. Valid concerns. How do we kill the enemy without modern weapons? Absolutely valid position. Let me explain the idea in its entirety."

Farad tipped back in his chair. His eyes flicked toward an attentive Mullah Rockmani. "Alright, go ahead," he scowled.

The explanation was lengthy, but it clearly demonstrated the brilliant mind of the renowned surgeon/inventor/entrepreneur.

After purchasing the computers and installing them in a clean room, Leon had decided to approach the Jihad's original Lebanese businessmen/contributors with a proposition. It was, after all, their very own children who had first made them aware of the Silent Jihad.

Doctor Leon offered to pay their college-aged sons a handsome fee for some part-time work. His prerequisites were simple; the candidates had to be interested in computers and academically rated near the top of their classes. Leon's wife,

Nanette, was a professor of art history at the Beirut University. Student records were readily available to her. Leon already knew that 12 of the young men in question were majoring in computer science at the University.

Without informing Farad of his decision, Leon had hired the sons of the Lebanese Muslim aristocracy to run the Jihad's computer operation. Their clean room was concealed behind the back wall of a harmless-looking laundry in the poorest quarter of Sayda, 160 miles away from Beirut. Leon had code named them 'the laundry people.'"

The Laundry's job was to scan internet sites, search for potential terrorist activity, and spider the most promising ones. On a much smaller scale, their task paralleled that of America's National Security Agency (NSA). And just like NSA, the laundry people scanned blogs, secret groups, chat rooms, even CIA trap rooms. They were looking for suggestive subject matter, symbolic expressions, code names, veiled references, code words; in short, any communication that might be interpreted as 'terrorist or anti-American.'

But unlike NSA, the young Jihadists were not looking to uncover embryonic terrorist plots, they were searching for points of entry.

Leon suddenly stopped his description. "Are you with me so far?"

"Yes," answered Farad flatly, rolling his eyes at the obvious simplicity of the concepts presented thus far. None of this was rocket science.

"All right," said Leon. "Follow me then. NSA's listening capacity is the heartbeat of America's counterterrorism system. It constantly scans all broadcast media and 'red flags' any suspicious communications which it thinks might become the building blocks of future terrorist threats. So, I decided to create a make-believe terrorist plot."

After a moment of silence, Farad asked, "What the hell for?"

"Well," said Leon, "Stay with me for one more minute and you'll see. Using some 'red flagged' words, some American slang and some symbolic references, we began creating a few suspicious emails of our own. We entered them into known Al Qaeda chat rooms. Then we created our own chat rooms. Then we added fake responders, originating the fake emails from European and Scandinavian cities. The idea was to convince NSA that something suspicious was developing. At every chance possible we connected our make-believe developing plot to known al Qaeda sources.

"Next, in our chat rooms, we began dropping references to particular U.S. ports of entry, especially ones in the South; American ports that we already knew were considered marginal and were therefore poorly guarded. We suggested that some of them were great places to visit. Our chat rooms made veiled references to cities that were easygoing and friendly. We injected catch phrases that could be interpreted as code.

"During the last two months we began doubling the chatter, as if building toward some kind of specific event. Something that would be taking place along the southeastern coast of the U.S., something that we occasionally referred to as 'July's most dazzling show of fireworks,' as well as other less blatant references.

"We now suspect that NSA believes al Qaeda, in conjunction with other terrorist organizations, is planning to smuggle explosives into the States in early July. They think entry will be made through one or all of three southeastern American ports: St. Joe, Panama City and Fernandina."

Once again, Leon stopped talking and waited for a response from Farad. He was greeted with a stony silence.

From its inception, Farad had been purposely excluded from the Laundry project. As the silence continued, Mullah Rockmani realized that the young bomber was not about to acknowledge his lack of understanding, especially after Leon's long-winded explanation.

As always, the Mullah tried to smooth the animosity. "Farad, I know you've always been a student of war. So let me cut to the bottom line of Leon's very detailed explanation. We all know about America's successful landing at Normandy in 1944. It was the beginning of the end for the Nazis. The Americans used a series of elaborate diversions, some of them leaked as code, Morse Code, some of them on the radio. And some actually involved the construction of inflatable tanks and plywood ships moored far off the coast of France. German spies, viewing the wooden fakes from long range, thought the fleet was poised to strike at Pas de Calais."

A smile formed behind the Mullah's dense black beard. "Put simply Farad, Leon is attempting to do the same thing with the Laundry. He's creating a classic diversion. By the first of July, while the American fools are focused on Fernandina,

St. Joe and Panama City, while their sniffing dogs are looking for al Qaeda explosives, while the mighty SEALs and the Coast Guard are waiting to pounce on us in Florida, we'll be six states away.

"In the first week of April, your explosives will be coming in through Canada, crossing the Niagara River and trucked right into Lewiston. That's 1200 miles north of where they'll be looking for us."

Farad hesitated a moment, pretending he had understood Leon's description all along. "Yeah, well that sounds great. Real high tech. Great diversion if they go for it. I only have two questions, Leon. First, how do we know if they go for it?"

"The same way we found out about the Pit Bull Strategy. Next question."

"Why are we waiting until April to do it?"

Leon's jaw tightened, his chin pushed forward. "Because you told us the Semtex would be sitting on the dock in Milan on the first of March, Farad. That gives us a full month to get it across to Canada and into the U.S. Understand me clearly. Delivered by the first of March! That's what you guaranteed. There's no room for mistakes here."

"Don't get your beard in a knot, Leon. It's no problem. Like I already told you. Everything's set. Even if your big diversion doesn't work, my shit will be sitting there on six-one. Guaran-damn-teed."

Beneath Mullah Rockmani's heavy beard, his nostrils flared. Farad's constant use of American slang was just one more in a series of irreverent behaviors.

When Farad's function is completed, he'll be dealt with.

20

And the lamb will feast on the bones of the shepherd.
Allah be praised.

Traditional

The Facility – Malibu, California

"Get ready for something different," she teased, "I'm coming to visit."

Luke Towne was in the A-Lab at The Facility when Dave put Kathryn de Kennesy's call through. "Fantastic," said Luke, "You'll stay at the beach with me."

"No, no honey, I'm already booked at the Regency in Irvine. The Embassy set it up for me. It's right near the office of Immigration. I've got meetings there."

"I'll pick you up at John Wayne, then. Right?"

"I'm already here."

"What? Where's here?"

"Orange County. It was supposed to be part of the surprise. I was going to show up unannounced at your door and sweep you away. But stuff got delayed and extended, you know, typical Embassy crud. I've been here three days already, trying to get it all straightened out."

"What Embassy crud?"

"It's going to be part of the surprise; I hope it will anyhow. Now, no more questions, okay?" she purred. "But listen, I have something planned. It's part of your birthday present. Are you free Tuesday night?"

None of Luke's nights were free. The Mind's Eye Project was dangerously behind schedule. At least seven weeks had been wasted on 'The Strategy.' And although most of the delays had been caused by the Pentagon's own conflicted priorities, they still expected delivery "as per the original deadline."

Kathryn could hear the wheels going around. "Lukie, I'll make it worth your while if you say yes." She was using her throatiest voice on him.

"How're you gonna make it worth my while?"

"Just say yes, and I'll do the rest."

Aside from being the most beautiful, Kathryn was the most spontaneous, inventive and creative woman Luke had ever known. Her surprises always included something sexual. And when it came to sex (Luke's mind struggled for an apt metaphor) *When they were together... there was no way to adequately... no one had ever...*

Finally he just said, "Yes. I'm there."

"Ooooooo, good decision," she purred. "Wear your tux."

"Right, my tux. That's a good one. Remember me, the grunt? Special Forces. Sand in the pants. Twig for a tooth brush. I think my last tux was a rental. A plaid one."

"Plaid??"

"Yeah. 19...something. Senior Prom. Looked rather spiffy if I don't say so. Anyway....I'm sorry, don't own a tux, Kat."

"You do now. It's a black Armani. Gorgeous double-breaster. Satin lapels. Dave's picking it up on Monday. I can hardly wait to see you in it."

"What are we doing, honey?"

"Something a little different. You'll love it. I promise."

"Okay," he said guardedly. "What time again?"

"Seven thirty. Roadhouse Grill." She could hear the conservative guard going up. "Listen Lukie, don't be a poop head. It's just a little birthday surprise. Just go with it. You'll like it. Even though I think you're getting a little bit old for a young chick like me."

"Oh yeah hot stuff, we'll see who's young when the time comes."

Kat hung up, shaking her head. *Spiffy? Did he actually describe himself as spiffy?*

Sixty minutes south of LAX on the 405 Freeway, pushing 80 mph all the way, the limo sped past the city of Irvine, a smudge of tree-lined conformity that marks the epicenter of California conservatism; that long-nosed political *squint* known as Orange County.

Luke looked down at Kathryn's map. *Sixty miles to go.*

Further south, the 405 loses two of its digits and all of its right wing clarity and eases up gently and permissively into the 5 Freeway - San Diego.

The limo driver pulled off the 5 Freeway and headed East. As they wound higher into the hills of North County, Luke wondered how Kathryn had found out about his birthday. How did she manage to have the tuxedo perfectly tailored to fit him? It was strange; from day one, she seemed able to intuit his preferences, even some of his fantasies. He hadn't told her any of it.

The big limo maneuvered around a blind corner and there, in all its disheveled wonder, stood an old splinter-wood barn. The Roadside Grill – an American biker bar.

Ducati, Lotus, Maserati, BMW, Ferrari, Bentley, Saleen, and one little green Vespa. The dirt parking lot was already jammed with the most pricy pile of shiny chrome, sheet metal and polished resin that Europe had to offer. And it was only 7:30 p.m. on a Tuesday.

Only Kat would pick a place like this. Hell of a birthday this one's gonna be.

Luke climbed out of the limo, but as he tried to tip the driver, he was told, "Already taken care of, sir. Generously." *The woman thought of everything.*

Luke climbed up the three-wide wooden stairs and pushed open the door. Emblazoned on the slat wall to his right was a big red finger and the words "Screw you."

There were 20 rows of long wooden tables, a loud metal band, and a mass of weirdoes on the dance floor. A pink neon sign stretched across the back of the place. The words were in English: "Rockin seven nights a week."

Shit Howdy.

Four towering stainless steel brewing tanks stood behind the bar, belching out mass quantities of the sweet ale that earned the place its endearing local reputation. Another neon sign hung over the double wooden doors, "A good place to get your ass kicked."

He stood back in the darkness to let his eyes adjust. He was overdressed; or maybe he wasn't. No one seemed to notice. There were a hundred more interesting fashion statements being made out on the floor: gender benders, fag hags, men in drag, ballroom dancers, bikers, truckers, rockers, gawkers, cowboys, and a gaggle of plain old reliable Laguna Beach queers.

Someone for everyone. Luke smiled. *Perfect.*

The band had taken a break and the Juke Box was filling in. Tim Curry was singing "Sweet Transvestite." And everyone in the place knew the words. Luke shouldered his way into a seat at the bar.

"Bushmills and a water back," he yelled.

"Ten bucks," shouted the silicone Chest that eventually slid his order across the bar to him. It was hard to tell whether it was a male or a female so Luke just raised his glass and said, "Cheers."

"Party on, Bud," it said and strutted off to serve another mug banger.

A long stainless steel trench full of hot buttered popcorn was cut into the center of the black marble bar. Every 10 minutes or so, a management Chest would come by and fill it up again.

It was apparent that cleavage played a big part in the joint's successful employment system. According to the owner, Marcel Bluestein, retired pharmacist, expatriate and former speechwriter for Tom Hayden, the real secret to the joint's success was not the women, it was the smell of the popcorn. And Marcel loved to crow about it. "It's the stink, man. The popcorn stink! It brings 'em in and keeps 'em thin."

Although no one had shouted "Surprise" or "Happy Birthday" yet, the Roadhouse atmosphere was definitely working for Luke. He undid his satin bowtie, shoved a greasy handful of popcorn into his mouth and reached for his whiskey. There was already another hand holding his glass. French tipped fingers. A tailored sleeve. A scent of musky perfume.

It was Kathryn de Kennesy. But she was dressed as a man. A dark, double-breasted suit; thin lapels pulled in at the waist; tanned fingers; impossible blue-green eyes; aquiline nose; and a thin dark moustache etched above the pout of magnificent sensual lips.

Breathtaking.

There was no mistaking this exotic creature for anything but a woman. A black felt hat with a gray feather was pulled low across her forehead. A curl of smoke rose from her Galouise. As it slowly drifted upward past her dazzling eyes, they became even more mysterious.

"Tell your fortune, mister?" she asked.

"Why not?"

"I see a climax in your future."

"Is that a good thing?"

"What do you think?" A lascivious smile on her lips.

"Do I call you miss or mister?"

She guided his hand inside her jacket. When he tried to withdraw it, she pushed it deeper into her breast.

"It's Miss then," he said smiling. Kat was so good at sex games. From the beginning it had been one of his favorite things about her. It made her impossible to resist.

"Are you alone?" she asked.

"I'm meeting a woman," he said, thinking he'd get the upper hand.

A smile built ever so slowly on her lips. "Is she as beautiful as I am?"

"Possibly." It was all he could think to say.

She could always beat him so easily at this. It was child's play. Words were not his forte. He'd been trained as a soldier and a scientist. And although she was 21 years his junior, Kat de Kennesy was always able to keep up with both of them. *Rare. She had the perfect combination of talents.*

She crushed out her cigarette and took Luke's hand. She led him down the long length of thc bar and around behind the tall tanks. Somehow she seemed able to move through the spaces between people without causing them to step aside.

The lady's room was marked with a crude black "W," the men's with an "M." She made straight for the "M," pulling him behind her.

Six unoccupied stalls with doors open. She pulled him across to the last one, steered him in backward and pushed him down on the toilet. She bent close to him, the palm of her hand pressed against her thigh, staring down at his upturned face. With her free hand she peeled off the fake moustache and stuck it to the commode's black metal wall. She pulled off the hat and dropped it to the floor. A stream of honey blonde hair fell down around her neck and across his arms.

She stood upright, unbuttoned her jacket and dropped it on the floor. Naked to the waist, she stared down at him. Brazen. Beyond beautiful. She stepped in between his thighs and with her hands, gently forced them apart.

"Will this do?" she asked.

In the moment of silence that followed, she knelt down, never taking her eyes from his and slowly reached for his belt.

"I hope to God your name is Kathryn," he said, still trying.

She undid his belt and giggled. "Like you care." Reaching behind herself, she found the stall door and pushed it closed.

Later they came out from behind the stainless tanks looking very much like the two mischievous lovers they were;

he, still holding the image of his own hands jammed bloodless against the walls of the stall, she, with the taste of him still on her tongue.

They approached the space at the bar where Luke had left his drink. The Bushmills was still there, but a large biker had taken over the seat in front of it. He was stuffing one of the Roadhouse's "Big Eat" special burgers into his bearded face.

"Excuse me," Luke said, "I just went to the head. That's my drink."

"Snooze, you lose, pal." The big biker didn't bother turning around, he just continued shoveling in the food. He was working on a hand full of curly fries when Luke spoke again.

"Listen, Pierre, do you mind? I'd like to offer this lady my seat. But your fat ass is sitting in it. How 'bout you take your shit burger and your bad attitude over there in the corner and leave us alone."

The biker spun around on the barstool and looked at Luke for the first time. He stood up to his full six foot six advantage. There was a quizzical look on his face. He couldn't remember the last time anyone had dared challenge him on anything.

"Kiss off, faggot. Or I'll have to rip you a new one," he said. "You'd probably like that, wouldn't ya?" He poked a greasy finger into Luke's chest. "Wouldn't ya, faggot? A new one?" Another push of the finger. "Huh? Wouldn't ya. Me and the broad here'll get ya a big jar of Vaseline and..."

The words choked off suddenly. Luke had caught the biker's finger in his hand and snapped it backwards. The sound of the bone breaking put a silence on the room. The big man let out a howl of pain and grabbed the broken digit with his other hand. This left his rather large Adam's apple unprotected. Luke's right foot kicked up into the exposed throat. *Spluk*! The larynx snapped inward. The band stopped playing because of the commotion. The entire bar went silent. The noise of the big man's collapse on the concrete was sickening to those close enough to hear.

No one moved. The silence was eerie.

Still, no one moved.

Then a tiny voice. "Time to go Lukie." It was Kat taking his hand and doing her best not to break into a run as she led him towards the kitchen. Once through the swinging doors she bolted for the exit. "This way Poncho."

They burst through the push lever door at the back of the kitchen and found themselves in an alley. "My car!" She pointed toward the yellow Mustang sandwiched between a dark green dumpster and a Porsche Cayenne. They ran to the car and jerked open the doors.

Seconds later she was fishtailing out of the alley, laughing like a banshee. "What a blast!"

The road suddenly bent hard to the right. And without hesitation, still talking, she calmly put the Mustang into a four wheel slide and punched it around the corner.

No fear, thought Luke.

"Nee new, nee new," the siren and the spinning red lights went flying past them. The meat wagon was already on its way to scrape up the biker, who was still lying unconscious on the Roadhouse floor.

"Honey, I'm so sorry about that idiot. I hope it didn't ruin everything."

"No problem," he shrugged. "Nothing like a good fist fight to kick off a guy's birthday party."

"The party's not 'til later. This was just supposed to be the hors d'oeuvre." She gave him one of her most libidinous smiles, mashed down on the accelerator and pushed the car up to 90.

"You certainly handed that dude his lunch," she said. "Not bad for an old guy, actually. I can't wait to tell Nana about it."

"Tell her the eight-and-a-half-weeks-cross-dressing deal was your idea, will ya? I don't need your mother thinking I'm some kinda pervert."

"Luke."

"Yeah."

"Three things: first off, it's 'Nine and a Half Weeks;' Mickey Rourke and your girl Kim Basinger. Playing dress up, remember?"

"Yeah."

"Okay, second, My stepmother Nana is French. The French invented perverts. Duh! And third, this whole thing was her idea. She saw Nine and a Half Weeks on pay-per-view last week, called me up at work all excited and said we oughta try it for your birthday. Thought it might spice things up!"

He broke into a wide smile. "I wasn't aware we had a spice problem."

Kat leaned across the seat and snuggled her head into his neck. "Love you," she cooed. Steering with one hand, barely keeping her eyes on the road. "Almost forgot," she said. "Got something else for you."

"Thought I already got my present back at the bar," he grinned.

"Think you might like the second present even better."

"Hard to imagine."

She pulled on to the Freeway and mashed the accelerator again, pushing it up to 110 mph. Drifting into left lane, the Mustang seemed to hunker down, lowering onto its haunches. "Racing suspension," she beamed. "Pretty cool isn't it?"

"Go for broke there, Dale," he chuckled.

It took Kathryn just under an hour and 10 minutes to reach Santa Monica, a record breaking achievement given the distance. Weaving madly in and out of the traffic on Pacific Coast Highway, she arrived at the Malibu Colony gate in record time.

Skidding to a halt in front of Luke's house, she jumped out and came around to the passenger side, but found Luke still facing forward in his seat.

"Honey?" she said, opening the passenger door, "Something wrong?"

"My foot."

She reached for his leg. "Cramp?"

"Ah...broken toe, I think."

"Oh my god, let's go to the hospital. There's one back in Santa Monica, isn't there?"

"Not a big deal; if you could just sorta crutch me up the steps, I'll stick it in some ice. It'll be fine."

"Does it hurt?"

"Like a son-of-a-bitch."

"Oh Lukie, you should've said something."

"The way you were driving, I figured we were gonna die anyway."

"Very funny," she said, helping him toward the door of his little house. "I guess you Knights of the Round can't very well slay the big ugly dragon and then cry all the way home. Can you. Wouldn't be muy macho."

She closed the door behind them and helped him into the tiny living room. "Honey, you don't have to prove anything to me. I'm in; don't you get it? I've fallen for the whole package. Aging scientist and bright young ambassador-to-be. Has kind of a sweet sound to it, don't you think?" She turned on the interior lights and helped Luke to the couch.

"We'll see who's the youngest here in just a few minutes."

"Promises promises," she quipped and went off to get ice.

When she returned from the kitchenette with a flat pan full of ice, Luke was gingerly trying to prop his right foot up on a stack of pillows.

"Guy had a throat like a steel pipe," he said.

"Here, let me help with that. God it's swollen. Maybe you should leave the shoe on. Let's try to get the swelling down first."

Luke shook his head in surprise. "Never take a soldier's boot off unless there's blood in it. You knew that?"

She shoved his shoed foot into the ice water. "What kind of a surgeon's daughter wouldn't know that?"

"You said Leon's a brain surgeon."

"Basic pre med, Dude. Keep it in there for 20 minutes. Did you know, by the way, that Russian hospitals pack the patient's entire body in ice prior to surgery? It slows the blood flow. It lessens the amount of anesthesia they need. It also seems to promote faster patient recovery."

Then she noticed the perspiration on Luke's forehead. "Is it throbbing?

"Yes."

"Pain meds?"

"Left mine in my other pants," he laughed.

"No problem. Got mine right here. Bottle of Vicodin. Never leaves my purse."

His answer was a silent smirk.

"Let me guess, pain pills are for pussies, right?" She put two pills into his fist.

"What do these do?"

"Two 500s. Acetaminophen. Honey, relax. It's just Tylenol and a little sumthin' extra to make nice. It'll help bring down the swelling."

Kat returned with a glass of water and forced his lips open. "Be a good boy and take these. Takes them about 45 minutes to kick. And things will get much better."

He did as he was told. "Now, can we get to the show and tell part?" he asked. They had agreed to go home for Kat's second birthday surprise. She had something to tell him; he had something to show her.

"You're the birthday boy. Whatever you say."

"Okay, me first," he teased. From his pocket, Luke pulled out a silver PDA and tossed it to her. "Now point this thing at your face and push the middle button."

"Is it gonna squirt water at me? You know I hate that kinda stuff."

"Trust me, just push the button."

She examined the thing. It looked like a normal Blackberry except for its silver case and its slightly enlarged camera lens. Reluctantly, she pushed the center button.

In the corner of the living room, a big flat screen TV instantly came to life showing an immense, high resolution close-up of her face. It was evident that the little PDA was, among other things, a very powerful digital recorder.

"It's a Bluetooth camera, right, no wires," she said, swinging the tiny thing around and focusing it on Luke's foot in the pan of ice.

"No, actually it's a laser device. My guys have been working on it for months at the lab. They call it Phyllis. It does lots of other interesting stuff. I'll show you some more later."

He shifted his foot in the ice, took a breath and went for it. "Actually, I thought...well what I had in mind was...when we make love tonight, if we used it, you know, I'd be able to have it back here on my big screen, for...you know...for when you're back in Al Bēkä and I miss you."

A great Cheshire cat smile bloomed on her porcelain face. "I love you Lukie. You're so cute. I just love you. And the answer is, 'yes.' I would be delighted to star in your personal porn movie, but there's one condition. I get a copy to take home with me to use on the nights when I get wet panties thinking about you."

What she wouldn't know until she returned home to Lebanon was that Luke had called her parents and explained his intentions, to the total lascivious delight of Nana de Kennesy, and arranged to have a gigantic HD laser system set up adjacent her bed in her little house.

She moved to the couch and gently straddled him, being especially careful of the injured foot. When she was comfortably seated in his lap, she unbuttoned her blouse top to bottom. And after feeding his very wanton eyes for a moment, she guided his face forward and held it tenderly to her breast. "Lukie, before I become the next Danni Ashe, and I promise to give it my complete concentration, could I tell you your second birthday present first?"

Without moving his head from her breast, Luke answered, “Go for it. I’ll be right here.”

“Well, you know how I said I was going to have some meetings at the Immigration Board in California?”

“Uh huh.”

“My government is opening an office in San Francisco. They want me to make the arrangements. They want me to get a place in San Francisco. And in the Ambassador’s absence, I would act as Assistant Ambassador pro tempore to the United States. Can you believe that? Ambassador pro tem. The Immigration Department granted me a diplomatic visa for two years. That means I can come to California any time I want and we can be together. Not just a long weekend, but days at a time maybe.”

When she stopped to catch an excited breath, she heard the snoring; smooth, steady, dead to the world. She checked her watch; exactly 50 minutes since he’d taken the Vicodin.

She climbed carefully off the snoring corpse, gingerly lifted his frozen foot out of the ice and stretched the leg out lengthwise on the couch. When he was tucked in with blankets she’d brought from the bedroom, she stood back and smiled. “Happy birthday, honey.”

Kat lifted the ice bucket and tiptoed toward the kitchenette. She dumped out the ice, dried the bucket and put it back in the cupboard. The cell phone in her pocket vibrated again – it had been buzzing against her leg for more than two hours. She’d been ignoring it.

Kathryn slipped out the French doors into the darkened patio and quietly opened her cell phone. There were 10 text messages demanding her attention, all of them from Leon’s new email address in the States.

In order to better direct Phase 3 of the Silent Jihad’s U.S. operations, Leon had closed down his practice in Beirut. Forty days ago, he and Nana had flown to the U.S., and moved into an expansive home behind the gates in Bel Air California.

Luke had happily assisted them in their search for a new home. He’d recommended several potential areas, finally enlisting the help of a long time friend and realtor who ultimately found them the Bel Air mansion.

Months earlier, Dr. Leon had applied and been accepted as a senior consultant in Brain Stem Research at LA's Children's Hospital. Landing such a surgeon and renown inventor of surgical equipment was considered a major coup for the hospital. For Leon, it was a strategic necessity. In the eleventh hour, a Commander *must be close to his troops.*

Both of the de Kennesys had quietly left their lives and their careers in Lebanon for a greater calling. *The will of Allah.*

For Kathryn, the new closeness was wonderful; starting a new job in San Francisco and having her beloved parents just a short plane ride away was a dream come true.

But of late, Leon had become a bit overbearing. In this case, his 10 persistent emails had all asked the same cryptic question. "Have you eaten?" Dr. Leon wanted a progress report.

Has the lamb devoured the bones of the Shepherd ?

Kathryn promptly erased all 10 of Leon's messages, and crawled into Luke's bed.

Bel Air, California – The New de Kennesy Mansion

California's creamy smooth coast line, its redolent night breeze, its luxuriant profile; the whole thing was transcendent, a departure from the acrid, pockmarked visage of Beirut. For Leon de Kennesy, the move was an idyllic release from tension. A respite. No curfews. No covert meetings. No gunfire after dark.

For Nana, the move was a leap of opulence. She had done a remarkable job making their new Colonial house in Bel Air, feel like their former mansion in the hills of Deir el Qamar. The art work, the silk Persian rugs, the new dishes, linens, textured walls and sconces, she'd spent thousands on new treasures, yet managed to make it all look familiar. Leon's new library was almost an exact duplicate of the previous one.

Forty days in this immoral paradise and Dr. Leon was already adapting quite well. The trip to Children's Hospital in downtown Los Angeles was relatively simple, once he'd learned to avoid the rush hour traffic. And the weather was spectacular.

At night, the palm trees behind the pool house whispered softly to him in the Pacific warmth. Life behind the gates of Bel Air was languid. His consultancy at Children's Hospital was a source of calm, a welcome release from the rigors he'd known at Beirut Orthopedic.

His army had silently moved into position. It was his time to regenerate. To pray. To prepare.

Phrase 3, the sacred moment of redemption, was at hand.

21

8 PM - Topanga Canyon, California

Darnel Davis was driving "some stupid white guy's BMW" up Topanga Canyon Road, knifing the corners at 75 plus. He was seeing two of every telephone pole that hurtled past his wide-eyed, 19-year-old face and enjoying every brainless second of the ride. *What a trip, man.* He couldn't feel the tip of his nose; he'd lost all feeling in his front teeth; his lips were so numb his saliva had run down his chin into a sloppy wet circle on his FUBAR sweatshirt.

It was Friday night and he was down from Bakersfield staying the weekend on campus at Pepperdine with his rich cousin Lonnie. Lonnie and his buds were doing valet parking at some gay party in Topanga Hills; it was supposed to be a chance for the cousins to hang.

Darnel Davis, known up north as 'Double D,' was a wiry, black, high school dropout, son of a single mom, with a police record. Darnel didn't exactly fit in with his cousin's college friends. So, in order to even things up, he'd done two lines of blow to each one of theirs, just to show who was a pussy and who wasn't.

By 8:30 most of the cars had been parked and it was time for chow. Darnel, seizing the moment, jumped into one of the guest's silver sports cars and hauled ass up the Canyon Road, shouting "Double D out." The other boys, college students at Pepperdine, all had their own small exotic sports cars or drove their parents' bigger ones. Darnel had never driven a sports car; never even sat in one except for the big Mercedes Diesel he'd tried unsuccessfully to steal. (No one had told him you couldn't hot wire a diesel.)

Valroni's Pizza was a popular take-out pizza joint tucked under a stand of oak trees and wisteria bushes that bloomed in mass along Topanga Canyon Road. It was about halfway in from the coast. By 8:50 p.m., Darnel was passed out in front of Valroni's, his head tilted back against the Beemer's headrest, dreaming about being rich. Six minutes into his dream, the rapid, cocaine-induced thundering of his heart snapped him awake again with a start.

"Shit!" he shouted, scaring himself back into partial consciousness. Disoriented, sucking in large gulps of air, trying to slow things down, he eyed the polished wood dash, ran his finger tips along the BMW's black leather interior, then remembered where he was. With a big smile, he addressed the BMW logo in the center of the steering wheel. "Double D be needin' us one mo hit." Then he burst out laughing at his own complete and total coolness and began searching through his pants pockets for the little glass vial. In his present condition, finding, chopping, and snorting his next line would prove to be a major production.

9 p.m. Doctor Cynthia Teller was tired; on her way home from The Facility after an intense week of 16-hour days trying to get the Mind's Eye project back up to speed. Luke's absence had thrown a giant anchor into the depths of their progress. 'Anchor' was the appropriate metaphor, as Doctor Cynthia Teller (co-director of The Facility) also still held the rank of Captain in the U.S. Navy.

She was heading up the Canyon toward her home, in no mood to cook. As she drove the winding darkness of Topanga Canyon Road, it dawned on her that there hadn't been anything cook-able in her refrigerator for months.

"Valroni's," answered the voice on her cell phone.

"Hi Jeff, it's Cynthia Teller."

"The usual, Ms. Teller? Half cheese, half pepperoni?"

"See you in five," she said.

"You got it."

A glass of wine, a few minutes in the Jacuzzi, half a crispy pizza, part of a DVD and into bed by 10:30 p.m. Boring, but mandatory.

She pulled her Lexus into an open slot in front of Valroni's and headed for the take-out counter. The smell of the place was fantastic; it never failed. She couldn't wait. She always had to pry open the box and take just one small bite before leaving the restaurant.

As she was getting into her car, chewing on a mouthful of pepperoni, some kid in a silver BMW lowered his window and called out to her, "Hey baby. Lookin' tight."

He was a wild-looking black kid with a lot of teeth. She nodded her head slightly in acknowledgment, gave him a small but polite smile, closed her car door and hit the power lock.

On the way home she smiled to herself. Kid must have been about 19. It was nice to think that someone that young would still think she was hot.

Six minutes later she turned into her driveway at 64 Sunshine Terrace. Waiting for the garage door to open, she waved to the green Buick parked across the street. A different CIA agent had been stationed there every night since her meeting with Quentin Hawk. She imagined they were probably there 24/7, even when she was out of state. It was definitely unnecessary, a waste of taxpayers' money, but she was secretly flattered that they thought enough of her to provide round-the-clock protection.

And as to Quentin Hawk – she had thought about his impertinence several times since their meeting. Why did all men think they had "the formula?" Such arrogance. This CIA man's corny attempt at boyish charm, sort of an "aw shucks ma'am, I'm harmless" approach, hadn't fooled her. It was just plain annoying.

Once inside her house, she set the pizza down on the kitchen counter and stretched her aching back. "Ten minutes in the water. Gotta do it," she said to herself, and began stripping off her work clothes.

Across the street in the green Buick, Agent Angie Dumont was eating a meatloaf sandwich and reading Oprah. It was an unusually hot evening in the Canyon, so she had removed her coat, unfastened her holster and placed them both on the passenger's seat.

She barely noticed the silver BMW as it parked in front of Doctor Teller's house. She did notice the tall black kid when he got out of the car, but when he headed for the house next door, she relaxed, took another bite of sandwich and went back to her magazine.

When she looked up again, the black kid was hanging from a neighbor's tree limb letting himself down into Doctor Teller's backyard.

Agent Dumont went into panic mode.

She hit the "Emergency" button on her cell phone and leapt out of her car. Sprinting up to Teller's front door, she hit the bell and began banging the brass knocker as hard as she could. When no one answered, she jumped down from the porch and ran around to the fence that enclosed the backyard. It was made of smooth plaster and stretched two feet above her head; too high to jump and too smooth to gain any kind of hand hold. She understood why the kid had used the tree; she would have to use the same method.

In two moves, she was straddling the second thick branch which extended into Teller's backyard. From her vantage point she had a clear view of the yard, the deck and the Jacuzzi.

"Oh shit."

The kid had pulled Cynthia Teller out of the Jacuzzi. He was sitting on top of her chest. Her arms were pinned under his knees. In his right hand he was holding a knife to her throat. She wasn't moving.

As quickly as she could, Agent Dumont inched further out on the tree branch. Quietly she let herself down into the yard. The kid's back was to her. She darted across the grass and stopped behind a little palm shack that housed the Jacuzzi machinery.

She reached for her weapon and came up empty; no holster, no gun. She'd left them in the car. "Oh God." Her eyes swept the area; she peeked into the Jacuzzi shack. Nothing. Not even a stick to use as a weapon. She had to do something!

Taking a breath, she stepped out into plain view. "Dude," she yelled.

He looked back at her, his eyes wide, a crazed look on his face. "Don't come any closer or I'll cut this bitch's head off!"

"No problem, man," she said. "Listen, I just got one question. What's a fine lookin' G like yourself, lookin' to do wit' some dried up old white broad? You know what I'm sayin'?"

An idea was forming. She took a step forward into the light. Then she turned in profile, slapped herself on the ass and stuck her butt out as far as she could. "Why ain't you after some real booty like this here?" And she slapped her ass again.

Darnel pushed the knife harder into Cynthia's throat. "Don't move bitch," he said. Then he turned to get a better look at the woman in the yard.

Angie Dumont was, in every physical sense of the expression, an Amazon woman. Skin the color of Bailey's Cream, huge almond eyes, full lips, auburn hair (the product of a Jamaican distance runner and an Irish mother) and the sinuous lean body of an athlete.

As Darnel stared in confusion, Agent Dumont ripped open her blouse, revealing a skimpy chartreuse bra, supporting a pair of firm chocolate breasts which were glazed with perspiration and heaving up and down in abject fear.

"Get chew some real pussy, man," she said. "Right here! I got what ya need. You not scared of a real woman, are ya? That what this about?"

Darnel lifted himself off Cynthia's body, grabbed her by the hair and jerked her to her feet. Holding the knife across her throat, he began pushing her along the deck toward the half-naked agent. "Double D do both of ya, bitch! This a dream come true."

Cynthia Teller tried to push back against his body but she was no match for his size and strength. He pulled the knife away for an instant and slapped her in the head with his free hand. Then he grabbed on again and pressed the knife inward, choking off her wind. "Double D do both of ya," he said again and pushed Cynthia forward.

"Bullshit!" shouted Dumont. "I'll bet you dick's too small. Only ass you ever get's off your baby sister."

Darnel's eyes grew wider, anger fueling his already hyped mind. For a moment he stood frozen, unsure of his next move, his body throbbing with lust, his brain amping with rage.

"What's a matter? You some kinda fag?" Dumont unzipped the fly on her jeans and jerked down on the waist band, lowering it to her thighs, revealing her panties. It was all she could think of to do. Bait him. Distract him.

The fag insult went deep into Darnel's hood-aged ego. A direct hit; like a shovel in the face. He let go of Cynthia, and jabbed his knife out in front of his chest.

"How 'bout you eat some a dis, bitch," he said. Then he charged across the deck toward Dumont.

With her jeans pulled down around her thighs, she was almost immobile. She tried to lunge sideways but only moved about 10 inches.

A few steps before he reached her, Darnel launched his body into the air, his arm elevated, the knife angling down at her from above like an archer's arrow.

There was a loud bang.

Darnel's body suddenly jerked upward and stopped in mid air, like he'd smashed into an invisible sheet of glass. He crumpled backwards into himself and dropped heavily to the ground. The knife jammed into the ground just three feet from Agent Dumont' chest.

Quentin Hawk jumped down from the top of the wall and ran forward, his Glock extended in front of him. His foot found the knife blade and kicked it aside. He stared down at the corpse. Then he removed his jacket and carefully covered the bloody face and head. Only then did he holster his weapon and look up.

"You all right Doctor Teller?" he asked.

She was sitting on a chaise lounge next to the Jacuzzi. Gently she rubbed her fingers across her throat, then answered, "Fine, Mr. Hawk. I'm fine. No damage."

"You sure?"

"Yes."

Quentin immediately turned his back on Cynthia and walked quickly to Agent Dumont. She was embarrassed, pulling at her clothes. Her shame at mishandling the assignment was obvious. She flicked some moisture from her cheek and turned her face away.

"You okay Dumont?" Quent asked quietly.

"Sorry sir," she answered, head bowed.

"Forget your piece in the car, did you?"

"I'm sorry sir," she said again.

"Well, listen Dumont, under the circumstances, I'd say what you did here was...amazing work. Creative...courageous. I couldn't have asked for more."

She was stunned. Raising her eyes, she asked quietly, "You aren't gonna suspend me for forgetting my gun?"

Quent smiled. "No. I'll bet you won't forget it again, though. Like I said before, Agent Dumont, I'm proud of you. Unless of course you're gonna change careers?"

"I don't understand, sir."

"Striptease. Got some real talent there, you know what I mean? Shame we don't have video. The guys would probably enjoy it a lot. You ever worked with a pole?"

Cynthia Teller was amazed at what she witnessed. Agent Hawk was a tall man. He towered over his female agent. His manner with her was rough as befitting a big man with a tough job. But the care behind his dealings with her was deep and sensitive. His priorities were evident. His agents came first. Although his care was less than delicate, it was touching.

Cynthia waited until Quent had moved away from his agent before approaching him. She extended her hand. "If you hadn't come along... I hate to think... Thank you Mr. Hawk. Thank you very much. You saved our lives."

And then it happened again. At the touch of his hand, a subtle quiver crept up her spine. "I'd like to apologize for my attitude last week. Combination of military ego and overwork."

"Understood and forgotten."

Something about the straightforwardness of his words was disarming. Or maybe it was something about his eyes. A moment passed as she searched for something else to say. "My partner, Luke, will be returning to California in a few days. I'd be happy to arrange a meeting for you if you'd like."

"Both of you were on my list, Doctor Teller. That would be great. Thank you very much. I appreciate the help."

22

The Basement – 1600 Pennsylvania Ave – Washington, DC

The room was almost completely dark. A gigantic plasma monitor occupied one entire wall of the private viewing suite. On screen, Kathryn de Kennesy stood naked to the waist, her breasts heavy, her hair unpinned cascading down her outstretched arms. Slowly she knelt down between Luke's open legs.

General Orin Pierce paused the DVR and pushed a button on the console. The outer door's deadbolt slammed into its slot in the steel jamb. The red sign in the hallway ignited, 'In Session.' The studio was unavailable.

Anxiously he rechecked chroma settings, although it wasn't necessary. Line stabilizers kept the voltage constant, so the color temperature would never vary. Because Pierce was right eye dominant, he'd had the pin spots programmed to adjust themselves automatically to the modulations of his right iris.

The huge monitor was a prototype screen, boasting 8000 crystalline electro pixels, an experimental medium being developed at NASA for the Central Intelligence Agency; yet no one at CIA was aware of its existence. The project had been taken from the CIA and rerouted to the President's Special Team; more accurately, to General Pierce himself.

The screen was currently producing a resolution 10 times greater than the human eye could register. The results were spectacular. The tiny creases in Kathryn de Kennesy's lipstick looked like deep canyons in a massive landscape of slick red pudding.

The single star on his shoulders gave Orin Pierce personal access to such exotic technology. Exclusive access. Everyone knew the general's position of authority. They also knew the raw political power that came with it.

No one knew about his unfettered pornographic appetite. No one knew the depth of his spiraling perversions. His position at the top of Washington's power elite shrouded his exotic tastes and preempted any question of his personal motives.

Tilting his oversized head forward, Pierce reached across the black leather armrest of his Neve mixing console and pushed the play button. The bodies of Luke and Kathryn animated once again. Pierce leaned in closer, his chin resting on the palm of his hand. He watched it twice from start to finish, transfixed by the intimacy on the huge plasma screen. Then cued back to the *best part,* zoomed in closer and watched it again in slow motion. His skin prickled. He arched his back, willing himself away from his own desires; forcing his mind back toward the inductive possibilities of what he had just seen.

He hit the eject button, a haughty smile on his thin lips. "What a goddamn surveillance coup," he murmured, "having the crap house bathrooms bugged just in time for their tawdry little romp."

He had sent young Ollie Jordan to Orange County to handle the surveillance of Kathryn de Kennesy. The zealous kid had gained entrance to her room at the Regency Hotel by climbing a trellis, going in through the open balcony doors and copying her day runner.

Illegal as hell; and certainly inadmissible in court.

But then operations of this kind had nothing to do with the law. Indeed, high-level Washington surveillance had its perks. Watching this beautiful woman on her knees on the floor of a dirty bathroom stall in a biker bar was more than titillating. Pierce felt intoxicated by a heady mixture of self praise and overpowering sexual stimulation. His mind was spinning.

"Into the men's bathroom right under my cameras. God what a performance. Totally uninhibited. The woman's a find. A sexual predator; far too skilled for this bumpkin soldier. Beyond question, a very skilled enemy agent."

He marked the disk with a Vietnamese character; roughly translated it meant "honey pot." He slipped it into his breast pocket, locked the door behind him, and walked down the gray basement corridor toward his own windowless office.

The Basement had no need for windows.

Sitting behind his desk, spotless, polished, organized as only an anal mind could demand, Pierce took a sip of tonic water, closed his eyes and tipped his chair back.

The de Kennesy woman is an amazing fake.

The First Lady had been correct (for once in her vapid life) in asking the question. Pierce himself had asked it months ago. *Suddenly she's the Colonel' constant companion. What do we know about her?*

The woman's file was dense; addresses, habits, friends, phone calls, patterns, preferences, memberships, even the damn body wash she used in the shower. But no hint of impropriety.

Now everything had changed. The business in the Roadhouse bathroom had presented him the first real chance to see her in action. The demonstration of sexual prowess had confirmed his suspicions. *No girlfriend, no oversexed housewife, no amateur sex kitten ever performed like this one. Kathryn de Kennesy is a pro. A plant. No doubt about it.*

Although most people would not have found her sexual performance to be 'incriminating,' the omniscient Pierce saw it clearly! Answers were always found in the smallest details. She was too good. Too clean.

Now he would focus the assets at his command. Point them in the right direction. Where had the first 14 years of her life gone? Where was the information, the birth records, the schooling? Why was it missing? Where did she come from? Was there an orphanage? An illegitimate birth? Was she a runaway? How many natural-born Lebanese girls are blonde?

It would be easy from this point. It was just a matter of persistence. Ultimately, the trail would lead him to the real enemy. The ones who'd sent her. The terrorist bastards trying to bring down his world. Pierce's resolve was unshakeable. He was going to enjoy this.

As expected, the omniscient Pierce had already made a second breakthrough. When Ollie Jordan handed in the copy of the de Kennesy woman's day runner, Pierce uncovered a damning revelation. A giant arrow pointing directly at his suspect.

The Lebanese Council is opening an office in Frisco. And guess who they're sending to set it up? What a coincidence..

The general immediately ordered young Jordan to set up surveillance teams in San Francisco and in Malibu as well. Orin Pierce loved a good game of cat and mouse. And there was no cat in the universe more skillful than the great *Orin Christopher Pierce.*

He moved to the task at hand with great relish. There was additional work to be done in Paris. A little insurance policy just in case the mice went out to play. It concerned the Hotel St. Clair. Although his star Agent, Ollie Jordan, spoke passable French, Pierce needed someone more experienced; a seasoned veteran with a legal background. The job required a tough negotiator with a creative flair.

Major Pete Gideon and a three-man team were already on United Flight 604 to Paris.

Paris, France

The white Citroen sedan, its Ministry bumper flags and French Government license plates signifying its importance, rolled to a stop in front of the St. Clair Hotel. The car's rear door swung open and out stepped Chief Henri Perrault, the Head of the Paris Police Department.

"You fat pompous bastard," muttered Paul Rubinstein, as he peeked through the second floor shutters. His family had owned the quiet little hotel St. Clair since 1919. "Can't you just leave us alone for once and catch some goddamn criminals?"

A second man now stepped from the Citroen. He was tall, graying at the temples and wearing a highly decorated dress uniform of the U.S. Military; his rank was major.

"Oh merde, who's this army jerkoff?"

The nervous hotelier raced down the mezzanine stairs to the foyer to await their arrival. He had been notified the previous day that the police chief would be stopping by on official business. He'd immediately developed a case of diarrhea. He'd lain awake in misery most of the night.

For the past two decades, the Hotel St. Clair had been a cherished and most discrete rendezvous for lovers; some famous, some infamous. Part of its charm was the over-stuffed furniture, the old-lady floral patterns and the garish Pierre Deux accents. Something about 'a grandmother's' style apparently gave patrons the feeling that it was safe to be adulterous at the St. Clair; a kind of 'your secret is safe here' vibe.

The last person any hotel patron wished to see at the St. Clair was a cop. And now the head cop was marching up to the front door. Rubinstein had offered to come down to the station on a moment's notice but, "No, the bastard had to pull up in front in the middle of the day, flapping his flags in the wind.

"Look at him. High stepping Nazi bastard. How can he be French and commit such an atrocity?" moaned Rubinstein.

The big oak door opened. "Ah, Chief Perrault," cooed Rubinstein, extending his hand as he scurried up to the rotund police chief, "An honor to have you here at the St. Clair."

You stupid monkey.

The chief made no response, choosing instead to blow his large nose vigorously into a big silk handkerchief which he then stuffed into his rear pants pocket.

Nice touch, thought Rubinstein, holding his eyes steadily on the chief's red face, waiting nervously to hear his fate.

"Mr. Rubinstein, I am here at the request of our friends in U.S. State Department. May I present Major Pete Gideon, special envoy from the office of the President."

"How do you do," said Major Gideon. "So nice of you to see us on such short notice. Is there somewhere we could sit for a few minutes?"

"I'll be in the car answering phone calls, Major," said Chief Perrault. "I'll take you back to the airport whenever you're ready. Good day, Mr. Rubinstein."

"Always a pleasure," answered Rubinstein, addressing the back of the chief's head as he was already halfway out the door.

"Right this way, Major," said Rubinstein, leading the way to the hotel's front lounge, a cozy room obviously designed for romantic intimacies. An ornate display of silver candlesticks provided a warm glow to the small space. Heavy velvet draperies screened out the daylight and a huge bowl of Casablanca lilies added their sweet fragrance to the dramatic ambience of it all.

The two men sat in oversized Windsor chairs in front of a wood-burning hearth, a Victorian coffee table between them.

"Will you take coffee, Major?"

"That would be welcome. Whatever it was they served on the flight over couldn't be considered coffee."

In moments a bellman appeared and began pouring an aromatic French blend into Major Gideon's porcelain cup. He did the same for his boss, bowed ceremoniously and left the room.

Major Peter Gideon took a long and satisfying sip of his coffee, then unobtrusively reached into his pocket and pressed a key on his Blackberry.

A small red light flashed on the dashboard of an unmarked panel truck parked in the cobbled alley behind the St. Clair. While the driver remained behind the wheel, two of the State

Department's finest electronics specialists exited the truck and began their assignment.

The installation of the St. Clair Hotel's Hibiscus Suite would take them 20 minutes. The wireless broadcast of sound and picture would utilize micro equipment. The miniature components would be carefully hidden in the furniture, the fabrics and various pieces of the room's antique décor. It was a costly operation. As General Orin Pierce would proudly declare later, "It proved to be a bit of inspired brilliance well worth the investment of manpower and resources."

The coffee poured and ingested, napkins folded, small talk concluded, Major Pete Gideon got straight to business. "Mr. Rubinstein, as you know, some of our most important statesmen and scientists have chosen to stay at your wonderful hotel over the years. We are continually grateful to you for your discretion as well as for your fine service."

Paul Rubinstein acknowledged the compliment with a polite nod of the head. "Thank you most sincerely, Major. We try."

The major continued. "My job is to protect these individuals, to insure their privacy, to see that they're secure from the prying eyes of the public. I think we share those goals; you as proprietor and I as a point man for our government."

"Without question. It's bedrock here; essential to the operation of our hotel."

Major Gideon took another sip from his cup. "I'm sure the very public arrival of the police at your door here today was...disturbing, to say the least. May I apologize and assure you that it was not of my design."

"Thank you, Major."

I wonder what the hell this bastard wants.

The next words out of the major's mouth provided the answer. "Mr. Rubinstein, we would like to reserve the Hibiscus Suite for the next 12 months on a round-the-clock basis for the use of our Secretary of State, our Secretary of Defense, a certain Colonel Luke Towne from our Department of the Military, as well as several other dignitaries who may need accommodation this year."

Rubinstein spoke up, his tone preemptive. "Major, our exclusivity is such that I'm afraid we can't really..." He was cut off in mid protest.

"Before you open negotiations, Mr. Rubinstein," said the Major, "Let me assure you that we know how discreet and very exclusive your establishment is and has been historically. In fact, the bureau has studied that history and found that during the last 10 years, Room number 6B, renamed the Hibiscus Suite in the Fall of '99, has had an occupancy rate of 226 days per year, and that on that basis, it nets your family a total of $56,082 per year.

Rubinstein was stunned to silence.

"For the accommodation I have requested, we would like to propose an immediate one-time fee of $112,000, or twice the room's yearly revenue."

My god he's taking out his check book!

"There are two additional requirements," added the major. "One, that we have periodic access to sweep the room for security reasons; and let me assure you our technicians will be a good deal more discrete than your local police."

With a tip of his head, the major then directed Rubinstein's attention to the two men now standing soundlessly behind the proprietor's chair. Rubinstein hadn't noticed the men enter the room. He tried hard to cover his astonishment.

"These two gentlemen, Master Sergeant Michel Vanderson and Specialist First Class Glen Bell, have just entered the St. Clair through the service door off the alley. They have completed a sweep of the Hibiscus Suite as we have been having coffee. You are dismissed gentlemen."

The two technicians left. Major Gideon continued without hesitation. "The second requirement under our proposed arrangement, Mr. Rubinstein, is that you mention this agreement to no one, and that you bill our personnel as you would any other guest."

Rubinstein was sure he had misheard. "But that would mean double billing. I'm... not sure I understand, Major."

Gideon didn't answer immediately, but opened his check book, wrote in the name "Paul Rubinstein" followed by the amount of "$112,000," and placed it on the coffee table between them.

Then he answered most congenially, as if the business at hand were a fait accompli. "Most all of your guests view the St. Clair as a unique, romantic hideaway to which they can escape unnoticed and undocumented. They are more than happy to pay for the privilege of staying here. We know that you and your staff work very hard to maintain that atmosphere. We would simply like to perpetuate their expectations in exactly the same way as you do. These are special people who need and deserve what you so elegantly provide."

Then the Major stood up promptly and extended his hand. "I assume we have a deal then?"

Paul Rubinstein eagerly shook the major's hand. Bowing his head to further signify his acceptance, he answered, "Thank you so very much, Major, for your understanding and your generosity. I will see to it that your requirements are followed to the letter. And please, if there's anything else you might ever need, I will see to it personally."

Rubinstein waited until the major had passed through the door before snatching up the check. His eyes grew large as he stared at the unbelievable amount of money. His money. The signature at the bottom of the check read "Brigadier General Orin Pierce, on behalf of the Office of the President of the United States of America."

Paul Rubinstein sat back down in his chair in front of the fire. He shook his head and began rocking back and forth. "America! Jesus! The rudest. Unsophisticated. No class; uncouth bastards. Goddamn it, I love 'em."

23

The Pentagon – Office of the Secretary of Defense

The purpose of NSA's Signals Intelligence mission at Ft. Meade, (SIGINT) is to screen all communications, regardless of source, country or medium, for 'suspicious indicators.' Key words, phrases, content vectors, websites or individuals are then analyzed by NSA linguists and cryptologists in an attempt to forecast potential threats to the security of the U.S.

Every Monday morning, Secretary of Defense Morton Ramsey received NSA's thick report covering the previous week's intra-world communications. On the second Monday of the month, having had a restful weekend at Martha's Vineyard, Ramsey was in early and anxious to get a head start on the week. Taking a swig of the black Arabica coffee he drank throughout his work day, Ramsey propped his Cole Hahn loafers up on the edge of his desk and began the laborious task of reviewing the NSA report. At the top of the title page was a paragraph that stopped him cold. It was labeled "Special Alert," a term he had never seen used in an NSA report.

He quickly scanned the summary of what the NSA experts termed 'suspect communications.' These were bits and pieces of conversations and text messages culled from numerous internet, short wave and cell phone sources. Ramsey then carefully read through the complete, detailed work-up of all the available information. After reading it a second time, he ordered his assistant to produce 12 copies.

Ramsey called an emergency meeting of the Special Intelligence committee.

Over a period of 12 months, using their multithreaded Cray XMT supercomputers, NSA cryptologists had detected an increasing amount of covert 'chatter' indicating a developing terrorist plot. Initially the communications had emanated from Lebanon, but as months progressed, there was a growing response from various locations on the East Coast of the United States. Tangentially, there were chat rooms, emails and cell phone communications that appeared to be related to the same subject matter. The cell phone calls originated in Qatar, Iran, Afghanistan, England, and Amsterdam.

Taken in combination, the body of evidence was pointing to an elaborate plan to smuggle explosives or other component liquids through so-called 'soft' ports along the southeastern border of the U.S. Some unnamed terrorist group was planning to begin their offensive around the first of July.

NSA suspected al Qaeda as the prime movers.

Ramsey's emergency meeting of the Intelligence Committee was convened in the Pentagon's counterterrorism boardroom in record time, just four hours after he had announced it. The Committee was minus only one of its members. The chairman of the Senate Select Committee on Intelligence could not get a flight out of Chicago in time to attend. In his place was one new participant, Admiral George Berkus, the former Head of Naval Operations, who was now consulting with NSA on potential seaborne terrorist threats.

Secretary Ramsey felt the admiral's input would be vital.

After three hours of review and discussion, the Committee recommended a massive increase in covert border surveillance along specific areas of the Florida coast plus the addition of secret land-based teams of SEAL interdiction forces to be inserted near the suspected ports of entry, Fernandina, St. Joe, and Panama City.

Admiral Berkus added an important additional element. The Navy would contribute its newly-designed speedboat-style 40' vessels. These high-speed snooper craft were created to look like pleasure craft, but were armed with infra-sensitive electronic detection equipment. Their concealed equipment would identify the suspects, track their vehicles and relay coordinates to the land-based SEAL teams.

Before the meeting adjourned, following Pentagon protocol, Secretary Ramsey's assistant, Dan Durban, collected all of the documents and notes except the master sheet which was retained by the Secretary of Defense. Durban then handed the collected documents to Mary Schulenburg who fed the papers into the shredder under Durban's watchful eye. Then, using the Secretary's master sheet, Durban would convert the Defense Secretary's notes into a formal document and returning it to him ASAP.

Because Mary Schulenburg was a whiz at formatting and punctuation, Durban would often ask her to check his draft for mistakes before he delivered it to Ramsey. Occasionally when Mary had redlined a significant number of errors in his work,

Durban would ask her to 'go ahead and make the corrections herself, input the thing and leave it on my desk.' The Pit Bull Strategy had been just such a document; 11 pages of complicated verbal interjections, revised wordings and Durban's incorrect grammar.

The current NSA report was high pressure. The Defense Secretary wanted the draft 'immediately.' Durban stood in front of Mary Schulenburg's desk. "Mary Mary, one more time. He's waiting for it. Check it for me would you. The grammar and stuff."

She quickly scanned the document and handed it back to him. "Perfect Mr. Durban," she beamed. "Pretty soon you won't need me at all." As he trotted off to his office, she was already reducing her own mental notes into a few illegible scratches.

Speed writing was a talent Mary had kept hidden from her employers. It was an archaic shorthand technique from the 50s which looked much like the scrawl of a child – a series of jerky lines, circles and unreadable symbols. Mary Schulenburg had made sure that her notebooks and yellow pads were covered with circles and squiggly lines and unreadable symbols. By now, the appearance of some extra pages of doodling on her desk raised no suspicions.

Mary had used her hidden talent on the Pit Bull document, surreptitiously duplicating it in its entirety before returning the corrected version to her boss.

The three pages of notes from the NSA meeting required very little translation. Its essence was easily captured.

On her way home, it was Mary's habit to stop at the local Starbucks, order a double macchiato and do a little web surfing. Among her favorite sites were Nordstrom's, Candy, Zappos and a popular international artists' website called arteria.freeform.org.

This last website was a free forum for artists. It posted modern art in myriad variety, accepting submissions from amateurs and professionals alike. Mary's occasional artistic entries featured angular shapes and contours filled with random masses of squiggles, lines, dots and abbreviated words. To the critical taste of the sites' owners, her work was reminiscent of 60s art phenoms Corita Kent and Ed Ruscha.

To the software on Leon de Kennesy's home computer, the squiggles, lines and dots were perceived for exactly what they were – speed written text stolen from classified Pentagon documents.

Leon's uniquely designed software scanned its target websites every five minutes, looking for coded messages. When Mary's *artistically rendered* text was recognized, it was immediately copied, translated into idiomatic Farsi, and sent to the printer in Leon's new Bel Air library.

The head of Leon's Laundry Team had designed the software himself and declared it foolproof. Although NSA utilized the most sophisticated electronic listening and spidering equipment in the world, websites featuring paintings and art work were not considered relevant. Furthermore, had their equipment come upon the website arteria.freeform.org, speed writing would not be recognized and parsed as a valid format.

There was an additional precaution. Within five minutes of their initial appearance on the site, Mary's pictures were automatically removed at their point of origin (Starbucks). Removals happened frequently as artists often had second thoughts and withdrew their work in order to make changes.

The de Kennesy Mansion – Bel Air, California

Sitting in his library, beaming with pride, Leon read and re-read Mary's purloined report. They had done the impossible! Months of effort by some college kids in Lebanon, the sons of his benefactors, using some hot-rod computers. And they had done it. They had scored big time. His Laundry people had pulled off a communications diversion that rivaled NSA's cryptologists and their mighty Cray XMT supercomputers.

While the U.S. Coast Guard and the SEALs and their dogs and all the other NSA bastards are waiting to pounce on Florida, Farad's Semtex will be floating quietly across the Niagara, untouched and unnoticed – right into Lewiston, 1200 fat miles away.

Leon immediately booked a flight to Lebanon. He needed to meet with his partners to coordinate the last details of the greatest coups of his career. He was about to hammer the final nail into the coffin of the Great Satan.

The trip would also be an opportunity to demonstrate the use of his medical video suite. Since his sudden move to the States, and the reduction of his practice, no one at Beirut

Orthopedic had been schooled on the new techniques nor on the procedures required to operate his cutting-edge video instruments.

As the number of surgical operations using his medical inventions increased, so would his notoriety, his product sales, and his revenue. He had quickly discovered that maintaining the de Kennesy life style in the U.S. was a good deal more expensive than it had been in Lebanon. He and Nana were already becoming addicted to the good life – behind the gates of Bel Air.

Beirut Orthopedic Hospital, Lebanon

"Beirut Orthopedic. East Wing Surgery," answered the haggard nurse, cradling the phone under her chin.

"Doctor Leon de Kennesy, please," said a female voice.

"I'm sorry, he's teaching a procedure to our surgical staff. Can I give you his voice mail?"

"That would be fine," answered Nuriyah Saleh, a yellowed cigarette pinched between the only two fingers remaining on her left hand. Nuriyah was the 19-year-old apprentice to the legend Farad Aziz. For the young Muslim girl, to carry the blasting caps for such a fabled warrior of Islam was more important than life itself. The accidental loss of her fingers was a badge of pride.

She had placed the call from Farad Aziz's munitions workshop which was housed in the 100-year-old, red-roofed grain shelter, high in the limestone mountains of Tal at Musa, Syria. As the shop's primary apprentice, young Nuriyah slept on the floor under a wheat bin near the fireplace, and did whatever the schizophrenic Aziz told her to do. And whatever was done was done without question, including the passionate use of her beautiful body and sexual willingness.

Nuriyah didn't recognize the name 'de Kennesy,' so she simply waited for the beep and then spoke the message exactly as he had been instructed: "Doctor de Kennesy, your glasses will be ready for pick up on Wednesday."

Nuriyah then dialed a second number, but this time she knew the name well. It brought passion to the hearts of many a young Muslim in Lebanon, a name spoken with reverence. When the call was answered, Nuriyah again repeated the words exactly as her mentor had instructed: "Would you please inform the holy Mullah Ahmed Rockmani that his glasses will be ready for pick up on Wednesday?"

West Wing – Beirut Orthopedic – Beirut, Lebanon

At precisely 11 p.m. on Wednesday night, Doctor Leon de Kennesy and Mullah Ahmed Rockmani sat opposite one another in Op B. The coded message from Farad Aziz had summoned them to an emergency meeting.

Farad was late as usual.

A slight anxiety hovered between the two formidable chieftains. There had never been an emergency meeting before. Meetings of the powerful triumvirate had always been scheduled well in advance either by Doctor de Kennesy or by Mullah Rockmani. These two shared a mutual respect. Each had countless obligations necessitating a meticulous dedication to schedule. Their commitment to advance planning had resulted in a partnership of unparalleled success. There had never been a need for emergency meetings.

Such a sudden call to arms could only be the work of their unpredictable, schizophrenic partner Farad. Yet he had still not made an appearance.

But Dr. Leon could hardly contain himself. "Most holy one, something so important has happened that I was about to call an emergency meeting myself."

"Would it not be prudent to wait until our young partner arrives?" said the Mullah, always the mediator.

"I'll be happy to repeat it for him - as if I were telling it for the first time."

Such excitement was a rarity for the ascetic Dr. de Kennesy. A smiling Mullah Rockmani relented. "Yes, of course, Leon, we're eager to share any good news. What is it?"

"Holy one, the Laundry has accomplished its mission. The plan was a success. The Americans have taken the bait! The proof's right here in Ramsey's speech."

Excited, standing up from his chair, Leon handed the Mullah two pages of Mary Schulenburg's notes. "Right out of their emergency meeting. Look, here on the second page, Ramsey names the exact ports we fed 'em. The exact same ones! St. Joe, Fernandina, and Panama City."

The Mullah read aloud from the page in his hand. It was a direct quote from Morton Ramsey. "The ports of entry along the coast of Florida are gonna be locked down tighter than a bug's ass."

The Mullah stood up from the table, met Leon halfway round, and threw his burly arms wide open pulling Leon into a bear hug.

"Allah be praised. You've done it, Leon. The Laundry. You've done it. Come March, when we're picking up the Semtex, they'll be looking for the proverbial needle..."

Ka bang!

The OR's double doors suddenly flew open and in walked Farad. Without looking up, he slouched across the small room and dropped heavily into the chair opposite his two partners. The Mullah released his grip on Leon. Embarrassed, he nervously straightened his garments and his beard and seated himself. Leon did the same. The moment had been ruined.

No one spoke. Leon sat very still. *Waiting for this' idiot to explain the urgency of the meeting he called...* The silence persisted; the atmosphere far more tense than usual; the chieftains sat stone-like, waiting for Farad to speak.

The three were bound in a marriage of personalities as opposite as their attire; the Mullah's traditional robe of black wool, fully concealing his body; Leon's olive, Brioni couture business suit, proclaiming his wealth and achievement; and Farad's torn jeans, black knit cap and short-sleeved leather jacket, exposing his ornately tattooed forearms, demonstrating his permanent non-conformity.

Finally, Farad spoke. "I got some not very good news, gentlemen. But as usual, Farad comes through. I've got the good news to fix it. It's boom time... Let's get ready to RUMBLE!!"

"ENOUGH! Enough of this insolence, Farad!" shouted the Mullah, slapping the flat of his hand down on the cold aluminum table, impacting a visible dent in its center.

For a moment, the holy man stared toward the heavens and took in a long deliberate breath to calm himself. When he spoke, his rage was made all the more intense by the terrible quiet of his whispered words. "We have come here in righteousness. We are consecrated in the name of Allah. We have pledged our lives to a holy Jihad against the vile corruptions of the West."

He lowered his rapier gaze to the face of Farad Aziz. "I will not tolerate your disrespect any further. Your words, your dress, your attitude...you act like one of them! You look like one of them! You sound like one of them. You will not receive another warning. Do you understand, my brother?"

The Mullah's use of the endearment 'my brother' was so uncomfortably personal that the back of Farad's neck broke out in beads of cold sweat. In the world of Islam, the pronouncements of Mullah Ahmed Rockmani had become tantamount to religious law. His displeasure bore the will of Allah; the result, possible torture and death.

It was time for Leon to speak. There was nothing he could add to the Mullah's outburst, so he asked simply, "Farad, why are we here? What emergency has summoned us to this meeting?"

Farad's eyes widened; he knew things were about to get worse. "The man I sent to Ulster to inspect our Semtex was arrested. The stupid English cops were waiting for him. I think the whole thing was a set-up. The stuff never left port."

"What stuff? Our Semtex!" screamed Leon. "It's still in Ulster?"

Farad continued. "We can't send our guys over there to pick it up. They'd be sitting ducks. But..." He held up his hand to ward off the onslaught he knew was coming from Leon. "But...I found a way out of this. I've got a good contact inside the RIRA. The guy says for $50,000, he'll move it all out of the barn tomorrow night. His boys will pack it up with a load of lead crystal and put it on a freighter out of Rosslare. They can get it to Italy by the middle of April. The Camorra will hold it for us. Like I said before, the Camorra runs everything there. And I already paid them off."

Leon's brain began spattering like a runny egg on a fry griddle. "I gave you $350,000 for this Farad! That was two months ago." He slapped his hand on Mary Schulenburg's stolen report, snatched it from the table and squashed into a ball. He raised his massive fist. "I spent 10 months creating a complex diversion. A successful diversion. It WORKED! It's right here. It worked, you piece 'a shit."

Leon threw the wad of paper at Farad. It bounced off his forehead and fell on the table before him. "A sure thing," shouted Leon. "That's what you said, a sure thing. Now you're telling me my 70 bricks of Semtex are still sitting in some idiot's barn somewhere in goddamn bloody Ulster! Are you insane? Another $50,000? To get it to Italy by April? April is a month too late, you stupid, mother... Do you think our benefactors don't care what we do with the money they give me? What do I tell them when they ask me what happened?"

"I can tell you what I think happened. Maybe your people would understand if they knew what happened. See the RIRA is a splinter group of the IRA. They're holding all the Semtex while the Sinn Fein are pretending to hand over all the..."

Leon cut him off cold. "Shut your stupid mouth, Farad. I know who the RIRA is. I've had enough. $50,000 in blackmail. That isn't going to get me my Semtex, you fool! It's not going to bring back my goddamn 350K either! I spent 10 months setting up a diversion for June, based on your word."

Leon's head was shaking with rage. A drop of his spittle splashed down on the table with a gentle wet 'smack.'

Farad opened his mouth to defend himself and Leon exploded again. "DO NOT SPEAK. Do not say another word. Understand me Aziz!"

Leon groped awkwardly inside his jacket and clumsily pulled out a black Beretta 85S pistol. Hands shaking, he jammed the barrel into the scar on Farad's throat. "Understand me clearly," he roared, "I will blow your goddamn useless head off!"

The blood drained from Farad's face. He had pushed this arrogant 'hawk nose' bastard once too often. He held his breath, knowing his life was about to end.

Leon closed his eyes and swallowed down the bile burning at the top of his throat. He'd built his fortune fighting with CFOs and lobbying ignorant hospital managers. But this was different.

His palms were wet. The Beretta wavered an inch to the left then back to center. He held it steady. He knew the feel of cold steel in his hands, of cutting blades, of boring drills. He was a surgeon. *A surgeon.* The word reverberated inside his head – a salat in a massive mosque.

A surgeon. A healer. He waited. Time stretching across a cavernous divide. The gun held steady, jammed into Farad's neck.

He tightened his finger on the trigger. Then...gradually he released the tension and lowered the gun to waist level.

He opened the black lapel of his suit and slowly inserted the Beretta back into its leather holster. He turned to Mullah Rockmani and exhaled two long breaths, remaining still for a long moment after each one.

Anger is a raging fire. Whoever can subdue his anger, puts out the fire: whoever cannot, gets burnt himself. Anger is a raging fire. Whoever can... It was the first Hadith he'd learned as a child. He could hear it more clearly now, words from Ali ibn Abi Talib; the Maxims.

When he was satisfied with his altered state of mind, he spoke again. His voice had changed; its oily texture had returned. "From now on, I will handle the purchase of all explosives. Your only job, Farad, will be its detonation. That's the end of it. I don't intend to let this...misunderstanding interrupt the progress we've made together. I'm putting it behind me. Moving on to do the work we've planned. I hope we can all do the same. We have much to do. The work of Ad-Darr (The Harmer).

"I'm sorry, Mullah, that you had to be subjected to this outburst. I respectfully suggest that we adjourn this meeting and convene at some later time."

Without another word, Mullah Rockmani bowed his head, rose from his chair and walked from the room – as was the custom.

Ten minutes later as Doctor Leon's Mercedes began its climb toward his home in Deir el Qamar, the car's cell phone rang. He'd been expecting the call. Pushing the speaker button on the rim of the steering wheel, he answered, "Yes Ahmed."

The Mullah's voice was calm. "Leon, you're a surgeon, not an arms dealer. How are we going to obtain the materials needed?"

"He's finished. We agree, do we not?" said Leon, ignoring the question.

"When someone else can be found, yes."

"And the 10 college students at the Laundry. What am I going to tell their fathers?"

"Tell them the Americans are slow to act. Tell them the project needs more time. Tell them my cousin has come to our aid."

"I should mention Mullah Omar?"

"You and I both came to the same conclusion. Farad cannot be trusted. So I wrote to Mullah Omar as a last resort."

Leon was stunned. "And...what did he say?"

"He has proposed a solution. I didn't want to disturb your momentum at the Laundry, so I didn't tell you. I was praying that for once Farad would deliver."

"But why do you sound hesitant, Ahmed?"

"There is a stipulation."

The two chieftains chose not to discuss the details on the phone.

24

From the beginning, Mullah Rockmani had doubted the potential of Leon's Laundry project. Rockmani was a man of the desert. He knew technology was necessary; it was the wave of the future. But the old ways had worked for centuries. Rifles, bombs and knives produced immediate results. Rockmani did not voice his concerns to his partner; Leon had worked financial magic before, perhaps he could do it again with computers.

After the Laundry had been in operation for six months, Mullah Rockmani lost faith in the project. Whatever was supposed to happen, hadn't happened. As far as Rockmani was concerned, nothing was going to happen. He decided to use the only other means at his disposal. He would prostrate himself before his cousin Mullah Omar, admit defeat and beg for assistance.

His request for a second meeting was confirmed by a messenger who arrived at Rockmani's door with a basket of delicacies. Amidst the figs and sweets was a formal document, ornate calligraphy on a traditional scroll, inviting him to come again to Omar's home in Kandahar; and this time he was encouraged to bring his partner, 'the Doctor de Kennesy.'

The day of their visit was unbearably hot and their trip to Kandahar was strained. Leon had been forced to sell one of Nana's prized Picassos, a small drawing of the Bird of Peace, to raise the half million dollars he now carried with him. The irony of the choice was not lost on either man.

That had been the stipulation. Quid pro quo.

In return for "a pledge of faith from your partner, the Lebanese doctor," Mullah Omar had promised "to solve the Jihad's need for explosives." The inscrutable Omar, fresh from a secret strategy meeting with Hizb'allah chief, Hassan Nasrallah, had made no further explanation. Leon and Rockmani were expected to simply hand over the cash and take Omar at his word. Leon, the businessman, was extremely uncomfortable with such a nonspecific arrangement. Rockmani assured him that Omar was simply testing his faith.

But then it was not Rockmani's Picasso.

They were met at the door by Mullah Omar himself, dressed in uncharacteristic white robes and turban, an expression of pleasure and excitement enveloping his normally somber countenance. "Welcome my brothers. Please come into my home and take refreshment."

They were led into the library where cold tea and damp cloths were prepared for their comfort. Leon was already fully aware that to be invited to the home of this most holy cleric was and extraordinary occurrence. However, to be addressed by him as 'brother' was the pinnacle of Leon's Islamic life.

Midway through their refreshments, Mullah Omar addressed them calmly. "I have something of supreme importance to share with you." The two guests put aside their tea and comforts and focused their attention on the reclusive Omar.

When he saw that he had their complete attention, Omar began. "The glorious events of 9/11 have altered the flow of Islamic life as we understood it. There has been much thought and discussion on these matters. The means and ends of our efforts have been given a new perspective. The Islamic Brotherhood, Ayman al-Zawahiri and Osama himself now believe that your Silent Jihad is the most promising approach to restoring the Caliphate. Our noble brothers have given their approval."

He waited in silence for the impact of his epic statement to fully register on his guests, an expression of pride emanating from his learned visage.

Then he addressed Leon directly. "Doctor de Kennesy, I have worked closely with our brothers to deliver the resources you and my cousin have requested." There was an awkward pause.

Mullah Rockmani slowly reached out to his partner, Leon, his palm upward. Leon handed over a small bulging leather case. Mullah Ahmed Rockmani then bowed respectfully and placed the case on the coffee table in front of his cousin Omar.

A servant appeared and removed the money. "Let us dine together," said Mullah Omar. Accordion doors opened at the end of the room, revealing a long dining table piled high with delicacies. At the doors, three of the Mullah's wives (one of them Osama's daughter) stood ready to serve their guests.

No further business was discussed at the table. And when the meal was finished, the enigmatic Mullah Omar himself accompanied his sated guests to his front door.

As Leon stepped down from the porch, a servant spoke quietly to him. "Someone will contact you."

25

Beqaa Valley, Lebanon

Kathryn's Flight 712 from L.A. to Beirut took 20 hours and 35 minutes. The automobile ride from Beirut to the edge of Beqaa Valley took another hour and a half. By the time Kathryn arrived home she was exhausted. She walked through the living room and headed straight for the bathtub without ever turning on a light.

When she entered her bedroom to select a bathrobe, she was so startled she dropped her carry bag and backed into the door jamb.

A huge HD flat screen TV was now standing by the side of her bed; and on it, in crystal clarity, was a live image of Luke's house in Malibu. She could hear the sound of the Pacific surf and the distant mewing of a seagull. She sat down on the bed, her shoulders relaxed, the bath forgotten, and smiled into the screen. The image was so big, it almost felt like she was there.

During her brief stay at Luke's little house in Malibu, she had bought a tiny birdhouse and hung it from a branch in Luke's front yard. There was a sign on its tiled roof that read, "General Store." In the clarity of Luke's laser system, she could see three yellow-headed finches casually pecking away at the grain in its trough, splashing seed down onto the grass below.

Kat checked her watch - still set to Pacific time: 7:30 p.m. She rolled on to one arm and smiled in expectation. And it happened! Right on schedule. Two white Canadian geese, their brown-tipped wings folded across their backs, came into the TV picture, walking across the grass, quietly honking to each other, looking for their evening meal. Luke had called them "The Rabbis; two old men, hands clasped behind their backs, heads down, lost in the Torah, walking together, anticipating a meal."

Kathryn drank it in, wishing she were still there. The phone rang. "What is it?" said the excited voice. It was her stepmother, Nana.

"What is what?"

"The big surprise? Luke called days ago to find out how to get some installers into your flat. He wouldn't tell me what for. Said it was a surprise. So what got installed?"

"Well, it's the biggest flat screen you've ever seen," answered Kathryn. "Something special about how it gets its signal. A Laser something or other. They put it right next to my bed."

"You sound pretty happy, honey. What's so great?"

"Well, I'm sitting on the bed looking at a live shot of Luke's house in Malibu. It's almost like I never left. It's like having him here. I love that. And right now, you wouldn't believe it. Right now I watching the Rabbis.

"The who?"

"There're these two geese that show up at the house exactly at 7:30 every night for dinner. They look like two old men on their way to Seder. It's so cute, Nana, you should see it. We nicknamed them 'the Rabbis.'"

Nana de Kennesy did her best to conceal her alarm. "Sounds wonderful, darling. Enjoy. Listen my kitty, I love you. But I gotta run. Getting my nails done and they're here to pick me up." And she rang off.

Doctor Leon was in the midst of conducting rounds at Beirut Orthopedic when his cell phone vibrated. Nana's call was the only in-comer that vibrated and only when the call was urgent. He excused himself from a group of young interns and stepped into an empty waiting room for privacy.

"Everything okay Nan?" he asked, concerned.

"Sorry for the intrusion, dear, but it's Kathryn. I don't like the way she sounds."

"She sick?"

"No, more serious. I just got off the phone with her and she sounds...she sounds like some goddamn lovesick 12th grader. Like she forgot what she's supposed to be doing with this bastard."

"What!?" he asked in disbelief.

Nana responded with an imitation of Kathryn's girlish attitude, mimicking the sound of her voice: *Oh Nana, two cute little duckies, right outside our house in Malibu. So wonderful. Just like having Luke right here with me. Like I never left.*

"I'll go see her tonight. Stop this shit before it gets out of hand."

"My thought exactly. Be gentle with her though, Leon, she sounds pretty confused at the moment. You know, vulnerable."

"Don't worry. I'll handle it!" he barked. "I made her, didn't I? I'll take care of it."

In his own mind, the CEO of the Silent Jihad was fast becoming infallible.

Exhausted after her 21-hour flight from L.A., Kathryn curled up on her own bed in front of the big flat screen. She stared at Luke's cute little house, wondering what it might be like to live there.

She lay back against her pillows and closed her eyes. She lived in a remote section of the Beqaa Valley. At night nothing stirred but the crickets.

The silence was comforting.

As her breathing slowed, her eyes grew heavy and her thoughts began to gently pinwheel. Somehow the last few hours she had spent in Luke's home, in his shower, his kitchen, brushing her teeth at the little sink, the whole experience felt so comfortable. No pretensions. No press. No politics. Calm. Normal. As if somewhere in her forgotten past she had been part of such a life, or at least dreamt of it.

She rolled over and pulled her knees to her chin. It felt like Luke was her first boyfriend; like she was just a naïve young girl again; though she couldn't remember ever having been "a naïve young girl.

Four hours later, Kathryn came fully awake. The digital readout said it was 5:30 a.m. The jet lag was playing havoc with her internal clock. She was wide awake. After several failed attempts to go back to sleep, she finally gave up, got up, took a shower, dressed and headed in to work.

They missed each other in the dense morning fog that smothers the access road to Beqaa; Leon, in his Mercedes 600, angrily steaming up the hill toward her house; Kathryn, in her Jaguar convertible, happily cruising down the hill toward Beirut proper.

Light traffic from the Valley into Beirut put her in front of the Lebanese Consulate a full hour before its underground garage would open for business. She drove further down the main street of the tree-lined Ashrafieh district and parked in front of the Praline, a popular croissant shop.

She sat down at one of its little round tables and immediately realized she was starving. Orange County, to

Miami, to London to Beirut on British Airways – 21 hours of the worst food she had ever dumped into a disposable trash bag. When the waiter approached, she was more than ready.

"Man'ousheh, honey yogurt, Cardamom coffee and a bottle of Pellegrino please," she said. "And could you have them make the mah'ousheh extra crispy?"

The yawning waiter took in her light hair and fine features, and mistook her for a tourist, "Ah, that's a lot of food there, miss," he smirked, "Sure you don't want something a little ... lighter?"

She answered in Arabic. "Hemen!" (Hurry up with it). The surprised kid ran off without another word. Kat was used to being misread by people; beautiful people are usually not remarkable for their acuity.

Memories of her childhood began to play a dark and disquieting slide show in her mind's eye; then strangely, a flood of goose bumps appeared on her arms. She buttoned her jacket against the morning cold, took the coffee pot from the waiter's tray and poured some into her cup. The sweet taste of Cardamom danced on the back of her tongue.

The familiar warmth and sweetness of the local brew always made things better. But instead, she felt a kind of gnawing anxiety. She looked around the little café; no one else there, nothing to fear. Still there was an odd silence in the air. She looked up and down the street. No traffic. She turned back to find that her food had arrived. It smelled wonderful.

She looked around the little café again, then up and down the street. *Strange. No movement.*

Silence.

Then a deafening crash.

The bottle of Pellegrino exploded in her face. The air around her flashed into a liquid mass of bright orange and white. Shards of glass cut into her neck and cheek.

She squeezed her eyes to protect them.

Everything went black. Dead still. She'd lost consciousness for a moment. When she opened her eyes again, she was on her back on the ground. A hard pain in her chest. Everything smelled of firecrackers. Hard to breathe. She tried to draw in a breath of air, but instead thick black smoke forced its way up her nostrils and into her lungs. She coughed violently. When she tried to turn away from the smoke, she realized she couldn't move her head. Something heavy was on top of her.

She blinked her eyes. Blackness. Total blackness. And a frantic roaring noise coming from somewhere above her. Then suddenly, the smoke cleared for an instant.

The glimpse of reality was terrifying.

She was pinned beneath a huge commercial refrigerator, its double doors collapsed like a paper accordions – one on each side of her – entombed in a coffin of crumpled steel. On top of her body was a pile of jagged metal debris, so heavy that it was crushing her into the ground.

When she realized that all she could move were the toes on her left foot, she felt a sickening panic beginning to take hold of her mind.

She thought she could hear sirens, but they sounded a hundred miles away. She called out for help, but her voice seemed trapped within her mouth. Inside the box, the air was black and hot and silent. Outside everything was drowning in a wind storm.

Several minutes passed. The smoke thickened. She was completely blind. The heat was suffocating. She felt herself becoming light-headed. *No! You won't!*

Her anger forced her to remain conscious.

Then she sensed movement. Voices shouting over the sound of the wind. "I think there's someone under this! There's a foot."

She moved her toes as rapidly as she could; it was all she could do. A male voice called out above the noise, "Quick, over here. Something moved. Shine your light down there."

Light suddenly appeared on one side of her body. Part of the weight was raised from her chest. Then more light. Then the refrigerator was tipped upward on its side. Then it was rolled over and away.

Three burly firemen stared down at her; one grabbed her under the arms and stood her on her feet. "Are you hurt?" he shouted over the howling noise.

She moved her shoulders, then her arms and legs, "I don't know," she croaked. Then a retching cough stopped her words and she began gagging on the soot of her own breath.

"Here, let's get you out in the air." One of them walked her through the debris. When they reached an open space, he pushed a water bottle into her hands. She poured it onto her face and down her throat, and nodded her head, signaling that she was 'okay.'

He climbed up and over a stack of charred concrete blocks a then reached back and helped her over.

They both looked south. A gushing blanket of fire had reached so high it dwarfed the adjacent buildings. It spanned half the block spewing a volcanic shower of blazing rocks and soot into the air. Three new explosions suddenly rocked the ground beneath them. The heat became so intense they had to run north and dodge behind the Pump truck to keep from blistering.

The fire captain shouted down from his position in the cab "They blew up the Consulate."

Kathryn's mind jolted into clarity. "Oh my God," she gasped, but the roar of the inferno was so deafening, she couldn't hear the sound of her own voice. She peered around the huge fender of the truck. The fireman was pointing at a gaping hole where the smoke was gushing toward the sky.

It wasn't the Consulate. It was two buildings south. There had been a small four-story structure with a copy service on the ground floor, a service that her office used on a daily basis. The little building's front walls were now completely gone and its three upper floors had collapsed into the center of the inferno.

Kathryn's office had been obliterated.

Within the hour, the international TV broadcasts were reporting 16 dead and 12 missing. Witnesses said a panel truck crashed into the front window of the copy service and plowed through its back walls into the building's atrium. A tremendous explosion then rocked the area, smashing windows as far as two blocks away.

The Facility – Malibu, California

The door to Luke's office flew open and Dave Halter rushed in. "Luke..." he began, but then he saw the phone in Luke's hand and the news report on the TV monitor.

"I can't reach her, Dave, too much traffic on the lines."

"Have you called her parents?" Dave asked.

"No. Would you keep trying the Consulate for me and I'll try Nana and Leon." Then his cell phone rang. He grabbed it and shouted, "Kat?"

"She's fine. She's on her way home," said Nana's welcome voice.

"God bless you, Nana, that's great news."

"She was desperate to get through to you, Luke, but everything was jammed. She thought maybe your TV system would work, so she called us and then headed home."

"Everything okay with you and Leon?"

"Fine dear, we're fine thanks."

"Do they know who did it?"

"No, but the whole second floor of the building was an American travel agency. They handle most of the flights in and out of Beirut and Damascus. The TV here says it was the probable target."

"I'm sorry, Nana. The world seems to get uglier." (Beat) "Thank you so much for getting through to me here. I appreciate it very much. I'm going to race home and see if I can reach her."

Luke was already climbing into his blue 350 Z, cell phone pressed to his ear. The tires squealed as he spun out of The Facility's underground parking lot and accelerated down the hill.

The laser connection at Luke's Malibu house was perfect as usual. There was Kat, waiting on his screen, sitting in her bedroom in Beqaa. "I'm coming to see you," he said as he walked in the door.

"I'm fine Lukie, you don't have to fly across the ocean just because I cut my ear. I'm a big girl you know."

She showed him the little cut on her ear. Then she told him about the explosion, the Pellegrino bottle and the firemen who freed her from the rubble.

"It could have been worse," he said. "I'm coming to see you. It's decided."

"I won't be here, honey, I'm just about to pack for Paris. We've got a summit with some Syrian businessmen. Besides, you can't just leave with all you've got going on there."

"Paris! That's even better. I already have to be in Zurich. I'll move my meeting with Leica. What day do you get to Paris?"

"Next Tuesday. Three in the afternoon."

"See," he said, "I told you. It's already decided. I'll see you at the St. Clair."

26

Tal at Musa, Syria

By climbing out on the red-tiled roof of the old grain shelter, Farad Aziz could see all the way to the bottom of the gorge, 3000 vertical feet below. He watched three tiny cars appearing and disappearing in the fog, navigating the switchbacks, grinding up into the mountains of Tal at Musa. It would take them another hour before they reached him.

There had never been a meeting at his munitions workshop. In the past, Mullah Rockmani had always thought it too far to travel. The arrogant Doctor Leon de Kennesy had looked down his hawk nose and explained that a "surgeon's hands were sacred tools" and that his "were never going to be exposed to the unstable devices" used by Farad at his "bomb shop."

Farad couldn't quench the foreboding. *All of a sudden, a formal meeting! Held at my place? At the top of the Anti-Lebanon mountains? Unbelievable! How stupid do they think I am?*

Four days had passed since the meeting was set and despite the sexual distractions of his beloved Nuriyah, Farad had been unable to sleep. So menacing and so transparent were the intentions of his partners! *Mullah Rockmani had the audacity to order that no one else be present.*

"In 10 years," said the Mullah, "No one has ever seen the three of us together. That's the way it is going to remain. Take care, Farad, to insure that our security is not compromised in any way. No one is to be allowed anywhere near the area. It's simply a matter of security."

Farad didn't believe any of it.

He climbed back down into the cold interior of his workshop and stood for a moment, shivering. Then he ran to the tall stacks of firewood and began pitching heavy cedar logs into the massive brick fireplace that occupied one-third of the building's central wall. He kept at it until a cold sweat glistened in the sinews of his neck; still the exercise did nothing to quiet his nerves.

"Have you gone, Nuriyah?" he shouted.

"Leaving right now Master."

"And the others?"

"I told them not to come in today, Master."

"Don't you come back either, until tonight, you understand? We'll test the rest of the short fuses tomorrow." Under his breath he added, "If I'm still alive."

Then he jammed a 20-round magazine into the middle of his prized 12-gauge M87, and carefully fed the little sawed-off shotgun into its leather sheath on the underside of his huge work table. *We'll see who's left standing when this one's over, my bastard brothers of Allah.*

His eye immediately caught the small red light flashing high up in the charred roof beams; Abd-al-Jawwad was signaling. Three unknown vehicles had just moved past the tall stand of cedars at the west end of the old man's farm. As an extra precaution, Farad had hired several old farmers to act as lookouts.

Impoverished by time and circumstance, the Tal at Musa mountain farmers considered any source of money to be *a holy gift from Allah.* No questions were asked; no explanations were needed. Their loyalty was as solid as the granite mountains of southwestern Syria, the same granite that held up the 3000-year-old Roman temples in Baalbek.

The three-car procession of limos was still 20 minutes away, but their progress had slowed to a crawl; the road to Farad's *Facility* had become little more than a goat path. The few locals who chanced to coax their little herds across the path could see clearly into the limos; but those who dared to look, cast their eyes quickly to the ground. These passengers were holy men.

Mullah Rockmani always traveled with a group of scholars and clerics, all of them holy men, all of them garbed in black robes and turbans as befitting the Imams of Islam. As the cars jerked and struggled to find passage through the scourge of rocks and potholes, some of the holy black robes were thrown open, revealing hard-edged automatic rifles and handguns. These mercenary objects were not hidden from the eyes of the faithful. Bodyguards were as holy to the Jihad as the teachings in the holy book which empowered their actions.

Leon and the Mullah had chosen to ride in the third limo, an old tobacco brown 1972 Mercedes 600. As usual, they spoke of their Jihad; but this time all thought was focused on

Farad Aziz. Their strategy was simple. By traveling to his workshop in the mountains, they would appear to be honoring him and his contributions to the Jihad. They would make him feel needed. They would speak of his importance, his past sacrifices.

They would offer him a kind of super promotion. Hopefully this would gain his cooperation. Hopefully it would get them through one more month. *One critical, transitional month.* Neither of them had been able to find a trustworthy replacement for their bomb-making savant.

"Savant bullshit," said Leon. "Just another word for crazy unstable son-of-a-bitch! That's what we've got on our hands here."

"Is there anyone over there in the States?" said the Mullah. "Anyone good enough?"

Leon's frustration showed. "You know them better than I do, Ahmed. You trained them. You think anyone from Talib was good enough? This idiot's got 20 years on all of them."

The Mullah's lack of response confirmed what both men already knew. They were stuck with Farad. They would have to begin the explosive Third Phase of the Jihad with Farad's ever-rebellious, psychotic personality in charge of placing, priming and detonating the explosives.

The procession rolled on. And although the old Mercedes 600 was partially restored, its gas shocks were no longer able to support the great weight of the once proud and powerful limo. Avoiding each hole in the road caused the body to yaw widely as if it were disconnected from its wheels. "Feels like I'm back riding a camel," said the Mullah. Both men laughed heartily.

Both were trying hard to believe that this one last ploy would work.

Earlier in the week, while Leon was buying gas in Deir el Qamar, his COMSAT phone rang. Only three people had the number: his wife Nana, his partner Mullah Rockmani and his banker, Soliman Biheiri.

Leon answered his private line in Arabic: "*Al Wakt Min Dhihab.*" (Time is gold.)

Soliman Biheiri responded in kind. "*Al Hubb A3ma.*" (Love is blind). It was a code phrase the two of them had enjoyed for many years.

"Ah Soliman," said Leon, "How is my money?"

"I'm given to understand that you've recently spent a large pile of it."

Leon was immediately on guard. A beat passed before he ventured a response. "And tell me, Soli my old friend, how would you have come by such information?"

"Because I know what you bought with it, Leon."

None of the Jihad's dealings was ever made public, not even to their banker. Leon, always the cautious owl, waited for Biheiri to continue.

"Don't worry, Leon, we're all on the same side here. Do you know of a Doctor A.Q. Khan?"

"Yes, I've heard of the man," said Leon, still unwilling to commit to anything. Everyone in the Middle East knew the black market exploits of the infamous A.Q. Khan. It was rumored that Doctor Khan was putting together a deal between China and Iran to build a uranium hexafluoride plant in Isfahan.

"Well I've just spoken with him at his guesthouse in Dubai. And I transferred your 600 into his account."

Leon couldn't believe his ears. He stood by the side of his Mercedes, hanging on each syllable of his banker's explanation.

When Biheiri finished speaking, Leon disconnected the line, let out a great shout of glee, pumped his fist and leapt in the air. When his feet hit the ground, he slipped on an oil spot and landed flat on his buttocks.

The station manager panicked. Dropping the cash he'd been tallying, he rushed out of his office toward his wealthy customer. When he rounded the front of the Mercedes, he found Doctor de Kennesy sitting in the oil spot, laughing wildly, the cell phone still pressed to his ear.

"Are you hurt, Doctor? Should I call someone?" asked the frightened merchant.

"Never been better," shouted Leon. When helped to his feet, Doctor Leon pressed a wad of cash into the attendant's hand. "Get this oil cleaned up, Ali, someone might sue you."

Leon roared at his own joke and leapt into his Mercedes. As he pulled out of the station, he hit his automatic dialer.

"Allah be praised," he began, "It's happened, holy one."

"What's happened, Leon? Are you all right?" Mullah Rockmani was not used to hearing such robust happiness from his partner.

"Ahmed. Your cousin! He did it. Allah be praised. We now own a 700-pound drum of magic. We don't have to ship it from Canada or Ulster. We don't have to pay anyone to steal it. We don't have to bury it in a shipment of auto parts and sneak it in. That's because it's already there! In the belly of the beast."

"But how?"

"Ahmed, my brother, our 700 pounds is sitting safely in a warehouse in a place I'll identify when we're not on the phone. It was delivered by none other than Doctor A.Q. Khan. It's waiting to be sampled for viscosity; he's guaranteed it. It's waiting for us to sign off on it. It's waiting to be formed into chunks of malleable dough and shoved up the asshole of the Jew-loving American pig bastards."

Phase Three of the Silent Jihad had finally coalesced. Seven hundred pounds of C4 explosive was enough to accomplish all of the planned attacks – and then some. It was sitting in a warehouse in Houston, Texas. Only two pieces of the puzzle remained; install the explosives, and detonate the blasts.

Farad Aziz was the fulcrum.

Tal at Musa, Syria

Farad peeked through a crack in the brick wall of his workshop. The first of three limos stopped 100 yards away, turned across the center of the road, and shut off its engine. Six black-robed men stepped from the car and stationed themselves behind rocks and pine trees to watch for intruders.

The second car parked near the entrance. Its holy men spilled out and quickly formed a rough perimeter at random points around the building; each man withdrew his weapon, disengaged the safety, checked the magazine and began a very intense vigilance.

Doctor Leon and Mullah Rockmani stepped out of the brown Mercedes as if they were royalty and walked toward the old brick building. When they pushed through shop's old wooden gate they found Farad Aziz seated comfortably in the barn's main room at the head of his huge work table. Steaming iron teapots and bowls of fruit had been placed across from him, in front of the chairs they would occupy.

"Welcome, my brothers," said Farad. "Come in, warm your hands and your stomachs. The coffee is from my neighbor's bush. It's the finest I've ever tasted. You've come a long way."

They poured thick Turkish coffee and made small talk. The room smelled of burnt gun powder, wet straw and sweet apples. The Mullah's breath made puffs of steam in the cold air as he told of embedding the Level 3s in America, but his telling seemed to lack its prior verve.

Farad's right hand remained beneath the table, his fingers trembling just inches from the butt of his shotgun.

Next it was Leon's turn. To the real purpose of the meeting. "Gentlemen, it's time. It's taken us 10 years. And now it's time." He turned to Farad, his face exuding the pseudo-sincerity that was his art form. "Farad," he smiled, "We have had our differences, most of them catalyzed by the heat of battle. I have never had the occasion to tell you how important you are to our Jihad. Perhaps what I am about to share with you will change some of the past."

Leon withdrew a flat leather case from his coat pocket and placed it on the table before him. Farad could see the name *Ralph Lauren* etched deeply into the chocolate brown suede. "First of all, as you know, I myself have bought a house in Los Angeles. My wife and I are living there now. I need to be close to oversee the final phase of our plans."

He pushed the leather case across to Farad. "This is your passport, Farad. I can tell you now that I have rented you an office in the JP Morgan Chase Tower, in downtown Houston, Texas. It will give you a valid reason for spending time in the building you're going to obliterate."

An ugly smile cut through Leon's perfectly manicured beard at the thought of destroying the Morgan Chase Tower. He savored the moment and continued. "I have also rented you a home across the bridge in La Porte. You will take up residence there to supervise the distribution, installation and the detonation of all explosive events in America.

"Our Russian friend Ruslan, will have some additional papers waiting for you at Sultanatabad, some personal effects, a Blackberry, a secure cell phone, and the rest of your support documents. They'll be ready for you on Friday."

Farad was speechless. Leon had always treated him like a blue collar flunky. His hatred for the man was boundless. And now this.

The Mullah spoke next. "Farad, you are essential to this operation. I'm saying it again – *essential.* And you have been since the start. Both Leon and myself are in complete agreement about this. From this point on, we feel that the Jihad cannot succeed without you. So, it is important that you understand this. Every detail of your itinerary to the United States has been carefully worked and reworked and reworked."

The Mullah looked at Leon; the rubber stamp of his religious authority having been applied, it was time, once again, for Leon to tighten the nuts and bolts.

Leon picked up the strand. "Your itinerary will include numerous border crossings; Lebanon, Iran, across the border at Tayebad, to Afghanistan, on to West Germany, England, and into Canada. Some of the layovers and changes of documents are probably going to seem unnecessary to you. You're going think it's overkill. But let me assure you, everything we have learned getting 49 of our people into the States is being used to insure your safe arrival.

"Finally, there will not be another Level 3 trainee sent from Talib to join the fifth and final cell, because its leader is going to be you. In addition to your overall demolition responsibilities, you'll also be heading up the final cell yourself. You will already know some of the *amAtya* members, so it should fall into place for you."

Farad was overwhelmed. In his life, he had never imagined that he would ever leave Syria. And certainly never be promoted to any position of real power by the two men sitting opposite him.

They all heard the noise at the same time. It seemed to have come from behind a tall shelf heavy with tools and rusty containers. It sounded like a stifled cough.

"Who's there!" shouted Farad. In one motion, he turned toward the noise behind him, pulled his shotgun from its hidden sheath and fired. Knowing it would be one of the Mullah's nosey guards, he aimed the blast at the top of the shelf, hoping some of the pellets would catch the phony bastard in his turban.

"Stop, Farad stop. It's me!" A tiny voice. Then a rustling of debris and a frightened Nuriyah crawled out from behind the fallen shelving, her hands bleeding from the broken glass and shredded metal of the gun blast.

"Nuriyah," shouted Farad. "I told you to leave..."

"Who is it?" growled Rockmani.

"It's Nuriyah," said Farad, and he went to her.

"Who is she, and why is she spying on us?"

Farad helped the girl onto a stool and began wiping the blood from her hands. "She's my assistant, Nuriyah. She's no spy."

"I'm his lover," said Nuriyah defiantly.

The doors at opposite ends of the room banged open and two of the Mullah's bodyguards charged in, their weapons drawn. They closed quickly on Nuriyah, gun barrels pointed at her head.

"Stop," ordered the Mullah. "I'm safe. Put away your guns. I'm safe, there's no harm here." The bodyguards did as they were told. And the Mullah walked to Nuriyah; the force of his physical proximity causing Farad to step back.

"Child," said the Mullah, "If you love this man, why have you disobeyed him?"

Her answer was just a whisper. "You, holy one."

He waited calmly for her explanation.

"Farad has told me. I swear my life to Allah, to this holy Jihad. I thought only to kneel before you. I prayed I might touch your robe, holiness.."

"Sworn your life?" repeated the Mullah.

She knelt and pressed her forehead to the earth. "Yes, holiness." The Mullah's eyes moved slowly from Leon to the guards and back to the prone figure of Nuriyah. For a moment he remained in deep contemplation. *She could not know that voicing such a vow in front of a Mullah is a petition for martyrdom?* His eyes rose to meet Farad's.

The blood had drained from Farad's temples. His face was ashen.

In such matters, the Mullah's word was law; a holy rubric, a custom which could not be altered. No one was allowed to speak. The Mullah would issue a blessing on the supplicant to signify his acceptance of her as a martyr in the name of Allah. All of the men in the room understood the implications. Farad's face had frozen in despair, knowing the girl would be taken from him.

They awaited the Mullah's fateful resolution, a cold silence hovering among them. At last, the Mullah spoke, his eyes locked with Farad's. "May Al-Muhaymin guide you safely on your journey, Farad." And without another word, the Mullah pulled his robes around him against the cold and walked from the room. The others followed; except Farad, who collapsed to the floor, his arms closing around his spared Nuriyah.

Late into the night, Farad would lie in bed with Nuriyah, puzzled by his sudden good fortune. Rockmani must truly hold him in high esteem to have spared his woman. Such an act of kindness was unprecedented. He grateful to the Mullah for his mercy, vowing silently to carry out his duties in America with renewed respect and responsibility.

The tobacco brown Mercedes eased onto a paved section of the mountain road and increased its speed. It was 50 minutes after the meeting had ended. Mullah Rockmani put aside his prayer beads and reached for the limo's tarnished microphone. A bodyguard in the right front seat pushed harder against his earpiece and began writing the Mullah's orders.

"The girl's full name is Nuriyah Saleh. Have her brought to Talib on Friday night. Hold her there in comfort towards the day when she will make her beautiful and most holy sacrifice. *Al-Muhsi* (Allah the Accounter)."

27

Zurich, Switzerland

Luke Towne flew in to Zurich, drove down the Autobahn to St. Gallen and then into Heerbrugg, where he was welcomed by the chief engineer at Leica Geosystems. He was there to supervise a test of the Mind's Eye prototype Meniscus lens Leica was manufacturing for him. The lens was a multi-layered sandwich of glass and hydrogen that was both concave and convex, and required tolerances so critical that no other company except the venerable German camera giant had even come close.

It only took five minutes for Luke to discover a critical flaw in Leica's current version. It was a great disappointment and Luke's displeasure showed clearly on his face. "How could you have me fly all the way over here and still have a leak in the hydrogen seals? That's the simplest part of the whole assembly and it's the easiest to check! I'm paying you 2½ million dollars for this. The seals are only worth 20 bucks!" He was shouting at the humiliated project manager.

"I'm so sorry, Colonel. It's inexcusable. It was stupid of me to have missed it. And to have caused you this trip...I don't know what to say. If we bring in an overtime crew, I believe we could have a new assembly for you in three days. Would that help any?"

Luke's countenance immediately changed. "Thank you Ernst. That would be good. That would be very helpful. The problem is I'm <u>way</u> behind on this one. We're supposed to deliver a working system in 60 days. And we haven't even tested the damn thing yet. And we can't test without the new lens.

"I have something to get done in Paris. I can be back here in three days if you can have it by then."

The project manager, Ernst Gezy, let out a great sigh of relief and eagerly took Luke's proffered handshake. "Thank you, Colonel; thank you so much. I'll have it for you on Friday morning."

Luke turned west on Heinrich Wild Strasse and set out for the Zurich Airport. One hour and 20 minutes later he'd be in

Paris. He was on a mission. And, as with most endeavors in Luke's life, failure was not an option. The car bomb incident in Beirut had sounded a frightening klaxon in his head. He could have lost her.

Kathryn was already in the Hibiscus Suite, waiting in bed when Luke came through the door; and this time he remembered to bring the flowers; white peonies and fracas. He set the fragrant bouquet down on the bed. Their embrace went on and on, neither one wanting to let the other go. Finally he pulled loose and handed her the flowers with the little rectangular silver box attached.

"What a cute little box. I'll bet it's potpourri," she said sniffing at it. She untied the ribbon and unwrapped the box. Inside the first box was a second smaller box. A Tiffany box.

The ring inside it was magnificent. She was taken completely off guard. She closed the box softly and looked away, her eyes pooling thick with tears.

This was not part of the plan.

She couldn't speak. She swallowed hard several times, stopped by the noisy battle of thoughts in her head. There were words to say, but she didn't know which ones to choose. Her thoughts were overpowering. *This isn't supposed to happen. I don't want to marry anyone! Too soon. No weddings.* She felt cold knives stabbing at her temples.

Luke's eyes were filled with promise, the suggestion of a smile waiting on his lips, his heart willing her to say 'yes.'

He has no idea why I'm with him.

She opened the box again. The ring was breathtaking; cast in Georgian gold, a magnificent center stone of Lapis Lazuli with four emerald cut diamonds set in a blazing perimeter. The art of it was that the blue, asscher cut stone appeared to be floating above a sea of radiant white.

To find a Lapis stone that matched her flawless eyes had cost a great deal of money. Luke's little Malibu house had been mortgaged in the process. In his mind, the ring was unique as the woman who was to wear it; an opus to her eyes.

The tears flowed down her face. When she could finally speak, she said, "But Luke, it's so soon. There're things about me..." Her words trailed off. A surge of fear tightened her face and compressed her lips into a trembling line. "Luke I love you. More than you could know. More than I ever thought.

But...there are things. You could never understand. Things I can't tell you."

Blind to it all, Luke saw no fear in her; only beauty and the power of his own intentions. "I love everything about you. What I don't know, I don't care about."

He took her hand and slipped on the ring. "Our future together; that's all I care about. Will you marry me Kathryn de Kennesy?"

She buried her face in his chest, terrified by what she was feeling. Her loyalty to her father was clear. Unbreakable. The plan, the path, the battle of cultures – fundamental. Inherited strife, centuries of angers had been carefully ground into her pores.

The enemy so close, and the cruelty of his culture so alien to her own.

The thought of marrying Luke Towne was unfathomable. Her breath came in little gulps. Yet the same thought was intoxicating, narcotic in its power; forbidden and therefore overwhelming. She could feel her eyes growing large like a child's at Christmas. She put her hand down on the bed to steady herself as if she were losing her balance.

The lights seemed to blur. She looked into his eyes, hardly able to contain herself, stunned by her own words. "Yes," she whispered. "Yes Luke."

Then she lay down in his arms, perfectly still, and set her mind adrift in complete surrender to the answer she'd given. Their love making began without the usual urgency of separation, rather, a gentle slowness as if time ceased. As if there were no one else in the world. No fear. No thoughts of the future. Just now; an all encompassing now.

The vulnerability she had feared for so long had now become the source of all pleasure and joy. She had never dared risk losing her heart to a man.

"Lukie," she said, exhausted, "This has never happened before."

"With an old guy?" he grinned.

"With anyone."

He could see that she was serious; deeply so. He cradled her face in his hands, she laid her cheek on his shoulder and pressed herself into him.

They fell into a blissful sleep.

An hour passed. Kathryn was sitting back against the pile of down-filled shams and crisp white pillows, naked to the waist, sipping Crystal from a long-stemmed glass. Luke was lying on his side in the bed facing away from her, dozing in the warm half-sleep of post love making.

Her question was tentative; almost inaudible. "Lukie, what's the Mind's Eye?"

"Huh?" he answered, half awake.

"The Mind's Eye, honey. You said it in your sleep."

"I did?"

"You did."

His response was slow in coming. "Work. You know, government thing."

"I know." She paused; then chewed on her lower lip; then added quietly, "But I don't know, really."

He rolled over and raised his head, supporting it on one arm, a warm smile building. "Look at you, sitting there naked; a little trickle of champagne on your breast; your beautiful nipples starting to harden right in front of me. And you wanna talk science?"

She blushed deeply, set down her glass and tugged the sheet up to her neck. Embarrassed. "No!" she announced firmly. "I mean, you know, not now, I mean some time when you feel like talking about it. I'd just like to know, you know, what you're...anyway, never mind, you probably can't tell me about it anyway. It's okay."

Luke persisted. "But wait a minute. Is something bothering you?"

"No, no, it's nothing; just a little problem I have sometimes. The male side of my brain starts working at the wrong time. I'm sorry. My dad used to kid me about it; said I played sports like a guy; thought like a guy. If I wasn't careful, I'd grow up and look like one."

"Right," said Luke facetiously.

"Honey just forget I said anything, okay? Just stupid girl stuff."

"Wait. Nothing's stupid. You're my wife...almost."

They both smiled at the sound of it. He paused happily, then pressed on with his train of thought. "Listen, no secrets ever, okay. Anything you want to know, anything, just ask. That's the deal."

"I just thought it'd be nice, you know, to know what my husband does every day. Unless of course, you want a dumb broad for a wife."

"Sex and submission. That's all I want out of this deal. You know that. Dress up nice. Cook food. And screw. That's it for me. A man of simple taste."

She stared at him, suppressing a smile.

"Ain't that what I'm gettin'?" he asked.

"You're gettin' champagne on the head in a minute."

"So ask. What would you want to know about?"

"I don't know... .whatever. The Mind's Eye. What's that?"

And so he told her. In a few paragraphs, he told her the essence of the Pentagon's most highly classified National Defense project. He told her in great detail about the positive byproducts of its ocular discoveries. And he told her the revolutionary advantage it would afford U.S. Top Guns, and the powerful destructive weaponry that went with it.

And the six digital cameras installed in the Hibiscus Suite by Major Pete Gideon sent it all directly to Washington and straight on to the desktop of General Orin Pierce.

Part II

28

Houston, Texas – JP Morgan Chase Tower

Farad Aziz looked out through the tinted windows of his 64th floor office in the landmark Chase Tower. Elbows resting on his teak desk, he could see across the bridge toward his two-bedroom house in La Porte. *Amazing!*

He had followed their instructions to the letter – the clothes, carry-ons, glasses, hair dye, magazines, smiles – everything *exactly* as instructed. Lebanon, Iran, across the border at Tayebad, into Afghanistan, on to West Germany, to Canada, then the landing at Hobby Airport, Houston, Texas. All of it had gone off without a hitch.

And here he was in Texas; beardless, wearing his American clothes, maneuvering into his underground parking slot each day, trying to look like he fit in. Of course, he would never fit in with these shiny-boot cowboys, who stunk of perfume and talked incessantly of sex and sports. He was repulsed by their women, whores who paraded the clubs and streets half-naked, blatantly offering themselves to anyone who'd buy them a meal of burned beef and barbeque sauce.

Americans are pigs. He could not stand to walk among them. But he could keep his eyes down, he could ride the elevator up to this vacant office in the sky, and he could pray to Al-Qahhar (The Subduer). *Make me your instrument. Let me end their blasphemy. Let me send them to Satan in a white ball of fire.*

He thought of the days to come. He would command each of the five cells. He would lay out the plans. He would carry the C4 with him. He would supervise its placement. He would set the fuses. He would...

Sitting alone in his furnished office, his brain began to bounce, pinging back and forth like a pin ball. He tried to shift his focus – back to a happier time. *Farad and Ahmad. The twins. Their band, Purple. Farad, holding a stolen soap on a rope, pretending it was a real microphone, hitting the high notes. Rock stars. Fame. His young voice soaring. CRASH. The sudden explosion that changed his life.*

He had tried to block the ugly image. But he couldn't. It always flashed in his head, ending the sweet remembrance.

He could feel it now, the hot steel mass ripping into his throat. Pain, smashing against the backs of his eyes.

Then came the odd dizziness. The disorientation. It was happening again. But this time he recognized the signs a little earlier. Rising angers, his throat closing – the onset of a seizure. He immediately gulped two more of the tiny white pills Doctor Leon had prescribed.

Leon, the smug bastard. Leon's got all the power, all the answers. Be careful! He knew that sometimes just thinking about the prick could overpower the effectiveness of the pills. *Relax. Float with it. Wait. Wait. Relief is on its way. One day the pain will have its purpose. One day soon, the glory will come. They'll write about me. Farad Aziz the one who made the bombs. The one who brought the American Jew-lovers to their bloody knees.*

Then at last, he felt the *whoosh,* a giant internal hand pushing down on the pain, covering it over, evening things out. Everything gone *smooth* again.

"Thanks be to Allah for the goddamn white pills," he whispered. "Ar-Rahim." (The Merciful.)

Farad Aziz sat in his ill-fitting Hugo Boss business suit, staring out of the 64th floor windows, waiting on destiny, waiting for Leon to call.

The Facility – Malibu, California

The sun was bright, the air pure, the visibility extreme. It was Monday morning. Luke had come in early, pushed through some paper work, and by 8 a.m. he was ready to get his hands dirty. Looking out his office window, he could see miles of cambered shore break all the way north to Trancas. He stared at a couple of Lidos dancing around the distant buoys at Zuma and his mind momentarily unhooked from the present. He thought back to the weekend. She was never out of his thoughts.

They had spent Saturday night and late Sunday on Mount Tamalpais in a tiny rental cabin. Luke and Kat, so content in each other's company, an old couple sharing a past they'd never had time to enjoy. *Amazing.* The power of their connection.

Luke walked out on the balcony and drew in a slow breath of appreciation. The wind was sweet. The world was full of possibilities. He watched a pair of golden eagles working on their nest in the top of a neighboring oak. There were three, brown-spotted eggs in the strongly woven basket the birds had formed together. The huge predatory creatures were unbelievably gentle with each other, their mutual respect seeming to blossom as the arrival of their eaglets drew near.

It was a privilege to watch them.

Luke heard a distant burst of static on his intercom. It was the voice of Dave Halter, his assistant: "Doc, you have a call from D.C., a Brigadier General Pierce."

Luke had never heard the name but he recognized the caller ID as authentic Pentagon. "This is Doctor Towne."

"Colonel Towne, this is Brigadier General Orin Pierce. I have a message for you. Singularity is calling."

The words hit Luke like a cement truck. *This can't be happening. Code words from a total stranger?* The effect was overwhelming. A five-second pause before Luke responded with the answer he'd memorized long ago: "T equals Zero. No one left standing."

The voice on the phone said, "Civilian dress; no I.D.; 1200 hours; number four South Beach Road. Auto pick up." The words were clipped.

"Message understood." Luke answered like the soldier he'd been most of his life.

The phone went dead. He sat motionless, the receiver still in his hand. The code words just exchanged were known only to a very exclusive group of Rangers. To his knowledge only four of them were still alive. And Brigadier General Pierce was not one of them. The words were created by his CO in a red mud cave in Kandahar, Afghanistan. It was a call to arms, to be used only under circumstances of life and death; to be answered without fail. A pledge to serve made only among the military elite. Nothing more sacred. Not family, not self, not faith in God. To these unique warriors, nothing would stand before service to country.

Luke had chosen to put down his weapons long ago. He had turned his considerable skills to science and technology in the service of country.

What the hell does this mean?

"Dave, would you have a car downstairs in 10 minutes, please. You're driving." It would take Luke only 10 minutes to complete his immediate task. Old routines were ingrained.

It was a procedure he'd developed in younger days. Before undertaking any Special Ops mission, he had been taught to put his affairs in order. He had no family left. He had already given everything he owned to his ex-wife when he left the service. His only possessions of value were some of the patents he held on the laser technologies he had pioneered. It only took 10 minutes to enumerate them and indicate the sole benefactor, Kathryn de Kennesy.

He placed the single page in an envelope embossed with The Facility logo, sealed it and placed it in his top drawer.

"Where to Doc?" asked Dave, as they pulled out on to Pacific Coast Highway.

"Let me off at the Starbucks, Dave, I feel like walking." It was strictly a military precaution. *Security measures.*

He walked the remaining distance to number four South Beach Road; the Chanticleer. He took a single table outside the restaurant facing the street and ordered a double espresso. Before the waiter returned to set the cup and saucer on the little table, the unmarked car had arrived and Colonel Towne was driven away. The shot of energy he had hoped to get from the thick Italian coffee was unnecessary. What was about to happen to him would provide enough adrenaline to last him several years.

The driver of the unmarked Buick handed a brown envelope back to Luke and never once looked in the rear view mirror. Inside the envelope was a wallet containing a new set of identification documents: credit cards, a laminated social security card and a driver's license with a current picture of Luke. All of the documents were under the name "G. Kennedy of Austin Texas."

Why do I need a fake ID?

The Huey helicopter moved directly out over the U.S. Carrier Henderson, which had dropped anchor in open sea just outside the U.S. Naval Yard at Point Hueneme. The sea below them was the color of dish water, somewhere between brackish green and dirt brown.

Luke hadn't been in a Huey since his last combat mission, bringing American military expertise to the beleaguered Mujahedeen mountain fighters – fighting the Russians.

How quickly the world changes.

The adrenaline pump that came before going into such combat had always been addictive for Luke, but the feeling in the pit of his stomach at this moment was just the opposite.

He jumped down onto the huge gray floating city that was the Henderson and immediately came face to face with the first lieutenant in charge of the flight deck. There was no salute. None of the customary protocol afforded military personnel.

"Welcome aboard, Mr. Kennedy," said the lieutenant, referencing the new I.D. in Luke's pocket.

"Thank you Lieutenant."

"If you'd follow me, sir, your meeting is set for 0200 in officer's state room A on the fourth deck."

There was no wind at sea. No sound on deck. Just an eerie flat silence everywhere as they moved smartly across the vast flight deck. Although he knew it was ridiculous, Luke was unable to quell the feeling that every sailor's eye was on him, that the officers were watching him from the windows in the con high above the deck.

What possibly can this be about? Certainly not a call to arms at this stage of my life, he thought. Although that was the intended purpose of the code words he'd spoken on the phone.

And who the hell is Brigadier General Orin Pierce? Perhaps it's my topographical knowledge of the Afghan highlands they're after.

They had descended four decks and Luke was now sitting alone at one end of a large officer's meeting room with a filled cup of coffee steaming on the table in front of him. Pristine; clean; antiseptic; functional -- the innards of every Navy vessel in the U.S. Fleet.

This has nothing to do with topographies in Afghanistan.

A knock at the bulkhead door broke the silence; then total shock, as General Malcolm Diggs stepped into the cabin. Luke's Special Ops commander approached with his hand extended.

"Luke, it's great to see you."

They pulled each other into an embrace of friendship reaching back 15 years into Luke's illustrious military career. General Malcolm Diggs was a legend in his own right, but in recognition of Luke's valor in battle, the general himself had made Luke one of the most decorated Rangers in the history of the Corps. They both stepped back for another look at each other. Luke was unsure and only half kidding when he asked, "We goin' back to work, General?"

"God I hope not," said the general with a warm smile. "Let's sit."

They took chairs opposite each other across the table. Diggs got right to the point. "Luke, you were the finest soldier who ever served in my command. I'll cut straight to the bottom of this. The only reason I'm here is to deliver this to you personally." He withdrew a sealed communiqué in a white envelope and passed it across to Luke.

"I have no idea what's inside. I only know it came from a very high level with a priority code higher than anyone I've seen since Nam." He exhaled deeply and continued. "I suspect they brought me out here to demonstrate some sort of...faith, or good will, or some such..."

He left his sentence unfinished and just stared into the eyes of his best soldier. No more needed to be said. The two seasoned veterans knew the significance of a general's visit. Extremely serious and most likely bad news.

They also knew the strict protocol for this sort of meeting. It was now over. They both pulled out their chairs and acknowledged the end of communication with a respectful salute. They shook hands. And before letting go of Luke's hand, the general stared into Luke's eyes with as much understanding and support as he could bring to bear nonverbally.

"If you ever need..." His eyes said the rest. He pulled the cabin door quietly shut as he left.

Luke now understood a small part of the mystery. No one on the carrier was to know who he was or why he was there. Not even the ship's captain. The communiqué was intended for his eyes only. It had all been planned with great care. Right down to the code words; and the final touch, the involvement of the one man he respected above all others in the Corps, General Diggs.

He knew he would not be disturbed. He was being left alone to read. He peeled open the clear wax seal and removed the contents of the envelope. It was a single sheet of stationery. The raised letters across the top of the page read: "United States of America. Office of the President." Luke's eyes shot to the bottom of the page and found the signature: "President Rundle Crowley."

Luke took in a slow deep breath of air. He exhaled very slowly and then began to read.

Dear Colonel Towne,

Only a matter of national security and of grave personal concern to me could have caused me to interrupt your life in this manner. You have served your country well and valiantly. The Medal of Honor I bestowed on you myself will attest to my sincerity.

You have not been chosen at random, but specifically because of your history, your loyalty, the special skills you possess, and your high profile reputation in the scientific community. I am ordering you to return to duty as a member of my personal Special Operations Unit under the direct command of Brigadier General Orin Pierce.

Luke knew about this group. They were considered invisible. Their efforts were permanently "off the books." They were granted complete autonomy and authority above all government agencies. Mercenaries. They reported only to the President. Luke continued reading the President's letter.

Colonel Towne, as you know, there are terrorist cells currently operating within the United States. We believe that some of them, notably al Qaeda, have probably had sleeper cells operating here since the mid '80s. Through their numerous business, religious and international charitable fronts, they are planning to finance violent operations against us. The names of most of these murders are known to us: Hamas, Hezbollah, Bin Laden, Al-Qaeda, Fattah, even Al Aqsa Martyrs Brigades.

However, a new group of these murders has come to our attention, a unknown Jihad, backed by the central figures in some of the other terrorist organizations. Our intelligence agencies believe this group has immediate plans to move explosive materials across our Southern borders in order to launch terrorist attacks against our citizens. In addition, we believe they could already have operatives in several of our cities planning to bomb major structures.

You are being called to active duty with a specific role; to infiltrate this nameless terrorist organization at the highest level possible. Your mission is to discover their plans and sources, and relay all relevant information to your control, Brigadier General Orin Pierce. At this moment, you have a vital and compelling opportunity to serve your country.

We have incontrovertible evidence that certain of this group's prime movers are well known to you; they are

Doctor Leon de Kennesy – a Frenchman of Moroccan decent, his wife Nanette Lahoud – a French Lebanese, and their daughter Kathryn de Kennesy.

Nooooooooooo! God, please. It's a dream!

Luke woke up screaming, in a bath of perspiration. It was still dark. He reached for the light on his nightstand and saw the wallet, his picture and the name "G. Kennedy." Next to it, the white envelope that had contained a letter from the President. A letter which he had burned before leaving the officer's conference room on the U.S. Carrier Henderson.

God help me it isn't a dream.

29

Malibu Colony, California

The coast line from Malibu north to Trancas is three times more exclusive than any other stretch of sand in California. There's no public access, all beaches are fenced, all require a key to gain entrance. But once your toes hit the sand, no one bothers you; it's part of the unspoken membership rules.

Luke's rage was so extreme he walked the shore break for more than an hour before looking up to see where he was. It was getting dark, the beach houses were unfamiliar; he had no idea how far he'd gone. His head was full of snakes.

The instant the government Huey dropped him at San Pedro, he called Kathryn, hoping the sound of her voice could somehow bring a touch of sanity back to his life. But she was unreachable. He had suppressed the desire to dump the whole thing on Cynthia. She already had enough on her plate. He would handle this himself.

Kathryn's a terrorist. My fiancé. What bullshit!

The whole thing was so preposterous. No evidence. No proof cited. The President had simply stated that Luke's loved ones were evil Muslim fanatics bent on slaughtering innocent Americans. And then, unthinkably, ordered Luke to prove it.

Unbelievable. A 50-year-old scientist in the prime of his career, back in the Army again? The Commander in Chief of the United States of America. Thank you Mr. President.

What a shortsighted moron.

At the bottom of the page, scribbled in the President's own hand, there was a "Thank you" in advance. Luke's cooperation was taken completely for granted. No opportunity to think it over for 24 hours and then do the right thing. The message was clear; unequivocal. You have no other choice. It was pure conscription; illegal; philosophically immoral; criminal.

It's a goddamn draft notice!

Supposedly, Luke had been trained to deal with the unexpected. It was his specialty. Twenty years of experience. Yet there was fear in his chest. An unfamiliar emotion. Something beyond his control; beyond the cinctures of military thought. For the first time in his life, he felt a resistance to serve. And he recognized it for what it was; a dangerous assailant in the life of a soldier.

It's why they take you when you're young, when you don't know better. Old men don't march off to war headlong and risk it all. Old men know there's more to life than drums and guns.

In the words of Luke's vaunted teachers at Bragg and Benning: "Vulnerability makes bad soldiering."

They were right.

These government bastards had found his vulnerability and set out to exploit it. It seemed his mentors had suddenly become his enemies. His response was a deep blinding anger.

The timing of this was unfathomable. The President had put him in an impossible situation. He was supposed to be inside The Facility overseeing the installation of the primary cannon brackets in the nose of the F18. There were 12 men in the A-Lab at the moment working on the welding, bolting and balancing of the equipment platforms. His presence was essential.

Simultaneously, the dimwitted President of the United States had given him new orders. Reenlist in the Military, turn traitor to his fiancée, and begin spying on the generous and loving family who had accepted him as a second son.

The Facility - Malibu, California

Five minutes after arriving at the A-Lab, he'd been unable to focus on anything but the President's letter and the kudzu it was making of his organized life. After a brief check on the installation progress in the A-Lab, he'd sought the serenity of some fresh air.

Luke stood on the hill above his office, trying to clear his head. The Malibu sun was unusually hot. It baked the lush pink bougainvillea into trails of florescence running down both sides of the canyon. Its shimmering pink tint was so intense it seemed to possess a heat all its own.

Wiping the perspiration from his eyes, he realized how exhausted he was. He hadn't been able to sleep a decent hour since receiving the President's letter. He went back into his office and stretched out on the couch. He closed his eyes and forced his mind to be still. Slowly the intense fatigue began to loosen his body.

And then, in that empty space between consciousness and dreams, came a moment of clarity. The Military had spent 20+ years training him to be a first-rate officer. Once an order was given by a superior, his job was not to question; his job was to execute. Put your shoulder to the wheel. No matter how great the load, shut up and make it roll.

Mr. President.

Colonel Luke Towne reporting for active duty as ordered. Please advise as to time and location of reactivation and briefing. It's an honor to serve.

Sincerely
Colonel Lukas Towne (ret.)

He emailed the short response to a coded switching facility in Tampa. From there it was checked, encoded and shuttled to another inspection facility; and, after it had been judged 'credible,' it was sent on to the White House basement.

Mission accomplished.

Luke fell back onto the couch and closed his eyes. *I wonder if I can trick my 50-year-old body one more time into believing this gung ho military crap?*

The Basement – Washington, D.C.

Orin Pierce already knew what Luke's response would be. "Perfect," he mused as he read Luke's email of acceptance. "Heed the call, soldier boy; duty first. That's what I like in a grunt; subservience."

This stooge is just like the rest of them; Special Forces, Rangers, whatever... peel off the medals and they're all made the same. Wind up robots. Use once and discard.

As usual, Pierce was prepared. Ever since Kathryn de Kennesy had suddenly appeared on the arm of the Army's most prized scientist, Pierce had ordered his teams of strategists and mathematicians to begin working on Luke Towne's files – mapping probabilities. What if the woman is a spy? What's the optimal play? How could we turn this to our advantage? The Goal is to identify who's behind her. How can we use Towne as bait?

Predicting Luke Towne's response was easy. But using Towne as bait was a highly sophisticated and daunting task. Predicting the enemy's response to that bait would require all of the resources at Pierce's command. Could they possibly convince the enemy that the colonel had defected? Would the terrorists let him in? Would they see Luke's defection as a gift from Allah? A divine intervention? Or would they recognize the ploy for what it was and simply kill him? Was it worth risking the life of a valuable laser scientist to penetrate a hidden network of terrorists and insure another four years of job security?

Absolutely.

The first step required a re-draft of Luke's venerable record of service. "Make him into a traitor," ordered Pierce. "I want anyone reading the colonel's bio to find a psychological train wreck. Deep seeded problems. Give him a new history. I want an ugly past. I want a set of circumstances that could lead him to turn against his country. And I want it believable!!"

Pierce was addressing his hand-picked team of strategists, an eclectic bunch he'd named The Disinformation Team. He loved calling them the DTs; the symbolic notion that he could inflict the DTs upon others added humor to his genius, or so he felt; although in four decades no one had ever heard him make a joke, nor ever laugh at one.

The Office of Disinformation

In designing their imposter, Pierce and his brain trust were following a time honored formula, 60 years in the making. The concept of 'disinformation' was conceived and perfected during the Second World War at Bletchley Park, England, in 1938.

As the British labored feverishly to break Germany's cipher machine (Enigma), they came upon an ingenious ploy. Led by the brilliant Alan Turing, they created an Office of Disinformation, a secret team of intellectuals whose job it was to provide faulty information to the enemy. The idea was to turn weakness into strength by planting false communiqués, documents and plans at sectors where leaks were most likely to occur, and then permitting the enemy to steal them. The false information was carefully seeded with half truths and bits of accurate revelation to make it believable. Such 'disinformation' forced the Germans into meaningless allocations of manpower and equipment. It led them into a quagmire of misguided, reactive strategies.

The Basement plan was similar. Luke's bio would be the initial document of disinformation. It would establish Luke's credibility as a potential traitor. Additional documents and events would be manufactured based on the enemy's need to know.

The Basement's highly-paid team of strategists, medical doctors, behavioral psychologists, researchers and historians snapped into high gear, working long hours to conjure an appropriate background for a potentially traitorous soldier. Motives were sculpted to suggest deep-rooted turmoil that might lead to defection. New members of Luke's family were fabricated: faithful, hard-working uncles and cousins who'd been grievously wronged by their hateful government bosses.

The career of Luke's famous scientist father was redrafted. Major Luke Towne Senior had actually pioneered a spray-on polymer which, when applied to an aircraft, would absorb ground-based radar signals. Without the expected bounce back, the coated aircraft would register as empty space on an enemy's radar screen, resulting in a virtually invisible aircraft.

In May of 1962, the U2, an American spy plane flown by Gary Powers, was shot down by Soviet munitions. The redrafted record now blamed the senior Towne and his miracle polymer for the loss of the U2. A footnote was added; the faulty polymer had put numerous American flyers at risk. As a result, Luke's scientist father was discharged from the Military and denied his pension.

Childhood traumas were invented for the young Luke; seeds of discontent fermenting in the subconscious; tantrums in little league; recurring issues with authority; peer conflicts, all indicating an ego in need of recognition.

A careful reader of Luke's new biography would recognize a underlying torrent of bitterness, a growing resentment at not being rewarded for his outstanding and diverse accomplishments. Ultimately, his rage would explode in his adult years, understandably directed toward the ungrateful government he'd given his life to.

Once the new bio was completed and approved by Pierce, it would be marked as 'Classified.' The simple red label, stamped on each page, was another Bletchley Park innovation. To any spy worth his clandestine pedigree, classified documents were always perceived to be of highest credibility.

Next, following the same procedure pioneered by the British code breakers, The Basement team would plant the altered files at sectors in the intelligence community believed to be the most vulnerable to theft. Luke's files would be secreted into the country's major intelligence organizations: the Army, the CIA, the FBI and most importantly, the Pentagon.

This specialized job would utilize The Basement's second team, experts at a different brand of stealth, a kind of cat burglary that fell under the catch-all heading of counterterrorism. Their job was the infiltration of our own government. Pierce referred to them as the "Friendly Spies."

"Do the Pentagon first," he ordered, addressing the four men who sat before him in his Basement office. Despite their uncomfortable military bearing, each of the men on the second team was dressed in expensive business attire; Versace suits, Dior ties, Ferragamo shoes. The fashion show was no accident.

"In my 40 years of government service," Pierce had written in his memoirs, "I've never ever seen an enemy agent wearing a decent suit. Apparently it's not in their budget. Such a gross oversight makes them easier for us to spot. It's blatant; ridiculous, but true. And it's an obvious mistake my people will never make."

Throughout his long career, Orin Pierce had been compiling notes and observations about himself, reflections on his ingenuity and his foresight. One day his memoirs would become a best seller.

It took the Friendly Spies just two days to penetrate the Pentagon. It had nothing to do with their haute couture. It had more to do with a pair of very tan legs.

Mrs. Olivia Cantu, tall, saucer-eyed, fair-skinned, Hispanic mother of two, could light up a room with her smile. When she wore one of her daughter's short skirts to work on the third floor of the Pentagon's massive Documents and Storage Department, she ignited wild bedroom fantasies for the 35 males who worked near her section. Should a security guard ask her to stop by for a moment, it wasn't to check her purse, it was to check her body.

It helped that she was an obliging flirt.

April 15th, 2005. It was a rainy day in Washington. Casual Friday at the Pentagon, the nation's high security hub, the fulcrum of military planning and strategy. Olivia wore a tight, leopard skin blouse over a pair of black silk culottes which stopped a scant three inches above her tanned knees. Olivia only wore name brands. She could only afford to buy them as seconds from Ross for Less and TJ Maxx; but nevertheless, she knew how to make it all work.

This day, inside her large, Kenneth Cole, leopard and black, ostrich skin purse, she carried the thick folder of Luke Towne's altered files. Six months of The Basement's finest work.

Her 2½ inch, slightly irregular, strappy Prada heels clicked across the building's hallowed marble vestibule.

"Holy forkin' big ass titty whistle," whispered guard Ornel Swink to his partner Rafael. "Will you look at that?" Both men stared in quiet, wanton, male hornitude.

When Rafael cleared his throat, about to ask Olivia to stop and show him her bag (though it was her legs that were calling out to him), Ornel immediately cut him off. "No man. No," he hissed, "Don't say a word. Don't say a damn word. Just watch. Look at that. Drink it in, dude. Look at that ass; two babies fightin' under a sheet. It's a beautiful thing. Don't spoil it. Don't say a word, man. Don't do nothin."

So they didn't.

And so Olivia Cantu breezed to her desk, straight into Section 10 of the Documents and Storage Department, carrying Luke's new files. She had brought in her own coffee from the Starbucks at 15th and I Street. She added some cinnamon she kept in her desk, and sat there drinking her latte, trying as hard as she could to look normal.

She waited 10 minutes. No one had come to arrest her yet. The usual swarm of male agents had started cruising by her desk, pretending they had something to do, trying not to look obvious as they gawked. But no one seemed interested in her purse or its contents. She took a deep breath, reached into her purse, lifted out Luke's files and carried them over to the document cage. She entered with her pass key and walked casually to the aisle posted "T."

Making sure no else was watching, she located the cabinet and quietly pulled out the appropriate drawer. She already knew exactly where to look because she had practiced her routine several times the previous day. She walked her fingers down the files until she located the tab "Colonel Luke Towne." Checking again, looking left and right, she removed the old documents and replaced them with the newer versions.

She returned to her cubicle and sat down heavily in her chair, shaking uncontrollably. *Act natural.* She began thumbing through the old pages as if she had retrieved them to do some assigned research. No one even looked up. She stood, reached for her purse, and headed down the hall to the ladies room, casually turning on her shredder as she left the cubicle.

Five minutes later she returned to her desk. And while the rest of the Pentagon labored to keep our nation safe, Olivia Cantu began quietly destroying a patriot – three pages at a time.

On the 15th of April, while Terebenev's statue of Blind Justice stood guard in an alcove, a file clerk in Section 10 of the Pentagon's Documents and Storage Department, following orders from the White House Basement, transformed Colonel Luke Towne into a traitorous double agent.

At the end of Olivia's day, when she was home and safely in her garage in Midland Heights, she opened the trunk of her 1997 Honda and removed a laundry bag. She knew what was supposed to be in there, but the Pentagon was hardly the best place to check it out. She had no idea how they had gotten the bag into her trunk, but she didn't really care. Hands trembling, she pulled the drawstring and turned the bag upside down. Tens and twenties and fifties; $20,000 worth of them fell out on to the dirty garage floor.

Later that night she lay tossing in bed.

"They're untraceable, honey," said her husband. "Relax."

"How do we know that?" she said, biting her lower lip.

"Trust me. These guys don't screw around."

There was every reason to believe Joseph Cantu, 6'2", 203 pounds, husband to Olivia and father of their two children. It was because of his job; a position he'd worked very hard at for six years. He was a special bodyguard by trade, assigned to protect a very private group of men. He didn't know their names, but it didn't matter, he knew who they were. And he was prepared to give his life to protect every one of their anonymous faces. He worked in the same building, in the same office they did; the White House Basement.

Joe also knew about an additional perk the Cantus were to receive if Olivia were successful. At the end of the day, when the deed was done, their son's college tuition at BYU would somehow, mysteriously, be marked 'paid in full.'

Joe smiled. He reached for his beautiful young wife and rolled her easily in his heavily muscled arms. He looked down into the dark eyes he'd loved since they were teenagers. "Told you honey, Joey got friends in high places."

Orin Pierce sat confidently in his darkened room, four floors beneath the White House. He had set the wheels in motion the instant Kathryn de Kennesy had entered the picture. She was an agent. He knew it. If this *idiot* Towne could now act the part of an emotionally believable military traitor, the package would be almost impossible for any terrorist network to resist. He was convinced the de Kennesy terrorist group would step forward and take the bait. It didn't matter that they remained 'nameless.' He had them in his trap.

30

Malibu Beach, California

It was 4 a.m. and foggy, 50 miles of mist from El Segundo north to the county line; the sea and sky had woven a heavy blanket of military green and hung it at the water's edge. The world outside was dead calm and desolate. Luke Towne stood in the dense, wet quiet on the deck of his beach house, trying to silence the hurricane of anger raging inside his head.

He'd tried to reach Kat several times; still no response. *Why?*

He'd thrashed about in bed for hours but couldn't turn his head off. Finally, at 4 a.m., he'd given up, gotten up and brewed a pot of coffee. Now he stood on his deck alone in the cold — the perfection of that metaphor making things even worse. Clenching a mug of steaming black in his hands, he paced, trying for the hundredth time to reason his way out of this.

He was not cut out for this kind of work. He knew he was not double agent material and he suspected they knew it also. He had spent 20 years as a soldier. The infantry handbook had no chapters on subtle conversation, or acting, or staging a tea house masquerade. His military life, his training and his experience were about fighting. Killing and winning.

Espionage was a completely different ball game. He didn't know the rules. Not a clue. To Luke, most of it sounded like bullshit. And Luke never bullshit anybody.

He was so caught up in his angers, he didn't hear his cell phone ring the first time. Not until she called again did he finally hear it, and then it took four rings before he picked up. It was his partner, Doctor Cynthia Teller.

"Yeah," he snapped, agitated at the interruption.

"Luke?"

"Yeah?" Still lost in the fog.

"Luke! Hello? We just landed at Langley. I hadn't heard from you. Are you okay?"

"Okay..." he repeated, still not quite returned to the present. Then reality slapped him in the face. *Cynthia has flown to Langley to begin interviewing the Top Guns. I'm staying here to prepare the F18 they're gonna use. What the hell happened to my brain?*

"Sorry, Cyn. Cell died. How was your flight?"

Cynthia knew something was wrong. But she said nothing. They both made a conscious effort to maintain a distance that allowed for personal privacy.

"The flight was smooth as silk," she said.

"Don't let those young hotshots turn your head, Captain."

"Right, 20-year-olds just can't get enough of me. So, isn't it a little early for you to be up?" The way he sounded gave her a bad feeling in the stomach.

"Just the usual work stuff, I guess. Drank a gallon of coffee last night. That could be it. Forget about it. I'm good. I'm fine. Call me tonight when you're through and let me know how it goes."

"Will do. Get your cell fixed." She clicked off.

Although Cynthia had always been able to read him like he was a Jughead comic book, Luke knew this was no time to burden her with in his personal problems. Testing the best fighter pilots in America's First Fighter Wing would require all her considerable skills. His confidence in her was unequivocal. She certainly didn't need a new distraction. He'd work this one out himself. Luke slugged down the rest of his coffee and began searching for his car keys.

Langley Air Force Base, Virginia

It was 88 degrees on the tarmac. Thirty F18 fighter pilots from the 1st Fighter Wing, United States Central Command had taken their seats in front of a lectern on the shaded side of the red brick Air Combat Command building.

These had been handpicked; the best of the best. They were to be tested in five specific areas; the areas that distinguished them as the best pilots in the world – the Top Guns. The tests would measure reaction time, memory capacity, eyesight, hand-eye coordination and depth of concentration. The tests would be conducted by Doctor Cynthia Teller, Luke's partner, and co-founder of the Military's revered Lasocular research laboratory.

The CO of Central Command called them to attention. "Gentlemen, you are about to meet Captain Teller, U.S. Navy. Doctor Teller is the head of neurosurgery at Eisenhower Research Hospital and co-director of The Facility, one of our specialized research units in California. The technologies being developed there are of critical importance to us. Very soon, your lives as pilots may depend on them. Whatever Doctor Teller wants, make sure she gets."

All eyes snapped toward the Air Command building, as the door opened and out stepped Doctor Cynthia Teller. She was 38 years old. She was born an *okay-looking* girl with long legs, a little boy butt and a flat chest. After her divorce, she had decided to treat herself to some long envied cleavage. The upgrade was a decade ago, but to this day she still had a problem with the reaction her new body evoked in men.

She was wearing chocolate Jordan heels and a camel chemise belted at the waist, which served to accentuate her stunning figure. Her auburn hair was tied in the back with a matching Hermes scarf, and her face was shaded by a USN baseball cap with her Captain's insignia on its bill.

Cynthia Teller was a frickin' piece of work.

This was definitely not what they had expected. As she approached the lectern, their initial stunned silence slowly built into a grateful crescendo of cat calls, applause and several "Yeah baby's."

She placed her ultra slim brief case on the lectern and calmly surveyed the group. "Thank you for that...vote of confidence," she quipped, immediately taking the high ground.

"Gentlemen, the 'Mind's Eye' laser response system has been designed specifically for F18 fighter pilots. Its name is classified 'top secret.' Other than the Joint Chiefs of Staff and the President, you are the first humans to even hear its name spoken outside of the lab in which it was created."

This woman didn't fool around. She had their undivided attention.

"For easy reference in non-classified discussions, the project has been appropriately nicknamed 'hubris,' from the Greek meaning an overabundance of self-confidence, or exaggerated pride."

Again she swept their faces, keenly aware of their very pampered supersonic egos. "It was not so named because you men are the most highly trained, highly skilled, elite flying force in the universe."

As she'd expected; great hoots of approval as their prowess was acknowledged; but her gutsy, off-handed punch line took them all off guard. "Actually," she mused, "the project itself is even more narcissistic than some of you are rumored to be."

She paused until their outburst had begun to fade and then cut them to silence with her next statement. "Project

Hubris is a scientific attempt at playing god. Simply stated, it will allow pilots to operate certain mechanical flight control functions...with their minds."

Several beats of silence. Then Captain Mo Morris, Squadron Leader of the First Fighter Wing U.S. Central Command, raised his hand. "Doctor, are you saying that at let's say, 750 mph, I can just think about doing a slow roll...and it'll happen?"

There was a moment; silence; all eyes on Captain Cynthia Teller.

"Yes," she said, "The result you describe is possible. By combining a miniscule laser mounted on the surface of your eye, and a CW generator about the size of a hair follicle, implanted adjacent the frontal lobe of your brain, you will be able to operate flight controls...by looking at them."

Pacific Coast Highway – Malibu, California

Luke hadn't been able to reach Kathryn. He'd left three more messages and she still hadn't responded. *Why doesn't she answer?* He told himself she'd call when she could. He was trying, unsuccessfully, to block the fear from his mind. *Move on. Stay positive.* It had worked for him in Vietnam under much worse conditions; it should work in L.A.

Don't be a pussy.

Instead of going directly into work, he turned north on PCH and headed toward Trancas. He cranked his little Z up to 80 and settled his shoulders into the car's coco leather seats. He took the silver Blackberry from his shirt pocket and snapped it onto a one-inch chrome stem protruding from the dashboard. The exotic little PDA was the same one he had shown Kathryn the night they celebrated his birthday.

The device was a prototype, still under development at The Facility. It began life as an ordinary digital PDA/cell phone; but it had morphed into something a great deal more powerful. Although it looked like a silver Blackberry, the similarity ended with the faceplate. Its innards functioned on a laser system rather than a digital one. More importantly, it had become one of the central and fundamental components of The Facility's Mind's Eye Laser System. The innocuous little PDA had become the fulcrum of the Pentagon's $300 million research program.

Since it retained its original Blackberry design, and continued to function as a souped-up PDA/cell phone, the scientists on Luke's team were constantly tinkering with its circuit board as a form of recreation, adding functions, enhancing its abilities, pushing its limits – just for fun.

At first, when no one could come up with an appropriate name or anagrammatic label for the device, Luke dubbed it 'Shit Face.' For two months, everyone enjoyed using the name; but then came a major modification which led to a more appropriate title.

The scientists added an exotic projection capacity. The new Shit Face could project simple visual images with amazing clarity onto any flat surface, much like an old-fashioned movie projector. They also discovered that the new lens could project images into the air – without the need of a traditional projection screen.

Instead of a flat surface, the newest lens was able to project its image onto the random particles normally present in the atmosphere. Modern holographic technology utilized a similar method. But the PDA's images possessed a much higher resolution, more opaqueness of color, and more than triple the light intensity of current holography. The resulting stills and even moving images were projected in almost HDTV-like clarity.

The technology was called Dual-Inline-Lens-Resolution, or DILR. Everyone automatically pronounced it anagrammatically – "Diller" like the comedienne Phyllis Diller. Luke's assistant, David Halter, started calling it "Phyllis," and the name immediately stuck.

Depending on the color saturation of the image to be projected, the density of particle matter present in the air, and the quality of the available light, Phyllis's projections could often appear to have physical substance.

The laser's intense light reflected color from particle to particle in a way that seemed to fill in the empty spaces between the particles. The effect was analogous to *tweening*, the animation technique of filling in the blank spaces between motion cells. The resulting images possessed a tangible, three-dimensional quality of such density that occasionally the DILR's projected images could appear to be solid.

For weeks, the techies at the Facility had been experimenting with Phyllis, using it to project what appeared to be doorways in front of existing solid walls. Not a day went by at without some incident involving a Phyllis prank; an embarrassing crash of scientist and dry wall.

Luke encouraged laughter at The Facility. There was a constant self-imposed pressure to succeed amongst the very unique and gifted brainacks who worked there. He understood their need to blow off steam and permitted them their fun; just one of many reasons that Luke Towne was beloved by his employees.

Point Dume, California

As Luke's speeding Z approached the coastal community of Point Dume, the Sunday traffic on PCH suddenly slowed to a crawl. Bored, he pressed one of the unique buttons on Phyllis's faceplate. The little PDA spoke to him in a breathy female voice that brought a grudging smile to his face.

"Happy Sunday Luke. S'up?"

"Phone calls?"

"Password please."

"Backside Mudslide."

A slight pause while Phyllis ripped through her data base. Luke's passwords rotated daily, And the techies hadn't had time to enter a reference for the latest one.

Phyllis was accustomed to having all the answers. The techies tried to keep her memory full of the latest slang. She uttered a phrase seldom used, "Uh...what's that mean, Luke?"

He laughed at the glitch, "X Games, Phil. Thought you'd have all the skate park lingo down cold."

"...Ohhhkeaaaaay." It was the sound the little computer made when she was recording new data. Luke smiled again.

Beams of light began to radiate from the device, projecting a small, articulate Lasocular image. It formed a line of green neon words floating in the air just above the dashboard.

"Larger, please," said Luke.

The words grew larger, spelling out the names of the callers who had left messages on Luke's home line:

"Kathryn de Kennesy; Nana de Kennesy."

"Play 'em," said Luke.

As Kathryn's audio message played, Phyllis projected her words as green neon:

"Hi honey, it's me. I hope everything is going well for you guys. I'm sure Cynthia will blow them away, doing whatever she's doing. I've heard a rumor that you're a pretty smart guy, although, as you've already guessed by now, I only want you for your body.

"Sorry I couldn't get back to you sooner, but you can't bring cell phones into chambers here, and I've been round-the-clock with the Syrian ambassador and his money guys."

A suspicious frown from Luke.

"The good news is I love you. The other good news is, I should be through a day early, so I'll see you for dinner at Mom's on Wednesday night. I miss you big time. Bye."

Hearing Kat's explanation for her delay in calling back didn't alleviate his discomfort. His logical mind wouldn't let go of it. The conference with the Syrians could not have lasted three days; he'd read about it in the Washington Post. The delegation had only stayed 24 hours, then returned to Damascus.

He and Kat had spoken almost every night since the day they first met, either by phone or by broadcast.

Now all of a sudden, no contact.

There was undoubtedly some logical excuse for it; but the President's terrorist accusation was playing havoc with his insides. In seconds, the slightest inconsistency or unanswered question could turn into full-blown suspicion. He couldn't control it.

On Friday, when he couldn't get through to Kat's cell phone, he had called her new office in San Francisco. Her assistant told him that it was a free day and that she could be reached on her cell. That wasn't exactly the way Kat's message had explained it. It sounded like she was covering something up.

"Shut the hell up," he shouted at himself. "You're acting like a pussy." He focused on dinner at the de Kennesys and decided that his life might actually begin to normalize, once they were all together in one place. The de Kennesys had already become a second family.

"Next one, Phyllis," he said to the PDA.

It was Kathryn's mother: "Hi Luke, it's Nana. We're expecting you for dinner on Wednesday. I've made rum tart for dessert. Leon and I are looking forward to seeing you. Take care of yourself, dear, don't work too hard. Goodbye.

"Oh wait," she added, "you'll be glad to know I've found out why my French countrymen are so difficult to deal with. I'm reading the autobiography of Charles de Gaulle. He gave us the answer way back in 1958 when he complained, 'How can I be expected to govern a country that has 200 kinds of cheese?' Bye bye dear."

Luke burst into laughter in spite of his black mood. Then instantly his anger resurfaced. "Terrorists!" he shouted. "Yeah. Both of 'em. Child rearing, tart baking, PhD's. Absolute murderous terrorists. Leon's probably down there right now at Children's Hospital curing some American kids so Nana can feed 'em tarts and then Kat can murder 'em. What a stupid...brain dead..."

His anger was getting out of hand.

"Disconnect," he snapped.

"Later dude," answered Phyllis.

He mashed the accelerator. The tires squealed. He hung a massive U-turn across PCH and headed back toward Malibu.

31

Malibu, California

The blue Z cornered violently into The Facility's driveway and skidded to a stop in front of the metal arm. Luke jammed his card into the reader and waited while the exterior security system scoped his car and his I.D. Three seconds later, the arm raised and admitted Luke to the underground parking garage located beneath the Avionics lab.

Work was Luke's hobby as well as his passion; he loved being in the lab. Hours would pass and he'd forget what day it was. It was a perfect escape from the problems that were now complicating his world.

Today, however, it was not going to work that way.

The Facility's underground lot was completely empty as Luke parked on Level Two and took the elevator straight up to the Avionics lab. The "A-Lab" was housed in a 4000 square foot building with 17' cargo doors at one end. The other end included a 3500 square foot clean-room shell that had been specially built for the Mind's Eye project.

Directly in front of the clean room sat the gigantic silver bones of an F18-C Hornet fighter. The plane was a prized weapon. Throughout the Gulf War, squadrons of U.S. Navy, Marine and Canadian F/A-18s operated around the clock, setting daily records in reliability, survivability and ton-miles of ordnance delivered.

The complete cockpit of an F18-C Hornet fighter had been disassembled on board the USS CORAL SEA (CV 43), flown to California and meticulously reassembled inside The Facility's Avionics lab. The cockpit plus its housing was then pallet-mounted on an electro-optical suite of roll-stabilized sensor units. The result was a functioning cockpit environment that could duplicate the actual physical responses of a plane in flight. It was accurate to a maximum of 20 degrees in all directions.

The Navy's F18-C Hornet strike fighter required numerous modifications for the Mind's Eye guidance system to be installed. Special cockpit lighting had to be designed to be compatible with the GEC Cat's Eyes pilot's night vision goggles. Hughes created a special upgrade of their AN/AAR-50 thermal imaging navigation set. Luke insisted on a redesigned touch-sensitive, upfront control display similar to the newer F/A-18E/F Super Hornets.

The most challenging modification concerned the Mind's Eye computer box itself, which had to be reconfigured to fit into the plane's nose compartment. But it had to be accomplished without interfering with the 20 mm M61A1 Vulcan cannon that was already installed there.

Luke was underneath the aft section of the Hornet's cockpit, replacing one of the pressure gauges, when the small wrench he was using slipped from his fingers and clanged down into the darkness at the bottom of the huge support structure.

"Damn it," he groaned as he crawled out from under the mass of hydraulics and went looking for a flashlight. He stood in front of the long, neatly organized tool silo. He stared at the rows of specialized equipment.

He stared...and stared...and stared. Almost half a minute elapsed before he realized that he'd forgotten what he was looking for. He had completely zoned out. The realization set fire to his already smoldering anger.

He jerked a bright red tensor flashlight off its wall bracket and flung it as far and hard as he could. It bounced off a support girder and splintered into a mass of shards that rained down on the engineering desks below. He stood in the cavernous silence of the huge lab, red-faced, jaws clamped shut, frustrated beyond his experience.

In the Military, Luke Towne was the consummate leader to his troops. To his team members at The Facility, he was a supportive and understanding boss. But when it came to his own performance, Luke was a vicious, unrelenting, unforgiving perfectionist. He paced back and forth amidst his machines and gauges, each of which did exactly what it was designed to do with zero tolerance for error.

The only marginal piece of gear in this whole lab is me! What a stupid, incompetent jerkwad!

He took in a long breath and let it out in gradual stages. Then slowly he climbed the 30' ladder that stretched up into the Hornet's cockpit. He slid into the pilot's seat and punched a button on the seat arm. The entire lab went dark. The angry lines in his forehead softened as they became defined by the green glow of the instrument panel. He sat back and again breathed deeply, trying to calm his mind.

He reverted to basic training. *Obedience. The first thing you learn. A good soldier always obeys his superior.* He sat for a moment, slowing his breathing, repeating the mantra they'd drilled into him. *A good soldier always obeys his superior.*

"But what if the superior isn't even a soldier? What if the guy's just an elected, politicized, corruptible, four-year son-of-a-bitch, whose only real agenda is preserving his own ass?" The words came boiling out through clenched teeth. "Whose politics am I supposed to believe? This guy's? Do I lay down my life now? Or wait four years for the next one do a 180 on me?"

"You bastards! My Kathryn is not a terrorist!"

The sound of the A-Lab phone suddenly interrupted Luke's rant and altered the mood. It was the private line; so it would be Cynthia, calling in from Langley.

"Tell me something good," he answered expectantly, trying to brighten things.

At the sound of Luke's spoken words, there was a whir of electronic switching on the line as the call was routed through a maze of blind connections and networks that guaranteed its security. There was no greeting, just the reedy emotionless voice of General Orin Pierce:

"Colonel Towne, be at Santa Monica Airport in one hour. The Harrier is already there on the south runway waiting for you. By order of the President of the United States of America."

The phone went dead.

32

Langley, Virginia

Something was wrong. It had started in the pit of Cynthia's stomach after she hung up with Luke; just a mild discomfort at first. Then gradually, it had morphed its way into a full-blown sense of dread. She could always tell when he was in trouble, no matter how great the distance between them. She was virtually infallible about it.

All cell phone communication to and from Langley had been purposely jammed for added security. She would have to wait until the following morning. By then her cell would be cleared for limited calls to selected phones outside the base.

But she tried again anyway. She waited while the Sprint lines located Luke's cell phone unit. The line rang. And rang. There was no answer.

She couldn't have known they'd made him surrender his cell phone at the Santa Monica Airport.

Santa Monica Airport

A British Harrier Jet GR7 sat on the dark runway, the unmistakable whine of the big Royce Pegasus turbofan silencing everything on the tarmac, a mirage of fuel streaming out the four nozzles beside its slate gray fuselage.

Why the hell do we need a vertical takeoff?

Luke strapped himself into the fighter's narrow passenger seat, his head full of questions. The Harrier Jump Jet (V/STOL vertical/short takeoff and landing aircraft) was designed to rise straight up into the air on take-off, like a hummingbird, then rotate the nozzles to the fully aft position to resume standard thrust and 700 mph acceleration. The AV-8B versions were the first Marine Corps strike platforms used in Desert Storm, specifically because they could deploy from advanced bases and remote tactical landing sites.

Who am I supposed to rescue here?

Luke had flown many a snatch and grab mission in the Harrier's bigger brother, the V-22 Osprey; but this beast they'd sent to get him was an old Hawker-Siddeley original — the workhorse of the Royal Navy. *Why?*

Thirty-eight minutes into the flight, exactly 404 miles northeast of Santa Monica, just over the corner of St. George,

Utah, the pilot handed Luke a sealed envelope containing his orders. Perhaps this would give him the answer. He peeled back the adhesive strip, expecting a meaningful explanation.

The directive was terse; Luke was incredulous. He was on his way to Washington D.C. to undergo an intense, 48-hour briefing on the tactics of counterterrorism. The crash course would be conducted by an elite group of Basement strategists under the supervision of General Orin Pierce. The orders were signed by the President himself.

What kind of last minute, spy-school bullshit is this? Two days' training and poof, I'm a double agent?

Luke punched the button on his helmet microphone and spoke to the pilot, his rancor booming. "Hey Chief, you think if we get there early, they'll give me some invisible ink and a shoe phone?"

He knew it was a dumbass remark, and he regretted it the moment he said it, but to a 20-year, boots-on-the ground Special Forces veteran, the whole Basement cloak and dagger business felt like Maxwell Smart.

As expected, there was no reply from the pilot. Luke was left to himself, strapped in the single passenger seat, going 700 mph to somewhere he didn't want to go, to be with some people he didn't respect.

At 4:30 p.m. EST, the Harrier gently lowered itself down like a giant insect, on top of an eight-story building. The site was hidden in a thickly-wooded nature preserve somewhere lost in the foothills of south D.C. The building was a monochromatic rectangle in ghostly grisaille, bleak, cold and out of place in the lush green landscape. Clearly it was intended to be inaccessible by land. That would explain the Harrier's V/STOL function.

Two armed MPs in dress blues escorted Luke from the building's helipad, down two flights of internal stairs and into a large conference room. The taller of the two men placed a notebook and a pen on the table and indicated that Luke should take a seat. He saluted crisply and said, "Mr. Kennedy, sir, General Clark will be along shortly."

On cue, both men did a crisp *about-face* and left the room, banging the door solidly closed behind them. Almost immediately, the door opened again, and General Eldon Clark entered, followed by the shorter MP, now pushing a long green chalk board in front of him.

Without a word of introduction, Clark began his lecture. The general spoke non-stop for two straight hours on the state of terrorist cells imbedded in the U.S.

Then he dropped his yellow chalk into the blackboard's little trough and spoke to Luke directly for the first time: "Grub; downstairs to the left."

What a charmer.

Luke would later discover that General Eldon Clark had no connection with The Basement Team, but was the Pentagon's leading expert on terrorist interdiction in the United States. He was undoubtedly jerked from his normal routine (just as Luke had been) and ordered to deliver a lecture to 'some newbie special agent named Kennedy.' That might explain his obvious anger and abrupt manner; something to which Luke could easily relate.

Following orders, Luke stepped off the elevator and turned left into a small rectangular space: a chipped, white Formica table, an industrial sized trash can, and a green wall of dingy food and candy machines.

"Nice lunch they put on here," he said out loud to no one. He debated a moment then pulled the lever for Ham and Swiss. The old machine groaned and squeaked. Nothing happened. Luke banged it with the flat of his hand. Clunk! A cello-wrapped sandwich hit the bottom of the trough, sounding like it was made out of plaster of Paris. Luke ripped off the wrapping. The bread had turned a dark pebbled green. In its center were two large Rorschach spots of florescent blue rimmed in fuzzy white.

"Real nice. Real nice. Class deal all the way. Just like this Pierce character. Guy doesn't have the respect to show up and deliver my orders in person."

Luke threw the sandwich across the room, walked back to the elevator and pushed the up button.

The briefing was scheduled to resume in a different room after the lunch break. Luke entered, keeping his head down, and took his seat. Across the front of the room were five decorated members of the President's Special Ops Team, shoulder to shoulder, standing tall, staring down at him. All were dressed in battle fatigues, their black berets set off at a jaunty angle.

Right, battle gear. So where's the frickin' battle?

Major Ron Beamon stepped forward and gripped the podium with his fat white fingers. He had an aggressive chin, a pound of fruitcake hanging on his chest, and 20 pounds of gut hanging over his belt. His superiors had declared Beamon 'too valuable to face combat.' As a result, his ego had grown even more bloated than his stomach. His kind were known as 'paper soldiers.' They were unconditionally hated by all enlisted men.

Major Beamon pushed out his chest, as if to emphasize his position of command, and began speaking without introduction. "We've got 48 hours, Colonel, to give you the benefit of our collective years of experience in counterterrorism, to prepare you for the very sophisticated task of becoming a double agent. Strict attention will be required for you to even retain a small portion of the knowledge here assembled for your benefit."

What an arrogant s-o-b, thought Luke, his temples already throbbing with suppressed anger.

"Fortunately, Our General Pierce recognized the potential danger of your situation very early in the game. We're lucky we had the benefit of such a head start."

Luke's face flushed. "What game are you talking about, Major? What's 'head start' supposed to mean?" Luke's voice was louder than he had intended. Without realizing it, he had raised halfway up out of his chair.

"Please, Colonel, I'm sure some of the terminology we use in the counter insurgency business is foreign to you. Don't mistake it for anything but shop talk." The major's patronizing tone was evident. "As to having a head start, you're very lucky General Pierce called us in early. We've been working on your file for six months.

"Now if you'll be so good as to remain in your seat, Captain Hinson, our chief of psychiatry, will take you through the changes we've made to your bio, your family history and your record of service. You'll need to have them memorized before leaving D.C. tomorrow."

Luke's mind was ablaze. *Six months! They've been watching me for six months?*

As Head of the U.S. Military's Department of Laser Research, Luke had a security clearance second to none. A retired colonel. One of the most decorated soldiers in the history of the Rangers. His own government spying on his personal life? *Inconceivable.*

His head buzzed. A massive shot of adrenaline pumped into his heart. He automatically snapped into attack mode. Each one of these arrogant desk monkeys was about to feel some pain.

These maggots are the real terrorists. Not the de Kennesys.

Luke's eyes swept across the five men standing in front of him, evaluating each one, noting height, weight, strengths, weaknesses. Whose belly was soft; whose eyes were the most aggressive; who was poised; whose stance was athletic; who was the leader.

He mentally arranged them in the order of probable attack. His jaws began clamping down rhythmically, his breathing deepened, his pulse increased, his pupils narrowed. He stood up from his desk and stepped slowly away from the chair.

He extended his arms in the air and bent down toward the floor in a languid stretch, as if his body had needed a break, a change of position from the hours of sitting. He held the pose for a few seconds, and in that instant, a buzzer went off in his brain. A moment of clarity.

Stop.

He sat back down in his chair. Twenty years of military training had finally come to his aid. This was the world of black ops. Different battlefield. Different rules. Different goals. Boundless resources. No records. No court martial. No explanations. No accountability.

Luke picked up his pen; his face went completely blank. Obedience. No tales to report back to their boss. *Hold your position. Neutralize your emotions. Concentrate on winning the war.*

When the lecture began, Luke retreated into his mind. He went back to Nam, crouching in the jungle, tracing a map in the mud, sending his men out on patrol. Nineteen-year-olds with letters from home stuffed behind their flak jackets, protecting their hearts; all of them scared to death, and all of them eager to serve. No paper soldiers. Real soldiers. Some came back with reports on the enemy; some would never come back.

Luke felt his skin crawl. The President's men were not warriors, or soldiers, or men of honor. They were called mercenaries for a reason. In a very real way, they were part of the enemy.

His first day with the boys from The Basement had been arduous, nonstop, 8 a.m. to 7 p.m. When the last lecture concluded, he was sent directly to the top level of the strange gray building in the forest. The entire floor had been sealed off to provide him with 'privacy to digest your reading materials.' As he walked down the hallway from the lavatory, he could see his own reflection in the green and white squares of decades-old linoleum flooring. It felt like a minimum security prison. In prowling around the open hallways, he discovered the doors and the elevators were locked down at 10 p.m.

"Something is very wrong with this picture," he said into the emptiness. He was a retired colonel, a salaried scientist on the Pentagon's payroll with a personally signed request from the President to return to active duty. He had agreed to undertake the very critical and dangerous assignment.

And they had locked him in his room!

His overnight living quarters were Spartan; faded gray walls, a single bed, a metal night stand and a straight-backed chair. *Nothing to do but work.*

At the end of the first day's lecture, Luke was given a cardboard box full of documents to be studied. Among the files was a copy of his altered bio. "Learn this backwards," said Major Don Byrne. "Double identity can become a confusing posture, especially to a rookie. Learn who you're supposed to be."

Luke devoted two hours that night and two more early in the morning, to learn who 'Luke the traitor' had been as a youth.

At the start of the second day Luke was moved to a different location. He was taken to the very public Hoover Building, adjacent St. Thomas Square in the heart of D.C. The day began with a test; a journey into his new past.

The man administering the verbal quiz was obviously some kind of social scientist; a small man with granny glasses balanced atop his balding pate. He didn't fit with the others, his bearing was decidedly un-military; his attitude thoughtful, his manner kind. His name was Norman Erlich.

As a member of Pierce's Basement elite, Norman Erlich rarely left the bowels of the Washington office; but this was an important exception, a clandestine intelligence operation with enormous potential, one in which he had already played a critical role. Norman was the chief architect of Luke's rewritten bio; the brains behind the detail.

They sat on comfortable couches in the building's enormous foyer. The sparsely decorated waiting area was set off in mahogany and leather, a failed attempt at warmth. The interview was designed to replicate a social situation in which Luke might encounter some questions about his past.

"Heard you had quite a temper back in school," said the little scientist, trying to sound casual. "Ever punch anybody out?"

Luke waited a few seconds before answering, as if he were reaching back into his past, searching for a good example. "Well, I was a pole vaulter in high school," he began. "Our coach was an Olympic weightlifter; got a bronze medal in Rome, I think it was. Big buddies with Randy Matson. Anyway, I was also the third best shot putter on our team. So junior year, we made it to the City finals. But our genius coach decided I should only compete in one event. 'Needed to concentrate,' was what he said. I could have earned three points if he'd' a let me compete in the shot; but he wouldn't. We lost by two.

"After the meet, we got into an argument about it on the bus. I went after him with a track shoe. Sent him to the hospital. Forty stitches in his face. Guy never came back to coach. Goddamn pussy is what he was. So they kicked me out of the athletic program. Had to sit out my whole senior year. I've hated the Jesuit bastards ever since."

Luke paused a beat for impact, before delivering the final bit of anger. "You know what? If I had it to do over again, I'd've beat him up worse."

Luke's answer had been fabricated for him by The Basement Team. For anyone reading his bio, it was to be one of many psychological signposts, indications of his deep-seated problems: anger, instability, a need for revenge. These were the makings of a traitor.

Luke dubbed the process "Tom Cruise 101." Actors, *guys who played pretend for a living*, were way down on his list of people to be taken seriously. Yet in spite of his own skepticism, in spite of his admitted thespian shortcomings, he strove to be letter perfect.

This little guy Norman seems to know what he's doing.

The interview continued, Erlich asking pointed questions, Luke enjoying himself, fielding each question with a high degree of dexterity. Finally, Erlich sat back in his seat and closed the files on his lap. The test was completed.

"Do you have any questions, Colonel Towne?"

"How'd I do?"

"May I make a suggestion?"

"Please."

"You were letter perfect, Colonel," said Erlich with great pleasure. "But most folks don't remember their own real history as well as you did your fake one. So if the situation ever arises when you have to recall any of this information, lose a bit of clarity about it and you'll be fine."

Then came a shocker.

"Colonel Towne, there's another part of the process you should be aware of. We expect this information – I'm talking about your new bio – we expect it to be stolen by the enemy. In fact, we're planning on it. I suspect the theft will probably occur at the Pentagon, although these people seem to have some access to the files at CIA as well. But I think their best bet will definitely be the Pentagon. It will probably happen sometime within the next 10 days to two weeks. So don't be surprised if you need to draw on what you've memorized very soon."

Luke couldn't restrain himself. "How can you be certain about this? Pardon me for saying it, but you seem almost, well, sort of blasé about it all. Am I understanding you right?"

"Not blasé Colonel," Norman replied easily, "Positive. You see, there's a mole. We don't know <u>who</u> he is; we don't know exactly where he is, we just know he's there. As a matter of fact, at the moment, we don't really care where. We're just glad he's there; because he's going to become very useful to us."

"So there's an acknowledged hole in the Pentagon security system, and you're going to supply some disinformation through it. Is that it?"

"Exactly correct Colonel. Except it's you who's going to supply the disinformation. Correction! Actually, it's you who is going to <u>be</u> the disinformation. A classic ploy in the espionage business; and you're probably going to be very successful at it. The battle rages on, Colonel. You can win this one."

That said, the little man smiled, shook Luke's hand, stood up and walked on tiptoes, quietly across the lobby and into the open elevator. The metal doors came together; and that was the last Luke would see of The Basement's 'little man with the big brain.'

Luke sat staring at the huge golden shield etched flawlessly into the foyer's white marble floor. The Hoover Building was vast and silent; strange territory. No boots, no troops, no enemy fire. No plans traced in the mud.

So where are the soldiers, covered in dirt, blood on their hands, fear in their bellies? Where are the warriors? The nation's finest?

He was already supposed to be among the nation's finest; at least that's what they claimed to be. These guys were the strategists, the architects, the planners. The intellectual chess players. Clean white shirts and comfy shoes.

He thought about what Norman Erlich had described. The newly created bio would be stolen from the State Department by a mole, a guy operating inside the Pentagon. But they didn't know who he was. And they didn't care. A terrorist hiding in the house and nobody cares? *Amazing.* The entire operation was based on something they had no control over. Unscientific. Unmilitary. Unbelievable!

Someone get me back to the lab. These are not my people.

He took the elevator up to the fourth floor classroom where the second day's briefing was to resume. He entered and took his seat in the empty room, five minutes early as was his usual custom. As the clock struck 9 a.m., in marched the group of five; as before, their berets set at an angle, fatigues pressed.

Ridiculous.

33

The second day was to be devoted to learning the subtleties of working with the enemy; provoking his interest, leading him on, gaining his trust, acting out, role playing.

Tom Cruise 101.

The lectures began; and for rest of the day, five arrogant, know-it-all intelligence officers talked down to their audience of one. Some of it bravado, some of it useful. All the while a stoic Luke Towne kept his head down, paid close attention and made detailed notes.

He had assumed that at some point there would be a review of the evidence linking Kathryn de Kennesy and her family to terrorism. It seemed logical that a double agent should know as much about his enemy as possible. As the day drew toward its conclusion, nothing had been said, so Luke requested a show of evidence.

"Could one of you gentlemen review the evidence against Kathryn de Kennesy and her family for me?"

Major Beamon stepped forward. "I'll take that one. I think we need to send a message here." He let out a sigh of condescension. "Colonel Towne, agents are almost always compromised by their own knowledge. We've lost too many men because of their, shall we say, closeness to people. In our business, we categorize such people as 'compromised.' We don't want that happening to you.

"Now follow me here. The less you know about her, the less likely you are to make a mistake. Right? Remember these terrorists are brilliant in their ability to deceive. Their cunning seems as boundless as their capacity for evil. There's no explaining it. There are just some people the world would be better off without."

Luke's response was unemotional, his words measured. "You're saying my fiancée is a terrorist. And you're unwilling to show me the evidence. Is that correct, Major?"

"It's for your own good, soldier." Beamon spat out the word with all the disrespect he could muster. "We know how to maintain our assets."

"Blindness is never an asset, you fat douche bag," growled Luke.

Beamon's face flushed a bright red. Such disrespect could not go unanswered. Drawing strength from his four cohorts standing tall in their battle garb, Major Beamon pushed out his chest, clenched his fists and began a bulldog strut down the aisle toward Luke's desk. His posturing afforded Luke ample time to stand, step away from his desk and prepare for attack.

This jerkwad ain't no field soldier.

Beamon arrived in front of Luke, his face contorted. He reached out for Luke's shirt front, expecting to pull him in nose to nose like a tough guy in an old Cagney movie. "Gonna teach you a lesson, punk," he snarled.

It was a bad miscalculation. Luke's hands came up on instinct; both of his thumbs poked hard and deep into the major's eyeballs. He followed that with a right-footed sweep which dumped the major on the floor, hands covering his eyes, writhing in pain. Luke brought the full weight of his own body down on top of Beamon's right kneecap, snapping the joint backwards, shattering the femur.

Luke stood up and addressed the gang of four, who stood frozen in their battle gear at the front of the room. "When you boys file your report with Pierce, you'll find this kind of action described in Section 12, paragraph 2 of the code."

Luke pressed his boot heel down on the neck of the unconscious major and continued calmly. "It's called 'Permissible combat.' General Walker and I wrote the guidelines for this kind of thing when I was Director of Special Forces at Benning."

A reflexive grunt of air escaped from the major's throat. Luke continued. "Gentlemen, I am aware that counterterrorism is <u>your</u> specialty. Thanks for sharing. As you know, warfare is <u>my</u> specialty." His eyes flicked down at the unconscious bully on the floor, then back up at them. "Right now I'd be happy to share some more of it with you; one at a time, or as a group if you like."

The President's men remained silent, four stunned bullies cowering in their costumes. When it was clear there would be no response, Luke removed his foot from the major's neck, rendered a proper salute and left the room.

Santa Monica Airport

The black F-18 touched down on Runway B, its predatory space age design causing the old Santa Monica Airport to look like the cow pasture it had once been. The military's exclusive passenger drop was nothing more than a worn white circle on the ground. The moment Luke's feet hit the tarmac, before he was even clear of the wings, the F-18 began moving backwards toward the runway. In seconds it disappeared in a jet blast of gray exhaust. It felt like they were glad to be rid of him.

For Luke, the feeling was mutual.

He took a cab from the airport to the large blue and white Standard Station on PCH, right in front of the Malibu Colony's main entrance gate. From there he would call up to The Facility and Dave Halter would come down the hill to pick him up. No one knew where he had been. The less anyone knew about his comings and goings, the better he would fare as an inexperienced agent for the White House.

As his cab turned into the station, Luke's eyes caught the reflection of the dark blue Galaxy speeding north up the hill toward Point Dume. They had been on his tail since the cab left Santa Monica. Why wasn't he surprised? They'd been watching him since Paris. He just hadn't known to look. It was beginning to feel like a goddamn Ludlum novel. And he was enraged by the whole thing.

Luke retrieved Phyllis from his briefcase, pushed one of her buttons and said, "Call my *control*."

Orin Pierce was waiting for Luke's call; his greeting laced with bile. "Have a little change of heart, did we Colonel?"

"Do you have some specific instructions, General Pierce, or are we on a fishing expedition?"

Pierce snapped, "Let me begin this operation with a little reminder, Colonel. The President has placed you directly under my command. I brook no insubordination at any time from my team members, no matter how important they believe themselves to be. Are we clear on that?"

"We're clear on this, General. I'm a retired Army officer. I'm not part of your team. The President himself asked me directly, and I quote, 'To do the best I can under these very difficult circumstances involving my family.' I will do what the President has asked of me. Nothing more. His request does not include kissing the ass of a bunch of desk jockeys. I suggest a different perspective. Since we're talking about spying on my fiancée and her family, if you don't like my attitude, you're going to have a difficult time finding someone else to do the job. Wouldn't you agree, General?"

There was a prolonged silence on the line. The great and powerful Orin Pierce realized at once that he was *stuck with this goddamn tin soldier.* The finality of Luke's logic was a difficult reality. No immediate rebuttal came to mind. This was an unfamiliar position for Pierce, so he tried to save face with a bit of forced bravado. "You're on thin ice, Colonel. I suggest you control your temper and concentrate on the task of counter-intelligence. It's what we do here. It's not your field, and you're going to have to assimilate the rules rather quickly in order to fulfill the President's request."

No response from Luke.

Pierce continued quickly. "So let me tell you how this is going to go. You'll be receiving a visit from our psychiatrist, Captain Hinson. I believe you two have already met. He will bring you up to speed on the various gambits we expect from this Doctor de Kennesy. Captain Hinson will walk you through the responses you'll need in order to maintain your believability. I'll expect a complete report from you after each encounter. That is all for now."

Pierce disconnected the call.

What an idiot! One didn't have to be a career soldier to sense an impending disaster.

As Dave drove him back up to The Facility, it took all of Luke's control to act as if nothing had changed. He would not offer an explanation. And Dave knew better than to ask.

Once back in his office, Luke locked the inside doors, poured himself three fingers of Bushmills and stretched out on his brown leather couch. He closed his eyes and considered his two-day trip to spy school. Of necessity he had destroyed his notes before leaving the Hoover Building in D.C., so he had only his thoughts.

Gradually the sounds and smells of his own office helped to soothe his overheated brain and he dropped off to sleep. But he was jolted awake almost immediately when the glass slipped from his grip and fell to the carpet. He awoke, still angry, and began cleaning up the spill.

On the flight back from Washington, the F-18's pilot, Captain Happy Quinlan, had recognized him. They had served together on two occasions; both were search and rescue missions, one in Vietnam and one in Afghanistan. But on this flight, the genial pilot had his own orders. He spoke but four words. "Welcome aboard Mr. Kennedy."

Welcome to the make believe world of espionage.

Luke had used the hours of quiet time in the plane to work out a story. He'd gone missing for two days. His mood was dark and he was a poor liar. He would call the two women in his life and tell them both the same lie.

Kathryn answered her cell on the first ring, "Is it another woman, or are you just too old for so much sex?" she said without hesitation.

He had decided to avoid the subject of his unreturned phone calls. "I had to design a new bracket for the Meniscus. It was faster to just go to Leica and do it on site. Sorry I couldn't reach you, my cell phone doesn't seem to like Switzerland. We worked around the clock, but we got it done."

"You never have to apologize Lukie. Work demands, we answer. I know all about how it works. Sometimes there's just no choice. Enough said? Okay. Now let's talk about dinner at Nana's and what I'm going to do to you for dessert."

The fake story worked fine with Kat; everything was easy with Kat. He had reached her at her parents' house. She responded to his missing two days like she did to most every difficult situation he brought to the relationship. *No big deal. The most important thing is 'I love you.' Nothing else matters.*

On the other hand, Cynthia would know his story was bogus. And it would matter. She was walking down the gray carpeted hallway of the Rickenbacker Building when her cell phone rang.

"Doctor Teller."

"Cyn, it's Luke. Got a minute?"

"What's the matter, Luke, is everything okay?"

"We need to talk, is all."

"I was worried. I couldn't reach you."

He couldn't force out the fake explanation. He just didn't say anything.

"Are you okay Luke?" There was no malice in her voice.

He knew she knew. He knew she was giving him space to work out whatever problem he was having. "Cyn," he said finally, "You're the truest friend I've ever had. You know that don't you?"

"Whatever you need," she said, true to form.

"How's it going with the pilots?"

"Well, at the moment, I'm on my way to tell 'em who made it through the first round. Then I'm on the Prowler headed home for a day, do my laundry and head up to Riverton. Get 'em ready for you. Are you sure you're okay?"

"The real answer is no. I can't really talk about it on the phone. So, maybe I'll show up at Riverton early. We can talk then."

"That would be good. The sooner you're there to show them what we're talking about, the better."

"Safe flight."

She made her way to the front of the room and waited for the attention of the pilots. All 30 of them were still seated at the long tables where they had completed a form at the end of their first round of testing. She was worried. Luke's call was a major concern. She did her best to cover.

"Gentlemen," she began, "Colonel Towne and our staff are back in California fine tuning the system which 20 of you gentlemen will be testing. We'll be moving you to a new location where you'll begin training in the simulator. Those who meet the final qualifications will be carrying the Mind's Eye into battle conditions.

"The full description of the Mind's Eye project is still highly classified. Suffice to say that it is designed to help you become better F18 pilots by increasing your ability to multitask while under enemy attack.

"We know how skilled and how competitive you men are. So an additional word of explanation should provide consolation to those of you who were not chosen. The first series of tests you were given – hand-eye, reaction time, and so forth – all of those applied to skills over which you had some control. So in a sense, the top 20 of you did win that one.

"However, the next round of tests will measure the strength of the electrical current produced by your brains. The brain is like an electric motor; it puts out amps as it functions. You have no control over that; it comes with the package at birth. So the final 12 of you will be chosen strictly by virtue of the electric circuitry passed on by your parents.

"Our scientists back in California have a nickname for the finalist pilots, the 'brain advantaged' ones. There's no reason you can't label these guys the same way we do. We call them 'amp heads.'"

She'd set it up perfectly. Most of the tension in the room dissipated immediately, as laughter, big cheers and applause followed her announcement of the names of the 20 pilots chosen to continue testing.

She turned the remainder of the meeting over to the officer of the day and headed back down the long gray hallway. She hurried out onto the tarmac and climbed into the truck that would take her out to the runway and the waiting Prowler Jet.

Her stomach had warned her in advance that something was wrong. She and Luke had always felt it imperative that they speak daily. When 48 hours had passed without contact, she knew he was in some kind of danger. The temptation to hand the Mind's Eye test process over to an assistant and jet back to California had been constant. And the impossibility of choosing that course of action had fractured her ability to concentrate and turned her stomach into an acid pit.

What has he done? How can I help?

Cynthia knew better than any other living person the complexities of Luke's mind, his strengths, the power of his will. She knew the refinements of his moral code. His habit of putting himself in the line of fire. His dedication. She knew the sadness in his past. All that and more, Cynthia understood in the unique way that only an ex-wife of 16 years could.

34

Houston, Texas

The name on his driver's license read Dominic Genero, an alias befitting the imposter's dark eyes and dark skin. The truck he drove, a 2002 Isuzu diesel, had a big Thermo King KOLD Refrigeration Unit sitting high above its cab. Stenciled on its side panels was a fat Guernsey cow munching grass in a green field. And just below the cow's hooves, in red, white and blue letters, was the company's counterfeit name: *National Dairy Company – Friendly Service since 1955.* On the truck's roll-up cargo door, a milkman carrying a little rack of Carnation milk bottles, had almost disappeared from the door's constant usage.

Farad Aziz's used refrigerated milk truck appeared harmless, one of a thousand other service trucks crisscrossing the highways of America. Its 10' square body was packed to the roof with Carnation powdered milk products: 30 cases of 10-gallon containers, 20 cases of two-gallon containers, 20 cases of Cremora and 10 boxes of Coffee Mate. A respectable load, about 3500 pounds of wholesome dairy products, all purchased at Smart & Final – for cash.

On the passenger seat was a book of manifestos cataloguing the company's deliveries to restaurant clients across the country. As it happened, many of those restaurants were located in high rise office buildings. The truck had been waiting in the subterranean garage of the Chase Tower the day Farad arrived in Texas.

Farad immediately snatched up his cell phone and called Leon. "You've made a mistake, Leon. This thing's got a big freezer unit on it. Powdered milk doesn't need refrigeration."

Leon did not usually explain his actions, especially to Farad. He tried to reel in his anger. "Listen closely to me Aziz. I told you once you got there, there would be no phone calls! I made it very clear. Absolutely NO DIRECT PHONE CALLS! Messages go to the blind answering machine. You have the number. It's for your protection and everyone else's. I thought this was an emergency or I wouldn't have answered it. Do not make this mistake again. You understand?"

No response from Farad.

"Do you understand?" Leon said again.

"Yes great one, but what am I supposed to do with a goddamn refrigerator truck?"

Leon took in a breath. "Well, Farad, you can tell me if anywhere in the world, anyone has ever heard of a bomber driving a refrigerator truck."

No answer from Farad. As usual, Leon's planning was brilliant.

Leon continued. "When you get a chance, unscrew the back panel of that 'big freezer unit' you're so concerned about and look inside. Make sure no one's watching when you do it." Leon smashed down the phone.

Delivering powdered dairy product to fancy restaurants seems, on its face, a very wholesome occupation. Add water to the cartons stacked around the perimeter of the truck bed and you get nutritious milk. Add water to the rest of the cartons stored in the middle of the stack and you get something else – cyclonite, the deadly, plastic explosive known to the U.S. Military as C-4. To the casual observer, it's virtually impossible to detect the difference between powdered milk and powdered cyclonite. More of Leon's brilliance.

The Silent Jihad was ready to go public. Doctor Leon had moved to California to act as its commander in chief. The complex terrorist operation had been two decades in gestation; it was massive in scope and infinite in detail.

It was D-day. Farad Aziz and his milk truck were being sent into the center of the United States to install 200 pounds of C4 explosive at the first carefully chosen location.

The slaughter of millions of American citizens was not going to be a random set of events. Leon had targeted five different cities using specific criteria. Among his considerations: target accessibility, population density, lack of predictability and maximum emotional impact.

Chase Tower, Houston, Texas

Farad had already made his first installation of C4. As the lessee of an office on the 64th floor of the Chase Tower, the National Dairy Company received a pre-assigned storage unit. Leon had not selected the office for its view. He had chosen

Office 6404A based on the location of its storage unit – a 10' by 10' basement room abutting the support girders on the northeast corner of the building.

The architect competing for the design work on Leon's bogus skyscraper told him that there was a structural weakness in the Chase Tower (the building Leon proposed to duplicate). It was a design flaw in support structure of the Tower's lobby which occupied the entire northeastern corner of the building.

"Our design will not contain such a defect," said Wesley Townsend, the president of Townsend and Lemert, AIA.

"As soon as I've completed negotiations on the land, I'll be back in touch, and we'll do the final review of your design," lied Doctor Leon. He promptly arranged to lease Office 6404A on the 64th floor of the Chase Tower, in downtown Houston, Texas.

No one even noticed Farad as he moved his cartons of Carnation products into the locker. It was a simple, one-man job. He mixed the ingredients and left the dough-like C-4 in the original powdered milk cartons. There was no need to pack the explosive securely around a bearing girder and disguise it with paint. The storage unit itself was already next to the building's support stantions. The explosives were easily concealed from view by simply closing and locking the storage unit.

The second installation would be more challenging.

Leon was unusually manic about Phase Three security measures. The cities and the targets within them had never been mentioned on paper, in conversation or even by inference.

Farad's actions were triple blinded; untraceable. "There will be no paper trail. Nothing written down. No one's name will be spoken. No records will be kept. No phone calls. No exceptions."

All procedural matters would be messaged to Farad's Palm Pilot. He was to read and erase them. The messages themselves would be inscrutable, never more than two words. And they were always non sequiturs.

The first message to appear on Farad's Pilot was typically enigmatic: *'xerxes overlook.'* Taken by themselves, the words were meaningless. Only Farad would know that the two words named an intersection somewhere in the middle of the continent.

Entering those two words into the milk truck's programmed GPS device would yield a two-digit number corresponding to one of the 50 states. Farad had memorized the states by the number.

From that point, the precautions were again double blinded. Once the milk truck arrived within the boundaries of the appropriate state (in this case #35 for Minnesota) the GPS would produce the name of the target city (Bloomington). When arriving in Bloomington, Farad would reenter the name of the city, and the GPS would present graphic directions to the intersection of Xerxes Avenue and Overlook Drive.

Farad was to crisscross the city at a leisurely pace, making sure to pass through the intersection of Xerxes and Overlook several times. Eventually he would pull the Milk truck into a parking spot, climb into the passenger seat and wait.

Bloomington, Minnesota

The city of Bloomington forms a rough isosceles triangle with the Twin Cities of Minneapolis and St. Paul. It boasts a population of just under 100,000, most of whom are involved in technology and retail sales. Two-thirds of the population own their own homes, mostly single family dwellings with a median value of $147,000. The city is rated one of the safest in the Midwest.

Of all the potential American cities that might be targeted for a terrorist explosion, Bloomington would be among the least likely. That was one of Leon's primary reasons for its selection. His secondary and most spectacular reason had been shared with no one but his wife Nana and his partner, Mullah Rockmani.

Two years prior to Farad's arrival in the U.S., a six-man cell of extremists, all graduates of Talib, had moved into the outskirts of Bloomington. Very quietly, one by one, filtering down from Canada, they had inserted themselves into the community, acquiring menial jobs, buying groceries, attending baseball games, eating at home and keeping to themselves. Their assignment was to map the target and wait for orders.

Farad arrived in Bloomington on a Friday afternoon at 5 p.m. Terrorist cell leader Abou Hamed had been alerted by

Leon at 6 a.m. via his own mobile phone; the one-word text message: '5 p.m.' The leader ordered his watchers to take up their strategic positions around the city at 12 noon, a full five hours early. Abou Hamed was a thorough man.

Farad's brightly-painted dairy truck was made even easier to spot by Bloomington's Friday afternoon bumper–to-bumper traffic. The watchers tracked Farad's progress for more than two hours as he circled through town, repeatedly doubling back on his route so as to expose anyone who might be following. At 7 p.m. he parked the truck in front of Coogan's Hardware Store – one block north of the intersection of Xerxes Avenue and Overlook Drive.

The text message was simple. "No one following."

When Abou Hamed received the same text message from each one of his five watchers, he moved from the back of Coogan's Hardware store to its front window to peer out. He stood for another 15 minutes, eyes searching the streets for anything suspicious.

Convinced at last, he walked quickly from the store, jumped up on the dairy truck's running board, pulled open the driver's door and slid in behind the wheel. He handed Farad a pair of opaque black glasses and snapped his seat belt in place. Only after turning the ignition key did Abou Hamed finally speak: "*Ar-Raqib.*" (Allah the Watchful.)

"*Ash-Shakur*" answered Farad (Allah the Grateful), completing the predetermined code. Abou Hamed pulled away from the curb and headed north on River Street. The ensuing 'blind' drive took 15 minutes and ended at the cell's safe house, a nondescript, beige bungalow-style house in the low-end residential community of Baytown.

Farad would never know his exact physical location (a safeguard against capture), nor would he learn the identity of the target until he was secure and comfortable inside the safe house.

As the truck pulled into the gravel driveway, the garage door slid open, the truck pulled in and the door slammed shut.

"It's safe to remove the glasses, now, Master Aziz," said Abou Hamed. "Please follow me." But Farad stopped short in the middle of the garage, his eyes taken by the roof-high pile of neatly organized FedEx and UPS packages.

"What is this?" he asked.

"Items purchased off the internet," replied Abou.

"What kind of items?"

"Those are GPS devices," said the cell leader, pointing to one group of packages. "These are boxes of regular cell phones and these are the ones with prepaid cards. We've got sleeping bags, survival knives, some night-vision goggles, and two pairs of tennis shoes for each man."

Farad interrupted. "Who paid for this?"

"A man in California sent us many stolen credit card numbers and a list of the names to go with them. He's the one who notified us that you were coming."

Farad was unaware of Leon's arrangements with the rest of the terrorist membership, especially with the imbedded cells. Leon referred to it as a 'need to know;' but Farad understood it differently. *Leon is purposely keeping me out of the loop.*

"Of course. My assistant in California. And for security purposes, you don't know the man's name. Is that correct?" he said, attempting to sound authoritative.

"That's correct, Master Aziz."

"Good, let's get inside."

Abou Hamed guided his guest into the living room and seated him in a tattered overstuffed chair. Kneeling on the floor before him, their foreheads pressed to the ground, were six Islamist soldiers eagerly awaiting his orders. For them, Farad's arrival was a blessed event. He was a holy man whose words embodied the blessings of Allah. They had been preparing for this moment for years.

"Al Hamdu Lilah Wa Shukru Lillah" said Farad. (All Praise and thanks belongs to Allah) The soldiers immediately sat upright being careful to keep their eyes averted in solemn respect for this messenger from Allah.

This worshipful treatment was heady wine for the orphan of Beirut. No one in his life had ever paid Farad Aziz such respect. Certainly not his partners. It took every bit of his self control to conceal the sense of power and fulfillment he felt in the presence of these committed martyrs of Islam. The shabby overstuffed chair suddenly became precursor to a throne; the six bowed heads were the makings of an army. His army. *Farad-Mumīt.* (the Bringer of Death) *Farad-Muntaqim* (The Avenger)

Leon had set out a precise routine in minute detail for Farad's initial meeting. It was meticulous, the de Kennesy thumb print on every detail.

Farad ignored all of it, choosing instead to follow his gut. He began by sending all of the soldiers out of the room. "You, leader, Hamed, you stay!" he barked. "Sit."

The startled cell leader did as he was told.

"Hamed, do you have any idea why you were chosen as the leader of this cell?"

"No sir. I don't," answered Abou Hamed. All orders were presumed to be the will of Allah as meted out by Mullah Rockmani.

"I chose you myself," said Farad, closing his eyes, doing his best to appear spiritual. "Two days and nights of prayer before it came to me. It was your faith in Allah, your ability to follow orders, but most important my brother," Farad's eyes widened dramatically, "It was your loyalty that led me to choose you."

The statement was an absolute lie, but its effect was extraordinary. Abou Hamed was struck dumb at such praise. To have his performance considered in any way by an elder of the Jihad was a rare honor.

From behind his spiritual poker face, Farad observed the effect his words were having on the enraptured cell leader. It was time to affect a subtle transfer of power, to shift the authority from Leon to Farad.

It appeared to be working.

As Abou Hamed waited anxiously for the next utterance, Farad produced a special hand-rolled joint and pinched it into an ornate silver roach clip. He fired its end and drew in a deep ceremonial breath of smoke. His eyelids closed in a moment of solemn silence. Then, exhaling slowly, he proffered the joint to his honored listener, as if to consummate a relationship of reverence and obedience.

As the calming smoke curled skyward from Abou Hamed's nose, Farad began to inquire warmly about the cell leader's family members, his city of origin, his Mosque, and his history of worship. As tensions eased and Hamed's answers lost their guardedness, Farad withdrew his Palm Pilot and laid it on the worn arm of his chair. As the friendly interrogation continued, Farad began entering some of Abou Hamed's information into the device. Occasionally, he would confirm the particulars before entering the data.

While it was a tribute of holy ascension to be included in Farad's personal notes, it sent Abou Hamed's insides into a nauseating plummet of fear. Knowing the intimate details of one's family, his place of worship and the identity of his friends

– this was dangerous information. Hamed tried to calm himself. He was sitting before a holy man, a messenger from Allah. His faith told him that there was nothing to fear; his stomach told him he was stepping on a land mine.

Farad continued warmly, feigning personal interest, until he felt the deal was *inked*. This would occur when he sensed that his notes were sufficiently damning to lock his man into a pact of fearful obedience. Then it was time to conclude the intimidation and bring things to a holy conclusion. To cement the new relationship.

He took hold of the cell leader's forearms and stared into his eyes. "Abou Hamed, my brother, you and I will destroy this corrupt country. Together we will resurrect the Caliphate. Allah's will be done. We will stand together knee-deep in their blood. Fear not. I will show you the way. We will burn them alive and send them to the hell they deserve. This holy Jihad will earn us our ultimate reward. I have come here as Allah's witness, to lead you and your men to heaven. Praise be to Allah."

Farad called it his resurrection speech. He'd thought of it the previous night in the Bide-a-wee Motel. He was brushing his teeth when the bolt of inspiration hit him. Wiping a little circle in the grime on the bathroom mirror, he took a long pull on a freshly flamed joint and stared at himself proudly. "You know why this is so goddamn brilliant?" he asked his heavy-lidded visage. "The brilliant part is..." For a moment he lost his train of thought, took another pull on the joint; then suddenly, it was back again. "It's brilliant because they won't even know it's happened to them."

His fantasy was to create a coup of his own; a secret militia within the Silent Jihad. They would become his personal militia, an imbedded force hiding under the shadow of Leon's arrogant hawk nose. They would become his insurance policy.

By now his angry battles with Leon had escalated in fervor and frequency; the hatred between them was barely kept in check. It was only a matter of time. No matter how much they claimed to 'value' him, he knew they were biding their time. Waiting for him to finish. He knew that on the day he set the last timer, Leon was planning to kill him.

But a man with his own army could become invincible.

35

The Mall of America

Minnesota's famous Mall of America is the largest fully-enclosed retail and family entertainment complex in the U.S. – 4.2 million square feet of humanity – waiting to be taken.

The terrorist cell members had spent 30 months infiltrating Minnesota's Baytown community, scouting the target site and carefully mapping the routes of attack and escape. Their accomplishments were beyond anything Farad had expected.

Two of them were working at a mobile hot dog stand in front of the Multiplex at the very center of the Mall. Both were on a first name basis with many of the shop girls and security staff. A third cell member had gotten a job as a clean-up man on the Mall's maintenance staff. A fourth was making daily pizza deliveries to the office personnel in the Mall's Administration Plaza.

It was 6 p.m.; the huge Mall was teeming with hungry Minnesotans. Three delivery men, dressed in "Carnation Co." T-shirts, entered the east end of the Mall on the street level. Two of them were rolling dollies stacked with large red Nestle crates labeled with the words, "Nestle Goodness." Behind them came Farad, wheeling a hand truck loaded with red and white boxes of Carnation powdered milk.

Midway into the Food Court, two security guards stepped in front of the trio and held up their hands, signaling 'stop.' Farad's forced himself to remain calm. He looked off into the crowd, his mind racing, trying to look casual. *What do I say to these pigs?*

The larger of the two guards, a perspiring hulk of a man with a huge fat stomach, addressed the smaller of Farad's two helpers. "Elon," dude, that's a big stack a' shit for such a little man. You need some help with that?"

A big toothy smile lit up Elon's face. "You eat too much taco, man. Pretty soon you bust and I have to clean up you mess."

Amazing!

The four of them began laughing and poking each other (two guards and two terrorists) like they were high school buddies. Then both guards decided to help out by providing crowd control. They walked ahead of the group, moving the crowd aside so Farad and his men could get through more easily.

When they reached freight elevators on the Food Court Level, the fat guard reached for the call button, "Up or down?"

"Never mind, we got more," answered Elon.

"Check you later, then." And the two guards moved off into the mass of shoppers.

Not understanding the idiom, Farad leaned close to Elon, "They're coming back?"

"No way. They be smoking now at dumpster."

"Alright, let's get going."

They carefully stacked all of the cartons in three waste-high piles in front of the service elevator. Then left the concealed explosives unattended and retraced their steps as if heading back to their truck for more boxes. Leaving the explosives in plain view was one of Farad's time honored axioms: *Nobody notices what you don't hide.*

When they reached the exit, the two helpers continued out the exit toward the loading zone. Farad turned left and headed for the 'All American Hot Dog Stand.

He shouldered his way in among the customers and shouted, "Long dog and a Coke. And give me a side of curly fries with that." In two decades of planting bombs in the Middle East, Farad had developed several of his own axioms. At the moment, leaning nonchalantly against the counter, he was practicing the most important one: *the bolder the behavior, the less noticeable the deed.*

As he reached out for his food, Farad got the feeling that someone was watching him. Casually, he looked across the rectangular booth and got caught in the gaze of a very tall, 20-year-old, blue-eyed girl. He looked down immediately, grabbed a plastic bottle of putrid yellow mustard and began squirting it on his onion-drenched dog. He bit off a giant mouthful and tried to concentrate on chewing. When he reached for his Coke, he snuck a quick look across the booth. The girl was gone.

He took a long, grateful swallow of Coke and turned away from the stand. She was now standing directly in his path. Her fish white legs were sticking out of some faded shorts, her feet were shod in pink flip flops. Her light-colored hair was buzz cut so short, her head reminded Farad of a ripened cantaloupe. The blue tendrils of a flower tattoo snaked up the right side of her neck. The hoops poking through her thick dark eyebrows made her look like a beaded caterpillar.

"Hi, I'm Nicole, my friends call me Nicky. Are you from Iraq?"

"Ah...I'm, I'm a Serb. I'm from Serbia," he said.

"Cool, where's Serbia?"

Nicole didn't know where Serbia was and neither did Farad. "You know, it's over there in the Mid East." Mind racing, he shoved half of the hot dog into his mouth.

Farad chewed. They stared at each other for an awkward moment. Finally she spoke again. "So what are you doing here, shopping or something?"

"Waiting for my...girlfriend." *That ought to do it.*

"I think dark men are hot. Wanna hook up before she gets here? Bet I can get you off faster than she does."

"Ah...I, you know, well...I'd like to...hook up. Thanks anyway, but well, you know, we're betrothed."

The big smile vanished. "Whatever, dude. Your loss." Abruptly, she turned her back and walked off into the mass of moving shoppers. Looking back, she pointed directly at him, and yelled, "Gay!"

Farad quickly turned the other way and as calmly as he could, walked to the trash can. He dumped in the remains of his hot dog and looked at his watch.

Five minutes late. That bitch.

He dashed into the aisle and raced to the entrance of Sam Goody. Waiting for a break in the stream of shoppers, he finally forced his way through the flow and ran to the handrail. He looked across to the elevators. His sigh of relief was audible. A small perimeter was marked off with orange tape and plastic cones. A 'Men at Work' sign was stretched between two of the cones. An 'out of order' sigh had been neatly taped to the doors of the utility elevator.

He could see Lookout man #1 standing close by pretending to read the newspaper. *This is good. This is very good, so far.*

In the weeks after 9/11, the management company at the Mall of America had doubled the size of their security force. They had installed new digital entry systems on all floors. And as an extra precaution, they had installed video cameras above every door in the complex.

Gaining access to the support structures of the Mall had seemed an insurmountable problem. It had taken the Bloomington cell six months of reconnaissance to solve it. It was Nizar, the Mall clean-up man who discovered the *way in*. On one of the previous dry runs, he had also succeeded in dismantling the elevator's alarm system.

At 7 p.m., it started. Farad nervously watched as 'his soldiers' began executing the steps they had rehearsed so often.

While lookouts #1 and #2 made sure that no one approached the service elevator, Nizar began moving the stack of Carnation cartons into the elevator. When the doors closed behind him, he would secure the elevator in the *stop* position.

Farad began his descent, pausing to look through store windows, killing time, checking his watch, counting the minutes.

Inside the elevator, Nizar was to use the struts of the hand truck as a ladder. He would climb to the top of the car and open the hatch. Then, choosing the heavier cartons first, he would carefully push the load of C4, one carton at a time, up the rails of the hand truck and through the opening until they rested on the top of the elevator itself.

Twenty-five minutes later, Farad climbed over the yellow tape and approached the service elevator. When he pushed the elevator 'call' button, the doors parted. He stepped into the darkened elevator and quickly pushed the 'close' button. When the doors were completely closed, he pushed the red 'stop' button and looked up. He was greeted by a pair of feet, shod in Air Jordans, hanging through the open hatch.

"Nizar?" he whispered.

"I am here."

Using the struts of the hand truck, just as Nizar had done, Farad climbed up through the opening and crouched down on the top of the car. The air was black, the odor of grease stifling. The atmosphere felt heavy and claustrophobic. Farad reached out to steady himself, found the greased cables in the center of the car and grabbed on. "I'm adjusting my eyes."

"Let me know when you're ready," came the reply.

In a few moments, the slight outlines of shaft and cables and 'U-beams' began to take shape in front of him. Another minute passed. "All right. Show me," ordered Farad.

Nizar clicked on a small flashlight and trained its beam on the side wall of the elevator shaft. Sticking out of the dirty black concrete, Farad could see a utility ladder made of individual iron rungs, each one protruding about five inches. The ladder ran vertically from the bottom of the shaft to the roof.

By stepping off the car and climbing up and down the rungs, repairmen could gain access to any floor by virtue of the open crawl spaces cut into the shaft wall. Each floor had its own crawl space designed to permit repairmen quick access to the control boxes on the interior walls of each floor. As the crawl space was not considered an entrance, no cameras were installed.

Carrying one 45-pound carton at a time (strapped tightly to their shoulders via backpack harnesses), it took Farad and Nizar 74 minutes to navigate the precarious climbs up the narrow elevator shaft, through the crawl space and out on to the Machinery and Maintenance floor.

Once Farad and Nizar had maneuvered the heavy cartons into the middle of the maintenance area, Farad's signaled a three minute break. The two men removed their harnesses and began chewing voraciously on power bars to recover their energy.

Powdered C4 explosive is a mixture of three primary elements: binder, elastomer and explosive. With the addition of water, followed by some distillation and filtering, the mixture becomes a relatively stable and malleable explosive with the consistency of modeling clay. When triggered, it expands with devastating effect, as in the 2002 bombing of the Sari Nightclub in Bali, which killed 180 people and injured 300.

Farad had already catalyzed the mixture, tripling its weight in the process, and left the resulting plastic dough in the five-gallon containers of Carnation Milk.

In its present state, the C4 was quite stable. Only a proper detonator could set off the blast. However, fearing a loss of control, Farad had encouraged the belief in his gullible cell members that handling the explosive was a life-threatening task.

Carefully wielding a wide-handled Xacto blade, Nizar made precise cuts through the edges of each carton, and cautiously peeled away the cardboard sides exposing the lethal dough.

Farad inspected the support pillars, making sure he had selected the optimal location for the blast. While Nizar gathered up the cartons of cardboard waste and carried them off to the interior trash chute, Farad climbed in behind the central support pillar. and began wedging the explosive dough into a wide crevice at the main pillar's base. The process took almost 20 minutes.

After assuring himself that the load was secure and properly placed, Farad climbed out and motioned Nizar in to take his place. Using a small can of beige touch-up paint, Nizar began painting the surface of the C4 to match the exact color of the surrounding concrete. As one of the Mall's clean-up men, Nizar had easy access to a large storeroom of exact paint colors which were used to cover the constant scrapes and grease marks left by the Mall's repairmen.

Painting the C4 with fast-drying water based paint was the final step in its concealment.

After inspecting the paint job, Farad flashed Nizar a 'thumbs up' and hurried back to the crawl space. He wiggled through the narrow opening, climbed back down the rung ladder and stepped carefully across to the top of the elevator. Easing through the open hatch, he lowered himself down to the elevator floor; then carefully replaced the ceiling hatch. Straightening his clothes, he took a deep breath and pulled out the alarm stop. The elevator took him down to the parking area.

He stepped out of the elevator and walked to the blue Toyota parked in the handicapped zone. In the back seat of the car was a pile of colorful shipping bags. He selected two from the Gap, one from Smith and Hawken and one from Eddie Bauer and hooked them over his arm.

He joined the flow of other shoppers and rode the escalator up to the second level. There he ducked into a Chuao Confectioners and purchased a small bag of liquor-filled chocolates. Moving as casually as he possible could, he walked to an adjacent food court and seated himself at a small table.

He couldn't stop his hands from shaking. The pressure behind his eyes was building. Panic! *I left the hand truck in the elevator!*

He jumped up and started to go after it. After a few steps, he remembered. *That was the plan. Nizar is gonna remove it. Part of his regular duties as 'clean up man.'*

He walked back to the little table and sat down again. His heart was pounding harder. The voice in his head was screaming, "Run! Get away. Now! Run for it." He fought to restrain the impulse. Hands still shaking, he stuffed three bittersweet candies into his mouth.

"Can I get you something, sir?" The voice came from behind him. His body went rigid with fear. Slowly he turned around to face his accuser. She was an overweight, middle-aged waitress, wearing an orange paper hat and a red and yellow jumper. The words 'Orange Julius' were printed on her blouse.

Farad Aziz stared at her *disgusting fatness*, commanding his mind to work.

"Sir?" she asked again.

"What??" he shouted.

Her eyes pinched together in a squint of confusion and disapproval. "Never mind," she said finally. And she waddled off toward another table.

A moment passed. Another moment. The stream of shoppers continued, moving past his table in noisy little clumps. No one seemed to notice him. The hint of a smile appeared on Farad's lips. *Safe.* Was he safe? Was anyone looking? Were they on to him?

Awareness crept into the corners of his brain. *No one's looking. They're not looking. No one knows. Relax. No one knows.*

He fished into the little bag of Chuao candy and chose a piquante. Savoring its tinge of spice, he stared over the railing at the mass of shoppers moving like ants along the aisles below. Then his eyes swept up and across the scores of hungry eaters jammed into the tables around him, queuing up in front of the purveyors of food. There were 40 different stalls within his view; and 50 more across the huge arboretum shading the center of the Mall.

One day very soon, the world will bear witness. They will honor the name, Farad Aziz.

His mind began to spin, visualizing the fruits of his labor; girders twisted into molten shoestrings, shock waves moving at the speed of sound. Concrete turning liquid, black/orange lava flowing into the aisles torching all in its wake. A howling death-storm. Flesh vaporized, bones charred into black powder.

He looked down at the thousands of diners in the Food Court below. The collapse of the massive concrete third floor, would kill them all. But more perfectly, its molten weight would cascade down into the Mall's 500 shops and the nightclubs and the theaters, crushing them under a river of fire and vengeance...the death toll would soar...tens of thousands. Infidels burning in hell fire. Hundreds of thousands before it was done. By the power of *Al-Mumeet (*The One who renders the living dead.)

By 11 p.m., all of the cell members had returned to the safe house. All were assembled in the living room. Farad took up his position, royalty enthroned in a tattered brown chair. It was his turn to play Mullah.

"My brothers, Allah be praised. You have lived with the *kaffir* (infidel) all these months; you have endured their stench and their depravity. Your loyalty to the *umma* (worldwide Islamic community) shines like a ruby in the mighty Sword of Allah.

"Today you have fulfilled the dreams of our holy Mullah. Through me, he sends you his prayers and his gratitude and his blessings. Our Muslim existence has been threatened by Jews and Christians for a thousand years. But praise be to *Al-Qahhar* (the Subduer)*!* Our revenge is at hand. The evil Satan will perish in hell fire. You are truly the blessed sons of Allah."

Their cheers echoed against the walls, each man welcoming his own death, each man lusting for its heavenly rewards. Hidden behind enemy lines, living in the *belly of the Beast*, six soldiers of the Silent Jihad danced around their empty living room in the quiet neighborhood of Baytown, Minnesota. They raised their glasses and drank great swallows of wine.

For a few minutes Farad indulged his troops, clapping his hands as they continued to embrace each other, shouting their joy to Al-Azeem (the Great One).

Then he raised his arms and called them to order. "Only the most holy Mullah can determine when the final day of glory will arrive. On that day I'll return to set the timing of the blast.

"In the meantime, your duties are even more important!"

Farad's eyes moved slowly from face to face, holding the gaze of each supplicant, imposing the call to blind obedience. "Should anyone suspect your mission, should one of the policemen attempt to take you into custody, in the name of Al-

Muhyi (the Giver of Life), you must fight to the death and receive his blessing. Your reward is as certain as his holy name. You will commit yourselves to the arms of Allah the Merciful. Is that understood?"

The response was an immediate, unified and deliberate "yes" from every soldier in the room. Farad nodded his head, maintaining a stern countenance, comporting himself as he imagined a wise and holy leader would.

He left them without further fanfare, backed the milk truck out of the garage and drove off headed for Highway 59.

Back on his own. End of charade. Reality suddenly crashing down on him. It's back to the gutter. The orphan of Beirut. Alone. No idea where to go. Not even the direction he should be driving.

Farad was lost. Caught in the belly of the Beast. Waiting for Leon's next set of instructions. *Like a goddamn puppy dog. Just the way Leon planned it.*

36

Riverton, Virginia

After a 10-hour flight, Colonel Luke Towne, in full military dress, stepped off the U.S. Marine Corps Harrier Jet at Riverton, a remote military landing field in north Virginia.

In the 40s and 50s, Riverton had been an active Marine Air Station, supporting 2500 troops engaged in Lighter-than-Air (LTA) blimp flight training.

These days Riverton was a ghost town; row upon row of forlorn camouflaged barracks surrounded by miles of crumbling, blackened airstrips. To all those passing on the rural roads, Riverton was an apparent wasteland; 40 acres of tall brown weeds.

The only living creatures at Riverton were the several hundred turkey buzzards who roosted in the debris of the military's dilapidated wooden structures, plus the countless packs of night howling, black-eyed coyotes driven there by the low cost housing developments to the North. The place was remote by anyone's standards. Even the local residents called it 'The middle of nowhere.'

But Riverton had one distinguishing feature. In its center was one of the largest concrete dirigible hangers in the United States. It was an enormous structure, 1087 feet long, 290 feet high and 300 feet wide, the interior of which had been permanently and secretly maintained in pristine condition by the Marine Corps.

Doctor Cynthia Teller and a crew of 20 scientists and engineers from The Facility had already spent weeks inside the giant structure, preparing it for the test phase of the Pentagon's highly classified Mind's Eye Project.

Although the first phase of Top Gun auditions was held at Langley, a more secure location was needed for the hands-on phase. The complex test equipment had to be assembled at a secure and completely isolated location. And Riverton with its enormous hangar was the perfect choice. The process was costing the Pentagon an additional six million, over and above the 300 million they had already committed to the project's development.

Twelve aviator chairs were set up at one end of the immense hangar in Riverton. They were arranged in two rows of six and placed just under the nose of an angry-looking, black F/A-18E/F "Super Hornet" fuselage – a $60 million killing machine with 13,700 pounds of external ordnance tucked under its 45' retractable wings; its shark fin Tailerons spiked straight up in the air; its Twin F414-GE-400, 22,000 pound thrust engines with their gaping, black rimmed, jet exhaust ports sticking out of its ass end.

A mass of greased hydraulics and mechanized support struts held the behemoth aircraft above the floor like a hungry tyrannosaurus looking down at its human prey. Twelve of the country's 1st Fighter Wing Top Gun pilots sat in the chairs beneath it.

They were anxiously awaiting the arrival of a legend.

The clock struck noon. The gigantic 10-story concrete doors at one end of the hangar parted and without fanfare, Luke Towne stepped through them and made his way down the aisle between the two rows of seats. When he turned to face the men, he was standing directly under the nose of the big jet, wearing the full dress uniform of his rank as a Lieutenant Colonel in the U.S. Special Forces. As the second most decorated soldier in the history of the Corps, his chest was heavy with the medals of his distinguished service. The men stood as one, applauding this famous soldier/scientist whose presence they had been promised, and whose arrival was long awaited.

"Gentlemen," he began, "The Mind's Eye project represents the cutting edge of our country's defense system. It is fitting that you should become the recipients of our most advanced technology. You are the best of the best. At the end of your training, you will be personally endowed with the power of a modern day Excalibur; knighted by your inclusion in an elite group of ultimate warriors. A killer force with an enhanced ability to do battle – with your minds. It is my honor to be addressing you today."

There was an eerie silence. Luke used it to maximum effect. With great reverence, he removed his little silver PDA from his breast pocket and set it on the table in front of him. After a beat he said, "All right, now that you've heard the marketing bullshit, let's see if this little pecker really works. What do you say?"

A hearty male cheer reverberated off the rafters of the cavernous building. There was a reason Luke had succeeded as a leader of men. Luke called out a name. "Squadron Leader, Captain Mo Morris!'

Captain Morris jumped to his feet. "Present sir," he answered, amazed that Luke knew his name.

"Captain Morris, imagine you're flying this F18 right here in front of us. You're in combat. You need to change course. Pick a random adjustment in wing attitude."

"You mean like, 'so many degrees right rudder,' sir?"

"If you like."

"All right, 15 degrees right rudder," he barked; then remained standing to see what was about to happen.

Luke turned his profile to them, clasped his hands behind his back, and stared directly at the little silver Blackberry PDA sitting on the desk in front of him. His eyes registered a tiny squint.

Zzz-Pssft! A metallic sigh whispered behind him; the chrome hydraulics under the huge F/A-18C Hornet hissed into motion. There was a subtle meshing of gears; a vibration in the big fuselage. Then its sleek black elevators eased downward, and the deadly jet fighter tipped its massive wings in an arcing 15 degree turn to the right.

The sight was magnificent. The enormous prehistoric creature suspended above them had freely turned its head before swooping to claim them all as prey.

Their unison gasp of disbelief was audible. No one spoke. Luke stood quietly in the silence, acutely aware that the event had more impact than any words he might add.

Then, sensing the right moment, he continued. "Gentlemen, let me explain what just happened here. In my mind, I ran through a rapid key code. Those word-thoughts produced an electric impulse in my brain based on my own cranial electronics. That impulse of electricity then triggered a tiny laser load from the lens on my pupil."

He pointed to his right eye then to Phyllis, which was placed on the desk next to him. "I directed the laser shot from my eye to the receptor in that silver Blackberry – which looks like a Blackberry but is actually something very different. We have nicknamed her 'Phyllis,' and that little pecker moved the F18 15 degrees."

The nation's most sophisticated, highly trained Top Gun pilots were still clearly awestruck by the demonstration. To a man, each one's brain was off on its own speculative journey, imagining the implications and possibilities of this new technology. Luke saw the questions coming.

"Hang on to your questions for a second. I'll see if I can pull it together for you a little more clearly. We've had you here undergoing brain scans and synapse testing for a reason. It's not because we question your mental capacity. We already know you've got plenty of that. And I'm told, some attitude to go with it. Doctor Teller tells me that some of your heads no longer seem to fit in the E/F's new AWL sensor helmets. Is that true?"

At that moment, Doctor Cynthia Teller entered and the men's laughter turned to warm applause. It was the first time they had seen her wearing her own captain's uniform in the U.S. Navy. She rolled a large blackboard up to Luke, handed him a pointer and took a seat with the men.

On the board was a complicated schematic of the Mind's Eye laser technology, which Luke used periodically to highlight his explanation.

"As you know," he continued, "The brain generates its own current, puts out amps as it functions. We have been testing you to find out how your personal brain generator works, because, unfortunately, no two brains function exactly the same way."

Luke sat on the edge of the table top and made himself comfortable. "I'm going to tell you how the Mind's Eye technology was born. The conception was easy. Took about nine minutes. Happened in the line at a Burger King. Three minutes to think it up; three minutes to stuff in a cheeseburger, three minutes to write it all down. The execution was not quite that easy: took us six long years to get where we are today, given the brilliance of a most gifted ocular surgeon, Captain Cynthia Teller, and a team of creatives at our Facility whom Captain Teller and I would rate as second to none in the world.

"The Burger King version goes like this. If the brain produces electric impulses, we should be able to process those impulses just like any other signal. Next question. Do distinct thoughts produce distinct repeatable signals? Yes they do. So why not convert those signals to laser pulses, miniaturize a laser gun, mount it on the human retina, focus it on an external receptor, shoot the signal to the receptor, connect the receptor to a solenoid and move mechanical objects in space?

"Result: I think the thought; a chip converts my brain current to a laser pulse; my eye focuses on a receptor; the laser pulse is amplified by the chip in my head and broadcast from my eye through an exotic set of Doctor Teller's lenses to the receptor; the electronics in receptor move the solenoid and the desired mechanical function is accomplished.

"It seemed to me that a man might operate and control external electronic devices with his mind...by looking at them. Hence the name, The Mind's Eye."

There was a deafening silence as 12 of the nation's smartest and most proficient Top Guns tried to assimilate Luke's fast food explanation of the Pentagon's $300 million research project.

Captain Mo Morris raised his hand. "Colonel, did I understand you correctly to say something about a chip in your head?' Would that mean that there are two operations; one in the eye and one in the head?"

Luke laughed. "Correct, Captain. One in the eye; that's the laser gun on the retina; and one in the head; that would be the power chip back here," he said, pointing to the back of his own head. "The power chip isn't actually invasive to the head, Doctor Teller just sticks it under the skin and gives it a stitch to keep it in place, right behind the occipital bone.

He let them chew on it for a time and then held up his hands to change the mood.

"There is one other critical element in this process that needs a word of explanation." He picked up his little silver PDA and held it high in front of them. "This amazing little can of broadcast resources functions like a normal PDA. But it performs at a level quite beyond anything you can buy at Wal-Mart. Its unique laser capacity is so powerful it'll be riding with you permanently in the cockpit of your F18; and from now on, in every fighter jet aircraft the U.S. sends up.

"Its internal processor is called Dual-Inline-Lens-Resolution. The anagram for that is D-I-L-R. It took about five seconds for my smart ass scientific team to name her Phyllis."

Luke set the little silver PDA back down on the table. "Let me assure you, gentlemen, Phyllis doesn't need me to explain her multiple functions. Phyllis can literally speak for herself."

And she did.

She was standing in a slightly darkened alcove to the right of the blackboard – a red-headed woman, wearing the uniform of a captain in the U.S. Air Corps. She possessed a minutely detailed, highly articulated physical form; her material substance appeared to be wholly tangible. She was rendered in perfect three-dimensional space, no transparency, no noise at the edges, no glitches in resolution.

Her voice was amplified by Yellow Tooth, The Facility's wireless laser amp system, so that she could be heard by everyone in the group. The sound of her voice was sultry, but her tone was serious.

"Good afternoon gentlemen," she began. "First let me say I don't appreciate being called 'a little pecker.' As you will observe, the name doesn't fit."

Phyllis was projecting her own personal avatar into the space in front of them. A Mind's Eye miracle; a breathing, three-dimensional, full color holograph that appeared in every aspect to be completely real.

As with most holographs, any sudden movements could destroy the impression of true *solid matter* by revealing the dark areas within the image – spaces between the air's reflective particles which give the image its form, as well as its halo effect – an outline around the image differentiating it from the light of its real environment.

In order to mask these imperfections, The Facility's scientists had designed an innocent looking alcove inside of which to project the moving holograph. The combination of slight darkness plus a concealed grid of reflective strips along the alcove's perimeter was enough to compensate for nature's shortcomings.

As a result, there appeared to be no perceptual difference between Colonel Towne and the woman who was now standing three feet to his left.

There was no reaction from the men. They thought she was real.

"You may call me Phyllis," she continued. "The technology of my laser projection chip affords a clarity of image that is unsurpassed; a material quality that surpasses HDTV."

Luke saw the eyes of two pilots in the back row grow wide in shock with the realization of what they thought they had just heard.

Phyllis continued, "As Colonel Towne will tell you, I may eventually save your lives in combat. I will be flying with each of you. I will be there in the cockpit awaiting your mental instructions. The more proficient you become at this new form of communication, the more I will be able to help you; the more tasks I will be able to perform. I am the perfect woman; treat me well and I can be anything you want me to be, except a little pecker."

Then, in one stunning revelation, right in front of them, Phyllis's red hair turned blonde, her age dropped 10 years, and her uniform dissolved into a skin tight evening dress.

Holy Crap! She isn't real.

There was an audible gasp of disbelief. Their eyes had deceived them. The woman had appeared completely real. Normal. And such bullshit metamorphoses were tricks for television and music videos. But this woman had occupied physical space before them. She was real.

She wasn't real.

Slowly the Top Guns rose en masse; single claps turned into groups of two and three until they stood united in one continual thunderous round of applause.

Phyllis eventually raised her hands and the group quieted. "Projecting my image into the air is a parlor trick. It's not part of my operations manual; nor does it have a purpose other than entertaining you and the scientists who created me. Perhaps one day they will find a use for it. In the meantime, Doctor Teller and Colonel Towne felt you could use this little bit of cheese ball levity after your arduous concentration and testing. Your efforts will be critical to the success of this project, and gentlemen, you are appreciated.

"But now let's get to the point. Let me return us to the purpose of your lives; your calling as pilots in our country's 1st Fighter Wing."

The blonde avatar morphed back into a mature but attractive red-headed captain in the U.S. Air Corps. There was an audible 'Ohoo' of disappointment from the men as they lost their blonde bombshell.

"I thank you for your ardor," she said. "My circuit board thanks you as well. Now, as Colonel Towne has indicated, this Mind's Eye technology is unique in the world. With it, our national defense system will take on new dimensions. Your responsibilities will be increased one hundredfold. Your brains, your abilities, your determination and the force of your will, will shape our airborne defense systems from now on.

"Say goodbye to the fun and games, gentlemen. Together, we have an awesome opportunity to shape the future. We will depend on each other. I will learn with you. I will go with you into battle. I wish you Godspeed in your commitment to defend our country."

With that, the feminine avatar dissolved into space right before their eyes, leaving only a little silver PDA resting harmlessly on the desk.

The Top Guns were on their feet again, united in one continual cheer.

37

Riverton, Virginia

Luke's participation at the hangar went on for two days. He worked closely with the pilots, answering every question, responding with genuine interest. He demonstrated a personal sensitivity to each man, an amazing trait which reminded Cynthia of why her former husband had become a military icon.

"Here's how the internals work," said Luke, addressing the 12. "There is a series of steps you must learn in order to control the Mind's Eye software. The first step is a state of 'unthought.' Some would call it a *blank slate*. I call it 'going to your room.' How many of you remember Brian Wilson's ballad, *In My Room?*"

No one responded.

"You know, the Beach Boys? *In My Room.* The anthem to male youth and solitude."

Not a single hand went up. (Old man consciousness.)

"All right never mind." He shrugged at Cynthia. "Think of it this way. Remember as a kid, your room was a place of complete and total safety, right? Peace and quiet; loud music if you wanted; cheat sheets; whispered phone calls; smuggled girlfriends; big plans, big dreams. The point is, whatever your room was, it was yours. All yours. Your concept, your choice.

"Well, in this case, make your room a zone of total calm; a place of perfect unthought. So that when I say 'go to your room,' you'll be able to shut off your mind at will." He snapped his fingers in the air. "Stop all thought. Instantly, just like that.

"Gentlemen, that's the first thing you'll need to master.

"Once you've got that, you'll move on to step two. You'll learn a pattern of simple key thoughts; rote; repetitive, like your own name. And those thoughts will arm the laser gun on your cornea. Once you've mastered that, you'll be able to fire mental commands at Phyllis and she will execute them for you flawlessly. That's what she lives for."

He saw some of their eyes begin to glaze over. "Remember now," he said quickly, "Thoughts in your brain create electronic current; the same exact current every time you think the same thought. For example, every time you think 'long legs,' the same repetitive electronic current is created. You think 'D cup' and your little brain powers up the 'D cup' impulse, right?

"So, if you think 'fire cannon,' your brain makes the 'fire cannon' impulse every time. Actually, your brain creates electronic current and our chip converts it into a pulse; a laser pulse. But you're getting the picture, right?"

One of the pilots raised his hand, but before Luke could call on him, Cynthia Teller approached with a look of concern on her face. Luke excused himself from the group of pilots. He could see whatever news she had was not positive.

His voice lowered. "What's happened?"

"I just got a message from Dave. Apparently the spot welds holding the main platform should have been bolts. Three of them cracked this morning. The computer slipped off and fell to the floor of the cockpit."

"Shit, I knew I should have stayed until it was finished."

"It gets worse. The computer cables held tight. It pulled the entire lens platform down with it. Every lens is cracked."

A big sigh of frustration from Luke. "Well, guess I'm outta here. Sorry to leave you in the middle of this, but..."

"I already notified Captain Lewis. The plane's fueling now. They'll be ready by the time you get your stuff." Together they began walking toward the living quarters at the opposite end of the hangar.

"Luke, I know something else is going on. I know now's not the time. But I'm worried. When you're ready, I hope you'll let me help."

He scooped up his gear, barely unpacked, gave her a peck on the cheek, and headed for the door. "Thanks Cyn. We'll talk when you get back. It's no big deal. Nothing I can't handle."

And off he went.

Nothing I can't handle. She'd heard him say it a thousand times. But as she watched the Prowler vault into the air and bank a lazy arc to the south, she could feel the acid dumping into her stomach.

The Facility – Malibu, California

Luke spent the next three weeks locked in at The Facility. Most nights he didn't bother going home, choosing instead to sleep in his office. There was far too much to do in way too short a time. The nosecone accident had set them back at least a month, but it had also presented opportunities for product improvement.

The implementation of each upgrade took endless hours. Circuit boards and housings were reinforced to guard against future impact bound to occur in combat; all welds were eliminated in favor of bolt-on superstructure; and the work had only begun.

Through it all, Luke and Cynthia spoke several times a day, updating each other with data that enhanced progress at both ends. Cynthia reported that several of the pilots had begun to master the mental techniques necessary for signal transmission. The optimal time was 10 seconds to establish communication with the cockpit receptor.

Practicing on a computerized version of Phyllis, 10 of the pilots had learned to connect visually in just under 60 seconds. These were prime candidates for ocular surgery. And although no human operations could be performed until approved by the Pentagon's medical staff, all of the participating pilots had eagerly signed the Navy's experimental surgery waivers.

During his the first week back, Luke and Kathryn de Kennesy were also back in daily contact. Her job as the Lebanese Consulate pro tem in San Francisco had quickly become a permanent 12-hour/day assignment. Luke had arranged to transport her laser teleconferencing system from her home in Beqaa, Lebanon, to her new apartment in Russian Hill. Their nightly visual connections had grown even more intimate, not in their sexual expression (which had not abated), but in their emotional closeness. Kathryn's vulnerability had apparently been greatly affected by her time at the little house in Malibu.

Of course Luke had said nothing about the President's ridiculous accusations against her family, nor about his supposed role as spy. *Why shatter her life?* It was all too absurd to discuss anyway.

He had real work to do. And work was his passion.

His stress levels were starting to burn off like so many mornings of California coastal fog. There had been no contact from Orin Pierce. No more government goons in his rear view mirror.

But why?

Luke had given the question many hours of speculation. They send him an engraved invitation from the Commander in Chief. They have it delivered by the one soldier he admires most in the world, General Malcolm Diggs. They send him to spy school, create a personalized course of studies with his name on it, then suddenly drop him like a hot grenade.

Why?

His years in the Military had given him the answer. And in retrospect, it was quite simple, predictable even. When class was over, he'd been tested. They had simulated some of the pressures he would have to face in the real world of clandestine operations. They'd purposely baited him, pushed his buttons, and threatened him physically in order to determine his viability as a double agent.

Not only had he failed, but he'd gone psycho on them. He was trained to be a soldier and he had responded like one. In spite of their overnight sessions in 'spy training,' he had defaulted to his original skill set; physical violence. He had warned them from the start that he was not qualified for the job. It now gave him a degree of pleasure to realize that, unknowingly, his actions had proven the truth of his prediction.

I flunked.

The Military functioned on a single tenet; the principle of authority and control. No military organization could accept a member they couldn't control. In the world of clandestine ops, unpredictability could be dangerous to the health.

A refusal to obey orders could easily result in death.

Given a bit of time to understand what had taken place, Luke had managed to shove the spy business into a dark closet and mentally slam the door. His productivity at The Facility increased, no doubt helped along by having Kathryn so accessible to him in San Francisco. His ability to concentrate was back. His role as a double agent had faded into the background. He was once again focused on the upcoming Mind's Eye presentation.

He had been to the de Kennesys' new home in Bel Air on several occasions. Leon and Nana de Kennesy had invited him over for fantastic home-cooked Sunday dinners, even when Kathryn was out of town. He had seen no indications of terrorist leanings, no philosophical discussions; no attempts to pump him for information. He had found no boogie men in the de Kennesy closets.

As he had suspected, the terrorist activities manufactured by Pierce and the President were just that; manufactured. Why else had they refused to present evidence at the Hoover building when he had demanded it?

The answer was simple. *They had none.*

38

Malibu, California

The next morning, Luke was up at six, heading north on Pacific Coast Highway, thinking about a modification on the nose cone brackets. As he turned east and accelerated up Canyon Road, Phyllis began playing the old rock standard 'Stairway to Heaven' and a line of green text appeared in the air hovering above the dashboard.

"Good morning, Luke," said Phyllis's voice.

Luke smiled at the little PDA mounted on his dash: "Didn't know you were a Zeppelin fan, Phil."

"Old school rules," she answered. "Did you sleep well, Luke?"

"I was completely faithful to you Phyllis, I swear."

"I feel so much better now that you've told me, sir."

The scientists at The Facility were always trying to embarrass him by loading Phyllis's banks with juicy remarks and personal knowledge about him.

"I'm sure you do, Phil. So what do you really want?"

"I have a guy on the phone who says he's with the CIA. Wants to speak with you. Says his name is Quentin Hawk."

Luke struggled to place the name, then remembered. Cynthia had told him about being rescued by the young CIA agent.

"Okay Phil, put him on."

"Colonel Towne, my name is Quentin Hawk. I'm an agent with the CIA. May I say first that I'm familiar with your Military record, sir, and that it's an honor to speak with you. Thank you for taking my call."

"Thank you for that, Agent Hawk. But I'm the one who should be thanking you. What you did saving my partner was extraordinary. I could have used you many times on one of my recon teams. I owe you one."

"Well sir, thank you. I had help you know. I'm just glad we were on guard. Which brings me to the purpose of this call. There are some security matters I need to discuss with you. Is it possible to meet with you in person? I'm not at liberty to discuss such subjects over an open line. And I'm aware that your cell phone is probably laser based and encrypted by your own scientists. The problem is, mine isn't."

"Who told you about my cell phone encryption?"

"To be honest, sir, I really didn't know about it. I just took a wild guess based on your position as head of the Pentagon's laser guidance systems."

"Wait a minute," said Luke, his memory pulling up an old image. "Quentin Hawk – the football player? Independence Bowl catch. Gophers beat Clemson?"

"Yes sir, I'm afraid that's me."

Luke's comfort level jumped up several notches. "First off, you can stop calling me sir. Luke will do fine. Second, you know Stellini's restaurant in Beverly Hills?"

"'Fraid I don't, Colonel."

"Corner of Santa Monica and Doheny. How about lunch in two hours?"

"Thanks Colonel, I'll be there."

When the connection had gone dead, Luke again spoke to Phyllis. "Get Dave for me would you, Phil?"

"Right here, Doc," answered Dave almost immediately.

"Dave, check the CIA data bank and see who this guy is, would ya? I'll wait."

In 30 seconds Dave Hall was back on the line. "There was a guy named Quentin Hawk. He was based in Duluth. The record says he retired five years ago. No one by that name currently listed in CIA personnel, Doc."

"Doesn't mean he's not real though. Could be black ops."

"Should I go deeper? Langley's probably got tabs on everybody."

"Negative," shouted Luke. "No contact with Langley. Remember my instructions about phone calls? Let's extend that to research as well. No electronic trails outside our building. Nothing goes out, nothing comes in. Until I tell you otherwise. Clear?"

"Clear."

Luke shook his head. *The most brilliant assistant I've ever had. Top of his class. Wants to bring in the Army. Jezz, that's all I need.*

Stellini's Bar and Grill - Beverly Hills, California

Quent got to the restaurant first, parked his rental and went right in. Stellini's was a small bar and grill frequented by sports celebrities along with a regular base of very hip regulars. The owner, Joe Stellini, had once been the maître'd at the Luau, one of Beverly Hills' most legendary bars. Joe knew everyone.

His place was small; his food was terrific and every drink was a double. Quent took a seat at the small bar and just sat there staring. His jaw actually dropped open. His eyes were fixed on the sports mural behind the bar.

He was in it!

There, painted on the wall behind the bar, was OJ, Kareem, Gene Washington, some Olympian swimmers, John Wooden, baseball and football greats from USC and UCLA, and some guys he should have recognized but didn't. But the thing about it was, Quentin Hawk was in the goddamn thing. *Bigger than shit.*

"Thought you might be interested in that painting," said a voice from behind him. "I'm Luke Towne, glad to meet you."

"Holy shit, Colonel, that was very...I appreciate this very much. Thank you."

They hit it off immediately. After a great lunch of sea bass, house salad, potato skins and small talk, Luke pushed back from the table. "So what exactly is this about, Quent?"

"I'm Assistant Chief in charge of a covert CIA intervention program, Colonel. Its purpose is to protect certain of our most valued American assets from danger – before it happens. By danger I mean potential kidnapping, blackmail or any kind of terrorist assault.

"Based on your military background in Special Forces, I thought you'd like to know ahead of time; some of my people will be hanging around. I don't need to find any of my agents in a dumpster somewhere because you got pissed off at being followed."

Luke smiled. "You think I need protection?"

"Off the record, Colonel, I think the whole idea is whacked. 'Stop criminals before they commit the crime!' Run around trying to guess who's a target and who's not. Right. That'll work! But it's at least an attempt to head off some kind of unpredictable 9/11 event from happening in our own backyard. The best I can say about it is, it's a start."

The last thing Luke needed as a double agent was someone else following him around. He assumed that Pierce's snoops would soon be hiding in the bushes, watching his every move. "I appreciate you telling me about this. But I don't like being followed. I don't need it. Let me be clear. I'm in the midst of a government operation. I can't talk about it. But any kind of outside surveillance at this point could seriously compromise my position. That's all I can tell you, except to say, I want it called off right now. I know you've got your orders, but would you see what you can do about it for me? I'd really appreciate it."

"Absolutely, Colonel. I understand completely. Here's my cell phone number. If you ever need anything, please don't hesitate to call me. And I'll get on the surveillance thing right away. I'll let your office know as soon as I have something."

"Thanks Quent. It was good meeting you."

"Same here, sir."

39

#10 Colonial Road – Bel Air, California

It happened the next day. Kathryn was due home for the weekend and they were invited to one of the de Kennesys' 'family' dinners. Inheriting Kat's family had been one of the truly unexpected pleasures of his relationship with her. Doctor Leon was an eclectic, intellectual powerhouse; Nana was a charming French sprite who could cook like an angel. And of course, Kathryn was an angel. His angel.

They had just finished an incredible five-course dinner, crowned by Nana's main course of roast pork and calvados; and as usual, the conversation had been diverse, challenging and spirited. Luke and Leon were having a Turkish coffee in the de Kennesys' book-lined study. The girls were doing the dishes and preparing Nana's famous rum-drenched strawberry shortcake.

The kindly doctor came straight to the point. "Luke, does your rank as a colonel give you any influence at any of the Marine bases around California?"

"They still salute me, if that's what you mean." Luke had been coached to play it totally straight should anything like this come up.

The doctor moved right in. "If I made you a business proposal, could we leave Kat out of it? Keep it just between us?"

"If you like, sure."

"As a doctor, albeit a children's doctor, I've noticed some fluctuations in your political temperature."

"Meaning?" Luke continued to play dumb.

"Seems to me you're not totally happy with some of your government's policies. Especially in Afghanistan; some parts of the Middle East; even Palestine."

Luke knew the moment was at hand; the door was opening. He had been warned by Pierce's Basement team not to grab the handle too quickly. "You must not seem too eager. Finesse is your best ally."

Luke was a trained soldier. *Screw the finesse. Go for the kill.*

"What do you want, Leon?" he asked bluntly.

"It's not so much what I want, Luke, it's more about what's good for my people. What serves the common good."

Common good. Jesus, there it was again. Pierce's goons had said the same thing. All of these bastards used the same lies, no matter which side they were supposed to be on.

"What do you want, Leon?" he asked again, looking straight into the eyes of his potential father-in-law.

"I want the kind of help that someone in your position can provide."

Then, like some hack magician producing his moth-eaten rabbit for the hundredth time, Leon de Kennesy delivered his big finish. "And my people are prepared to pay you a significant premium for it."

Luke asked with unabashed confidence, "Two questions, Leon. Why would you think I'd consider providing that kind of help to you in the first place? And second, why in the world would you think that money could ever persuade me to do anything?"

Doctor Leon sat back in his overstuffed chair and drained the last of his demitasse. A subtle metamorphosis was taking place behind the fungible mask that was his face. No more clumsy sleight of hand, this response would be a demonstration of skill and precision.

"Second question first," he began. "And please, I mean no disrespect in what I am about to say; I am just expressing what I consider to be the reality of the situation.

"If you had decided to bring your considerable scientific skills to the private sector instead of toiling nobly for the Military as your father did, your laser patents would by now have made you a very wealthy man. But you chose otherwise.

"Now enter the beautiful Kathryn. Because of her extraordinary qualities, our Kathryn has been courted by some of the most prominent men in Europe: industrialists, statesmen, princes, athletes – all of them wealthy men.

"Please let me finish," he said, sensing Luke's need to respond.

"Since the two of you have been together, she has enjoyed extensive travel, the best hotels, opera, the finest foods; anything she could possibly want, you have graciously provided. To put it simply and crudely, Luke, to keep her in your bed, you've had to maintain her lifestyle.

"I'm not saying she isn't drawn to your character; I've never seen her so happy with anyone; but the sad fact is, on a scientist/soldier's salary you simply can't possibly keep this up. I regret to say it, Luke, but the size of her engagement ring speaks volumes."

A profound silence.

What a smart, cold-blooded bastard he is.

The initial salvo had drawn blood. And Luke's silence had borne witness. In his idyllic relationship with Kathryn, money had been a big problem. And was getting bigger.

Leon knew he had struck home. But he wasn't finished. His tone changed to one of sympathy. "But Luke, it's your first question that surprises me. Why do I think you'd provide us with that kind of help?"

He lifted the little silver coffee maker and poured more of the Turkish brew into Luke's cup. He was confident.

"Luke, you're an idealist; an altruist. I suggest that you have deep resentments against your government. They don't practice what they preach. They don't value the same qualities you do.

"Your own father literally gave his life to them and how did they repay his family? $978 a month to a widowed mother with a 7-year-old kid to raise? Disgusting!"

"But worse than that...your brother. No effort by the State Department to bring him back. If not for you, he'd still be in North Korea rotting in a bamboo hut. And sadly, all that's left of him now is a post traumatic vegetable. Thanks to the care and support of the U.S. Army. I'm sorry to be so harsh, and to bring up such a personal sadness, but it seems to me that you have more than enough motivation to help our cause."

Luke was speechless.

He had no brother.

Leon had just quoted the *traitor's bio* almost word for word. The Basement experts had said Luke would need deep psychological motivation for his defection to seem believable. And there it was. Verbatim. The altered bio. The background data. His reason to defect. His insurance policy.

He was overwhelmed by Leon's cold-blooded words. And even more stunned by the scope and accuracy of Orin Pierce's predictions. Pierce already knew Leon was dirty. He knew that Luke had been duped. He had known there would be a security leak at the Pentagon. He had made it part of his plan. He understood his enemy. He had predicted they would take the bait. And the ugly truth was, they just did.

Luke had thought Pierce's exotic biographic alterations were ridiculous and had said so after his briefing at the Hoover Building. He had called Pierce and questioned some of the "...hocus pocus contrived by your desk jockeys."

"My job is clandestine operations, Colonel Towne," replied Pierce. "I'm an expert. I'm given to understand that your expertise has been war. There'll come a time in the field when you'll need all that war experience. It's part of the reason you were selected. But until that time, Colonel, stick to what you know. Ignorance doesn't become you."

The garroted artery in Luke's neck had bulged a bright red; but before he could fire back a response, Pierce had hung up.

And now, before he could respond to Leon's traitorous proposition, Nana called from the kitchen. "Okay, you two, enough business. It's time for dessert. It'll be ready in three minutes."

She knew exactly what Leon was doing. Of course she did. They're in it together. Just as the President's letter had stated. Nana had just given the signal to wrap it up. It wouldn't do for Kathryn to walk in and overhear something she wasn't supposed to hear.

Right on cue, Leon withdrew a plain white business envelope and placed it on the table next to Luke's cup. "Inside is an access code. It's to a bank account in the Caymans. Untraceable; and only accessible to the bearer of that account code. There's $100,000 waiting for you. It's yours no matter what you decide. Just access the account, change the initial code to one of your choosing, and no one else will ever be able to access it but you.

"It's a down payment. Yours to keep, no matter what. Should you decide to help us, all future payments will be made to the original account and you'll access them the same way."

All smiles and laughter, Nana and Kathryn approached with dessert. Leon quickly added, "You don't have to answer now, Luke. We never have to speak of this again if you wish. But if you see things clearly, as I think you will, just change the access code and we'll be in touch."

We'll be in touch. Sweet Uncle Leon, the gentleman terrorist.

The enemy had the expertise to steal an American agent's files, right out of the Pentagon's file drawers. They had the depth to determine which psychological buttons might assist in 'turning' him against his own country. Luke was faced with some important realizations. Leon and his group were terrorists. They were obviously very well financed. They were organized, highly educated and very capable of penetrating American social structure. They were not some rag-tag band of foreigners forever doomed to stick out in a crowd.

They apparently had multiple resources. And they definitely posed a major and immediate threat to America's national security.

For the first time in his Military career, Colonel Luke Towne was emotionally involved but strategically unprepared.

40

Norman Erlich had given Luke the private line for The Basement's operations department. By dialing it directly, Luke was able to avoid Orin Pierce. He was immediately connected to Captain G.R. Hinson, the project's lead psychiatrist. It was Hinson's job to advise on the subtleties of communicating with the enemy.

Luke was instructed to wait 10 days before responding to Leon's invitation to treason. The Basement experts would use the time to carefully map Luke's initial decent into the treacherous wormhole of counter-espionage.

They predicted that the enemy would suggest an 'initial gambit' to test Luke's verity. The request would probably involve something small. It would be of minimal risk to Leon and his friends, but it would most certainly put Luke at risk. It would authenticate him as a traitor, and verify his usefulness.

It went exactly as the President's men had forecast. Luke waited a week before responding to Leon's offer. Then, ignoring the precise wording specified by his Basement mentors, Luke rose to the bait in his own style. He and Leon were sitting out by the de Kennesys' pool house drinking some of Nana's lemonade.

"On that matter we discussed the other night, Luke, have you given it any thought?" asked Leon.

"Who'd I have to kill for that kind of money, Leon?"

"Far from it, my friend, far from it. Let me suggest an initial venture. Something to cement the relationship with my future son-in-law. As it happens, I know of a group of soldiers outside of Dbayeh who are in desperate need of small bore firearms. A few rifles should be quite easy for you to procure; but they would be an enormous help to the freedom fighters in my homeland."

"I'll look into it," was all Luke said in response.

The Basement experts spent the next few days evaluating options. Although the operation would be staged, there must be a reasonable chance that the perpetrators could be caught. Without the presence of real danger, Luke's credibility could be destroyed.

After evaluating 25 locations, the experts suggested the theft of some ancient Kalashnikov rifles which were in storage at the El Toro Marine Corps Air Station in Irvine, California. The Base had been officially closed in 1999, but a part of it was still being used as a storage depot for automotive parts, outdated equipment and PX supplies.

Cal State Fullerton College was now located on the El Toro's 3700-acre site. There was heavy civilian traffic; 4000 students passed through its gates each day. The California Station was considered a low security installation. It seemed the perfect choice.

The Basement experts suggested six rehearsal sessions with Luke to develop the subtleties in his critical presentation to Leon. Luke ignored them completely and put the question to Leon over nachos and beer in a dugout box at Dodger Stadium. He made it simple. "Been working on your request. I provide the maps; you provide the manpower?"

Leon's immediate handshake set the process in motion. The enemy had taken the bait. Captain Hinson labeled it "Operation Back to College."

The Basement

General Orin Pierce was now saddled with a Pandora's box of speculation. Late into the night, he sat at his desk compiling his notes, re-writing, revising, attempting to narrow his focus to the essential elements:

1. *Providing manpower – de Kennesy responds immediately.*
2. *He's only been here two months. Where does he get the men to do it?*
3. *Is there a sleeper cell in California?*
4. *Would the enemy actually risk being discovered over the theft of a few rifles?*

As the day of the operation approached, his questions continued to multiply. The answers eluded him.

Nothing to do but wait.

El Toro Marine Air station, California – 12 p.m.

Mustafa Al Moud drove his battered blue Chevy truck up to the guard gate at the El Toro Military Base. The few remaining military storage facilities in the U.S. maintained a cursory guard at the main entry points. A formality.

Mustafa was passed through the gate without even a look. The man in charge, Corporal Michael Peavey, was on his Bluetooth, talking to his girlfriend in Fayetteville. Acting like all the other male students at ICA, Mustafa Al Moud cruised around campus for a while, checking out the chicks, then finally parked between the yellow lines in the newly black-topped area marked 'student parking.'

He walked leisurely around to the back of his truck and lifted the fiberglass tarp about two inches so air could circulate to the four men concealed beneath. Then he climbed back into the cab, slipped on a pair of Sony headphones, propped his Apple MP3 player on the dash and went to sleep. To the passerby, this was a typical student, most likely hung over from last night's clubbing.

At 10 p.m., Mustafa was awakened by his cell phone alarm. From this point on nothing was leisurely. Everything had been worked out to the second.

He slapped his hand twice on the outside of his driver side door to signal the others. Then he pulled slowly out of student parking and turned right onto Military Road. At 20 mph, he would be passing Storage Building #43 in about 30 seconds. His team had been over the process many times. He was to pass the building once. If the solitary overhead light at the rear loading dock was on, he was to abort the mission. If no light was on it would confirm that the single sentry was on break. There would then be approximately 14 minutes to gain entry, load five cases of Kalashnikov 7.62 millimeter assault rifles into their truck, and drive away.

Mustafa had been at building #43 the previous night. It had taken him 11 minutes to cut through the thick, rolled steel Schlage lock. He had had just enough time to replace it with his own lock and get away on foot.

It was 10:15 exactly. There was no light. The guard was on break.

It was on!

He turned the key noiselessly in the lock and hoisted the overhead door up to chest level. Four burly, dark-skinned men ducked inside while Mustafa stood guard. Each two-man team was to carry one of the heavy cases between them, slide it into the truck bed and return for a second case.

Mustafa checked his watch. Thirteen minutes had elapsed. There were four cases in the truck; one case remaining. Then he saw the small head lamps of the guard's golf cart coming back up Military Road.

The bastard is early!

The men inside heard his soft whistle. They set the remaining case down and raced to the loading dock. Mustafa already had the overhead door pulled three quarters of the way down. They ducked under and scrambled into the truck bed, squeezing between the stolen cases. Mustafa jerked the key out of the lock, climbed back into his idling truck and eased away into the darkness of the vacant runway behind building #43. It took him three minutes to arrive at the exit.

Giggling to himself, Mustafa Al Moud, the 25-year-old terrorist, pulled up to the gate and motioned to the guard. "Dude," he said in his labored slang, "I making burger run. Over to Big Mac. Got six order for chili fries. Want I should bring you back something?"

Twenty-year-old Private Second Class Darrin Canfield from Cabin Creek, Virginia, flashed him a toothy smile. "Thanks bro. Next time." He waved them through.

Mustafa turned left onto Sand Canyon Road and accelerated.

"Yeah. Thanks bro!" he howled, then banged his hand repeatedly on the door panel. Cheers boomed into the warm night from the truck bed.

Sixty powerful rifles had been delivered into the hands of the enemy.

It was Luke's first act as a double agent and it had gone flawlessly. Four members of Pierce's Basement team had arrived a week earlier at El Toro to set up the play. No detail was overlooked; the Marine guard normally stationed at building #43 had been delayed an extra few minutes at the PX. The gregarious Marine who bought him a second beer was one of Pierce's men.

The Kalashnikovs had been originally confiscated by U.S. troops at an Iraqi outpost in Mosul. Most of them were destroyed in the field, but five cases had found their way back to El Toro.

One week later, a routine inspection on base would discover the replaced lock, but no investigation would be ordered. Amidst the old junk kept in Building #43, a couple of missing cases of something would go unnoticed. After all, El Toro had become a bunch of classrooms now with an old airstrip sticking out of its west end. The place had all but lost its military bearing. Tire companies had begun using the airstrip to demo their latest low profile racing tires. And as to the replaced lock, it was probably just the work of frat boys trying to find where the Marines stored their pallets of beer.

Luke couldn't explain why he felt the need to visit the scene of the crime. Perhaps it was 20 plus years in Special Forces. His colonel's ID drew a crisp salute from the regular guard. "Go right in, Colonel, sir," he said unlocking the front door to Building #43.

Luke had received a report on the operation from Leon. He was aware that a single case had been left behind.

The remaining case of Kalashnikovs had been moved to the rear of the building and covered with a green tarp. No one at El Toro knew or cared what was in the wooden crate; they had just moved it out of the way to keep the aisles clear.

Finding the missing weapons was a simple matter of following the scrape marks down the center aisle which led Luke directly to the tarp. He pulled it to one side and stared down at the battered wooden crate. It looked exactly like a hundred other weapon's crates he'd handled over the years. He stooped down and inserted his car key into the space under the lid and pried upward. The lid came lose easily in his hand.

A tiny alarm triggered in his mind.

He removed the oil cloth from the top weapon, hoisted one of the rifles and slammed open the breach. *What the crap?* He saw it immediately. There was a small dark line etched across the diameter of the detonation rod. Only a weapons expert would have noticed the irregularity and known its meaning. The firing mechanism had been machined neatly in half. When the trigger was pulled, the sheared rod would break apart and improperly detonate the live round. The magazine would blow apart.

Luke examined the rest of the weapons in the case and found the same treacherous modification; all of the weapons had been rigged to explode in the shooter's face.

"Doctor de Kennesy here," the phone was answered in two rings.

"Uncle Leon, this is Luke calling." It was a code they had worked out. The next words spoken were understood to be of critical importance to their mutual project, and would be continued later when both men were at pre-arranged public locations that insured secure lines.

"Go ahead, Luke."

"Do not distribute those presents yet at Children's Hospital. They need to be wrapped and I've got the paper and ribbon."

Luke disconnected and dialed a series of numbers which connected him to an exchange in Washington. When he heard a new dial tone, he punched in the remaining numbers, which would in turn connect him to a secured, direct line to Pierce's office under the nation's White House.

"The whole screwing lot of them were booby trapped," he shouted.

There was a slight pause at the end of the line before General Pierce responded. "I guess the Iraqis must have done it before our boys got there."

"Bullshit! Those pins were machined. You can't do that in the field, Pierce. It's obvious. You did it! Who the hell do you think you're dealing with here?"

"I'm dealing with an inexperienced hothead who's out of his league." He continued with an ugly vehemence. "Did you really think I was going to release 60 Kalashnikov rifles in working condition to a gang of terrorists operating inside our borders so they could use them on us?"

Luke fired back, "The Kalashnikovs were your call, Pierce! Not mine. The first time one of these rag heads blows his head off trying to fire one of these things, my life isn't gonna be worth shit. Is that the way you take care of your own, General?"

The President's man allowed a moment for the smoke to clear.

"Let's put the exalted value of your life aside for the time being, Colonel Towne, and see if you can follow a direct order. Get on the phone to your father-in-law and tell him the Iraqis booby-trapped these weapons trying to injure our men. No one knew about it until you, in all your brilliance, discovered it.

Are the lights going on yet? You saved their pitiful lives. Praise be to Allah. You get to be the hero you already seem to think you are. They'll pay you double for this one. Whoopee you're an insider! Just like we planned it.

"Oh and by the way," Pierce added, "Rigged Kalashnikovs don't hit anything unless the pins get replaced. Those KLs are 40 years old. You couldn't find an original pin in the factory at the Kremlin. And Leon's boys don't have any either. That's of course unless you gave them some, because we sure as hell didn't give them any."

"Check your manual, General Dipshit, they're selling AK-47s off the racks at Wal-Mart these days. They're still using the same pins. They're interchangeable."

"Stop playing games, Towne, this one's over. You've already called 'Uncle Leon' and fed him the whole story anyway, just like we knew you would. So in the future, just keep in step. Understand? We'll do the thinking. You do the marching. Are you there, Towne?"

There was a deadly silence on Luke's end of the line. His next words had a different sound to them. An icy control. Very deliberate. Very quiet.

"Listen very carefully, General. You've had your turn playing God. That's over! No more surprise endings, no more 'look how smart I am;' no more hidden agendas; no secret plans within plans; no last minute gotchas. If I don't have the full story from the beginning, if you hold anything else back from me, even one small detail, you're going to lose my services. You'll have the worst rogue agent you could ever imagine. A goddamn live weapon. And you, General, will be standing tall, right in the crosshairs."

General Pierce looked through the double glass panels separating him from the wall of recording equipment. Satisfied that the conversation was still being recorded, he spoke.

"Is that a threat, Colonel Towne?"

"No, Pierce, it's a promise."

This time, Luke disconnected the call.

41

Dien Bien Phu – Vietnam

Colonel Ari Shine hated everything Vietnamese; he hated their food; he had a difficult time with their stupid sing song language; the women were too thin; the waiters pretended not to understand; even the air didn't seem to agree with his nose. He had a large nose, but then he was a large man. A highly decorated veteran of Israel's Elite 2nd Mossad Group, Ari Shine was an intimidating presence. Handsome, dark complexioned, about 6'2", 240, one of those guys you wouldn't want to cross.

At 3 p.m. on this afternoon in August, Ari Shine was on special assignment, sitting in a bar in Saigon, dressed in civilian clothes, tailing a rag head (an Arab). This Arab was a businessman suspected of funding an act of terrorism against Ari's beloved homeland.

Ari did like wearing civilian clothes for a change; in this case, a polyester Hawaiian shirt, jeans, and a pair of ES skateboard tennis shoes. Pretty snappy was the way he'd described himself to his 11-year-old daughter, Rachael, as he kissed her goodbye back in Haifa.

"You look like a geek in that, daddy," she teased. "My friends think you look studly in your fatigues though."

"Very important what your friends think, Chicken. Perhaps I should bring them back a present instead of my no good daughter!"

"I take it back. I take it back," she squealed. "Seriously. My friends are losers. I hate all my friends, really. Really I do." She waited a second. "You buyin' any of this Pop? "

He hoisted her up to eye level as if she were a weightless paper doll. "Anything you got to sell, Sweetheart, I'm buyin'."

Ari had lost his wife of 15 years to a suicide bomber. It was two years ago. A Saturday. Little Rachael and her mother were in a grocery store in Haifa. By chance, his daughter had run out into the parking lot to see a schoolmate. It saved her life. There was nothing left of the grocery store.

Ari was proud of his country and proud to have earned his position in the Mossad. But after more than two decades of service, he was tired; his body was starting to show signs of wear. But retirement was out of the question. His daughter, then his job; in that order; it was all that mattered; it's what kept him alive.

He was staring down into his melting ice cubes, thinking about his daughter, when the ugly waiter slapped down another gin and tonic in front of him and stuck out his oily hand. "You pay please."

"Add it on to my lunch tab, asswipe."

"You pay please!"

"All right, how 'bout this? What's the best thing ya got here for lunch?"

"Ah! We got Wang Soy salad with fresh cobra meat. Make you 12 o'clock all time." (Twelve o'clock was Viet slang for springing a woody.)

"I'm not interested in getting laid, pal, I just want to eat."

The little waiter said nothing, just stared as if he'd heard nothing. Expressionless.

Patience was not one of Ari's strengths. "Look, when you were back in the kitchen, what looked like the best thing to eat?"

The answer was delivered with big toothy smile. "We got spice Wang Soy salad with fresh cobra meat. Make you 12 o'clock all time."

Anger flashed like a lightning spike in the eyes of the grizzled commando. He grabbed the waiter by his collar and pulled the little man's face close. "Do I look like a man with a dick problem, you ass face?" (Pause) "Well do I?"

"No ploblem. No ploblem," came the terrified answer.

"You got beer nuts over there?"

"We have. Yes." Sweat was now pouring down the sallow cheeks.

"Then get the hell away from me and bring 'em over here." Ari shoved the waiter's face away from his own and swigged down half the gin and tonic. Then his cell phone rang.

"Yeah," he barked.

"Is this the handsome and mysterious Captain Shine, the one who likes to play with matches?" said the voice.

It took a second, but a slow smile broke out on Ari's tanned face. His reply was whispered. "Right. And is this the cute little nursey who blossomed into the prettiest captain in the U.S. Navy?"

"Hi, Ari," said Cynthia. "It's good to hear your voice. How are you? And how's your beautiful daughter?"

"Both of us are a lot older than the last time we saw you. And we're both fine. But I sense that all is not well on your side of the water."

"Prescient as usual, Ari. What was it that tipped you off?"

"Well, first off, there was the incident in Paris. Some ancient schmuck of a colonel acting like he's a big time scientist. Pissing off the frogs. Getting his ugly mug in the French newspapers – while I did all the real work. And now a call from his beautiful partner. Doesn't take much to put it together. I know you didn't take the trouble to find me in this mole hole just for giggles. How can I help?"

"How busy are you, Captain?"

"Well, they've sort of put me out to pasture. Younger guys running things now. So I get surveillance jobs. Courtesy shit, nothing important. I been sittin' here for 10 days, waitin' on some sand spook to show his ugly face. I'm essentially a free man. Please give me something to do."

"Thanks Ari," said Cyn. "You got somebody to look after Rachael?"

"Staying with my sister. I'm ready to go. Now."

"There's a first class ticket to Virginia waiting at your house. Some technology stuff I think you'll enjoy."

"Couldn't come at a better time for me. Thanks Cyn. See you when I get there."

Doctor Cynthia Teller was changing uniforms. Reverting to form. Twenty years of Military procedure was ingrained. It was time to marshal the forces.

42

Omaha, Nebraska

Ten days had passed since Farad installed the C4 in the Mall of America, in Bloomington, Minnesota. To his complete surprise, Leon's next target had turned out to be something much less challenging; a Mormon Temple in Omaha, Nebraska. The thought of it made him laugh. *A huge granite building, 16,000 square feet of pious believers, all destined to burn in raging hell fires. The Mormons call it the Winter Quarters.*

Unfortunate choice of name.

The Omaha *amAtya* was even better prepared than the cell in Minnesota. Two of the younger Talib graduates had actually joined the stake (congregation) of Latter-day Saints and were attending weekly instructions at the temple. They had told their religious recruiters that they were Iraqis, thus explaining their unusual accents. They volunteered to help with the Temple's landscape work. The two of them, tilling the gardens, had become a familiar site to regular churchgoers.

Under the circumstances, three men carrying cartons of powdered milk into the basement of the Visitors Center was hardly a suspicious act. Farad, dressed in black pants, a white shirt and black tie, was introduced as a visiting missionary who was helping with the load. One of the rectors even unlocked the pantry for them.

The Mormon Winter Quarters and Visitors Center only held a few thousand believers. When the C4 was eventually detonated, the carnage would be comparatively small. The Mormons posed no unusual threat to the Muslim faith. The city of Omaha had no essential industrial value, nor was it of any great Military significance; but Leon had chosen the target for very specific reasons. The majestic temple itself was located in the center of the American heartland. It was to be a psychological blow. A demonstration of power. The Silent Jihad was reaching into the very guts of the beast. No one was safe. Not even the humblest church member.

Mason City, Iowa

It was 3:30 a.m. Farad had left Nebraska and was already 100 miles into Iowa; no lights on the highway, endless rows of green vegetation splayed out to his left and right, racing through the flat fields of middle America. The Mormon installation had gone down exactly as planned. *Fi Amanallah* (In Allah's protection)

Ten minutes outside of Mason City he began looking for the *Wayfarer Inn* Motel. And suddenly, there it was, on the right, just where Leon said it would be. Another tired flop house, five letters burned out on its sign, no cars in the lot, unthinkable for most travelers. "Welcome to the Wayf...er..Inn Motel." *Good enough for Aziz the ignorant bomb maker.*

On his initial thousand-mile journey north from Texas to Minnesota and now west toward Iowa, Farad had spent his nights in an endless drudge of low rent motels, each one of them the same. The beds were old, the springs poking up through stained batting; the curtains worn thin, the smell of industrial detergent nauseating, the water cold, the surroundings squalid.

At this hour of the morning, the room key would be taped to the manager's door. Farad opened the envelope and read the enclosed note. "Wayfarer Rates: Room #6, one night, $33.75 – Paid in Advance. Check out time 11 a.m."

The door to room #6 was ajar. Its knotty pine walls were the color of dog crap; the bathroom sink was circled with permanent rings of rust, the shag carpet had surrendered its color decades ago. Farad had grown up in the alleys of Lebanon. Rats, filth and hunger were part of his country's inherent poverty. But he was tired. And he was struggling with his present surroundings.

These things mean nothing. My will is strong. My faith is deep. Al-Muqit. (The Nourisher)

He rolled into the declivity in the center of his double bed and stared up at the perforated squares on the ceiling, scourged brown from water leaks and cigarette smoke. The rumble out on I-35 added a constant tremor to the bed pillows. "They probably tell these stupid pigs the goddamn bed shaking helps put them to sleep," he said out loud, attempting to humor himself.

But it didn't work. There was nothing funny about his situation. He was becoming increasingly uncomfortable. *Americans are truly the children of Satan. Disgusting fast food. Filthy animals. In need of cleansing. Whores on the street corners. Bibles in the drawers. They deserve to die in the fire.*

He pushed himself off the bed and began pacing around the dingy room, silently repeating his mantra: *My will is strong. My faith is deep. Al-Quddus.* (Allah the most pure.)

His faith was deep, his will was strong, but his mind would not be still. A sudden noise from the bathroom shook him out of his malaise. Grabbing a statue of the Virgin Mary off the night stand, he sprang through the bathroom door.

"DIE, you American mother fu...!"

There was no one there. At his feet, a herd of cockroaches clattered across the linoleum, finding safety under the tub. Farad stood for a second, the Virgin poised above his head. *Shit.*

Embarrassed, he stepped into the shower and slammed the corroded little window closed. "These shitty motels are not safe, Leon, you hook nose bastard," he screamed. He smashed the cheap statue against the shower wall and climbed out of the tub. Returning to the bedroom, he flopped down on the bed and forced his head between the pillows.

For the last four weeks, sleep had become impossible without several shots of liquor and a handful of Ambien. His first aid kit lay open on the night table; sleeping pills – several brands of them. In addition, there was Morphine, Percocet, naproxen, amoxicillin, Betadine, Silvadene and Xanax. Leon had thought of everything.

Twenty minutes later, when the drugs finally squashed him into unconsciousness, he dreamed the same horrible dream, the recurring nightmare of his present life. A tapestry of fear and failure. Trapped in the middle of this horrid country, dependant on a man he despised, geographically lost until the next cell phone message from Leon. He was permanently vulnerable.

His sleep was intermittent, every sound a threat, every movement an intruder. Truck horns dopplering down I-35 morphed into screeching police sirens and big booted captors surrounding the motel, breaking down the door – jerking him out of his restless sleep.

Only a dream. Only a dream.

At 5 a.m. he finally gave up, rolled off the bed, splashed some water on his face, packed up his stash of pills and walked out to the milk truck. After gassing it up, he headed out onto I-35.

For Farad, the milk truck had become his only source of comfort, a mental security blanket. He had recently taken

Leon's suggestion and unbolted the grill plate on the big Thermo King Kold Refrigeration Unit on top of the truck's cabin. The radiator coils had been replaced with a hidden cache of emergency weapons.

To his surprise, he was now the owner of an ancient 1982 surface-to-air Stinger missile launcher with two warheads, an Ak-47, a Glock 21 and a Glock 27, a large stack of ammunition, a land mine, one Browning Savage bolt action rifle and several crudely made dynamite vests.

At least he had control of something. *Always more comfortable in the truck. Safer. Take a lot of them with me if it ever comes down to it.* He pushed it up to 75 and rolled down the windows. Sweet earthy scent of warm, green vegetation. Clean. Fresh. Pure. Unlike the people he was on his way to slaughter.

The little bit of cocaine he'd snorted out of the truck's center ashtray was just enough to clear his head. He was starting to feel better. Out here on the road alone, flying through the middle of the corn fields, things felt different. The sun had come up, the air was warming. He was back in Baalbek, ditching grammar school, hiding in the white rocks along the Litani River.

At 11 years old, Farad would sneak off to his hiding place by the river to dream; lying on his back with the sun on his face, he would imagine what he might become; Farad the rock star, Farad the powerful, Farad the famous; known round the world for... what? For something he had yet to imagine.

Now, pushing the truck up to 90, he felt the sun on his face and for a moment felt free again, as if all of it were possible. He thought about the Mall of America. He imagined the concrete structure collapsing on itself, just like the Twin Towers. *This would be even better.* The results would be cataclysmic. In one magnificent day of explosive euphoria, the American heartland would be brought to its knees. Bloomington's everyday citizens, believing themselves safely tucked away from the mainstream, protected by their lattes and their shopping bags, these *kaffir* would be fried like the immoral arrogant pigs they were. The whole of America would be frozen in fear.

The same thing was going to happen to the Texans in Houston, the Mormons in Omaha, the filthy Mall whores in Minnesota, and in...in wherever the other two disgusting temples of sin were going to be. He would destroy them all.

He sensed the blood rushing through his veins. It was accelerating his heartbeat. The feeling was big. It was in his chest. For a moment he struggled to name it. It was like a feeling of power. The idea struck him like a slap in the face. It was power. His own power!

Farad Aziz is going to be famous. Never mind what Leon had done. Never mind the meticulous planning and the sleeper cells and the Mullah's money. "Never mind all that," he shouted into the wind. "Never mind what the bastards have done. It's about me! It's Farad who's gonna get the credit."

He backed off the throttle, set the cruise control at 65 and stared out the window just in time to see another one of those big pink signs which promised 24-hour service for 'The best flapjacks in Iowa.' Breakfast would give him some time to think. He pulled off the interstate to 'Drop in and taste a little stack of heaven.'

The place was warm and it smelled of butter and bacon. He chose an empty corner in the back and slouched into a U-shaped booth. When the waitress finally approached, he hoisted the menu in front of his face and pointed to the words 'Special.'

Ten minutes later in Belle's Diner, home of Iowa's 'heavenly stack of flapjacks,' while stuffing his mouth full of dough and maple syrup, Farad experienced a second epiphany.

His head grew dizzy at the thought of it. *Leon's completely dependent on me! Since the first day I got here.* It was startling. The exact opposite of the way he'd been looking at it. Suddenly, the success of the Jihad had become totally dependent on his demolition skills. *They can't do anything without me!*

He stuffed a bite of chicken-fried steak into his face and chewed hard for a second, thinking it over. Then he threw down his fork and went looking for the pay phone. It was time to assert himself.

Leon de Kennesy was in his rosewood paneled library, finishing a little bowl of Crème brûlée when the analog phone on his desk rang. Only two people had the red phone's number: Mullah Rockmani and Farad Aziz.

Farad's voice was unusually strong. "I want a meeting. I'll probably be ready in about 20 days. You name the place."

"A problem?" asked Leon, gritting his teeth.

"Just hurry up and message the damn magic words to the next targets. We'll talk when I'm done." Farad slammed down the receiver and strutted back to his pink plastic booth. "Bring me another order of those round cakes. And a lot more of that thick maple juice."

The big-haired waitress, doing the night shift at Belle's, nodded and shoved the order up into the kitchen spindle. She spun the shiny wheel around toward the cook. "Gettin' more weirdoes every year, Buck. I swear to Buddha."

43

Gardena, California

Farad's meeting took place three weeks later at the Helix, a tiny, four-table Greek restaurant in Gardena, California. The fact that there was a terrorist agent living in Gardena, managing a Greek restaurant, was a frightening testimony to the depth of enemy presence within the U.S. The town of Gardena was perhaps the most unlikely city in California from which to expect any kind of unlawful international activity.

The Helix Restaurant had closed its doors on the second Friday of the month to accommodate this most private of parties. One table had been set up in the center of the restaurant's kitchen. Eating in the kitchen was what made the Helix a favored spot. To the patrons, it was like coming home again. Except the swarthy characters who showed up on this Friday night were a long way from home. And dining was only a secondary purpose.

Leon was already enjoying an order of grape leaves when Farad sauntered through the door. Stunned by what he saw, Leon jerked up from his chair and tried unsuccessfully to choke down his mouthful of oily leaves and rice. Swallowing hard, unable to get the words out, he began waving his hands frantically in front of his chest, signaling stop!

Farad had brought someone with him!

Before Leon could speak, Farad and his companion pulled two chairs up to the table. Leon was left standing, working a napkin back and forth across his beard trying to conceal his shock.

"You can sit down now," said Farad.

Unable to find words to express the torrent of anger in his gut, Leon fumbled with his chair then cleared his throat before replying.

But Farad cut him off and began making the introductions. "Ali, this is Leon de Kennesy. Leon, this is my new apprentice, Ali Yusuf. Ali's a Level 3 from Omaha. Brought him along with me. Gonna use him on the next job."

Leon de Kennesy, veteran of a thousand verbal wars, recognized the ploy at once; the expanded chest, the smug expression, the extended chin; it was an amateur's attempt to score points in front of an underling. Leon drew in a long breath, silently masticating his angers into a fine powder, buying time.

Turning such a moment to his own advantage was one of Leon's strong suits. Facile as a chameleon, Leon's expression altered, his pupils widened, his face went smooth as a dark stone. A broad smile parted his thick beard and he extended his hand. "Ali Yusuf," he said warmly. "Your reputation has preceded you. Your teachers at Talib have given you their highest marks. Allah be praised. Welcome, my friend."

"Honored to meet you, Doctor," answered Ali. His accent lacked the crudeness of most soldiers from the Talib. His high forehead and penetrating eyes suggested a high degree of intelligence, an asset rarely packaged in such a large frame. Ali stood 6'1" and weighed 290.

"You don't look like a native Lebanese," said Leon.

"I was born in Oslo," said Ali. "My father is Dutch, my mother Egyptian."

The mutuality of their exchange was not what Farad had intended. "So listen, Leon," barked Farad. "Let's get something straight. About this Colonel Towne. I don't need some big shot American scientist snooping around. I've already built more bombs than this guy'll ever see in his life."

Leon's mind flashed; absent for a second. Realizing he had made a mistake; broken one of his own rules. Afraid that too much *alone time* was dangerous for a personality as schizophrenic as Farad's, Leon had sought to bolster the man's emotions with some positive news from home. Leon had emailed a cryptic message that included what he hoped was a coded insider's reference "...Towne's coming over to our side."

"Are you listening, Leon?" shouted Farad. "I don't want him. You hear me? I don't like it. How do I know he's not a spy?"

Discussing the inner workings of the Jihad in front of anyone, even an apparently bright Level 3 from Talib, was anathema to Leon. "Have you forgotten the lives saved in the matter of the rifles?" he asked calmly.

"So he saved a few of us from dying with the broken Kalashnikovs," growled Farad. "This proves nothing! He risks nothing for this. Real proof! I want real proof. Will he kill for Allah? That is proof. Get us proof, Leon. Our brothers from the Talib agree with me. You might have brought a spy among us. If this is true, you will die for such a mistake."

Leon turned to Ali Yusuf. "Over there," he barked, pointing toward the kitchen. Ali Yusuf fled quickly from the table and disappeared through the door marked 'άτομο,' (Men's Room) Leon's eyes bored into Farad's. "Listen very closely bomb maker. The passport that got your impudent carcass into Texas, I paid for it! Correct? Your little sex kitten Nuriyah comes from the Al Thawra – am I right? I persuaded the Mullah to spare her meaningless life. Am I right? Now hear me. Discussing any part of our business in front of anyone is unacceptable. Bringing this Level 3 here is also unacceptable. You have stepped over the line, Aziz. One more mistake like this and you will end up tied to one of your own bombs. Are you hearing me?"

"No, you listen! Don't threaten me, Leon. You get me proof this American isn't a spy, or I won't go near the last goddamn target. I won't detonate the rest of them either. Make a few phone calls and it's over."

"What are you talking about?"

"Cut the bullshit. I've got some new friends, remember? They work for me now. You think they don't know about each other? You ever heard of cell phones, Leon? You thought maybe my people wouldn't talk?"

That was precisely what Leon thought. Each imbedded cell was supposed to be a separate unit. Completely isolated. Independent. No one in Minnesota should even be aware that another cell existed. And certainly no information should be passing from Minnesota to Nebraska.

Leon was rocked. He had built a foolproof system. The Jihad was inches away from victory. Suddenly in the eleventh hour there was a potentially fatal breach in security. His mind raced for answers. It was called the 'Silent Jihad' for a reason. No one had ever heard of them. They had remained invisible for two decades. Now, they were inside the devil's belly and...

"Listen *Doctor*," shouted Farad, pushing his face across the table. "You think I'm going to wire some target in the same city where your bloody scientist lives? Did you think about that? You trying to tell me it's all just a coincidence? Bullshit. I'm not getting near the place. How do I know they're not waiting to arrest me?"

Leon knew he was cornered. He heard Farad's claim that the imbeds were *his* people. He maintained an air of supremacy, hoping for a way out. "All right genius, what do you suggest?"

"I don't know. Have him kill someone. How about that?"

"Brilliant," said Leon. "Kill someone. Let's have him kill the Governor? That'd be good. Why don't we send the cops a personal invitation? Call as much attention to us as we can. Would you like that?" Leon's head was shaking with rage. "Let's get us all arrested. Did you think about that?"

A slight furrow appeared in Farad's brow, the wheels spinning for a moment as he grappled with the problem.

Leon pressed his advantage. "Why don't you go ask your new assistant over there? He looks like a real smart guy, hiding over there in the Greek shithouse like a girl."

Farad sensed he was losing control and blurted the next thing that came to mind. "I don't know Leon. Make him prove he's real. Have him steal me some butane tanks. Or some dynamite. Something I could use. Get him to do that."

Leon snapped back, "You've already got C4, remember? What the hell are you going to do with dynamite?"

At the mention of C4, Aziz's brain fired. "You've got me running all over this goddamn country planting C4 everywhere. But you forgot one thing. How am I supposed to make them all go boom on the same day when all I got is a bunch of 24-hour fuses? You're too damn cheap to buy me anything with a real timer on it, Mr. Computer Specialist. So make it detonators. That's what I need. Get me some bloody detonators with electronic timers. See if your laser spy can pull that off."

Almost all of Farad's previous failures could be traced to a singular weakness – the fuses. He was forever without the resources to buy reliable timing devices. As a youth, his fame had come from his ability to improvise; a wind up clock, a powdered fuse, a stray piece of wire. It was only after Leon raised the initial funding that Farad graduated to mechanical blasting caps. The commercial grade devices improved his success rate by about 35%, but his improvised timing mechanisms still failed more than half the time.

Then he created a series of inventive cell phone timers, which saved Jihadist lives by allowing the installers to distance themselves from the blast. His success rate soared by another 30%. Finally, with more money came the time pencil, a chemical device that wears down gradually and detonates the charge at a fairly predictable interval. But Farad had been denied access to the more modern E Cell delay detonators, which used sophisticated electronics and which would have raised Farad's success even higher.

Leon had always insisted on spending his funds on the acquisition of explosive materials. The only exception was the famous computer system at the Laundry. It was a definite blind spot, created perhaps by Leon's growing hatred of Farad. Without realizing it, the great mastermind doctor had created a flaw in his own methodical process, crippling Farad's potential, and blaming Farad for it.

Leon had always enjoyed taunting Farad about his so-called 'street smarts.' "I'll provide the gunpowder, Farad. You're the savant, you figure out how to blow it up."

Upon hearing Farad's plea for detonators, Leon saw his chance to regain control. His expression turned thoughtful. The anger in his face dissolved. His gaze dropped to the table, then slowly drifted back up to meet Farad's pinched stare. "Now that's the first really smart suggestion you've made in a long while, Farad," he said, playing him like a trout. "Detonators. Let me see what I can do. You and your assistant rent yourselves a couple of rooms somewhere in town. Go see a movie. Relax. Take a couple of days. Maybe you're right. Giving Colonel Towne another test might not be such a bad idea. You know I've always said, 'It never hurts to be cautious.'"

Score one for me, you bastard, thought Farad. He sat back in his chair to savor the moment. When he looked up, Leon was already heading across the room toward Ali Yusuf who had emerged from the bathroom.

As they shook hands, Leon pressed a card into the young Muslim's palm. He spoke quickly and confidentially. "Ali Yusuf, the most holy Mullah Rockmani wishes to speak with you in private. Use this number tomorrow, but only when you're alone. You understand, Ali? Only when you're alone. Allah be with you."

Twenty minutes into the ride home from Gardena, Leon directed his limo driver to pull off the 405 at Centinela and pull into the Hillside Memorial Cemetery. "Make a right at that statue up there. Drive to the top of Calvary hill; then go take a walk."

When the driver was out of earshot, Leon pushed a number on his Inmarsat phone. For its high paying mobile customers, the Inmarsat company's IP technology provided an 'always-on' connection. And the digital signal was always strongest from a point slightly above the surface streets. The call was pinged from the ground terminal in Westwood to one of the company's 11 satellites, then down to a ground terminal in Beirut and directly to the sat phone in the reading room of Mullah Ahmed Rockmani.

It took but a few seconds for Leon to bring his partner up to date. "He could easily destroy two decades of work, you know that Ahmed. Now he's got the cells talking to each other. He's calling them his people. You should have let me kill the son of a bitch when I had the chance."

"Patience Leon, patience. As I remember it, he was all we had then. He's all we have now, is that not the truth?" answered the less agitated Mullah.

"Of course you're right. We have no choice. At least until he finishes the installation." Leon let out a sigh of frustration. There was a silence on the other end. Then the Mullah spoke.

"About the scientist. What is your...?"

The sat phone connection suddenly went dead.

It took the Limo two hours to negotiate the heavy traffic on the 405, then weave its way up Sunset and through the Bel Air gates to Leon's mansion at #10 Colonial Road.

Leon needed to finish his conversation with the Mullah, so he broke another of his own rules and used the red phone on his desk. True to form, he was more guarded when speaking from his own library.

"You asked about the friendly scientist," said Leon, picking up where they had left off.

"Yes, do you think he might be helpful with our man's new demand?"

"Actually, the idiot's demand turns out to be an excellent idea. And providential as well. As you know, he's always had a problem with... matches. Well as it happens, my scientific friend is quite an expert at such matters. Perhaps the perfect person to supply some... shall we say, state of the art match books. Maybe they'll have some clever New Age designs on the covers."

"I shall pray for it," said the Mullah. "By the will of *Al-Muntaqim* (Allah the Avenger)."

"Al-Muntaqim," answered Leon, I'll be in touch."

44

The Basement – Washington D.C.

Although the tape machines in the tech room of the White House Basement had captured every word of the library conversation between Leon and the Mullah, there was a problem. Since moving to Bel Air, Nana de Kennesy had not left the house for more than an hour at a time, sending her house man to do most of the errands. Pierce's tech specialists had only been able to stay in the house long enough to install one tiny bug in Leon's library. The rest of the house remained uninstalled.

Pierce was furious at his team's limitations. There had been but two calls recorded on the library phone. And The Basement analysts had not been able to provide their boss with much information about the first call. They could only describe the caller as "...an angry male (name unknown) who called from a public phone (location unknown) to demand a meeting."

Pierce didn't need their analysis for the second call. He already knew who the 'friendly scientist' was. And Leon's use of the term 'matches' was fairly transparent, an obvious reference to some kind of detonation device. Pierce inferred from the nature of the conversation that Leon's terrorists must already have a quantity of explosive stored somewhere. It sounded like they were planning to ask their *spy* to provide them with some modern detonators.

The call implied an impending event which could have disastrous effects on U.S. soldiers abroad; or worse, it could foretell a planned attack on American soil. Knowing the details and the location was critical.

Unfortunately, Towne was the key.

Pierce resolved *to jerk his chain a little tighter.*

Two nights later, Luke and Leon sat together in the de Kennesy pool house, Nana and Kathryn having gone to the movies so the men could 'solve the world's problems.' Leon got straight to the point.

"Luke, I know this isn't your fault, and I apologize; but here it is. Bottom line, my friends in Syria are skeptical about the Kalashnikov incident. There's one in particular, Aziz. The ringleader. He's tried to block me every step of the way. Ever since I brought you in. He keeps demanding proof. More proof. I've tried to explain that by alerting us to the broken firing mechanisms, you saved lives. Actually you proved yourself twice; by providing the weapons in the first place, and then by alerting us to the danger. But several of the influential chieftains... well, plain and simple, they want more proof."

"What the hell kind of proof do they need?" said Luke. He had prepared long and hard for this moment. He knew his role. "I'll give you some proof," he shouted, "How about we blow something up? Hit one of their goddamn verification labs. They're supposed to be so 'state of the art.' The bastards up in Monterey have never been satisfied with anything I do.

"How about we wait 'til they go home to their big houses then blow their 'perfect' lab into outer space. I'll tell you what, Leon, I'll fix it so you can detonate the son-of-a-bitch right here on the couch. How's that for proof?"

Luke had rehearsed and rehearsed, trying to make his manufactured emotions sound believable. The knee-jerk soldier. The years of disrespect. The angry scientist out for revenge. Luke knew he was a lousy actor. He'd warned Pierce's goons about it.

The moment had come.

And it was over in a heartbeat. Leon was quiet for a time, just sitting across from Luke, staring out at the pool. Finally he asked, "Luke, what did you mean 'I could detonate something from the couch?' Are you saying I could trigger an event somewhere else in the world, say in Lebanon for example, from here?"

Luke hesitated an instant. The fake passion disappeared from his voice. There was no need to put on an act. He spoke as a scientist, his tone serious. "Yes."

"Do you have access to such technology?"

A longer hesitation. And a deadly stare from the spy/scientist. "I invented it."

It was Leon's turn to be silent. He had read the stolen bio over and over. Yet he allowed himself a millisecond for review.

Even a novice can see the psychological problems in his past; his deep resentment of authority. They've kept him out of the limelight as a soldier. They've screwed him as a scientist - in spite of his remarkable achievements.

The look in Leon's eyes was telling. He wanted to believe. Yet he wasn't going to jump in prematurely. He was convinced Luke was for real, but he was going to wait; take it slowly. *It's never a bad idea to be cautious.*

Leon rubbed his beard as if in thoughtful speculation. "Is there a way...?" He stopped himself. *They've got to think the detonators are going to the Middle East.* Leon started over. "Would it be possible for me to use this technology...against my enemies in Al-Shab?"

"It would take more money than you could afford," said Luke, sensing the fait accompli.

"Give me the number, Luke, and let me be the judge."

Luke let out a sigh. *The rebellious scientist would not have had time to place an exact dollar amount on his traitorous deeds.*

The Basement goons had prepared him well. He massaged his forehead. He worked his lips as if computing the risk. Finally, in faux frustration, "I don't know. The price would be awfully steep. Maybe 750. Maybe more."

Leon's answer was solemn. "I'll get back to you, Luke."

On his way home from the de Kennesy mansion, Luke reflected on Leon's surprising knowledge of The Facility's laser accomplishments. It seemed no coincidence that Leon asked for a device that Luke had already developed. Once again, it caused him to question the 'chance' meeting with the woman he now loved.

After showing Luke to the door, Leon stood at the peephole, watching until Luke's blue Z had disappeared down the driveway.

A smile of victory on whitened teeth showed from behind his gray and black beard. He led Nana into the bedroom. And decanted a magnificent Lalique crystal of Colheita port he had purchased on a visit to Portugal's Douro Valley. After pouring them each two fingers of the aged tawny wine, he raised his glass in a toast.

"My dear, I would like to give brilliance its due. You raised her; you worked so tirelessly and so diligently at every detail. You took what was just a suggestion from me, breathed life into it and formed her into a holy instrument. An infant succubus. She has become a sword of Islam.

"I now truly believe daughter Kathryn has delivered us a weapon beyond anything I could ever have imagined. To use their mythology, I believe this American scientist can become our Goliath.

"To you, my love, I bow my head in respect and in praise of your accomplishments. I am blessed to share your bed. I remain in awe of your beauty, within and without."

With that, he drank a measure of port and placed a small wrapped present in front of his delighted and teary-eyed Nanette. It was an antique Cloisonné Patek Philippe watch, formed in the shape of a camellia. The petals were tipped with pink diamonds. The inscription on the back was meaningful on many levels.

Our time has come.
Love, L

Malibu Colony, California

Luke sat on his porch, drinking a beer. A domestic one. In a can. He was not celebrating. He was waiting. He had put out the bait. Now all he could do was wait.

It only took 48 hours. The call came through at The Facility during a lunch break. Leon tried to sound calm and matter of fact, but Luke could hear the suppressed excitement in the bastard's voice.

"Hi Luke, how are you?"

"Very busy, Leon, how are you?"

"Let me get right to the point then. I spoke with some of the board members at the hospital yesterday and they think your offer of gifts could make this year's Christmas the best one ever for the children. We'll be happy to cover your expenses. Your generosity is accepted with our deepest appreciation, I can assure you. So...now, how long do you think it would take your staff to collect that many presents?"

"With everything else I've got going on, it'll probably take me three or four weeks to collect them all and have them wrapped."

"That long?" Leon's voice registering suspicion.

Luke could hear the admonitions of the Basement psychiatrist: *You're scared. Make them believe. You're a frightened scientist about to become a traitor.*

Luke responded accordingly, "Leon, you wouldn't want me to get fired for slacking off on my job? I can't let that happen."

"No, no. You do what you have to do. It's fine. Four weeks will be fine. You know what you're doing. Whatever you're comfortable with."

It had worked exactly as the Basement's man predicted.

"So alright, I'll be in touch," said Luke.

"Excellent," said Leon. "But you know, I just had a thought. You needn't bother wrapping the presents. I'll have my staff go through them first, make sure nothing is broken. You know the delicate ones can get damaged in transit."

You phony bastard, though Luke. "Yes, you should definitely check each one before wrapping. Wouldn't do for any child to get a broken one."

"Thanks, Luke. Just give me a call when you're ready to...send them over."

Luke made no response; and the line went dead.

45

The Facility - Malibu, California

Work is the solution to all problems. If that doesn't fix it, work harder. Classic Luke Towne. True to form, he'd been working around the clock. Although the basic D-12RS detonator units already existed, Leon's request for 10 of them mandated a complexity of new functions; a new cone design, a laser amplifier, beacon transmitter, new timer, circuit board and some additional retro fittings. None of these changes had as yet been conceived, fabricated, assembled or tested.

Luke was under the gun, working alone. He had created a mental prototype and was now bent over his work table, intently focused on rendering a new blueprint. When it was completed, he would call in his team, pull them off the Mind's Eye, and give them their new assignment.

He continued to ignore the green light flashing on his desk panel. And he'd been unresponsive to Dave Halter's earlier attempts to reach him, so Dave walked to the open door between their offices and poked his head in. "Doc, there's a Mr. Shine who'd like to speak with you."

Luke brightened and picked up his phone. "You fall down a hole or something? Or did you just get too old to tango?"

"You're older than I am, gramps."

"Hey Dave," said Luke, holding up the phone's hand set, "There's no one on the line."

"That's because I'm standing in your office, shit-for-brains," said Ari Shine.

Luke turned away from his desk to see the huge figure of Ari Shine filling up most of his doorway, a mischievous smile on the giant commando's face.

"What the...?" Luke came around the desk and stepped into a bear hug with the big Israeli; then he stepped back still in shock.

Ari spoke first. "Hey buddy, if this is a bad time for you, I could go back to Nam. It's only about 6000 miles away."

"Let me guess. You finally pissed off too many people and got fired, right?"

"No, I missed your birthday. Had to pay my respects to the elderly."

"Seriously, you on assignment or something?"

"No, I was invited by a very beautiful woman who said her partner was too proud to ask me for help."

"Cynthia did this?" asked Luke.

"How come her schmuck partner didn't have to balls to ask me himself?"

No answer from Luke, just a shake of his head.

"She said you were in some kind of trouble. Said she couldn't discuss it, but figured you'd probably need me as a backup. I told her I'd talk to you about it myself."

Luke was incredulous. "She called you last week from Riverton? I hadn't told her anything about it yet."

"She's an amazing person, Luke. Maybe the two of you should get married."

Luke acknowledged his friend's good-natured barb. "Thanks for the tip there Sigmund. We can talk marriage later. But I still can't believe you came all this way. You're a true friend."

"No problem, Luke. So, what can I do to help?"

"Why don't we have dinner at my place. I'll tell you about it there. And, there's someone I'd like you to meet."

The ride down the hill from The Facility to Luke's house in the Malibu Colony usually took about 15 minutes. Luke pulled out of The Facility and hit the first left-hand curve going 85 mph.

"We late or something?" asked Ari, trying to pry himself off the passenger door and stuff his seat belt into the slot.

"Oh...no. Well...yeah, kinda. I want you to meet Kathryn and she's gonna be there in six minutes."

"She's got a key, doesn't she?"

"Sure, but she's in San Francisco," answered Luke, as if his explanation should make perfect sense.

"San Francisco? Okay. Ah...Luke, how about you pull over and let me drive?"

"What?" asked Luke, oblivious to his own behavior.

"You're acting like a Jew on a pig farm, man. Slow down."

The big Israeli was always making jokes and this one got through. Luke let off the gas and began laughing. "Jew on a pig farm?"

"It was the best I could do at the time, ass face. How 'bout you let the little woman wait a goddamn five minutes and tell me what's going on with you."

Luke pulled into one of the scenic turnarounds that overlooked the canyon and skidded to a stop. He turned off the engine. "Sorry, man, I guess I'm a little screwed up. The shit storm my life has turned into..." He looked nervously down at his watch. "I'll give you the short version."

"Shoot."

"After 9/11, everyone in the whole damn country started pointing fingers. Everyone was suspect; Army, Pentagon, CIA, *everyone* was responsible for letting it happen.

"The 9/11 commission concluded our intelligence agencies were at fault because they weren't talking to each other. We weren't sharing our info. They were absolutely right. And that's the way it's always been. President Crowley decided we should all share resources."

"Yeah," quipped Ari, "We had a running joke about that one. Martha Stewart told him to assemble all the ingredients and bake 'em together in one big cooperative cherry pie. Mmm good. Homemade and delicious."

"Yeah. What a great idea. When the stupid pie came out of the oven, the shit really hit the fan. War at the core. Everyone fighting for dominance. The Pentagon is never gonna eat from the same bowl as the CIA. Same goes for the FBI or the state police.

"It's worse now than it was before 9/11. Nobody shares anything. So, right off the top, I get called in to the Pentagon. They're damn well not gonna lose out to the CIA or NSA or anybody else. They're gonna win this race big time. The President wants to send a clear signal to everybody. They wanna know, do I have anything in development they could use to send the message?"

Luke paused, an expression of resolution on his face. "All the research we do at The Facility is funded by the government. We're a union shop so to speak. The laser guidance systems I have in development are for the use of the Military. They know what I'm doing. They oversee it. They authorize it. They pay for it. They decide exactly how and when and where they'd like to use it. As a scientist, I don't work for the President. I work for the Pentagon."

Ari interrupted, his understanding crystal clear. "But as a soldier, you're supposed to be working for the President, right?"

"You've been there, I take it?"

Ari just smiled.

"Next thing I know, I'm in the Oval Office listening to the grand plan. The President's exact words were something like, 'I'm planning on a second term here, Colonel. And you're the perfect emissary to kick this thing off.'"

"Political football."

"Right. So that's what I did. I mean that's what we did in Paris. And I can never thank you enough for your contribution. It was great to be working together again. Felt like I was working with myself."

"Loved every minute of it, Luke. You know that."

"Actually, the technology we used was just a mini version of what we've really got," said Luke.

"I figured as much. Then when the call came from Cynthia, I figured you were out flanked. If you were planning some kind a' lone wolf operation, I wouldn't want to miss out on all the fun."

"I already had you penciled in, I just didn't have time to call you yet."

"There is one other matter though," said Ari. "Cynthia said it wasn't her place to talk about it. That if you wanted to tell me you would."

"I will always love Cynthia, Ari. You know that. She's more supportive than anyone will ever know. No matter what I do, she's in there for me."

"You've met someone else, my friend. Haven't you?"

"At the Paris convention, I met a woman; I fell in love with her; I met her family; they were wonderful to me. We got engaged to be married. Suddenly she got a new job. She and her family moved from Lebanon to the U.S. I helped her mother and father find a house in Bel Air. Everything fell magically into place like it was predestined.

"I was never so happy in my whole life; even when I was married to Cynthia. And that's saying a lot. Anyway, the exact day they moved into their new house, I got a phone call out of the blue from General Orin Pierce, a man I'd never heard of. He dropped me on a carrier off Point Mugu. There was a personal letter from the President waiting for me on board. It said Kathryn and her family were terrorists; plain and simple."

"Jesus."

"The president ordered me back into the Army. My new in-laws are a 'terrorist cell.' I'm suddenly a double agent. My job is to lure them into the ultimate death trap. All for the greater glory."

The big Israeli was stunned. His face contorted in disgust. "Are they serious?"

Luke's jaw began to flex, his anger palpable. "I knew it was all bullshit. Kathryn's no terrorist. I didn't say anything to her or anyone about it. And for a while, nothing happened. I figured it was just another example of bad intelligence work.

"Then, one night after a family dinner at her parents' house, her father offered me $100,000 to get him some classified information. My life has been hell ever since."

Luke looked at his watch again. "Shit. We're late." He cranked the engine, spun thc wheel and shot out onto the pavement. Ari was quiet for the next two miles, deep in thought. Finally he said, "What's your fiancée's name, Kathryn what...?"

"Kathryn de Kennesy."

"Are you kidding me?!" Ari shouted. "Lebanon? The Ambassador's assistant? That Kathryn?"

"Yes, Kathryn de Kennesy," said Luke.

"Do you know who she is?"

"I hope so," said Luke.

"I mean, of course you know who she is. But I mean, she's famous. She's a big time socialite. High profile. She's at every international event. Even my office staff in Israel knows who she is."

"Yeah..." said Luke, "I knew all that. And what I didn't know, she told me. And very modestly too." Luke was missing the point.

Ari spoke emphatically, "Well it's preposterous. Everyone knows who she is. It's totally preposterous! She's no terrorist."

"I believe that. I know that. But her father sure as hell is."

Luke pulled into the little parking place in front of his house. There were deep lines in his tired face. The two men sat in silence for a beat.

"I've said nothing to Kathryn about any of this," said Luke finally.

Ari said, "I understand."

They got out of the Z and went up the path toward Luke's front door. The house was dark as Luke led Ari into the living room and turned on the lamp. "I thought she was here," said the Israeli.

"She is," answered Luke. Then he pointed Phyllis at the huge HD flat screen in the coroner of the room. The image snapped on and there stood Kathryn in her San Francisco bedroom, arms crossed leaning against a door jamb, waiting for Luke's appearance.

"There you are," she said happily. "Hi Lukie." She was wearing faded blue jeans, one of Luke's blue dress shirts with the sleeves rolled up and a flowered bandana pulled across her forehead holding back her hair.

"Hi Hon," answered Luke. "There's someone here I'd like you to meet."

"Would that be the infamous Ari Shine??" she beamed. "Luke has told me lots about you. It's an honor to meet you, Ari Shine." Her brilliant smile lit up the room. She was speaking to Ari in flawless Arabic. "And how's Rachael? Luke said she's the star in your galaxy."

"Well thank you very much, Ms. de Kennesy, the pleasure is mine," answered Ari, also speaking his native Arabic. "Rach is fine; and thank you for asking. She is my galaxy. She's grown another inch last month." Then he switched to English. "But now tell me something; where the heck are you? You look like you're in the next room."

"At my house in San Francisco. Sorry I couldn't be there in person. This was the next best thing. Luke's fancy laser stuff makes it so clear. It keeps us close on those cold lonely nights, if you know what I mean."

She winked at Luke and flashed him a seductive glance. "So okay, my turn again. Speaking of the next room, what brings you all the way from Asia clear over here to California?"

Ari knew he was not to divulge anything about Luke's plans or his own participation in them. "Oh, I was watching after one of our dignitaries, Moshe Ya'alon; so I was in the area."

"I spent the last two days in a meeting with Mr. Ya'alon. I didn't see you there," she said, no accusation in her voice, but the question was enough.

"That shows you how good I am, Kathryn. You're not supposed to see me." She had caught him in his lie, but Ari was lightning quick.

They both smiled.

Then Ari added, "Just kidding. Just kidding. I dropped him at LAX and a colleague of mine took over at SFX. I thought it would be a lot more fun visiting my aging pal here."

"The old coot still looks pretty good to me," she laughed; then shifted effortlessly back into hospitality mode. "So are you guys ready for a home-cooked French meal?"

Luke answered. "I got everything you sent, Kat, plus some stuff Nana sent over. We're ready. You just gotta tell me what to do with it all."

Under Kathryn's guidance, Luke baked the entrées, heated the bread, chilled the salads, cooled the desserts and poured the wine. Then she bid them 'Bon Appétit,' clicked off the screen and left them to themselves.

While the wine was airing, Luke motioned Ari out on to the porch, sat him down at a weathered wooden table and proceeded to bring him up to speed.

He began with Pierce. "The guy's ego is gonna put lives at risk. It's a sure path to failure. I've seen it happen a hundred times. I'll bet you've been there a few times?"

Ari just laughed in acknowledgment.

"There's only one way to do this. As much as I hate the term, it has to be what you guessed; a rogue operation. And it's got to be done very quickly. I've been living at work, spending my nights at The Facility trying to speed up the process. It has to look like we just pulled these detonators out of stock, shined them up and delivered them. It can't look like we've re-tooled anything trying to pull a fast one."

For Luke Towne, 20 years as an expert field commander, winning battles was all about momentum. On the contrary, for Orin Pierce, an expert at counterintelligence, winning battles was not about speed, it was about gathering information. Luke's recent overnight absences from his Malibu house had given Pierce a strategic opportunity.

Four nights earlier, a pair of The Basement's black ops techies had silently entered Luke's house and successfully installed three tiny bugs: in the kitchen, the living room and the bedroom. The devices themselves were state of the art. And due to their minute size (slightly larger than a hair follicle), they were practically impervious to detection. However, because of their low voltage, the devices had a limited broadcast range. A digital recording machine had to be placed in close proximity to the bugs to catch their weak signals.

In Malibu Colony, the original older houses (like Luke's) had been built extremely close to each other. That made it much easier for Pierce's men. The small recorder was placed inside the meter box of the house directly next door to Luke, a distance of only a few feet.

Anything said within Luke's house would be picked up by the bugs. But as long as Luke and Ari were seated outside on the porch, their conversations were safely out of range of Pierce's snoops.

The sun lingered for a moment, hanging above a dead flat Malibu sea as if waiting for Luke to finish his briefing. Ari Shine was an accomplished soldier, a retired Colonel in the Mossad; his observations were invaluable to the success of the proposed action.

Luke was clearly uncomfortable with the very un-military nature of his 'rogue operation.' He paused briefly and asked, "You ready to bolt yet, Ari?"

Right elbow pressed on the table top, chin resting atop his huge right fist, the big Israeli demolitions expert laughed. "Still here."

Luke moved on. Leon de Kennesy was planning a large scale series of explosions involving multi-targets located somewhere in the Middle East. The man was for real. He had already demonstrated his ability to pay for illegal services. His second request was specific. He wanted detonators that could be triggered from long range. Luke was going to provide them.

"The detonators, all of 'em will be duds, right?" asked Ari.

"No. All of them will be live and fully functional. These people are obviously gonna have to randomly test at least one or two detonators to make sure they're all active. So I haven't any choice. I can't give him duds. They'll all have to be live.

"The fail safes?"

"We have several. Every half-hour, each detonator broadcasts its own exact geographic coordinates. It's done with laser pulses. Above normal radio frequencies. Nobody has the laser equipment yet to monitor them, so the signal beacons are virtually undetectable.

"You and your guys will have the only equipment that can read the signals. When the detonators are delivered, somewhere near Lebanon most likely, you'll be able to pinpoint their exact location, track their transportation, and determine their ultimate destination. No matter where they go, you'll be able to cordon the exact location of the target.

"Depending on how long it takes the terrorists to set up targets and install the explosives, your teams should have enough time to track the main perpetrators and identify their strongholds. You may even be able to locate some additional hidden weapons caches.

"Since you'll always know the exact target locations and the precise positioning, we should be able to alert the local authorities before anything happens."

Ari spoke. "I hear you. And if we miss something? If we make a mistake, what's the next fall back?"

"Two of them. First, we've got some counterstrike weaponry for your team to set up. Should things come down to a negotiation, we'll be able to threaten an unprecedented destructive response."

"You're talking about the little B B gun we shot off in Paris, right?"

"Yeah, a somewhat larger version. It's called a Lasocular Cannon. We built it for the Pentagon. It' their most guarded and most lethal weapon. It has the power to combust solid matter into a gaseous vapor; a massive annihilation... only to be used as a last resort.

"But we've got one <u>even more effective</u> safety measure than that. I can disable all of the detonators from here. That ability is the essence of the Mind's Eye technology. It literally happens with the blink of an eye. It's what Cyn is training our Top Gun pilots to do. When you get to Riverton, she'll give you a first class demonstration."

"When do I leave?"

"After dinner we'll head down to Santa Monica. The Harrier's already waiting for you."

Ari would be spending the next week with Cynthia Teller in Riverton, learning the fine points of the Mind's Eye system. And while at the hangar, he would experience the Pentagon's most guarded weapon system.

In a matter of days, he would be in the Middle East charged with two tasks: first, recruiting a response team to monitor the location of Luke's detonators; and second, setting up the Mind's Eye laser cannons behind enemy lines.

As Ari was about to ask another question, the silence of the evening was interrupted by a beeper – coming from the kitchen. "Let's eat," said Luke.

They immediately abandoned their shop talk and headed for the kitchen – unaware that the feast would bring them within range of Pierce's bugs.

During dinner, the two old friends told stories, reminisced and talked about sports. Then, as they dug in to Nana's peach cobbler, Ari asked a very telling question. "With everything that needs to be done, the guys I'll have to recruit, their equipment, the detonators and the rest of the hardware, it sounds like this is going to be a costly operation."

Just under the dining room table, Pierce's tiny bug was picking up each word in pristine digital fidelity, and sending it straight out to the recorder in the meter box.

Luke answered, "I've set up two different bank accounts for you. One at the Otsar Hahayal bank of Israel, the other at the Al-Baraka in Byblos. There should be enough to cover everything. But if something comes up and you need more, we'll just extend the line of credit."

The Basement

Retrieval of the digitized conversations from Luke's house would prove to be a source of tremendous frustration for Orin Pierce. After Ari had left for the airport and Luke was headed back to The Facility, Pierce's men made their first attempt to recover the recorder.

It was 3 a.m.

The Basement men crept quietly through the bushes along the side of Luke's house. When they arrived at the meter box, it was gone. Luke's neighbor was in the midst of a kitchen remodel. His workmen had moved the power lines to the opposite side of the lot. The old meter box had been discarded under an enormous pile of dry wall and lumber and bent rebar. The load was too heavy to lift and, under the circumstances, too noisy to even attempt.

Pierce's men (threatened with dismissal if the information were lost) were forced to post a sentry in an unmarked car, waiting for the lumber to be removed by the workmen.

15 days later the lumber was finally removed, the recorder was retrieved and the information was presented to an infuriated Pierce. One listening confirmed his worst fears. A highly financed rogue operation was being planned without his knowledge. There were two banks mentioned, one in Israel and the other in Greece. This nameless Jihad was planning an action somewhere in the Middle East and Towne was in it up to his laser brain.

Pierce's rage was immediate. Sitting at his desk, alone, he screamed into the silence, "Kill this bastard tin soldier. Now!"

The outburst was followed by the Pierce snarl of self affirmation. He snatched up the phone and punched in an oft used code. The omniscient Pierce had already prepared someone for the job.

When a male voice answered, Pierce spoke calmly. "Concerning the accidental death of Doctor Luke Towne. Proceed...at your own pace."

"Yes sir."

46

Cynthia Ann Teller left Queen of Angeles Nursing College and entered the Army when she was just 17. The opportunity to become a doctor on the government's tab was compelling for a youngster whose father made barely enough money selling refrigerators at Sears to keep her family of five in Kool-Aid and casseroles in their little house in Riverside, California.

She met 23-year-old Corporal Luke Towne when they carried him into the base hospital on a stretcher. He'd had his bell rung in a platoon football game, and when he came to, he found himself looking into the large, concerned, doe eyes of Nurse Cynthia. Of course, he'd faked the injury. A buddy had told him the new nurse was 'hot looking,' and so he devised a foolproof plan to get himself some immediate hands-on attention.

The plan worked well; extremely well, as the two young lovers were married just five short months later. But it took 16 long and passionate years of togetherness for them to finally admit that they had drifted apart.

Their divorce was amicable. He loved the road and stayed on it, fighting in different countries around the world. She loved surgery and saving people's sight and so, chose to remain in California, making their ranch style house in Topanga Canyon her permanent home.

In retrospect, Cynthia had a good-natured explanation of her youthful marriage and break up with Luke: "We were two career-minded, type A personalities, pursuing totally different goals. We just grew apart together. It's a wonder we didn't kill each other."

But then three decades later, on January fourth (Cynthia had made a note of it) they chanced to meet at a party in Malibu; it was a fund raiser for Cesar Chavez and his farm workers. The two were delighted to see each other again, and after some energetic conversation, both realized the power and potential synergy between their mutual interests. By then Cynthia had become the Army's chief ocular surgeon, and Luke had risen to become the head of laser technology for the Defense Department.

It was Cynthia's suggestion that they apply for government funding; and with that as a starting point, they had cofounded The Facility. The combination of their very divergent specialties had yielded spectacular results. Together they had pioneered some of the country's most sophisticated defense technology. The Facility had rapidly become the Military's premier research laboratory.

"The best unworkable team in the world," she'd say proudly when asked about their successful reunion as research partners.

San Fernando Valley, California

The moon over the San Fernando Valley Airport was huge and pale and mysterious, like some eerie crystal ball balancing itself on a long bent finger of cloud.

When the Navy's Prowler Jet rolled to a stop, Luke pulled out on the runway. Cynthia walked across the gravel toward his car absent her normal sprightly gate. The long hours at Riverton and the added pressure at Langley had exacted a price. Her cheerful greeting and prolonged hug was an attempt to cover her deep concern for Luke.

He had never before asked for her help, and she was afraid.

On their way home from the airport, Luke carefully avoided the real purpose behind their meeting, choosing to ask a barrage of questions about the Top Guns, the equipment and the progress being made in Virginia. Cynthia was content to answer everything in detail, knowing he'd get to the real subject when he was comfortable.

A star-filled calm embraced the canyon, triggering the scents of white gardenias and jasmine. Once they arrived at Cynthia's, she mixed a pitcher of Mojitos, he lit some split logs in the patio fireplace and they sat down together on the outdoor couch. The night was dark and warm.

They had never kept secrets from each other. It was no secret that Cynthia was in favor of trying it again as a couple. She was a very self confident woman and had never been the least threatened by Luke's revolving girlfriends. They came and they went; but Cynthia felt that the power of the couple's initial connection had always remained. She was confident that their conversation wouldn't have anything to do with women.

"I knew something was wrong the minute I got on the plane," she said, filling his glass. "I called you when I got to Riverton but your cell was down. Dave didn't know where you were either."

A chest-heaving sigh was all Luke could muster.

"What is it?" she said. "Are you all right?"

"Cyn, I proposed to Kathryn de Kennesy. And she said 'yes.'"

"The Lebanese girl?"

"Woman; Lebanese woman. She's 14 years younger than me, Cyn. And yes, she's the one." He tried to be gentle but failed.

There was a moment of silence.

"Well, aren't you the mystery man," she said finally, in a futile attempt to cover her shock, "I had no idea." She raised her glass. "Congratulations," she said nobly. "I wish you all the happiness in the world."

"Thank you Cyn." They both drank and set their glasses back down on the coffee table. Luke took a slow breath. "A few weeks after that, I got a call from the White House. Brigadier General Orin Pierce. Never heard of him before. Special assistant to the president. Guy works in The Basement."

Cynthia knew what 'The Basement' meant. Her forehead creased into a deep, two-lined furrow. She braced herself for the explanation.

"They dropped me on a carrier, five miles outside of Mugu. There was a letter from the President. Under white seal. My eyes only. Malcolm Diggs, in person; handed it to me himself."

Cynthia Teller held the rank of captain in the U.S. Navy; she knew who General Malcolm Diggs was, and she knew people's lives could be destroyed by such 'white seal meetings.'

"God what is it, Luke?"

"The President said my fiancée was a terrorist. That her father was a big time financier of Muslim extremists. That my marriage was a direct threat to national security. He ordered me back into the service as a double agent — to spy against my new wife and her family."

"They can't do that!" she shouted. "Did they show you the proof?"

"I love you Cyn. Your loyalty means everything to me."

"To the end," she said simply.

"The first thing I asked them for was proof. They didn't have any. Or wouldn't show me any. Some bullshit about if I had full knowledge, it would make it more dangerous for me. Anyway, it wasn't necessary because it turned out they were right about her family."

After a stunned pause, it was her turn to sigh. "God, I'm sorry, Luke."

He told her everything: Leon's offer; the booby-trapped rifles; his fury at Pierce; and, as gracefully as he could, a few details about Kathryn de Kennesy.

Cynthia took it all in silence. "I'm so sorry, Luke," she said again and took his hand. Then, as delicately as she could, added, "And you're sure Kathryn's not part of it?" She was surprised at how difficult it was for her to speak the woman's name.

"Leon purposely asked me to keep her out of it."

Cynthia hesitated respectfully before asking the next question. "You know I'm on your side, our side Luke; but the woman is his daughter. How can you take his word on anything?"

Luke had questioned Kathryn's allegiancc a thousand times since hearing Leon's true intentions. In roundabout ways, he'd tried to test her, each time feeling like an unfaithful lover. And each time she had emerged untainted: a loving, caring, supportive partner; the partner he knew she was. He detested his own suspicions. He found his own behavior hateful and traitorous.

But he knew Cynthia was correct. Leon's words meant nothing; and perhaps they were even more suspect when he was speaking about his daughter.

Luke just stared into the fire.

Cynthia's own reactions disturbed her greatly. She could feel Luke's passion for Kathryn de Kennesy; this wasn't just some fling with a younger woman. She was not prepared for the way it made her feel; possessive, angry, threatened, jealous; these were unfamiliar emotions to a woman as beautiful and accomplished as Cynthia Teller.

There was even a terrible shadow of joy knowing that her rival might be fatally flawed.

She would conceal all of her feelings from Luke, but she could not hide her fears for his safety. "There has to be some way to get you out of this thing," she said finally.

"I haven't been able to talk to anyone about it. It's been driving me crazy. I apologize for being such a zero at the lab, but at least now you know why."

"Forget about the lab. It's you I'm worried about."

Luke breathed an audible sigh and put his arm around her shoulders. "Thanks Cyn, you could always make me feel better; even clear back when we were kids."

His poignant comment only made it worse. She just rested her head on his shoulder and said nothing. All was silent, except for the occasional snapping of oak embers drifting up the chimney into the night.

Cyn showed her frustration. "How are we supposed to get Mind's Eye ready for the Joint Chiefs while you're out being a spy? The pilots are ready to get their implants. How's that gonna work?"

Luke just shook his head.

"All right, how about this?" she said. "The Pentagon's got $300 million into Mind's Eye so far; they're not going to want to just throw it away." She sat forward, excited by her own idea. "What if I make the presentation by myself? I'll explain where we are and admit that I've already done the implant on you. Then I'll make the case that we can't go forward without you? We need you in the lab. Not out hunting terrorists."

"The President says I'm to put everything else on the back burner. It's national security."

"And when we miss the deadline, what's the Pentagon going to say about that?"

"You think the Pentagon is gonna end run Crowley? You know the climate on the Hill. All he's gotta do is say the words 'national security' and it's game over."

It was Cyn's turn to stare into the fire. They were partners in The Facility. They built it together. What was hers was his and vice versa. Frustrated at her own lack of solutions, she expressed the obvious. "Well you know I've got a million five left in the Ocular grant. It's there to use if you want it."

Luke took a few sips of his Mojito and set his glass down on the wicker table in front of them. "I knew you'd say that Cyn. Thank you."

A moment of silence between them. She could sense the wheels turning. "What am I hearing in your voice?"

"I didn't say anything."

She stared at him for a moment. Then her eyes fired. "Don't tell me you want to do this cloak and dagger stuff? Please tell me I'm wrong, Luke. After all we've accomplished. You're not gonna play cowboy again. Haven't you had enough? You managed to kill off a marriage with it. Please don't let the same thing happen to the project."

The moment the words were spoken, she regretted them. She had stepped over a line they'd agreed on years ago. She didn't need to see the look on his face. She quickly held up her hand to stop his reply.

"Wait a minute Luke, please. Wait. I'm sorry. That was way out of line. And it was wrong. Please forget I said anything. You had just as much right in our marriage to pursue your goals as I did to pursue mine. You know I mean that. You know I believe it. Just erase that...stuff and tell me what I can do to help. Let's figure this out together."

"Forgotten," he said. And it was easy for him to mean it. She was an amazing person; the best kind of an ally; one who could listen to what you said and honestly change her position if you had a convincing argument. She was a great partner and a selfless team player if she believed in the cause.

And he needed her to believe.

He took a deep breath and began. "Well, I'll admit, there is some truth to the cowboy thing. Only it's not like you think; not like it used to be. But I do have an idea. And it'd take most of your grant money to pull it off."

He laid it out carefully: the live detonators, the Mind's Eye technology to turn them off at the right moment, and finally, the money to hire Ari Shine and the Mossad to pinpoint the detonator locations as well as setting up the Lasocular Cannons.

"Calling Ari for me was...beyond the call, Cyn. Thank you. It kinda felt like you already knew what I was thinking."

"Whatever you need." She knew her feelings for him were probably going to become a problem at some point. No matter. She extended her hand to shake on it. When he reciprocated, she squeezed his hand firmly and said, "You're not planning on telling Pierce are you?"

"No."

"Doing this alone?"

"You, me and Ari. Together."

"What about Agent Hawk, the young CIA man?"

"I think it's way outside CIA policy. I'd have that guy on our team in a minute but I can't imagine the CIA lining up against the Pentagon."

"That's probably right."

"You know," he said brightening, "If this works, it could turn out to be the ultimate proof of our whole Mind's Eye system. It could win the day for us."

Cyn's response was straight from the hip. "But we haven't tested it yet. Not the way you're suggesting. It could lose the day too. It could blow the whole thing. And if it doesn't work, you're completely exposed. You'd have no escape. They'd kill you in a second. And from the sound of things, a lot of Muslims or Arabs or Syrians could die."

Luke had no answer.

In attempting this rogue operation, Luke was leaving himself open to the unpredictable reactions of an egomaniac. Orin Pierce was not an actual soldier, he was political flake, a meddler, a control freak. And like most of his kind, he was deeply insecure.

Over the years, Luke had seen many such egomaniacs in the Military, all of whom used the same methods to secure their own beatification. Anyone who refused to conform to their personal brand of tyranny was exposed for some past indiscretion, then regretfully dismissed; or betrayed by friends, exiled, and replaced by the same friends; or simply made to 'disappear.'

Luke had seen it clearly on his first day of spy school. When the double agent operation was over, no matter what the outcome, Pierce had the power to make Luke disappear permanently.

That meant his partner and former wife, Cynthia Teller Towne, was now standing in the crosshairs with him.

47

6:30 a.m. – The Facility – Malibu, California

It was still cold in the huge A-Lab hangar. They were seated at one of the large design tables, steam rising from their coffee mugs, three scientists and Luke.

"Thanks for coming in early, guys. Let's get to it," said Luke, his tone unusually serious. "I need you to put something together for me quickly. No one's in the loop on this except the three of you and Doctor Teller. Let me clarify. If something should happen to me you are authorized to discuss this with Doctor Teller only. No one else. No congressional committee under oath. Not the president of the United States. No one! Understood?"

At Luke's mention of a personal mishap, the general atmosphere ramped up from serious to high alert. There was a moment of quiet. Finally, the senior scientist, Arthur Clark, spoke. He motioned over his shoulder toward the huge F-18 fighter behind them and asked nonchalantly, "Ah Doc, you're not pulling us off the Mind's Eye project, are you?"

"Until this is done, yes," said Luke.

The F-18 Mind's Eye Project was the most important operation in the 10-year history of The Facility. To be pulled off the project at this point was inconceivable. Luke had not mentioned 'national security,' but in the minds of the scientists, that had to be the only possible explanation.

Luke unrolled his new blueprints and spread them on the table. "All right, here's what I need. Ten D-12RS detonators. Satellite synced. Phyllis controls 'em all. You can use the new lenses we just got in from Leica."

Arthur Clark's forehead constricted. "Clarifying, Doc... you want us to take the prototype lenses out of the F-18 and put them into Phyllis? The new ones. The Fish Eyes, with the bolt-on brackets. The ones we just installed. Is that correct, Doc?"

"Yeah," said Luke as if was obvious. "You with me so far?"

"Yes sir," all three answered in unison.

"Good. Next I need a hidden signal generator in there. Maybe fabricate it into the twist cone. (He pointed to the spot on the blueprint) A ten-second beacon every half hour should be adequate. And finally, I want the on/off mechanism to reside solely within the DILR system."

"No shut off on the detonator itself, correct?" It was Clark again.

Luke nodded his affirmation, then pushed back from the edge of his chair and waited. The senior scientist was expected to summarize the directive once more and then ask for confirmation from the others. It was part of the way they worked; a system of checks and double checks.

The three scientists continued looking at the blueprints and scribbling in their notepads. After a few moments, all three men looked up and nodded, almost in unison. Arthur Clark, the senior man, cleared his throat. "All right, to summarize then, you need 10 D-12RS detonators set up for long range. You want to reach them via satellite. Full Mind's Eye protocol. You want to use Phyllis to send the *fire* signal. You want to turn her on and off by lookin' into her pretty little eyeball. Right so far, sir?"

Addressing Luke as 'sir' was a rarity at The Facility. It underscored the unprecedented reversal of focus mandated by Luke's new directive.

"Right," was all Luke said, adding further gravity to the ambience.

Clark continued. "Next, you want us to conceal a transmitter in the twist cone. You want the detonators to broadcast a 10-second 'find me' signal every half hour. I assume that's a covert signal. How strong does it have to be?"

"Sixty...70 miles should work," said Luke.

"Sounds doable to me," said Clark. "Anybody else got anything?"

Alex Bell, the 24-year-old electronics expert, spoke up. "Ah Doc, two things. How 'bout a failsafe combo inside Phyllis? So if someone's eye transmission doesn't engage, you could punch her out of commission from right there on the faceplate."

"Done," said Luke.

"And about the on/off switch? How about an a/b/c switch instead? It'd give you one additional option; on, off, and other. So, for example, if you wanted to detonate some other ordinance, or signal a different part of the globe, you and Phyllis would be able to do that."

The collective brain power amongst The Facility's scientists was a shared treasure. All of them felt the same spike of adrenaline from the young scientist's thoughtful input.

"Excellent, Alex," said Luke. "So...put your heads together. Let me know how soon you can get this done. I'll be upstairs."

Before Luke reached the stairs, Arthur Clark called out, "Doc?"

"Yep."

"Best guess would be about three weeks' time."

"Whatever." Luke climbed the stairs two at a time and disappeared down the hallway.

There was a kind of unexpressed gravity at the table after Luke had left the room. At no time in their experience had they ever heard him use the expression, "Whatever." Such an obvious expression of resignation from the brilliant and precise mind of Luke Towne was unheard of. Or was it surrender? Whatever it was, it was definitely un-Luke.

He sat at his desk, watching the fog creep down from the hills, holding its ground at the edge of the Pacific. The view north was cut off by a dense wall of blackened mist.

Walls.

The Basement shrink, George Hinson, had used the expression 'sleeping with the enemy.' The words had become a dark refrain whispering in Luke's head.

At 'spy school,' Pierce's agents had repeatedly intoned vile incriminations against Kathryn's family. Now, with each subsequent set of instructions, they continued to bombard him with more of the same. And although he had rejected most of it, each implication carried with it a pall of uncertainty.

In spite of Luke's toughness, it was getting to him. A sick foreboding had begun leaking into his consciousness. In truth, since the day he met her, he'd been unconsciously questioning Kathryn's credibility. He fought to keep it all out of his head.

It's just another ploy.

Luke walked from his desk to look out at the darkening water. His eyes drifted northward toward San Francisco. It felt like a betrayal to keep anything from Kathryn even for a moment. The idea of spying on her was unthinkable. He suppressed the temptation to call her, tell her the whole ridiculous thing and be done with it.

Yet he had instructed Dave that for the next few days he was to 'take messages from her,' rather than put her through directly as he had done in the past.

Kathryn, his wife to be.

Finally, at 2:30 a.m., Luke shut off his computer, drove down the hill to his small yellow house and climbed into bed. His mental burners flamed out almost instantly and he drifted into a restless sleep. But at 4 a.m. a persistent ringing next to his bed woke him again. In his drowsy innocence, he assumed that no one would be calling at this hour but Kathryn.

"Hi," he answered, still in half sleep.

The whir of electronic equipment in his ear jolted him awake. In seconds Orin Pierce was on the line. As usual, there was no greeting. "You were given a direct order to update this office on Friday the 2nd. My records indicate no report."

"Your line was busy," snapped Luke.

"When one of the president's Special Ops agents fails to report in, Colonel Towne, I have four alternatives to consider: he's dead, he's a defector, he's missing in action, or he's AWOL. AWOL agents are subject to immediate arrest and imprisonment. Any offense may be considered capital and punishable by fatal injection."

"Right, that's 'absent without leave.' I could have sworn you just reached me at my home number. Doesn't sound absent to me."

"Listen closely, Colonel, I didn't authorize the use of any excess funds. And I most certainly did not order detonators! Nor did we discuss anything of the kind. What the hell are you trying to pull, Towne?"

"I don't need your authorization for shit," said Luke. "When the Secretary of State asked me to run our missile guidance program he never mentioned you."

"You're very confused, Colonel Towne. I'd say even bordering on psychotic. Your delusional behavior has left me no choice but to terminate this whole operation and you along with it. You've become a security risk."

The words came blasting out of Luke's mouth like the spent shells of an M16. "Don't threaten me, Pierce. I'm a double agent, remember. I'm inside where you put me. I'm on the payroll of a major financier of terrorism. I eat dinner with the bastard once a week. Oh, and by the way, I'm also engaged to marry his daughter. You want to put me in jail? Go for it. You know where I am. You got guys tailing me everywhere. You want to kill me? Do it. Except you haven't got the balls or the talent. What are you gonna do about it? It's your move, asshole."

Pierce was livid. No one ever challenged his authority. He'd had his ass kissed by prime ministers and presidents for three decades. And suddenly this arrogant punk soldier was calling him out.

His hands shook. He hit the mute button. His foot bounced up and down like a jack hammer. He breathed in deeply, then out again, then demanded his superior intellect to scan the variables.

Towne's infiltration of this nameless terrorist organization was unprecedented. From the sound of it, the group could even have assets within U.S. borders. In the eyes of the President, the operation was already considered priceless. Almost holy. There wasn't *a goddamn thing* Pierce could do about it.

"You still there, Pierce?" Luke shouted into the muted silence.

The mute button was released but Pierce said nothing.

"What do you want?" said Luke.

"Two weeks ago on December 21st, after a meeting with some Lebanese businessmen, your fiancée went missing for the day. We followed her from San Francisco down the coast to the city of Burlingame. But somewhere in a maze of tract houses she managed to evade us. She was gone for nearly three hours. We picked her up again later leaving Holy Name Cemetery in the north end of town.

"Fifteen seconds behind her was a car driven by a Syrian arms dealer named Shadi Ammad. We didn't know he had left Iran. We don't know how he got into the country. We know in 1983 he was the mastermind behind the Hezbollah's bombing of our Marine barrack in Beirut. It killed 214 U.S. troops. He's number two on our most wanted list."

Pierce was barely controlling his own angers, suppressing them because of the importance of the operation. Inside he was boiling. His voice was a guttural growl. "This situation has already gotten dangerously out of control, Towne. Hear me. Nothing goes on without my approval. I'm giving you an order. From now on you don't even take a breath without first reporting it to me. Or you'll be taking your last breath. Are we clear?"

No answer from Luke.

The unflappable Pierce was now shouting into the phone, "You need to separate your bloody whore from your bloody hormones. Or I'll cut you up into so many pieces they'll never find you."

Luke jerked the phone cord out of the wall, ripping the faceplate off the wall with it. He rolled over and stared at the ceiling, his mind churning*...and churning. "Missing for the day, Syrian arms dealer...Beirut...214 killed. Your fiancée, missing for the day... your fiancée ...missing for the day....*

The words circled around and around in the dark, diving at his head, cawing and pecking like a haggle of vultures.

48

San Francisco, California

The American Airlines morning flight from LAX was halfway to San Francisco. Luke was sitting in business class. He'd called her 10 minutes after hanging up on Pierce. When she finally answered, he'd made up an excuse about needing to be in the city right away. *Probably not the smartest move.*

She was delighted. He was manic.

It wasn't all 'I miss you' and 'I want your body' like he'd made it sound. It was really about December 21st; the day Pierce said she was in Burlingame; the day she'd passed off as 'just real busy, honey.'

The time had come. He needed to ask her some questions, but he wasn't sure he wanted to hear the answers.

It was 11:30 in the morning when Kathryn opened her door. Her shades still drawn, the light dim and smoky; it looked just like a TV commercial for Victoria's Secret.

She was barefoot, her toenails pearlescent. She wore a black lace bra and a black silk wrap around her hips that was about the size of a head band. Her body looked like Tara Banks; all thighs, calves and cleavage.

"Baby," was all she said. Then she wrapped herself around him and, with one hand, pushed the door closed behind them. She opened her lips and pushed her tongue into his mouth, pulsing it against his in a gentle throbbing rhythm. She moved them both back against the wall.

Then, like a graceful white spider, she climbed down his body clutching his limbs and nipping his skin with little bites and kisses as she moved toward his stomach.

She flattened her palms against his Pecs and pulled downward. Their connected bodies slid down the wall until they were stretched full length on the soft carpet.

The blinds cast thin shadows across them in the darkness. They made love again and again; their passion fueled by absence and longing. And when he awoke for the nth time in the midst of tangled sheets, the sun was already on its way down behind the bay bridge. He found his beautiful Kathryn gazing down at him with a worried look on her face.

"What is it?" He struggled to lift himself, body and mind, out of the mélange of his blissful dreams.

"I love you Lukie, you know that."

"Yes." He nodded his affirmation. *Oh god, what's coming?*

"I've never felt this close to anyone in my life since I was a little girl. So I want you to know everything there is to know about me. No secrets. You know what I mean?"

"Kathryn, I don't need to know about the past. All I care about is now. Whoever you were with before...it doesn't matter."

"Lukie, this is about me. It's about who I really am. About the only white lie I've ever told you. About Burlingame, about everything. And it's time you knew."

Luke took a deep breath. "Kathryn, I love you now. And no matter what you have to tell me, when you finish telling it, I'll love you just the same."

She kissed the side of his face. "You're the sweetest man on earth, Luke. Thank you."

The story she told him began in 1988, and it lasted well into the night.

1988

Ronald Reagan was in the White House; Steffi Graf beat Martina Navratilova at Wimbledon; NASA scientist James Hansen warned Congress of the dangers of global warming; Ben Johnson was stripped of his gold medal at the Summer Olympics in Seoul; Dustin Hoffman won the Oscar for "Rain Man;" the Song of the Year was "Somewhere Out There."

Burlingame, California

It was the first day in May, 1988. In San Mateo County, the old-fashioned city of Burlingame was sleeping soundly alongside the San Francisco Bay – most of its 26,000 residents unaffected by ecosystems, politics, sports or movies.

Thomas Bowen was already hidden in the bushes at Riverdale Park. The 8th grade class of St Brendan's grammar school had just arrived for a day of supervised fun. The boys in their salt and pepper cords and the girls in their light blue starched blouses looked crisp and innocent. It was that innocent look, in fact, that had enabled them to sell enough subscriptions to the Tidings Newspaper to win this free day at the park.

Thomas Bowen, freckled-faced, 12-year-old geekster, was not one of the innocents. At least he was trying his hardest not to be. Yesterday, he had hidden in the girls bathroom at school, hoping to catch a glimpse of some bare skin, when he overheard something that could make him famous. Something that might get him closer to the "cool guys" who hardly acknowledged his existence.

Hiding on a commode, with his knees pulled up to his chin, Thomas heard Cathy Jenrette tell her best girlfriend that she was planning to sneak away from the others at Riverdale Park and meet her "lover" – a high school junior named Blaise.

Cathy Jenrette was amazing! She was the best setter on the volleyball team; she was head cheerleader, she was by far the prettiest and most popular girl in his class, and she also had major breasts. At 14, little Cathy already had the body of a 19-year-old and along with that, a kind of natural maturity about everything.

Unfortunately these 'qualities' made her practically unapproachable on a sexual level. Nonetheless, she remained the gooey provocation of a hundred 8th grade hormonal fantasies.

Bowen hid his dad's new Polaroid instant-shot camera in a lunch pail and convinced his mom to drop him at Riverdale Park 20 minutes before the busload of his classmates was due to arrive. He stationed himself behind a stand of sycamores just off the parking lot so he could keep an eye on Cathy when she got off the bus.

Twenty minutes later, the bus arrived. No one but Thomas was watching when Cathy ditched the others and snuck off through the brush to rendezvous with the famous Frankie Blaise.

Everyone knew who Frankie Blaise was. Several months ago, the "Blazer" had stopped by St Brendan's school yard during basketball practice. Just for fun he had slapped the ball away from one of the 8th grade players and casually knocked down a 20' jumper from the corner without ever looking at the basket. All the more amazing was the fact that he had performed this prodigious feat while never taking his eyes off Cathy, who stood nearby watching practice with her girlfriends.

Cathy had already said 'no' to Frankie Blaise on three separate occasions; she knew it drove him crazy. No girl had ever said 'no' to the Blazer. Even at 14 years old, little Cathy Jenrette was already a master technician, an absolute killer.

Cathy was raised by her single father, Dave Jenrette, a syndicated journalist and regular contributor to Rolling Stone.

Several times each month, Cathy would miss school because she was out on the road, covering a concert with her dad.

Of course St. Brendan's didn't approve of the absences. In Dave Jenrette's mind, missing school was unfortunate but just couldn't be helped. There was no way he would consider leaving his daughter at home alone.

In private moments Dave would admit to friends that missing school at St. Brendan's really wasn't that big of a deal. "The only reason she's still in Catholic school is because her mother wanted it that way."

Nine wonderful years of being married to Cathy's mother had ended suddenly and unexpectedly when Melissa's heart had stopped beating. The doctors said her heart lacked glycogen; that it was a genetic disease; and that it didn't even have a name yet. No one knew she had it.

Cathy was only nine when it happened. Dave had immediately taken his little daughter out of school so the family could be together. That had been five years ago. And Dave had not even begun to recover from the loss.

When Cathy finally returned to St. Brendan's, half a year had elapsed and she was hopelessly behind. Although she was certainly bright enough to skip a year, Monsignor Dodge, the pastor, objected, and so Cathy was held back to begin the second grade again. From that point on in her schooling, Cathy would be 9 months older than any of her classmates and a good deal more mature.

In little Cathy's mind, Dave was the greatest father that ever lived. She'd been back stage at 50 rock concerts and some of the country's top rockers even knew her by her nickname "Jenner."

After she had finally said yes to Frankie Blaise and they began their most secret and highly illicit affair, she had gotten Jimmy Page to autograph a back stage pass with the words, "To Frankie Blaise – lights out shooting, man. Keep it up. All the best, J. Page."

She had given it to Blaise on his 17th birthday. He and his friends were huge Zeppelin fans. From that point on, the little grammar school cutie had become a minor celebrity at Dorsey High where Frankie Blaise was a starting guard and himself a major celebrity to be sure.

Thomas Bowen trailed Cathy to a deserted area of the Park. When he saw her spread a blanket out on top of a wooden picnic table, he had quietly climbed a nearby tree to insure an unobstructed view of the sexual gymnastics he was about to behold. He had only imagined such things before, but now he was going to see them for real.

Minutes later, Frankie Blaise arrived carrying a quart bottle of Ole. He climbed up on the picnic table next to Cathy, popped open the bottle and handed it to her. She took a long pull on the bottle and handed it back to him. He did the same and then set the bottle aside. Without saying a word, she undid the first three buttons of her St Brendan's light blue blouse and put her arms around his neck. The couple tipped slowly backward, Frankie on top, Cathy under him.

Thomas Bowen, tree snoop, was about to score big time. In a few seconds, the prettiest girl in his world, the sex goddess of his dreams, would be lying naked to the waist directly below his perch – her magnificent forbidden and heretofore only imagined breasts would be there completely exposed.

The couple sat up. Off came her blouse. Back down again.

Blaise struggled for several moments trying to unhook her bra with one hand while still lying on top of her. When that didn't work, he pulled her up, and struggled a bit more with both hands until the flimsy little lace contraption snapped off.

She helped him slip it from her shoulders and then the two lay back down. Supporting himself in a kind of half push up, Frankie kissed the naked stomach of the incredible woman-child Cathy Jenrette.

Bowen's hands shook. He leaned out from the tree a bit and snapped the first picture. Then, gingerly, so as not to make too much noise, he pulled the Polaroid exposure out of the camera and slipped the precious photo into his shirt pocket to begin developing. He'd seen his father do it many times. But never hanging from a tree.

In order to accomplish the move, Thomas had to hold on to the camera with his left hand and pull the exposure out smartly with his right. He never actually realized that he had let go of the branch with both hands until he saw the edge of the picnic table rushing up at his face. It all happened so fast; faster than his brain could compute. He didn't actually hear the sound of his left arm snap as he flung it out in front of himself to break the fall.

To Cathy and her man, the noise of Thomas's body crashing into the corner of their picnic table sounded like an atomic bomb. An earthquake. The ancient wooden table collapsed to the ground, its termite-riddled legs snapping like match sticks. The impact felt like they had fallen off a 10' cliff.

For a moment they both sat in the rubble, frozen in shock. Then, the "Blaiser," first string basketball hero, seducer of women, high school wunderkind, immediately leapt from the blanket and beat feet toward his car, using every bit of his legendary athletic speed and quickness to get him there.

"Frankie, wait!! He's hurt!"

His answer was shouted from the open window of his Dodge Dart as he brodied out of the gravel parking lot. "I can't. My scholarship. I could get in trouble."

Cathy tore a strip from her skirt, wrapped it around the gash from which Thomas's femur was protruding and calmly went for help.

It might have all ended right there. Thomas would have claimed that he'd accidentally fallen from a tree, and Cathy certainly would have gone along with that story. Except someone found the Polaroid camera hanging from a tree branch. The medics emptied Thomas's pockets and found the developed picture which, together with the camera, was handed over to Monsignor James Dodge, pastor of St. Brendan's.

The quality, automatic lens setting and perspective of Thomas's one picture were extraordinary.

So it was that Dave Jenrette and his daughter were summoned to St. Brendan's rectory on the Monday following the December 19 weekend of 1988.

Sitting opposite the Monsignor, staring across his huge mahogany desk, squinting in the dark severity of the room (a severity which surrounded everything the prelate did), Dave noticed that the man's high-backed chair was a good deal higher than the uncomfortable little stick chairs provided for guests. All proclamations thus took on the air of being "handed down from on high."

After a moment of dramatic silence, Fr. Dodge simply pushed the Polaroid photograph across his desk allowing it to come to rest in front of Dave Jenrette. He waited dramatically and then announced, "I cannot allow this sort of behavior in my parish."

Dave looked down at the picture for a moment, "Are you talking about the missionary position, or…sex between minors, or just promiscuity in general?"

"All of it!" snapped the prelate.

"I see. All of it. Well then, how do you propose to stop it, Father? You've already tried to convince them that sex is dirty. That didn't go over very well. 'You'll all burn in hell fire.' That one isn't working either. What else you got?"

"It starts with the parents. I intend to get the parents of these offenders directly involved."

Dave shook his head. "Offenders! Are you suggesting my daughter is one of these...'offenders?'"

"Pictures don't lie, Mr. Jenrette. I would have thought that was obvious."

Dave glanced down at the Polaroid. "Did Thomas Bowen tell you this was a picture of my daughter?"

"No he did not."

"That's good, because I hear he doesn't even remember being there."

"The paramedics brought this to me."

"Did you discuss this incident with them?"

"I have not."

"With anyone?"

"Mr. Jenrette, I'm not on trial here."

Dave held up the picture. "So you're saying that you know what my daughter looks like naked. Is that right? That you've seen her naked before? You must have. If you didn't discuss it with anyone, how would you know it's Cathy?" Dave's voice was gradually increasing in volume.

"I'm not saying anything of the kind, I'm simply saying...."

Dave cut him off. "Yes you are. Think about it lame brain. If no one else has seen this picture, and you're the only one who thinks it's my daughter...that makes you the only witness, doesn't it?"

Dave slapped his large hand loudly on the desk and abruptly stood up to his full 6' stature. "Listen, you self righteous little maggot, if I hear that you've ever said one derogative word about my daughter, that you've even mentioned anything about this incident to anyone, I'll have you in court for slander. But first, I'll drag you out of this little tax free hotel you run and beat the living shit out of you!"

He extended his hand to Cathy. "Let's go, honey."

As they neared the door, Monsignor Dodge made one vain attempt to recover his dignity. "Don't you threaten me! I have teams of lawyers."

"Bring 'em on you pervert. I'll make you look even more like a pedophile than you already do. We'll have a press party. In your honor."

It was quiet for a long time in the Camry as they drove home. Cathy moved close to her father and leaned her head against his shoulder. Finally, she said quietly, "Daddy, that is me in the picture."

"I know it, honey. You look so beautiful lying there. For a moment I thought it was me and your mom."

A full minute of silence. Then she said, "It's Frankie Blaise."

"I know honey, his parents called me."

When the light went green at the Larkspur onramp to the North Freeway, Dave accelerated into the sparse afternoon traffic.

"You guys had sex yet?" he said.

"No."

"You planning to?"

A hesitation; then, "I think so."

"Does he have protection?"

"I had one in my pocket Dad."

Then all Dave said was, "I love you Cath. You'll always be my girl no matter what."

She started to cry and he put his arm around her. "Aren't you going to tell me I'm too young?"

"You are too young, honey. But then you're too young to have the woman's body you got. You're too young to be as smart as you already are. Too young to see the things you've seen. Too young to lose your mom when you're eight years old. But that's just the way it is."

Deep in thought for a moment, Dave heaved a deep sigh of adult frustration and parental foresight. "Cathy, the bottom line is, I think you were born with an old soul. I think you're one of those people destined to contribute something important to life. Something the rest of us aren't capable of doing. Maybe even change the world in some way. You're an extraordinary being and I'm lucky to be your dad."

Two days later, on the evening of December 21st, 1988, Pan Am Flight 103 exploded in mid air. Pieces of the plane fell onto the Scottish Towne of Lockerbie, killing 259 people.

Dave Jenrette was one of them.

"Is this Cathy?" It was an unfamiliar voice on the phone.

"Yes it is," she answered brightly.

"Are you the daughter of David, the journalist?"

"Yes, who's this please."

It was 5:30 in the evening, three days before Christmas. The official from the Federal Aviation Administration did his best to be kind; but there's no kind way to deliver such a horrific message.

Cathy sat down on the kitchen floor. She never thought to question the caller. She was 14 years old, but she knew it was real. The room went topsy turvy around her. The blood pulsed in her temples. The pain was intense – an axe blade wedged into her chest.

The whole world seemed to have gone away. She was there all by herself. She began rocking back and forth. Tears welled up at the bottoms of her eyes. Then she swallowed hard and screamed out loud at herself. "NO." She drew in a huge breath and shouted again, "No, I won't!" She wiped away the moisture before it could run down her cheeks. "I don't cry!! You can't make me cry if I don't want to."

At the innocent age of 14, Cathy began to close down her natural emotions, to bury the aloneness that was too painful to feel. Push it away, force it down.

It was the only way to survive.

She crawled into the corner of the kitchen next to the stove and pulled her knees up to her chin. She stayed there for 20 heartbeats, counting them up. It was so quiet. Desperate empty silence. A huge black hole of it.

Totally alone. Both parents gone.

"It's just me, then. By myself."

Then suddenly her mind stopped working. No thoughts would come. Her stomach turned over. There was nothing. No place to go. Nothing to hold on to. Nothing familiar. No point of reference. Just an overwhelming sense of dread. Deep. Bottomless. Terrifying black despair.

"Fine," she said to herself. "It's just me. Alone. If that's the way it is. Fine. It's just me. Fine. I'll take care of it. And nothing...no one will ever do this to me again."

That one thought forced itself up from the bottom of her gut. She used it to kill off the black despair that threatened to obliterate her spirit. And she built it into a wall.

And over time, the wall would grow stronger and thicker and taller. She would find solace and protection behind it for the rest of her life.

The sound of a ringing phone cut into the kitchen silence.

"I have a person–to-person call from Ms. de Kennesy, for Cathy."

"Yes." Her voice sounded stronger than she expected.

"Is this Miss Jenrette?" It was the operator.

"Yes."

"Go ahead, please."

"Cat, precious. It's aunt Nana. Honey are you okay?"

Cathy started to answer but her aunt couldn't seem to wait. "I want you to come stay with us, dear. Leon and me. Can you be ready by tomorrow?"

"I guess."

"All right dear, dry your eyes. Doctor Blake from next door is going to take you to the airport tomorrow morning. Can you be packed by 7?"

"I'm not crying, Nana."

"It's all right if you do. Don't worry about what you need to bring. Just....just...can you get over to the Blakes' house in the morning? We want you here with us. Okay? It'll be just like last summer."

"Thank you, Nana. I'll be there. See you tomorrow."

Cathy hung up. She had things to do.

The note she penned to her best friend, Nicole, showed a focus far beyond the ken of a 14-year-old; a precursor of the organization skills that would one day enable her to become an agent of the Lebanese government.

Dear Nicki,

I won't be around for CIF finals. So I want you to take my place as head cheerleader. Tell Sister Brigit I said so. It's your turn to be "queenie." Ha ha.

Bye,
C.J.

P.S. Please take care of Mergie. She hates milk and will only eat Chicken of the Sea. My kitty's got nothin' but class.

Mergatroid was a 12-pound alley cat that had been sleeping nights on top of Cathy's head ever since it wandered into the house six months earlier.

Cathy Jenrette awoke with a headache in a strange bed in a darkened room. She stirred in the covers and quickly realized it wasn't just her head; everything ached; arms, neck, back, everything. She struggled to remember how she had gotten there, but nothing would come.

She raised up on her elbows and felt something pulling on her shoulders. It was a nightgown, a silk one. And it went all the way down to her toes. *Impossibly weird.*

Cathy had been sleeping in the nude ever since she turned seven. She had read in Cosmo that older women slept naked. It felt strange at first. But then at a Mamas and Papas concert she had asked Michele Phillips if she slept in the nude and Michie had said, "All the sexiest women sleep naked." That did it. Cathy sleeps naked! No question about it.

So what's with the silk nightgown? she wondered. Then a bit of memory broke through. Her neighbor, Doctor Blake, had put her on a plane. He'd given her a tiny blue pill and told her to swallow it after they'd taken off. The stewardesses were pretty. The seats in first class seemed huge...and that was all she could remember. Mercifully, her mind was still blocking out the realization of the terrible loss of her father.

She sat up. She was in a four-poster king-sized bed with tons of soft pillows and a puffy down comforter. *What a trip.* Still her head hurt so badly it was hard to make anything out in the darkness. "Hello?" she ventured.

"Cat, are you awake, honey?" The voice came from a figure wrapped in a white blanket, bundled on a chaise lounge next to the bed.

"Nana??" she shouted. No one but her beloved Nana ever called her Cat.

Instantly Nana was there, tanned arms tightly wrapped around her. "Oh Cat, it's so good to have you here," she said, and then began to rock her precious little niece back and forth slowly.

"I'm so sorry," she whispered and refused to let go until finally, deep sobs broke from Cathy's chest and the first tears began to pour down her pale cheeks.

49

San Francisco, California

The terrorist bombing at Lockerbie had taken place in 1988, a full 17 years ago. But Kathryn's re-telling of the horrible events surrounding it had reopened a deep wound. No river of tears would ever wash the pain away. And as Luke rocked her gently in his arms, she told him why she had driven to Burlingame on the 21st of December. And why she had kept the details to herself. It was to put flowers on a gravestone:

> *Dave Jenrette, beloved husband of Melissa,*
> *Devoted father of Cathy, struck down*
> *the 21st day of the 12th month of 1988*
> *above the glen in Scottish Lockerbie.*
> *May flights of angels carry you to rest.*

An hour had passed. Kathryn had cried inconsolably for most of it – a vulnerability she had vowed would never be seen by anyone. The vow was made by a 14-year-old on the kitchen floor on the worst day of her life. She had not broken it until this day.

Now she lay cradled in Luke's arms in half sleep. She was silent for a time, then stirred quietly and turned her face toward him. "I didn't mean to burden you with all this. I'm sorry. That wasn't what I was trying to do. I only wanted you to know who I was at the start of it all. At the beginning of my life."

"God, what a terrible, horrible thing to happen to a child. I'm so sorry. I would hunt them down and kill them for you if I could. I apologize for doubting you about things you hadn't told me. Just tell me what I can do to help," said Luke helplessly.

"I love you, Lukie. You don't have to do anything. Just hold me like this and listen to me like you do. I've never talked to anyone about it. I could tell you more. It isn't all bad. Some of it was even pretty great."

Kathryn would only tell him the good parts. She would describe *Al-Muqit* (Allah the Provider) *High School* as a garden of opportunity; a chance to learn, to grow, to thrive. Like being raised a second time, "...initiated into an ancient cultural heritage so rich and powerful and so completely different from my own."

Nana and Leon were heaven's angels. Upon graduation from high school, she had changed her name to theirs.

But there was so much she could not tell him. Her exterior was feminine and soft. But her instincts and her defenses were hammered into stone by the solitary upbringing she had endured in Beirut. Her step-parents were generous, but they had their own lives. They were older and always busy. Little Cathy was left to her own devices.

She had learned to trust no one.

From the beginning, she had no real relationships, she had arrangements; one after another; most of them sexual, predatory and political; arid as the desert that surrounded her, a constant quid pro quo of the heart.

Leon and Nana had raised her in Islam. She had studied the Koran as every student did. She felt their cause was in her blood, if not her genes. She had attended her junior prom with a young patriotic Syrian boy named Ayman Nouri – a grown man now, building suicide bombs for Hamas.

She couldn't tell Luke these things. She couldn't speak of Sarkis Jabara, a high school crush, now a feeder for the Hezbollah. Nor could she mention Hasan Al-din, her third 'older man,' who was now one of Interpol's 10 most wanted terrorists.

In her youth, she had slept with these men. Some because they were attractive men and she had been attracted to them; some because they had showed her kindness and she had mistaken it for love; and some because she feared she would be disfigured or killed if she refused.

Her fate had been decided for her when she was 14. Reborn into another world. How could she escape her upbringing? She had been reared in Islam. She had prayed with her Muslim brothers, pledged herself to the faith. She was an obedient and loving daughter.

She had met and seduced Colonel Luke Towne. She had made him fall in love with her. It was a simple request. She had served cause of Allah. To her Islamic brothers, Luke was a living archetype of Western civilization, the devil from hell.

To Kathryn de Kennesy, he was the most kind, generous, honest, loving and truthful human being she had ever known. She had fallen deeply in love with him.

Her civilizations had collided. She could not tell him.

Typical. LAX was crowded as hell. Luke was stuck in the line waiting to pay the automobile storage fee for his 48-hour stay in San Francisco. But he didn't care. His weekend with Kathryn had been transcendent. She had let him in. She had opened herself and shared her life's most painful tragedy; and the telling of it had cost her. He had seen the pain; he had dried her tears.

She had done that for him.

The missing day in Burlingame had turned out to be an incontrovertible snapshot of the person he knew she was; honest, courageous, strong and faithful. He felt like the luckiest man in the world, an intrepid believer.

He knew she had told him everything. There were no secrets between them. Except the one he was forced to keep from her. For her own good. For the good of their relationship.

He would preserve her bond with her adoptive family for as long as possible. She had suffered enough. She didn't need to hear about Leon the terrorist. There had already been enough painful truth in her life. He would face the truth problem when he absolutely had no other choice.

50

Haifa, Israel

4 p.m. The sun lingered above a dark and turbulent Mediterranean Sea. From Ari Shine's apartment living room, one could see the weekenders flying their brightly colored kites over the white sand of Tripoli's southern beach. But Ari saw none of it.

He was on hands and knees, plotting distances on a map of Lebanon: to the north *70 miles to Beirut;* to the East *550 miles to Baghdad.* After spending a week with Cynthia at the hangar in Riverton, he'd stopped in Malibu, picked up a trunk of electronics and flown home to Haifa and immediately gone to work.

That was 72 hours ago.

In just three days, Ari had already recruited 18 Mossad commandos, outfitted them with high-end USMC communications equipment, and instructed each man on the use of the special GPS receivers he had brought from Malibu. The handheld devices were preset to pull in the laser beacons broadcast by Luke's detonators. Their reach was accurate to a 60-mile radius.

Initially, the laser beacons registered on the PDA screens as geographical coordinates. The software would then project actual live locations (in real time) as updated regularly by NSA's satellite photography. The NSA data banks also provided current street maps which could be superimposed over any of the live coordinates.

With this equipment and the laser beacons hidden in Luke's detonators, they could identify the exact location of the explosives the instant they arrived. They could then create a tight perimeter around the terrorists and follow their actions, undetected. It was an unprecedented chance to corral a major Jihadist ring.

Felt tip pen in one hand, cell phone in the other, Ari was conferring with Luke on the placement of his resources. "How do we know where the bastards are gonna put 'em?" asked Ari.

"Well, at best, it's a guess," said Luke. "But I think it's a pretty accurate one. In every conversation I had with Leon, even before he came out of the closet, his statements were consistent. His *freedom fighters* were always in the same two general areas; '...struggling in Beirut, or in-fighting in Dbayeh.' There was a third one too. Occasionally he talked about a small army holed up in the mountains of Al Najaf."

"All right, that means I've got to extend the field all the way inland to Baghdad. I'm going to need at least 20 more handhelds."

"We're working on them now. I'll send them ASAP. But the ones you've got now cover the obvious entry points, right?"

"Correct. Airports and seaports from here to Beirut. The additional 20 would be for airstrips hidden somewhere inland, plus a few uncharted strands of coast line. Cynthia gave me some of the F18's new triangulation equipment. Amazing technology. When I get the rest of the handhelds, we'll have a very tight grid."

"Anything else?"

"Well, I haven't been to either of the banks yet. All my guys volunteered. Nobody even asked how much they're getting paid."

Luke answered, "Most of them have families, right? How 'bout we pay 'em all in advance? In full. Send the money to their wives."

Ari knew that Luke was considering the danger of the operation and the possible loss of life. "Thanks Luke. I appreciate that very much. One last question. When do you think you'll be sending the matches to Leon?"

"End of the week."

Children's Hospital – Los Angeles, California

One week later, the detonators were delivered by the Facility's Special Courier (Manuel Diego) to Children's Hospital in downtown Los Angeles. Doctor Leon de Kennesy was at his desk going over some patient files, nervously awaiting the delivery, when his assistant knocked.

"Doctor, we just got two cartons from Medico Precision Instruments. Would you like me to bring them in?" she asked.

"What does the label say, Vanessa?"

"It says 20 .015 Nylon syringes in solution, Doctor."

"Fine, just leave them out there with the rest of the boxes. We'll sort through all of it Friday. Thanks."

Over the past week, Leon had purposely ordered several cases of various medical supplies and told his assistant to let them pile up in the outer office until they all had arrived. He would then instruct her where he wanted them stored.

Leon could feel his heart beginning to race. He immediately popped a Xanax and tried to distract himself. In 45 minutes, she would leave and he could get to what he wanted.

Vanessa left work at 5:30. Leon waited until 6:15 before locking the outer door and turning off the lights in her office. Only then did he go to the stack of boxes, retrieve the two from Medico Precision Medical Instruments and carry them to his desk.

He sliced through the packing tape and opened the corrugated flaps. Inside each carton, there were five small wooden boxes fitted into a rectangle of thick gray Styrofoam. Gently, he lifted one of the small boxes out of its casing.

At first he could not find a seam. The boxes were sealed tightly by their own meticulous wooden construction. After a bit of experimentation, he applied a slight pressure to the edge of the box, and its top hinged open. There, pressed into a dense black form-fitting gel, rested a single detonator.

He lifted it carefully out of its packing. To his surprise, it was relatively lightweight. A gray metal cylinder about nine inches in length, pointed at one end, with a simple black dial fitted into the larger end. There was a small engraving just under the dial that read: 'D-12RS."

The instructions were simple; the job of activation could be performed by someone with no prior experience. *Insert the cylinder (small end first) into the explosive medium. Activate it by rotating the black dial a quarter turn to the right.*

The actual detonation could only be accomplished from the PDA Luke had already delivered. At the appropriate time, Leon would simply press three of the four small buttons on Phyllis's faceplate and the detonators would be armed. One final push and all the explosions would ignite simultaneously.

To certify their functionality, Luke had encouraged Leon to test any number of the devices in any way he chose. Leon had decided to ship one detonator to Beirut. His partner, Mullah Ahmed Rockmani, was to find a remote section of desert, away from prying eyes, insert one of the detonators into the sand (near or under a bush), twist the dial one quarter turn to the right and leave it unattended. A second detonator would be sent to Talib where it would be handled in a similar fashion.

When assured that the detonators were in place, Leon would sit down comfortably in his library, toast the Jihad with a sip of Laffite, and depress the buttons on Phyllis's faceplate in the proper sequence.

The signal would be lasered to one of the U.S. Military's permanent satellites and pinged down into the Middle East, 6000 miles away. The detonator's interior circuitry would electrically charge the alloy filament and ramp it to an extreme temperature sufficient to ignite the explosive.

Since there would be no explosive used in the initial tests, there would be no sound, no explosion; but the detonator itself would self destruct.

The result (the detonator's proof of function) would be a charred glob of melted aluminum buried in a ring of blackened desert sand.

Leon overnighted the two packages to Beirut on Emory Air Freight. Mullah Rockmani sent his most trusted bodyguard out to a remote tribal region in South Waziristan to deliver the first detonator to Talib. The Mullah planted the second detonator personally in a rice field adjacent his own house.

During the next 24 hours, Leon received two separate text messages, both of them spelling out the same word: "Ready." He immediately called Nana into the library to watch as he carefully pressed the three-button sequence on Phyllis's faceplate. Then he handed the little PDA to her. "The honor is yours, my love."

Nana pressed the last button and the two embraced. Twelve hours later, two more text messages appeared on his cell phone. Both were in Arabic: "Al-Mu'min." (Allah, The Affirmer of Truth.)

Proudly, Leon called out the good news to his wife. "Nanette, our son-in-law, the traitor, has delivered the goods. And so has his magnificent wife-to-be."

51

The Helix Restaurant – Gardena, California

Tuesday night. The tiny, four-table Greek restaurant in Gardena had closed early to accommodate an important customer. Once again, a special table had been set up in the center of the kitchen. Doctor Leon de Kennesy was served avgo-lemono soup, Spanakopitas, Moussaka, yogurt with honey and a double espresso; for the Doctor, a thoroughly satisfying meal.

After the table was cleared, he ordered another espresso, dismissed the kitchen staff, and bid 'good night' to George, the owner. While watching their cars pull away from the parking lot, Leon downed the second espresso in a single swallow and sat down to wait for *the ignorant street rat* to arrive.

He had planned this maneuver carefully, hatched it with Mullah Rockmani, and refined it with Nana de Kennesy, his ingenious and ever creative partner.

Leon heard the hard slide of tires on the gravel parking lot outside the restaurant. The moment had arrived. Seconds later, the door was yanked open and in strode Farad Aziz; black boots and jeans, a dark t-shirt with a grotesque white skull covered by a dirty leather jacket.

As expected, Farad was 20 minutes late. He did not speak, just jerked out the chair opposite Leon and dropped heavily into a slumped position, gazing into space as if Leon weren't there. Farad's contempt for the *hawk-nosed bastard* was palatable.

Leon spoke softly. "Thank you for coming." This from a man who never thanked anyone, especially Farad Aziz.

Farad's eyes remained vacant, his tone dismissive. "You said come alone. I'm here." Keenly aware he had almost exceeded his usefulness, Farad had come prepared. His left hand remained in his jacket pocket clutching the little Beretta PX4, pointed directly at Leon's groin.

"I asked you to come alone," began Leon, "because I have a message for you from our leader."

"Yeah?"

"After hearing my account of your installations, the most holy Mullah Ahmed Rockmani has ordered me to say these words to you." There was an unusual glint in Leon's dark eyes.

Farad's finger tightened on the trigger.

With great solemnity, Leon quoted the Mullah. "Farad Aziz, you bring great honor to our brotherhood. I am filled with pride in your accomplishments. Allah has blessed us all with your quiet faith."

Farad said nothing. Skeptical. His expression unchanged.

From a bag on the table, Leon produced a worn leather-bound book and passed it to Farad.

"What is it?"

"This belonged to our beloved Sayyid Qutb," said Leon. "It contains his personal notes for the last book of *Fi Zalal.* He wrote it in 1986, while he was still in prison. Three unpublished poems. It's written in his own hand."

From Farad's throat, there came a sudden involuntary gasp of breath. *Could this be true?* Blazing beneath Farad's psychotic mood swings, branded on his soul, was an intractable Muslim faith, a faith more passionate than even his most rebellious behaviors.

Farad, the savant, the back alley bomb maker, stared at the little book, trying to control himself. He swallowed hard. Embarrassed. Afraid to believe. *Qutb's masterpiece, Fi Zalal.* He had read it a hundred times. He had seen the great man's handwriting reproduced in libraries. *But the actual document?*

He let go of the Beretta and took the book into both of his hands. Gently he opened to the first page.

The words – the actual words. And the handwriting. And the signature.

Overcome with emotion, his chest heaving uncontrollably, he set the little book back on the table as if it were scalding his fingers. There simply was no response to equal the magnitude of such a gift. Sayyid Qutb's 20th Century writings were seminal; his legitimization of the holy Jihad was fundamental dogma to both Taliban and Al Qaeda movements. His words had become sacred text. To own something actually written in Sayyid's own hand was to possess a true relic of modern Islamic provenance. Mullah Rockmani's gift was priceless.

This display of affirmation from the powerful Mullah Rockmani was beyond fantasy. Farad opened his lips to speak, but there were no words. Leon took hold of his forearm. "Farad," he said warmly, "When you recognize the value of that gift, I think you will come to realize just how valued your contribution to this Jihad has been.

"The Mullah wants you to come home. He wants you to be reunited with Nuriyah. He plans to give you the full credit you deserve for the explosions you've courageously seeded. You will be recorded in the annals of our faith as the warrior that you truly are."

Leon paused a moment, and summoning as much faux concern as he could muster, he continued. "But when the world learns of your deeds, you will be in grave danger. Vulnerable. A public enemy number one. The Mullah wants to bring you home. He wants to reunite you with your beloved Nuriyah, and hide the two of you in the mountains of Talib. He has said to me that you must be protected as one of Mohamed's heroes."

Farad's head was spinning.

Leon continued. "The scientist spy, Towne, has delivered the detonators to me. I have already shipped them to the *amAtya*, to the leader of each family. I have chosen each man based on your dealings with them.

"You see, there is no need for you to be exposed further. The installation can now be done by anyone, even a child. Insert the detonator into the C4, turn the knob and leave. That's it. I can trigger them all on the same day, remotely, from my own house. No one will be able to connect anything to me.

"But realize, once the Jihad takes credit for this massive victory, you will be identified as the mastermind. You will become an international target of hatred. Hunted like Bin Laden himself. More important even than Bin Laden.

"There is more. The Mullah has told me that he sent Nuriyah to the madrassah in Kashmir. She has proven to be an eager student. The Mullah intends that some additional education will make the two of you even happier when you return."

Farad sat stone-like, trying to conceal his emotions. Finally, he said, "When...when does the Mullah want me...to?"

"There is one more task I must ask you to perform. You warned me that you didn't trust the spy Towne. I apologize to you now, Farad, for my stubbornness. You were correct."

Leon exhaled as if to underscore his guilt. He was now going to launch the fairy tale that he and Nana had concocted, hoping that it would result in the death of this psychopath.

"Recently, Nana learned that Towne and my daughter were going to be entertaining guests for dinner. Nana made them a favorite meringue dessert. Towne came to my home to pick it up."

Leon continued, his brow knotting. "As Nana was preparing it in the kitchen, she wondered if he had something in his car to keep it cold. So, she went to the library door to ask him, but she stopped in her tracks. She did not speak. She watched in disbelief as Towne inserted a memory stick into my computer.

"After copying the files, she watched as he put the stolen information in his pocket and jumped back on the couch; as though nothing had happened. No doubt he was hoping to discover the precise location of our targets."

Farad could not resist. "I knew that bastard was rotten."

"Your instincts were correct. But here's the point. I have paid him well. And he has delivered everything I need. We have tested the detonators and found them to be functioning perfectly. Three of them have already been inserted and primed; the one you did at Staples Center, the one in Bloomington, and the one in Tennessee. Omaha will be done within the week. And you've already done Houston. The point is, Towne is no longer important. He's a complication that needs to be eliminated."

There was an eagerness on Farad's smiling face. "With most honor and humility, Leon, I welcome the task. Allah be praised."

Leon withdrew an envelope from his jacket and pushed it slowly across the table. "This is from me, Farad. There is $20,000 in there. It is what I would have had to pay a mercenary to do the job. The Mullah suggested that you and Nuriyah might use the money to purchase furniture for your home in the mountains."

After saying goodbye to Leon, Farad pulled his rented Ford to the edge of the parking lot, but suddenly hit the brakes. Unable to distinguish between anxiety and simple excitement, he tossed a handful of anxiety pills into his mouth and began chewing vigorously.

He looked down to his right. There, on the passenger seat was the holy book he had been given; Qutb's priceless writings – to be protected at all costs. He was on a mission for Allah. *A violent mission.*

He climbed out of the car and walked the short distance back to the restaurant. Handing the book to Leon, he said, "Will you keep this for me, Leon, until I return from doing the work of Allah?"

Leon bowed as he accepted the book. "I would be honored, Farad."

Leon watched gleefully as Farad sped away – the sewer rat so eager to undertake the will of Allah. Bold warrior charging into battle. *Too stupid to ken the difference between the will of Allah and the will of Leon.* "This is my kind of battle," he whispered. "No matter what happens, I win."

52

1:30 a.m. – The Facility – Malibu California

Seated at his desk, drinking the last of some hot coffee, Luke Towne was a happy man. Gezy had come through with the new fish eye lenses. The 20 extra SBNS units were on their way to Ari. His rogue operation seemed to be proceeding as planned; and all of it without interference from Orin Pierce.

Time to quit while I'm ahead.

He took the elevator down the parking level, buckled himself into his Z, and fired up the music, *The Best of Earth Wind and Fire* (more old guy consciousness). As he headed for home, his shoulders dropped several inches; and for the moment, all seemed right with the world.

Malibu Colony

When he drove through the guard gate at The Colony, it was 2 a.m. A heavy fog had descended and visibility was nil. He sniffed at the damp sea air; something about it always felt spooky, like an old Conan Doyle mystery.

Moving very slowly he approached 22 Shore Drive. But as he neared his parking space, his eye was suddenly taken by a movement somewhere off to the right. He braked and stared intently through the windshield into the fog, trying to locate the source.

Nothing.

There is was again! A flash of light. Somewhere to the right. As he pulled forward, the fog thinned momentarily and he saw the source. His own house! Behind the shutters of his living room, a tiny circle of light was moving slowly, tracing its way around the perimeter.

He rolled slowly toward his assigned parking space. A blue Ford was parked in it. *Wearing Texas plates.* Luke pulled into the lanai of his neighbor's house and walked back to the Ford. The hood was still warm.

"Cowboy took my spot."

He slipped into the shrubbery along the side of his house, quietly moving the palm branches aside as he went. He climbed silently over the few small piles of lumber left by his neighbor's construction crew; the kitchen next door was taking longer than his neighbor anticipated. Stepping cautiously over the little white fence that rimmed his own backyard, he approached his back door. It was always unlocked. There hadn't been a prowler in the Colony in 15 years.

A smile. *Bet it's someone very special.*

Luke slipped noiselessly into his back bedroom and waited for his eyes to adjust to the darkness. When he satisfied himself that there was no one in any of the closets, he moved off down the hallway toward the living room. The second most decorated officer in the history of the Rangers was eager to greet his *special guest.*

Along the north wall of the hallway was an arrangement of baseball memorabilia: a fielder's glove, a favorite picture (*Willy's Catch),* some ticket stubs, newspaper clippings and souvenirs – a trove he'd been collecting since childhood. He removed a shiny black Louisville Slugger from its place of honor, ran his palm over the Stan Musial autograph and crept forward.

When he reached the threshold of the living room, he stopped short. There was a stocky man kneeling at the coffee table, hunched over his laptop, copying data onto a portable DVD recorder. The stranger's back was to Luke. The glow from the computer screen cast a silhouette around the man's head and shoulders. It seemed to Luke that he was of medium build and possibly foreign.

"Pssst," said Luke quietly, hoping the intruder would turn around and show his face before having his skull cracked. The man obliged. He stood up and turned around.

Apparently he was expecting to see someone else. His dark eyes shot open in surprise. Luke had turned his body slightly to the right, concealing the bat behind himself. He remained perfectly still, conjuring the roar of the crowd; *Stan hits one into deep center field.*

When the burly intruder rushed forward, Musial's bat flashed upward and connected with his upper lip, just beneath his large nose. The force of the bat's trajectory drove the cartilage straight up into the frontal lobe, dropping him to the ground. Abdul-Malik was dead before he hit the floor.

Luke let the bloodied bat fall to the ground and stepped forward to examine the crumpled figure in front of him. As he bent down for a closer look, he sensed movement behind him.

Too late. A large left forearm shot forward and clamped itself across Luke's windpipe, snapping him upright in an angry chokehold.

Automatic response. Without thinking, both of Luke's hands shot up above his right shoulder in anticipation of a potential knife strike. The seven inch commando blade in Farad's right hand was already slicing downward toward Luke's neck.

His thick wrist slammed hard into the 'Y' of Luke's grip. Instantly locking his fingers around the wrist, Luke jerked his own body forward. He could feel the wiry strength of his opponent whose body was now pitched forward against his back, toes slightly lifted off the ground. Decades of military combat had formed his musculature into a network of rote responses; he unleashed a violent backward heel kick aimed just above the attacker's instep.

There was a sickening 'crunch.' Farad's left trochlea joint shattered, causing a gross separation of the foot from the tibia. The effect was tantamount to having one's foot torn off below the ankle.

"Ahaaa!" Farad bellowed in agony. His body went limp. He began to lose consciousness. His chokehold released.

Sensing the moment, Luke lunged downward and simultaneously yanked hard on the wrist. A classic jujitsu throw. Farad's body flipped high into the air, stretching out full length, feet over head.

Under normal conditions, a completed throw would have landed an attacker flat on his back in front of Luke. But as he cart wheeled through space, his right foot caught in Luke's wrought iron chandelier and Farad's body was snapped to a sudden halt. Strung upside down like a helpless side of beef.

For an instant, his knife-wielding right arm continued its arc of motion. But its direction was inverted; the knife blade was now rushing upward toward his own face. Pushing against the force of Luke's grip, Farad struggled wildly, trying to ward off the blade. His effort lowered the trajectory but two inches..

Assisted by Luke's force, the knife buried itself seven inches into the soft flesh under Farad's upturned chin. The penetration made a sickening noise as it severed a cluster of veins and arteries.

Luke stepped quickly to one side, scanning the darkness, setting up for the next aggressor. As he listened into the surrounding darkness, Farad's hanging body danced a paroxysm of spasms and guttural grunts.

Gradually, the death tremors decreased, until the only sound was a small leak of air escaping from the open wound.

The glories of a Jihadist's life. Hanging upside down in the enemy's lair, impaled on his own sword. Farad's twenty years of violence, corrupted zeal and religious hatred had ceased. The invisible spirit of the legendary bomb maker hovered in the void. Waiting...waiting. Waiting...waiting for his ultimate reward. *Praise be to Allah.*

Incompetent. Poorly trained. Stupid. Luke's response was far less arcane. No time for fairy tales. He remained completely still for another minute, listening for the rest of them. But there was no other sound. No one else in the house.

Picking up the bat, he moved to the front door and stepped outside to survey the area. He approached the blue Ford. *Nothing changed.* He circled his house from the opposite side. Finally, satisfied there were no accomplices, he went back inside and flipped open his cell phone.

Twenty minutes later, at 3:05 p.m., Quentin Hawk and two of his agents arrived at 22 Shore Drive, Malibu Colony. When they pulled to a stop Quent jerked the key from the ignition and pointed to his subordinates. "You in the back; you in the front. Nobody in 'til I say."

Quent stepped out of the car and walked quietly up the steps. Luke had already turned on the interior lights, so the carnage was visible. The two men shook hands. Luke said nothing until Quent had surveyed the battlefield and turned to him for an explanation.

"Two in the house. No one else. Got home an hour ago, caught one of them copying files off my computer. The other one jumped me from behind."

"You try to make these rag head...ah, these two visitors comfortable and they both jump you?"

Luke smiled. "Thanks for showing up, Quent."

"No problem, Colonel."

The body was still spilling blood on the living room carpet. Quent helped Luke cut it down from the chandelier and together they lowered it to the floor. Quent stood for a moment looking down at the bloody face. "Know who this is?"

"Nope."

"Aziz. Number 4 on our most wanted list. Farad Aziz. Bomb maker."

Luke made no comment. He had committed all the faces on the most wanted list to memory during his preparation in Washington. But he knew the rules: the less information offered, the better.

"Ever seen the other one, Colonel?"

"Nope."

Farad's accomplice, Abdul-Malik, would not be found on any list. He had joined the terrorist *amAtya* in Omaha and was one of the last graduates from Talib to cross the Niagara Bar into the U.S..

Quent called his men into the house and gave them his initial instructions, then joined Luke on the front porch.

Luke said, "Since you were straight with me, I'd like to be almost completely straight with you. As straight as I can tell it."

"Shoot."

"We've been working on a project at The Facility for several years. It's Pentagon driven. It's critical. It's ground-breaking and it's highly classified. We're right on the verge. I described some of it at the Paris convention. I think you told me you read about it."

"Yes sir, I did. Pussy politicians can't seem to do anything by themselves. Sounded like someone sent a message without 'em."

"Pussy politicians?"

"Sir?" Quent responded, thinking his take on things was the most normal reaction anyone could possibly have.

"You always speak your mind like that, Quent?"

"A lot easier to get things done that way, seems to me."

"You ever decide to leave the CIA, you let me know. You'd fit right in."

"Thank you, sir."

"Anyway, I'm also involved in another government operation. An off the books thing. I can't talk about that one either. Long story short, any public knowledge of what happened here tonight, and both of these operations are in serious jeopardy. I'm talking absolute national security."

"Understood, Colonel, loud and clear. Say no more. I've already discussed this stuff with my chief. She told me to tell you this. You just stay on schedule and go ahead with whatever it is you're doing. We'll clean up here for you. That's exactly why this unit was created; surveillance and protection of our country's most valuable human assets. And you and your partner are certainly at the top of our list."

He looked down at the pool of blood and the bodies and shook his head. "Pretty damn dismal job of surveillance we're doin' so far. I apologize, Colonel. I can only say we'll do better than this in the future, sir."

"No apology needed. Ever. What you did at Doctor Teller's house was as good as it gets. I hope this little clean-up here won't put you guys in a bad light."

"Actually Colonel, you're doing us a favor. Everyone thinks 9/11 was totally our screw up. Eliminating Farad Aziz will be good for us. Make it sound like we're doing our job for a change.

"We'll take care of this easily. Set the scene somewhere else a thousand miles away from here. There'll be no connection with Los Angeles. With you. Or with The Facility. Guaranteed."

"Thanks Quent."

53

The Pentagon

The deadline for presenting the Mind's Eye project to the Joint Chiefs of Staff was fast approaching. It was an approval for 4th stage financing. Cynthia was right. They weren't going to make it.

Luke flew to Washington for a sit down with Secretary of Defense Morton Ramsey to plead their case. It was Ramsey who had orchestrated the Pentagon's special explosive presentation at the Paris convention. Luke was planning to subtly remind the Secretary of Defense that 'The Strategy' had cut two months out of the Mind's Eye production schedule.

The meeting took place on the fourth floor of the Pentagon in Ramsey's private office. Before Luke had uttered a word, Ramsey preempted any attempt at subtlety. "I know why you're here, Doctor. The Mind's Eye isn't going to make the deadline." His voice ramped up a level. "And you're going to attempt to blame us for your failures. And that's preposterous. With a $300 million budget, one missing PhD doesn't put the whole screwing project back 60 days."

At that point, the door to Ramsey's office opened and in walked General John Lennihan, Chairman of the Joint Chiefs. He had overheard Ramsey's shouted remark while waiting in the outer office. The General had been a supporter of the Mind's Eye project from its inception. It was Lennihan's troops who would benefit directly from the costly Mind's Eye laser technology being developed at The Facility.

"Good morning Doctor Towne, nice to see you." The 6'3" Lennihan shook hands with Luke, then turned toward Secretary Ramsey. "Sorry I'm late, Mort, how can I help?"

An experienced veteran of political in-fighting, Lennihan had expected Ramsey to try some kind of an end run – shutting him out of the meeting in order to render a negative verdict on the Mind's Eye. Lennihan's sudden appearance was a half an hour earlier than Ramsey had scheduled it.

In the moment of silence that followed his question, Lennihan pulled a file from his briefcase. "In case you don't have the actual details, Mr. Secretary, I can tell you exactly how many days it took all of us to design that spectacular little bit of theater in Paris. As a matter of fact, I was just with the

President and he told me to commend you for your work on it. It was a major success. Reversed the President's downward slide in popularity."

Lennihan turned toward Luke. "Doctor Towne, the President said to tell you he would always be in your debt." There was a momentary pause as the general allowed the impact of his words to crush all hope of a rebuttal from Ramsey. When he sensed that he had accomplished his goal, Chairman Lennihan continued. "So, Mort, I've got all the details here if you need them. As you remember, I was in charge of expediting the Pit Bull Strategy from day one. You gave me the job."

End of argument.

Because the personal jet usually provided for Luke Towne's travel had been called away suddenly, Luke had to resort to a commercial red eye flight to get him from D.C. back to California. It was in the Ronald Reagan National Airport (DCA) that he saw the newspaper headlines. "Nation's 4th most wanted terrorist killed by CIA in Florida."

Luke immediately bought a copy of every newspaper at the airport kiosk. He was poring over them before the wheels of United Flight 106 were off the ground.

Quent and his CIA team had done a brilliant job of concealment. The refinement of their disinformation was impeccable. They had even manipulated pieces of the story so that newspapers in different parts of the country would report slightly differing facts, just as they commonly do on all high profile stories.

According to the New York Times, the CIA had cornered a violent and most dangerous Al Qaeda soldier, Farad Aziz, at the Las Palmas Motor Inn, in Manatee County, Florida. Earlier in the day the disguised terrorist had attempted to board a Western Airlines flight to Rio de Janeiro. When his passport showed some inconsistencies, he bolted from the Sarasota Airport and evaded Bradenton police who were first on the scene.

Later that night, acting on an anonymous tip, agents sealed off a four-block perimeter around the Las Palmas Motor Inn. According to a CIA spokesman, Aziz was taken completely by surprise by agents who broke down the door to his room. At first he agreed to cooperate with the arresting officers; but when they attempted to handcuff him, he pulled a knife and a struggle ensued. Two agents were injured and Aziz was subsequently killed as he tried to escape.

Luke smiled at the thought of it. Florida was about as far away from California as one could get. He tried unsuccessfully to reach Quentin by cell phone. Although the airline had advertised otherwise, cell phones still didn't work in the friendly skies.

He scribbled a page of notes which he would later dictate to Phyllis; a feat he could not accomplish at the moment, due to the annoying housewife sitting next to him in coach, who insisted on telling him the details of what had led up to the latest episode of Survivor. By the time she reached the first immunity challenge, Luke was asleep.

22 Shore Drive, Malibu Colony

She arrived a day earlier than expected. The summer warmth on the Malibu coast line was a welcome change from San Francisco's evening fog; by this time of night, Kathryn de Kennesy's little apartment in Russian Hill would have been completely engulfed. She knew Luke probably hadn't gotten her message yet, but so much the better if he arrived home and found her there. She was excited about spending another weekend with him.

His house was dark as she walked up the path. Kat inserted her key in the door, stepped in and felt for the light switch.

"Oh my God!" There was blood everywhere. She looked down at the carpet and realized she had stepped in some of it. The glass coffee table in the living room was smashed. Broken shards crunched under her feet with every step she took. Luke's home had been turned into a war zone.

The CIA had focused its primary effort on removing the bodies to Florida. Next came the construction of a believable crime scene, and finally, a mixed pallet of stories to be released to the press. Clean-up was given the lowest priority.

In an instant, Kathryn understood it all. Nana had often mentioned Farad Aziz as one of the most disruptive members at Mullah Rockmani's entourage at the Mosque.

The violence in Luke's house told her what her stepfather had intended. He had known Luke would be home; he had planned on it. He knew of Luke's prowess as a Ranger and simply gambled with Luke's life in order to rid himself of an archenemy.

She screamed into the phone. "How could you send that butcher here to attack him? You know Aziz is insane, he could have killed him."

"You slept with the little prick, dear, I only sent him to break in. What are you yelling at me for?"

"You're a liar! You sent Farad here hoping he'd get killed! It wasn't a break-in. It was a suicide mission. You gambled with Luke's life!" Her voice broke. "Jesus, Leon, I was only 16 when I dated Farad. We were children."

Leon did not respond for a moment. Then he said calmly, "Whose side are you on my child? It worked didn't it?"

She screamed back at him. "You're a bastard. I was only 16. And don't call me your child!"

She smashed down the phone and sat down on the floor.

She looked at the big pool of dried blood next to her purse. *Is he hurt? Whose blood am I sitting in?*

The smell was nauseating. She ran to the Dutch door and gulped in some salt air to keep from vomiting.

She hit the cell phone auto dialer to call Luke. Immediately she hit cancel.

What am I not supposed to know? She had lost track of her cover story. The constant subterfuge was tearing at her emotions. Allegiance, love, passion, truth; hatred. *Which role am I supposed to play now?*

She dialed Luke's number again. He was still on the plane. She got his answer phone. "Luke, are you hurt? There's blood all over here. Where are you? Please call me. I'm at your house now. Please tell me you're all right!"

She hung up.

When he opened the door, she ran into his arms. "Oh my god, are you all right?"

He pressed her into him. "Yes, yes honey, I'm fine. I'm sorry you had to see this. If I'd known, I'd have had them clean it up before you got here."

"What happened? Are you sure you're all right?" She would not let go of him. So he lifted her into his arms and carried her to the couch. "My work at The Facility. You know, guidance systems, national defense stuff. Every so often, someone tries to find out what we're up to.

"I came home the other night and there's this guy at the coffee table, copying files off my laptop. I told him to stop and his buddy jumped me from behind."

He stopped talking and left it at that.

"Well, what happened?" she said. "You can't just stop there."

"I made them stop. That's all."

She smiled at his matter-of-fact macho. "What'd ya do, bury 'em in the backyard?"

"Shoveling dirt hurts my lower back. I have guys to do that stuff for me." He smiled.

It was over. She held on to him as tightly as she could. He'd made up a story, protecting her from the *truth* about her stepfather. This man was the love of her life. He still believed she was innocent. The fear of it made her cold. Fear. It was always there, dragging behind like a twin sister.

She held on to him and said nothing.

54

7:30 a.m. – Pacific Coast Highway

Luke was behind the wheel of his Z, driving into work, transfixed by the passionate images of his night with Kat. Somehow, she'd been able to dismiss the bloodstains and the ugliness. She'd wiped away the images of Farad's grizzly death, tucked it all away somewhere and focused her complete attention on him. She'd washed away his anxieties; familial, religious, patriotic, learned, imposed – all of it.

Old man Towne. The luckiest guy on the planet.

Forcing himself to concentrate on the road, he accelerated into the flow of traffic on PCH. A tone sounded and Phyllis's green letters began floating gently upward from the dashboard.

"Good morning, Luke, I have Manuel Diego on the line for you. He says it's important."

"Put him through, Phil."

"Doc, this is Diego. You know, the delivery guy."

"Of course I know you, Manuel. Packing and shipping. Two years now isn't it?"

"Ah...well, yes sir. Yes. Two years. Thank you. So okay. So right now I'm on my way to WTC Air Freight. I've got those 20 units for overseas. I packed them all in one box."

"Right."

"Well, I stopped at this traffic light a minute ago and all of a sudden they started beeping."

"Not to worry, Manuel. One of 'em probably got jostled. It'll stop in a few seconds." There was no response from the driver. "Hello, Manuel. Did you get that?"

"Yes sir. It's just that...it's not one of them. It's all of them. All of them beeped. All at the same time."

Luke swerved to the side of Pacific Coast Highway, jammed his foot on the brake and slid to a stop. "Okay, start from the beginning. You left The Facility with your regular load. And one of the boxes is making noise?"

"Yes sir. Except it's the only box. It's my last delivery."

Luke's hands tightened on the steering wheel. "Who's name is on it, Manuel?"

"Ari Shine. Tripoli."

Silence from Luke. Then, "How do you know all of them are beeping?"

"It was too loud to be just one of them."

Luke's concentration snapped into hyper drive – searching wildly for an explanation.

"Manuel, where are you?"

"In downtown L.A."

"Yes, but where? Exactly!"

"Ah...across the street from Staples Center."

"My God! Don't move. Park the truck. Stay in it. And keep your line open." Luke disconnected and shouted into the PDA, "Phyllis, get me Quentin Hawk. Now."

Ten seconds later, Quentin's voice sounded from Phyllis's speaker phone. "Quentin Hawk!"

"Quent, this is Luke Towne. Where are you?"

"Sittin' up on the hill at Pepperdine. Watching you from a distance. Driving in to work. Sorry, it's my day in the barrel."

"Forget it. Listen, Quent, I'm afraid I need your help again. Only this one's a May Day like I never experienced."

Luke explained as simply as he could, being careful not to reveal too many details on Quent's open phone line. There was an emergency unfolding in the area of the Staples Center. It required that the entire place be temporarily cordoned off. There were three hours before the scheduled concert. It was supremely important that the public be kept totally unaware of the true cause or that there was any potential danger. And the potential danger was enormous.

And the excuse for delaying the concert was going to be, (Luke improvised)..."ah...that the entire plumbing system at Staples got clogged. No one can be admitted until all toilets and water systems are repaired and verified as safe and pure."

All CIA and attendant personal that Quent could muster were to keep their public responses low key and friendly.

Quent's reply was instant. "Something like, 'All the shitters are out, dude. Nobody craps on Britney until we say so.' Something like that?"

"Perfect."

"Got it. How many people you think we need?"

Luke hesitated. "Forty, maybe 50."

"Shit. How about Staples Security Staffers? Can we use them?"

"Yes. Excellent idea. In fact, if all your guys identified themselves as Staples Security, it'd squash some anxieties.

Just as he was about to hang up, Luke remembered an important variable. "One more thing. I've got no clout at

Staples. Can CIA call someone and get the Staples people on board with this? Let them know I'm coming. But not explain exactly what's really going on?"

"We'll handle it. No problem. Anything else you can tell me?"

"Nothing on the phone. Except...this might be the most serious phone call I've ever had to make. I don't know how much time we've got. You read?"

"Understood."

Staples Center – Los Angeles, California

Even with police escort, it took Luke a full 75 minutes to get from Malibu to downtown L.A. The police motorcycles turned off their sirens and broke ranks just before reaching the freeway off ramp. There must be no visible reason for public anxiety. No hint of the emergency building inside Staples Center. Luke drove down the ramp without them.

As he approached the parking structure, he was stunned to see Staples security men posted at every entrance. Most were wearing security attire; others were dressed in jeans and casual shirts. No heightened public fears. *No suits, no cops, no haircuts – just ordinary security people waiting for Britney.*

Luke pushed his blue Z into the east street entrance and was stopped by a friendly wave of a security man. "Sorry, sir, all the crappers went out in the arena. Can't let anyone in until they're all fixed. Some kind of public ordinance."

"What about the Britney concert?" said Luke, certain he was addressing one of Quent's CIA agents.

"Dude, aren't you a little old for Britney?" came the laughing reply.

"My name is Doctor Luke Towne. Your boss, Chief Quentin Hawk, is expecting me. Could you let him know I'm here please."

"Sorry Doctor, staffers aren't allowed to have cell phones. You might wanna call him on your own phone. No offense, but I never heard of the guy."

Luke pulled away, amazed at what Quentin Hawk and his team had accomplished in less than an hour and a half. As he raced toward the Staples main pedestrian entrance, he was shocked again. There were six L.A. Sanitation trucks and five plumbing trucks grouped in front of the ticket windows. Each truck showing a different plumbing company name on its side panels. *A major plumbing problem indeed.*

Quent answered his cell on the first ring. "Hawk here."

"I'm at the main entrance, Quent."

"Be there in a second, Doc."

As the two men entered the arena, a woman wearing a Staples attendant's uniform approached, obviously awaiting orders from Quent. "Dumont, no one else gets in. If there's a problem, call me or Porter."

"Yes sir."

Luke was already walking toward the vendors' section, holding a small rectangular receiver called a SBNS (pronounced *Sssbens*) out in front of him. A green dot flashed intermittently on its screen. When Quent caught up, he could hear the quiet beep that sounded with each flash of the dot. Luke held up the device and said, "SBNS. I'll explain it in a minute." Then he moved quickly to the right. "Where are the elevators?"

"Main bank over there," said Quent, pointing to the right.

"No. The service elevators. Where?"

Quent unhooked a small transceiver from his belt and shouted, "Donnie, service elevators?"

The answer came back instantly. "Other way. Right past the vending machines."

Luke and Quent reversed their direction and the dot on the screen moved with them. They reached the service elevators and stepped into the first car.

"Bottom level," said Luke. Quent pushed "B" and the doors closed. As they began their descent, the frequency of the beep increased. Luke increased the volume of the beep.

"SBNS," he said. "Satellite-Based Navigation System. It's telling me there's one of my detonators down in the basement somewhere. It's most likely sticking into some explosive substance. Probably C4 or something close to it. I'll have to deactivate it by hand."

Quent was silent for a moment. "Is there more than one?"

The look of admiration on Luke's face said more than his answer. "Probably they've only used one detonator. It depends on how smart these terrorists are. I doubt they know anything about this kind of laser detonation. It hasn't been used yet. I'd guess we're probably only looking for one load of explosive material."

When the elevator doors opened, Luke stepped out and swung the meter back and forth. The beeping increased slightly when pointed right. They both headed off to the right.

Forty feet later, the beeping turned into an unbroken tone. Luke set the meter on the ground and depressed a button. The sound stopped.

The available light was dim. Before them were four huge concrete pylons rising into the darkness above. Quent produced a high-powered flashlight and shone its light toward the pylons. Luke said, "Those two mounted on the coiled steel. They're shakers. It won't be on them. It's the other two."

Each man approached one of the two pylons. "What am I looking for?" asked Quent.

"A small round lid about the size of a quarter. Sticking out about half an inch."

Luke embraced the massive circular pylon and began moving his hands slowly up and down, feeling for a slight protrusion. Quent followed suit. Each man went once round a pylon, starting from the bottom, moving his hands carefully upward as high as he could reach. "Nothing," said Luke, staring up into the darkness.

"Nothing here either. Except it sorta looks like this one's been repainted. Does that count?"

"Stop!" shouted Luke. "Don't move." Taking Quent by the shoulder, Luke gently moved him back and away from the pylon. "The repainted section. That's not concrete. It's C4. It's been painted to look like concrete. My detonator is gonna be sticking out of that one – somewhere."

Quent directed his light upward. Both men saw it at the same time. Fifteen feet above the floor, protruding from the back side of the pylon. A small black dial.

"Very thorough," said Luke. "Out of sight. Out of reach." He turned back toward Quent, but there was no one there. "Quent?" shouted Luke.

Silence. Then from the darkness came an answer. "Ladder." There was the sound of metal scraping across the concrete floor. Quent reappeared from the darkness, pushing a 15' rolling A-frame ladder. Luke jumped on the third rung and immediately began climbing while Quent was still moving the ladder into position.

"Hold it right there," shouted Luke. "It's right in front of me." Luke leaned out over the ladder and peered into the darkness. Before he could get any words out, Quent shouted, "Light comin' up."

Luke caught the flashlight in his left hand and turned swiftly back to the pylon. He adjusted the flashlight lens until the detonator cap was clearly encircled in its light, then he reached for the dial.

He touched its cold black surface, took a breath and turned the activation dial one click to the left. *Half way there.* Then, wedging his fingers under the dial he tried to take hold of the cone housing. But there wasn't enough of the cone protruding to get a hold. Groping for his wallet, Luke pulled out a credit card, slipped it under the black dial, and using one finger as a fulcrum, pried upward. No movement. He tried again at a different angle. The cone slid upward half an inch.

He was now just barely able to slip his thumb and forefinger in under the dial. He twisted the cone slightly to the left, and it gave. Tugging gently, and twisting at the same time, he carefully pulled the 9" tube out of the putty-like surface.

"Out of danger," he announced. Then, breathing a long sigh he climbed back down to the floor and set the detonator down next to the meter box. He pushed the audio button once more.

No more beeps. Both men drew in long slow breaths then exhaled. Luke said, "Can you have one of your people bring us a trash can filled with water? Safer to get the detonator submerged and bring it back to The Facility."

Quent called Angie Dumont on his GMRS and gave her the orders.

Staring up at where the detonator had been placed, Luke said, "All right, now you and I are going to have to peel the C4 off of this pylon. Can you get us a couple of large plastic garbage cans down here as well?"

"Is two enough?" said Quent, reaching for his transceiver again.

"I'd guess four 30-gallon cans oughta do it. In case we find another pylon."

Quent barked the order into his GMRS transceiver and reattached it to his belt. He couldn't keep the smile from his face. "I guess this means we're not gonna get to see Britney."

55

The two men began the delicate process, Luke at the top of the ladder, prying small chunks of C4 explosive away from the concrete pylon, Quent at the bottom, receiving the pieces and placing them carefully into large plastic garbage cans. As they worked in silence, Luke came to a decision.

He climbed down a few rungs of the ladder. "Quent, I think it might be a good idea if I explained what's really going on here. I get the feeling this is just the beginning of it. I could certainly use your help. And your department's help. It'd be easier if you knew all of it. You game?"

"Absolutely."

"First let me say your guys did an amazing job. And the plumbing trucks – brilliant work. Sold the whole thing to everybody. It looked like the Staples people even bought it. How'd the hell did you pull it off in such short notice."

"I had a lotta help. An amazing chief – Barbara Porter. The woman thinks like a field commander. Got a focus like a steel trap. Like no woman I ever met. Gave me carte blanche. Never seen anything like it. Never had a superior that good."

"Sounds a lot like a woman I know," said Luke. "You'll meet her one of these days. So, all right, enough with the bullshit, here's the story."

Luke began by explaining his role as a double agent; being sent off to weekend spy school in Washington; his overwhelming shock when his father-in-law-to-be quoted portions of his altered bio and then offered a six figure payment for 10 detonators.

Luke then gave a very general description of the Pentagon's most secret technology, thc Mind's Eye, indicating only that it would have a critical role in ultimately foiling the terrorist objectives. He said nothing specific about its actual function.

There were several parts of the operation that Luke did not include. He didn't mention that his plan was a rogue operation; nor did he say anything about breaking off communications with his immediate superior; nor did he reveal that he lacked the protection of even one single member of the U.S. Military.

When Luke concluded the debriefing, Quent said, "Thank you, sir."

"Please, it's Luke."

"Luke, I do have a question."

"Go."

"If all of the terrorists' targets are set up in the Middle East, how did this one get into the Staples Center?"

This kid Hawk is really smart.

"That's a good one. Here's the most probable answer I've come up with. I think Leon probably ordered the Staples installation as a bargaining chip. In case he's ever caught, he'd try and trade us information about the Staples location for clemency.

"In any case, I'm confident the rest of my detonators are gonna turn up in the Mid East. And I think it should only be a matter of days. We'll know the precise locations of each one. I'll give you the details as soon as it happens."

"Understood."

"One last thing," said Luke. "Can you guys arrange to get this C4 out of here and into lockup somewhere?"

"No problem. We'll take it from here."

"Any other questions, you've got my cell. You're one of us now. Call any time day or night."

On his way back to Malibu, Luke made two phone calls. The first was to Cynthia, who was still in Virginia working around the clock with the Top Guns. He brought her up to speed on the Staples Center and on Quent's initiation as part of the team. "I heartily approve," she said. "Quent's a good man." She was immediately surprised at how good she felt knowing that Quent was now part of the team.

And once she heard that the Staples business was safely under control, Cynthia's interest immediately jumped to the progress of her pilots. "Three of them are just amazing. They've learned to communicate with Phyllis like she's a baby sister. Nick is the fastest. It only takes him 12 seconds from initial eye contact to get her to execute a command."

"Great work, Cyn," said Luke. "Stay on them. I'll call you tomorrow with an update."

Luke's next call was to Ari Shine. The additional SBNS units would be arriving within the week. They would be delivered to Ari's rental house in Tripoli. Ari's response was similar to Cynthia Teller's response. He was glad to get the update, but he was more eager to describe the developments at his end.

Ari reported that his second team had successfully installed the Pentagon's Lasocular cannons at two of the four preordained sights. These cannons were the full blown version of the 'BB gun' Luke and Ari had demonstrated at the Paris Conference. Their capability for destruction was exponentially greater than the destruction of the miniature Arab house that was vaporized on stage.

"We'd forgotten something Luke," said Ari. "There are cable dishes everywhere over here. On every tall building and commercial structure in every major city. All over the place. They even got cell phone towers sticking up in rice fields and fruit farms. It was amazing. We just rolled up in our fake TV trucks and people let us right into their homes. No questions asked. They even moved stuff out of the way so we could use their balconies. No one ever even asked for I.D."

Luke couldn't stand the suspense. "Detonator signals?"

"Yes. The first one arrived late last night."

A great sigh of relief from Luke. "Tell me."

"We tracked it from the airport right into the heart of Baghdad. I've got a team with eyes on the package right now. And a mobile unit ready to move. But it's in a strange location."

"Where?"

"On a shelf in the Art Department of Beirut University."

"Fantastic. And you've got guys ready to go if they move it somewhere else?"

"Yep."

"Excellent work, Ari. You'll let me know when the rest of them arrive."

"Certainly. But...Beirut University? Don't you think that's a little weird? You don't even sound surprised."

"That's because I know the woman who used to chair the Art Department at Beirut U."

"You know her well?"

"She's about to become my mother-in-law."

A relieved Luke Towne sat down in his own living room, a beer in one hand and Phyllis in the other. He'd put off making the most difficult call. It was to San Francisco. Finally Luke said, "Phyllis. See if Kathryn's at home."

She answered on the second ring. "Hi Lukie, been trying to reach you. Did you get my messages?" Luke's assistant had not been putting her calls through for several days.

"Sorry honey, haven't had time to check. Been up to my ears."

"What else is new?" she said brightly.

"I was down at the Staples Center," he said, trying to keep his voice as normal as possible.

"Why, for God's sake? I thought you couldn't stand Britney."

"How'd you know about her?"

"I'm looking at my laptop right now. Headline. L.A. Times. 'Britney concert flushed. Leaky bathrooms at Staples Center cause postponement.' Gee, Lukie, I didn't know you did toilets, too."

Not one moment of hesitation. Happy as ever. But still he couldn't let it go. He had to press. After a beat he said, "Hon, "I've got a question for you."

"Anything you want, my dear."

"Farad Aziz." He said the name and listened hard into the silence.

One second later, she said, "Is that the question?"

"Yes."

Her answer came straight out. "I met Farad Aziz when I was 16. He was a kind of wild non-conformist kid. The kind little girls think are sexy. It ended quickly. We moved in different circles. I went off to school. He didn't. I haven't seen him since. But I know about him. Read about him. He's turned into a bloody killer. An extremist. Bomb maker. There are many people in my government who think he was involved in Rafik's assassination. Leon called me to tell me the CIA had killed him in Florida. He was very relieved. All of us were. Leon doesn't approve at all of the extremist Muslims. Especially their methods.

"So, I hope you're not jealous," she said. "It was a long time ago. I was just a kid." Then before Luke could prod any deeper, she skillfully changed the subject. "And now I have a question for you. What does Farad Aziz have to do with leaky toilets at the Staples Center?"

"I love you Kat," answered Luke. "And forget I asked. The answer is 'there's no connection.' And the next time I ask about some old boyfriend, you can cut off my supply."

"Not going to happen, Lukie. Ever."

When the call was over, Luke sat stone-faced, staring out the front window at the fog. It had rolled into his front yard and smothered his house. His brain was clogged with unanswered questions. They circled round and round. *Wheels within wheels within wheels.*

In San Francisco, Kathryn dropped the phone on the rug. Her hands shook. She pushed them into the crevices between her overstuffed pillows. *Does he believe? What exactly does he believe?*

56

Pepperdine University – Malibu, California

For Quent, the emergency at Staples Center had turned into an all-night affair. Moving the C4 out of downtown LA, playing Chief Sanitation officer, confirming the arena's water safety to the press – his was an endless chronicle of responsibilities. At 6 a.m. he was still at Staples Center.

After gulping down some grease fried bacon and eggs at the L.A. Pantry, he raced out the 10 Freeway toward the Coast. As he came out of the bridge at Santa Monica beach, he could see a thick cloud bank moving in over Malibu.

It was dark and overcast as he whizzed past the Colony gate and headed up the hill to Pepperdine College. Once there, he took up his position on the Bluffs, binoculars ready. From his regular spot in the school parking lot, he could see PCH from the Colony east to Malibu Canyon Road.

Turning on the car heater, Quent issued a command to himself. "Last day of this crap. No more Luke surveillance." *I should 'a had someone else up here from the beginning.* Spying on his friend (and now co-conspirator) was not part of the Hawk play book. He would delegate the job to someone else; someone not so closely involved.

At precisely 7:30 a.m., right on schedule, the mechanical arm at the Malibu Colony guard gate rose and Luke Towne steered his methane blue Z out onto Pacific Coast Highway. Luke settled in, depressed the lever and sent the car's hard top up and then out of sight behind the back seat.

No other cars were out on PCH at this hour. Luke eased the little convertible up to 110. The Z's special suspension pressed down hard. He smiled. It felt like the thing was on rails.

Up on the bluff, Quent trained his Steiner 80mm prism binoculars on the streaking Z. He stifled a yawn. *This is ridiculous. Assistant Chief of CLOPS crammed into this piece of shit Ford, watching Luke drive his hot little Z in to work. Waste of man hours.*

Quentin Hawk had just turned 35, and although he still looked and felt like 25, his body told him he was getting too old for this kind of *grunt duty.* He could probably still dunk a basketball backwards over his head, but at 6'4" his long legs always started to cramp after two hours of sitting *in this stupid two-door grunt burger of a car.*

He watched Luke's little machine eat up the turns as it rolled up Malibu hill. The car disappeared momentarily behind a strip of citrus trees then immerged again like a blue rocket. *He's smokin' today, man.*

Quent's cell phone rang. "Hawk."

"You still in bed?" It was Luke.

"No, at the moment, I'm watching some maniac drive his blue sports car up Malibu Canyon like he's got a frickin' death wish. I really oughta ticket the sucker."

"It's not nice to spy on your friends."

"Doing my best. Keeping my distance. Sorry dude; I mean Luke. You know. Just following orders." Quent set his speaker phone on the dash and tried to massage some life into his aching temples.

"Understood. No problem. Got two things for you; first, I want to thank you and your crew for what you did for us last night. Second, the first one of our packages turned up last night in the Middle East."

"That is great news! Very glad to hear that one. Confirms where the rest of them are headed."

"Exactly. And we've just added 20 more SBNS to what's already there. So our coverage is now doubled. Also, I explained to Cynthia that you're now one of us, and..."

Quent continued massaging his head with one hand, holding his binoculars with the other, listening to Luke's explanation; when suddenly, a tiny blur appeared in the upper left quadrant of his viewer.

He would remember it clearly.

At first he thought it was a bug. Then it grew in size. Then it flashed double silver in the sunlight. Then it ballooned into a huge multi-axel, double-tank gasoline truck about to run the stop sign at the only intersection on Canyon Road.

Quent screamed, "Look out Luke on your left. A truck..."

The crash was so violent it sent a visible shock wave up the side of the canyon. The tallest trees shook in the wake. Quent watched in horror as Luke's blue Z was catapulted into the air, turning end over end like a torn football. Blasted by 10,000 foot-pounds of accelerating metal, the car soared out over the edge of the canyon wall, covered in gasoline, flaming like a meteor.

As it flipped again and again, Luke's body was hurled skyward into the air above the smoking car, his body spinning horizontally like the bit in a power drill. Then both car and driver dropped below Quent's line of sight. Quent grabbed his cell phone and called the paramedics.

A second later there was another explosion at the bottom of the gorge. A fiery cloud spewed straight up from the canyon floor billowing inward on itself, spitting tongues of orange, then snuffing out as it dissipated into the high sky.

Quent slammed his car into reverse and tore out of the parking lot. Speeding downhill toward Pacific Coast Highway, he punched his cell's auto-dial for Cynthia Teller. It took a full 30 seconds.

"Hello, Doctor Teller, this is Quentin Hawk."

She was at Riverton, taking a break from her sessions with 'her kids.' "Hi Agent Hawk. Luke was just talking about you last night. It's good to have you on board."

"Doctor, I have some difficult news to report. Luke has been in a serious crash; just a few moments ago. I saw it happen. I'm in traffic on my way to him now. I think it's serious enough for you to be here in Los Angeles."

Cynthia's military training took over. "Details? Extent of injury? Any more you can tell me?"

"Only that he was struck broadside on Canyon Road by a speeding truck. I won't know more until I get there."

"I'm leaving now. I've got the Harrier. As soon as you know more, call me please? Leave a text if you can't get through."

"Will do. Safe flight." Quent had tried to state the facts without emotion. But it was difficult not to sound disconsolate. It didn't feel like he had done a very good job.

When he turned south on PCH, the morning traffic had already begun to stack up. He was trapped in a lineup of student cars stretching in both directions from Malibu Canyon Road all the way up the hill to the bluffs.

The traffic crept slowly along in both directions. His car had no siren. There was no dirt shoulder on either side of Pacific Coast Highway. With every signal change at PCH and Malibu Canyon Road, Quent could only make four car lengths of progress. *Requiescat in pace;* (Rest in peace) the phrase he'd learned as an altar boy. *What a horrible negative thought.* But it wouldn't stop. Next came the longer English version. *May the souls of all the faithful departed rest in peace. Amen...* Once a Catholic, always...

Suddenly a space widened in the traffic and he was able to turn up Malibu Canyon Road. *More traffic.* A very slow going.

Malibu Canyon is a swatch of green that cuts east into the rugged hills at the coast line and dumps out 35 miles later in the brown industrial heart of the San Fernando Valley. For the last six months, only three quarters of an inch of rain had fallen on the Canyon's dry chaparral. The big gasoline truck's aluminum tanks held 4,150 gallons of flammable liquid which had turned gaseous on impact. The spill had ignited a 50' section of the south canyon wall. In seconds the entire canyon was going to go up and thousands of homes and lives would be threatened.

But Malibu Hook and Ladder arrived, rolled out their hoses and had water flowing in under seven minutes. It was fantastic work. The police were right there behind them.

It took Quent 16 minutes to get to the crash scene. It was a gruesome sight. The huge double tank gasoline truck lay on its side, jackknifed across the center of the intersection.

There was a charred blue spot on Canyon Road where the Z had been crushed. The driver's seat, belts akimbo, was thrown clear of the car and was found in a clump of sage 20 feet away. The truck driver, who had walked away unharmed, was being interviewed by the police.

By the time Quent arrived, the investigation was already underway. Rescue teams had already set rope lines down the side of the canyon wall. Access to the bottom of the gorge was made more difficult by the morass of heavy brush which lined the walls of the canyon. Visibility was hampered by thick stands of palms and deciduous trees.

There was a sudden crackle on the walkie talkies, Search and Rescue announcing they had found the point of impact. It was at the base of a thick Eucalyptus tree – almost 200 feet down the side of a thickly wooded incline. They had found a dark slash of blood streaked across a stand of eucalyptus trunks. It was eight feet above the thick masses of spiny growth which littered the floor of the canyon. The blood was still wet. One of Luke's shoes with half its sole torn off was found hanging 30 feet away in a white azalea bush.

Quent listened as the head of the rescue team reported it all to his captain. He concluded with, "Sir, we covered a quarter mile both ways down to the dry creek. There's no sign of the body."

"Better take it out wider then," came the Captain's answer. "And take some medics with you. If the driver's still alive when you find him, he's gonna need some help."

Two hours later a heavy rain began spilling down on Malibu Canyon. A dark storm front had moved south from San Francisco. As the winds increased, so did the rain. Searchers were forced to rely on miner's lights to maneuver through the wet brush. After another hour of futile searching, the hunt was called off until the weather improved.

The next morning, the rain abated and the Marines took over. At the special request of Doctor Cynthia Teller, General Malcolm Diggs, the head of Luke Towne's former Special Ops Command, had ordered a unit of Coast Guard Search and Rescue brought in to aid local police. The Corps immediately widened the search perimeters and began a slow crisscross up and down both sides of the Canyon. Every five men were accompanied by a Wild Life Search and Rescue Canine Unit.

At 7 a.m. when Cynthia arrived at the Santa Monica Airport, she found Agent Angela Dumont waiting to drive her to the site. On the way, Dumont handed her a CLOPS team Blackberry and explained its unique functions. She was part of a special network, which included an emergency two-way radio mode, a secure conference mode, plus a second line and five exclusive CIA channels which could be used for scrambled communications.

Cynthia's Blackberry rang immediately. Quentin informed her that she was officially deputized to participate in the operation in whatever way she chose. He suggested that on the way in, they stop at Luke's house to get samples of Luke's clothing for the dogs to identify scent.

"Thank you Quent," she said. "I so appreciate your thoughtfulness. And about the clothes, won't the rains have washed away all hope of scent matching?"

"Probably. But I'd still like to try it anyway."

Quent and Cynthia spoke several times during her first day. By the end of the second day, Search and Rescue had completed four thorough sweeps of the impact area. They had pushed the perimeter three quarters of a mile outward in all directions from the bloodstains.

No body was found.

Lumber Yard – CLOPS Headquarters – Santa Monica

Quent was disconsolate. When he arrived at the Santa Monica Lumber Yard, a private email from the chief was waiting for him.

RE: Doctor Luke Towne

Chief Hawk, I have read the police report. Mistakes were made by the Malibu Police. But you are in no way responsible for what happened to Doctor Towne. Your duties at CLOPS did not include the prevention of this tragic accident.

I am deeply sorry for the loss of your friend. It is our country's great loss as well.

I'll be at Camp David for a few days, meeting with the Security Council. You are in command of all CLOPS operations. Please refer to the CIA Manual on your desk. Attached to the cover you'll find an insert dated January 1 of this year. Please read it thoroughly before taking further action.

Quent hated being told what to do, even by this most considerate of superiors. His respect for Barbara Porter was boundless. But he still resented being 'told.' In Quent's personal vernacular: *I'm a cow-head. It' just the way I am.*

Quent jerked the heavy manual out from between his bookends, a scowl on his face. The insert was easy to locate. It was the most recent. The heading was "CIA Jurisdiction Relative to Government Personnel and National Security." The insert addressed the conditions under which the CIA could legally supersede the authority of another law enforcement agency.

By the end of his first reading, he was already shaking his head in admiration. *Damn. What an amazing woman.* Barbara Porter was showing him how to remove the Malibu Police Department from the case and take command himself.

Quent slapped the manual down on his desk, grabbed his cell and punched in an *alert* to six members of his team. All six Responded within 20 seconds. All were automatically linked. Quent's instructions were simple, urgent and unequivocal. The team was to proceed immediately. Maximum speed. No sirens. Call when in position.

He disconnected the call and reopened the manual to the insert. When he finished, he read two additional chapters clarifying terminology and procedure.

His cell phone buzzed. *All agents in place.*

He dialed the Malibu Police Department and asked for Captain Roger Berry. When the captain came on the line, Quent identified himself and said, "Captain, I'm looking at your report on the Canyon Road hit and run two days ago. I'd like to go over it with you."

"Got it right here," said Captain Berry.

"What exactly do you mean by 'the truck driver left the scene?' What the hell is that supposed to mean?" Quent had raised his voice a notch.

Malibu Police Captain Roger Berry, in whose jurisdiction the accident had occurred, attempted to respond. "My men interviewed the truck driver at the scene. His wallet was burned up in the crash. The guy said his name was..."

Quent interrupted, "You list it as a hit and run and you're telling me you don't know who was driving the truck?"

"I'm trying to tell you Chief Hawk, we checked with the Old South Trucking Company. They have no driver named Charlie Smith. That was the name he gave us. We're working on ID'ing him right now. I've put two men on it. And I've got to tell you right now, I don't need any gov'mnt asshole tryna run my investigation for me. We clear on that, Chief?"

Quent waited a moment before responding. "Captain Berry, I wasn't always a Chief. During my 15 years on the street, there was always some dipshit superior sticking his nose in, trying to run my investigation for me. I understand your frustration in spades. I also understand that you can't hold the hand of every one of your men. I also know you gotta take the heat when one of them screws up. And we both know that letting the truck driver walk was a mistake. I understand. Believe me. I'm not calling to accuse anyone of anything. But there are some classified details that I need to make you aware of."

"Like what?"

"Like...the driver of the blue convertible is an employee of the Pentagon. A decorated soldier. A former colonel in the U.S. Special Forces. He is also a Military scientist whose work is critical to our national security. It is for that reason <u>only</u> that I've been authorized to take over your investigation."

Dead silence on the other end of the line.

Quent continued. "I appreciate your years on the force, Captain, and I understand your position thoroughly. At this moment, a team of my agents is arriving at your office door."

(Quent could hear the commotion in Berry's office.) "Please turn over all of your files and notes to them immediately. This case is rated as top security. No names released. No press. No one including yourself is to discuss anything regarding this investigation. The U.S. government is depending on your professionalism."

There was no response from Captain Berry.

Quent continued, "As to my being an asshole, I suggest you talk with Javier Camacho at Topanga Police Canyon station. We go back a ways. You might want to ask him about my character. And then do as you see fit. Because if I ever see you on the street, I'll be compelled to remind you not to let suspects walk away from a damn crime scene! And when I'm through, you're gonna need a plumber to remove your fat head from your stupid, lazy, incompetent Malibu ass. We clear on that one, Chief?"

When there was no response from Berry, Quent hung up.

57

Topanga Canyon, California

"Damn trucker never even hit his brakes." This from a ferret-faced short order cook behind the counter at the Fish Shack, a four-seat eatery on Canyon Road.

"You saw the crash, sir?" asked Agent Dumont.

"Well, not actually. I heard it though. I was out in the back makin' up some blueberry pancakes when we heard like this incredible explosion."

Agent Dumont stopped her note taking. "We?"

"Me and the shit heads."

"Sir?"

"You know, the busboys. Those two over there. Lazy black bastards."

The remark brought a tinge to her cheeks, but Agent Dumont moved right ahead. Strictly business. "I see. Did any of them see the crash, sir?"

A hesitation from the witness. "Well, no."

Quent had sent in two teams of his own men with orders to begin a new investigation from scratch. Twenty men were to concentrate on the mountainsides. Six others were to interview anyone even remotely connected with the crime scene. That was to include employees, campers, vagrants, and even local residents who had been absent the day of the crime.

There were 25 statements in all. In the end, only one person actually saw the collision - through a pair of Steiner prisms.

Agent Dumont's report was thorough but disappointing in its paucity of information. Other than allowing the prime suspect to leave the scene, the Malibu Police had conducted their investigation according to standard procedure. No press was allowed in. No names were published. No word of the accident had reached the public. The collision was recorded as a hit and run.

The Nissan Z convertible had been found at the bottom of the south gorge. The driver's body was reported as missing. And there was no new evidence that might lead them to the location of Luke's body.

The police report described the truck driver as a tall white male, 35 to 40 years old, weighing about 200 pounds, short dark hair and glasses, jeans and black shoes, wearing a John Deere baseball cap. Of the 25 people interviewed, no one had really noticed the truck driver. He had somehow vanished from the scene.

In Quent's mind, the facts were beginning to point in a different direction. It was starting to look like a professional execution.

And Quent was correct. It was a very professional job. But neither Agent Dumont nor Assistant Chief Hawk would learn the true motive behind the crime. Nor would they learn the killer's name, nor his country of origin nor his whereabouts.

The killer was known as Agent 1901 (Cantu), a newbie on the Basement's tactical team. Although the elimination of a single 'target' was a fairly routine assignment, Cantu was still being *evaluated* by his superiors; and so, he had charted each of his moves meticulously. The details in his carefully written report were more than thorough.

In the middle of his police interview at the crime scene, he asked to use the men's room. He already knew the only toilet was located in the back of the Fish Shack's tiny kitchen because he had been there before, rehearsing his moves.

He had assumed that the Malibu Police would be accommodating. And they were. The lead detective pointed the way toward the kitchen and suspended questioning until he returned.

Agent 1901 never returned. He entered the bathroom, removed his baseball cap, his glasses and his over-shirt and stashed them in one of the busboys' lockers.

Wearing an ordinary black T-shirt and jeans, he looked like one of the many restaurant customers. He climbed out the small bathroom window and walked away from the building and into the trees.

Unrecognized among the mass of firemen, plain clothes policemen, campers, diners and restaurant employees, he slipped away easily.

1901 walked north along Canyon Road until he reached his rental Buick, which he'd parked off-road behind a stand of oak trees. He drove slowly inland until he reached the 101 Freeway. He headed south, and merged onto the 405 Freeway. He turned west onto the 10 Freeway, remaining in the slow lane until he arrived in Santa Monica. The journey took two hours and sixteen minutes.

He reported in from a public telephone in the rear parking lot of Chez Jays Restaurant on Pacific Coast Highway. The report was brief. "1901 reporting. Mission accomplished; no witnesses, no survivors." Disconnect.

Orin Pierce listened just once to the recorded message, nodded his head in satisfaction and hit 'erase.'

End of problem.

58

64 Sunshine Terrace – Topanga Canyon

Doctor Cynthia Teller's home in Topanga Canyon was typical of many in the surrounding area; sprawling, ranch style homes, built in the 70s, mostly brown stained wood, a dog run on one side, and a scattering of fruit trees in the backyards. The house was just one canyon south of Malibu; for Cynthia, a 15-minute drive in to work.

Upon the news of Luke's accident, The Facility had shut down. The scientists and clerical employees had grouped themselves into shifts, taking turns, lending their support, bringing food, sleeping on the floor of Cynthia's house, keeping a vigil. Waiting for information.

By the end of the second day, when Luke's body had not been found, the gathering had gradually dissolved into a wake.

Quent had kept in close contact with Cynthia since the Topanga crash. When her cell phone rang, she knew who it was.

"Anything yet?"

"I'm sorry, Cynthia, nothing yet on Luke's whereabouts." He could hear the discouraged sigh on her end. "But I'm not giving up. I got teams out there constantly, combing every inch."

"Thanks, Quent."

"There is some new information, though. Would it be all right if I came over and talked to you about it in person?"

"You don't need to ask, Quent, you're like family. Come any time you like."

Quent and Cynthia sat together in front of a wood burning fireplace in the little room she used as her den. Walled in knotty pine, the room was an add-on, converting part of the patio and its fireplace into a cozy interior space for TV watching.

The rest of the mourners relocated to the living room and kitchen so the two could have some privacy.

"President Crowley just called," she said. "He wants to host a formal ceremony at the White House...to honor..." (her voice cracked) "...to honor Luke's memory. Defense Secretary

Ramsey called as well." She took a slow breath. "I'm sorry Quentin, I'm having trouble accepting this. I don't accept... I don't believe (a long pause)...it's too soon."

Another breath to collect her thoughts. "You said new information?"

Quent's way of being supportive was to stay focused on the investigation. "Yes. When you and I talked earlier, I asked if someone at The Facility could run a test on the gasoline that the tanker was carrying."

"Yes, Brendan."

"Well, according to Brendan, the liquid wasn't gasoline, it was jet fuel; Jet-8 Sulfur."

When Cynthia's expression didn't change, Quent realized his mistake. "I'm sorry, I should have given you the background information first. Number one, the truck was registered to a company called Old South. Old South is a gasoline shipper. They don't carry jet fuel. Number two, the police report shows they reported one of their trucks missing. But that was 48 hours before the crash occurred."

It only took her a moment. "Premeditation?"

"Yes. The crash was not an accident. It was planned in advance. Well planned. We think the jet fuel was an attempt to destroy all possible evidence. After Luke's car went over the edge of the canyon, I saw an explosion. It shot up from the gorge, lit up in a oval shape, and then flamed inward on itself. Your man Brendan described it as a high intensity thermal. He suggested they might have put a small container of jet fuel in Luke's trunk.

"That would explain what I saw. It could also explain why no body has been discovered. The intense heat would have reduced it to ash. I've been forced to change the case from hit and run to homicide. Premeditated murder."

Cynthia's face contorted in disbelief, her mind grappling with the details. Before Quent could ask the next question, she asked it for him. "Who would want to murder...?" She stopped short and stared into the fire.

A moment later she said, "Doctor de Kennesy?"

Quent nodded. "I've gone over it many times. The pieces fit. We know the detonators have been delivered. Luke was already paid for them. He already gave de Kennesy the DILR that triggers them. With Luke out of the way, there would be no primary witness to testify against him. It's pretty clear motivation."

"Enough to arrest de Kennesy?"

"Possibly. But there's a problem doing it that way."

"He could press the button before you could get the cuffs on him," she said.

"Exactly. He could do it while we're knocking at his door."

"Isn't there some other way?"

"I had a team ready go in and try to recover the DILR. I thought we had a shot this morning. Leon and Nanette went grocery shopping. But just as they drove off, two sentries arrived and took up positions at the front and back of the house."

"He's hired guards?"

"Yeah. And when husband and wife got back from shopping, two additional bodyguards showed up to help them carry in the groceries."

"He knows, doesn't he? It's pretty obvious."

"I'd say Doctor Leon knows a lot more than anyone has given him credit for. We did get one small break this afternoon. A friend of mine is captain of the Topanga Canyon Police Force. Javier Camacho. He's got a beautiful young daughter, Riki. She's 19.

"We sent Riki up to Leon's front gate. When she waved, one of the guards came over. She said she lived next door and her father had noticed them. We told her to say that her dad was a contractor and needed some security at one of his sites. The guy wrote his home phone number on the back of a card and handed it over. He works for a well known company in Westwood called 'Reliable.' They mostly do security work at concerts and games.

"We've made some arrangements. Starting tomorrow, two of the four guards will be ours. They know what the DILR looks like. If they're allowed in the house, we'll see. At least it's a start."

Cynthia was about to comment when Quent's cell phone rang. "Hawk." He listened for a moment. "Hold your positions. I'll call you back."

Quent turned to Cynthia. "You got cable?"

"Yes."

"Could you turn on MSNBC?"

Cynthia punched the remote. The MSNBC logo appeared. Slashed across the center of the screen was a red banner declaring 'Breaking News.' The banner then pushed off screen revealing a live shot of a spacious Bel Air mansion. The voiceover explained, “We’re looking at the home of Los Angeles doctor Leon de Kennesy. In just moments we’re told that the doctor, a surgeon at Children’s Hospital in downtown Los Angeles, will be holding a press conference.”

59

The MSNBC cameras pushed in closer. Ten white Doric columns stood proudly across the front of the de Kennesy house giving Leon's front porch a Colonial presence and an official bearing.

A podium had been set up between the centermost columns. Cynthia Teller's eyes widened. "Oh God, what have we done?"

Quent's cell rang. It was Barbara Porter. "I'm in route to the de Kennesy house. Where are you?"

"At Doctor Teller's house."

"Your Doctor de Kennesy claims he's received a threatening message from a group of terrorists. John Lennihan called and asked me to handle it. De Kennesy's lawyer has an unopened letter from the terrorists. I'm going there to accept it on behalf of the government. So far, no mention of Luke Towne, but I think we know where this might be headed."

"Where do you want me?" asked Quent.

"Right where you are. Lennihan thinks that Doctor Teller is the only remaining person who knows all of it. Make sure she stays alive. And find out what she knows. Apparently there's a lot going on behind this that we don't know about. I'll be in touch." She rang off.

Quent immediately called in additional forces, ordering his team to construct a double safety perimeter around the Teller home. When he finished, Cynthia unmuted the TV and they both refocused on the 'breaking news.'

The streets leading up to the de Kennesy mansion were jammed with TV trucks. Telescoping antennas were sprouting everywhere. The mass of camera crews and broadcasters struggled for position, crowding against the heavy iron gates at the bottom of Leon's driveway.

It was quite apparent that Leon had hired some guards. They were the athletic ones, prowling the corners of the lawn, their eyes ever vigilant, their dark suit coats bulging with firepower. Uniformed L.A. policemen were outside the gates, directing traffic and checking credentials.

The privacy of the wealthy remained very well preserved.

MSNBC cut back to their news desk. Close on anchorwoman Conchita Velasquez. "The L.A. police report they've surrounded the de Kennesys' home in order to insure the safety of the doctor and his family. Doctor de Kennesy has agreed to act as a mediator.

"The doctor himself called L.A. Police 24 hours ago, saying he had been contacted by an unnamed terrorist group. He was ordered to publically deliver their message to an official of the U.S. Government. He was told that his wife and members of his family in Lebanon would be slaughtered if he failed.

"Doctor de Kennesy is a renowned Lebanese physician, currently the Director Emeritus of Brain Stem Surgery and Research at Children's Hospital in downtown Los Angeles."

Quentin Hawk and Cynthia Teller sat transfixed. Neither one spoke.

Suddenly, MSNBC cameras pushed in close on two men standing at the podium; the celebrity of the moment, a dark-skinned, heavily bearded man wearing a pin-striped Brioni suit, and his lawyer, a bastion of silver-haired, practiced bravado, holding a Cartier briefcase, reeking of legal proficiency. The lawyer stepped forward confidently and adjusted the microphones.

"My name is C. Desmond Smith. As Doctor de Kennesy's counsel, I will attempt to outline the grotesque circumstances that have brought us here today. When I've finished, the doctor will make a brief statement. I would remind you all that the lives of the de Kennesy family have been threatened. My client is under extreme pressure. And I would ask that you to limit your questions appropriately."

C. Desmond Smith was himself a media star, as famous as most of his clients, most of them high profile, business and entertainment figures. Before beginning, Mr. Smith scanned the press corps, and acknowledged several notables with a slight nod. Then his brow furrowed and he began speaking extemporaneously.

"Twenty-four hours ago, a large unstamped envelope was delivered to this mailbox." Smith pointed toward Leon's unique letter box, a perfectly rendered miniature of the de Kennesy mansion. "In that envelope were typed instructions. Under threat of physical violence, the doctor was ordered to drive to a nearby library. Once inside, he was told to sit facing a particular section of books and wait for further instructions. He was warned not to turn around or he would return home and find his wife...and this is a direct quote, he would find his wife Nanette 'gutted like a salmon, and hung from the roof with piano wire.'"

C. Desmond Smith waited for the shock to ebb. Then he ran his fingers through his hair, as if adding his own gravitas to the horror of the words.

"The doctor did as he was instructed. He sat in the Beverly Hills library for 15 minutes. Eventually, from behind his chair, an unfamiliar voice spoke to him in Farsi. He was told to remain perfectly still. Then, a firm hand was placed on his shoulder and, without warning, the skin on the back of his neck was slashed open with a knife blade.

"Two hands restrained him. And once again he was warned not to turn around. A second voice joined with the first and together they said the words, 'Velayat-e faghih.' I am told these words are a terrorist battle cry meaning absolute Muslim rule of every human being on earth."

Again Smith paused, clearing his throat before delivering his last two lines. "Before leaving, the two terrorists pushed an envelope into the doctor's coat pocket. The envelope was sealed with the doctor's own blood."

C. Desmond Smith opened his briefcase and withdrew the bloodstained envelope. "My client has instructed me to hand this evidence to an authorized member of the U.S. Government." Finished with his part of the performance, the lawyer stepped back from the microphone.

For a moment, Leon de Kennesy fumbled nervously with the buttons of his suit coat – feigning timidity, unwilling to take the spotlight. His lawyer leaned back toward the microphone and said, "The doctor will take a few questions. Mr. Daniels, from CBS, you may have the first question." Leon stepped forward and placed his hands carefully on the sides of the podium as if to support himself.

The reporter from CBS called out, "Doctor de Kennesy, why you? Why did these people choose you?"

Playing the moment for maximum impact, Leon appeared flustered, a simple physician, bewildered by the attention of the press. He began haltingly, "Ah... my name is Doctor Leon de Kennesy. I am from Lebanon. In my country, our research facilities are quite archaic. The equipment in America is decades beyond anything we have at home. When I was offered an Emeritus position at Children's Hospital in California, I accepted without hesitation and moved my family here.

"You ask, why did these terrorists choose me? I don't know. I've never been associated with anything but medicine my whole life.

"I have never been involved in any religious movement. My wife taught Fine Arts at Beirut University. There were radical types on every campus. Perhaps that's how my name was known. I practiced in Beirut for many years. I speak several languages. Maybe because of that...I don't know. I have never been involved in politics. As I said, I don't know. I'm sorry."

Before Leon had finished his answer, a female reporter shouted an accusation. "But Doctor de Kennesy, your own daughter Kathryn is in politics. Lebanon's Ambassador pro tem. She's a major political figure. Is she a part of this?"

"That's it!" yelled C. Desmond Smith. "Interview's over. You people have no decency. For God's sake. This man's family has been threatened."

But Leon would not be moved from the podium. He insisted on giving a response. There was a look of benevolence on his face – almost a smile. "Miss, I am very proud of my daughter's accomplishments. She holds two advanced degrees from the Tyre Graduate School of Foreign Affairs. The two of us have an understanding. It goes back many years. I do not ask her to attend my surgeries. She does not invite me to the U.N. My Kathryn knows nothing about this. As a parent, why would I tell her? It will be hard enough on her when you write these things in your paper."

Leon turned slowly away from the podium. His arm was taken by a stalwart and protective C. Desmond Smith. The abused citizen was escorted back to his front door.

Cynthia Teller pushed back into her couch, shaking her head in disbelief. "Brilliant. That was...as good as I've ever seen. Amazing. I'll guarantee you everyone bought it. Poor Doctor Leon de Kennesy; faithful, loving, respectful father. Learned. Patient. Gracious under fire."

Her jaw poked forward in anger. "Leon the murderer."

Quentin gently pulled her against his shoulder. His response was quiet. "And a mass murderer if we don't do something to stop him."

Cynthia said, "Quentin, you're very good at what you do. I know you're trying to keep me on track. And I appreciate it very much. Thank you."

A moment later, Quent pointed to the screen. "That's my boss, Chief Porter."

Stepping to the podium, Barbara Porter took the microphone. "Ladies and gentlemen, my name is Chief Barbara Porter. I am the Head of the CIA's Department of Counterterrorism. Counsel for the de Kennesy family has delivered to me the unopened envelope received by the doctor. We will examine its contents under laboratory conditions. We will review our findings with the Pentagon and the appropriate actions will be taken. As soon as possible, my office will release all relevant information to the press."

There was an immediate harangue of shouts and questions from the news media; all of it loud, urgent and unintelligible. Chief Porter waited calmly until most of the noise had ceased. One last shouted question hung in the silence, "The public has a right to know."

"Ladies and gentlemen of the press, please bear in mind that the Department of Counterterrorism was created to insure the security of this country. The rights of the public are our primary concern. Our only concern. And our sole, I repeat, our sole responsibility. We will attend to our responsibilities. You will be given details when it's appropriate to the security of the public. Doctor and Mrs. de Kennesy have been most gracious and forthcoming under very trying conditions. I would ask the press to honor their privacy. Thank you."

With that Chief Porter was escorted to her waiting Town Car.

Two hours later, Quent's cell rang. It was Chief Porter. "How are you doing, Quent?"

"Chief, the Teller house has been secured. I've got a double perimeter. Do you want me to come in?"

"No, but call me back on the scrambler. We need to talk."

Quent punched one of the CIA's scrambler lines on his Blackberry and auto-dialed his boss.

Chief Porter picked up where she had left off. "The bloodstained letter has a list of demands. The terrorists doesn't identify themselves with a name. Their demands are what you might expect; sort of a combination of Hamas and Al Qaeda themes. They want the release of all prisoners, an international boycott against Israel. They want contracts with American companies to begin rebuilding Palestine and they want a commitment of $11 billion to start the work. They want some of the money to come from Israel as damages. Some of the other specifics are doable. Bottom line, they're giving us five days to deliver. If we don't, they claim they have numerous bombs already in place in our cities. They claim the destruction will be 10 times the power of 9/11."

"One moment, Chief, let me get some of these demands down."

"Forget about the demands. That'll be the President's problem. Is any of it real? That's our problem. Do they really have bombs in place? I'm going to read part of this letter to you. This part's important to write down verbatim. You ready?"

"Shoot."

"'You have given us seven tickets to eternity. We will use them to send you to hell. The walls will crush your heroes. The Arts have always been reality's decoy.'"

"Reality's decoy? What's that supposed to mean?" asked Quent.

"I'm hoping Cynthia will know. She's the only person still alive who might understand it all. No one at Langley has the faintest idea what's going on. It seems we were purposely kept out of the loop. I'm afraid you're on your own, Quent. And there's not much time. We need her to translate this for us. Is it real? Is it eminent? Because if the answer is yes, we've got ourselves one hell of a serious crisis."

"Question," said Quent. "Based on what we learned from Luke Towne at Staples Center, what's your opinion, Chief?"

"I think we're in trouble. Far as I'm concerned, Staples is conclusive proof. I'd say they've definitely got other bombs in place. I think Doctors Teller and Towne conspired to pull off some kind of rogue operation. I can't imagine why they chose to keep it a secret from the Pentagon, but it's done now. I'd say they got in over their heads. And it's obvious they underestimated Leon de Kennesy. The threats sound very real and eminent to me."

"Cynthia's asleep. She just kind of collapsed on the couch in the middle of the broadcast. They tell me she's been up continually since the crash. And she's pretty shaken up."

"I'm sorry the weight's on you, Quent. But it is. Get her up. And get her talking. Call me as soon as you get something. Godspeed."

60

64 Sunshine Terrace

Cynthia woke up at three in the morning. She made coffee and the two of them sat down at her kitchen table. Quent took a swallow. "We've got a real problem. Let's get to it."

"Okay."

"First, I need to ask you a difficult question."

"Whatever it takes. We're both on the same side."

"Okay, would you say that Luke's dealings with Leon were a rogue operation, I mean, outside the knowledge and jurisdiction of the U.S. Government?"

"Yes." She answered without hesitation, but said no more.

"So...it's you, me and some Israeli guy in Lebanon, right? No backup?"

"Pretty much. The techs at The Facility made the detonators, but they were never told the purpose. The guy in Lebanon is named Ari Shine. He's ex Mossad."

Quent was momentarily at a loss for words.

"Ask anything you think will help. Anything. Motives, accusations, whatever. Please."

"There's some kind of coded message in this terrorist letter. My boss thinks you're the only one who'll know what it means."

Quent pushed the flash memory on his PDA. It was Barbara Porter's digital voice, reading the words from the letter: 'You have given us seven tickets to eternity. We will use them to send you to hell. The walls will crush your heroes. The Arts have always been reality's decoy.'"

Cynthia asked him to play it again while she scribbled some notes. She sat staring down at them for a few moments, then grabbed her cell phone and hit auto-dial.

When Ari answered, she just said, "Ari, do they know you've got eyes on the package?"

"Yes, I'm sorry. They've seen us. But it was strange. Seemed like they already knew we were there. But what the hell is going on over there? It's all over television here."

"Emergency here, Ari. Explain it to you later. Stay close to your phone. But one more question, the 20 new SBNS units, are they in place?"

"Yes."

"Have they picked up any more signals?"

"Nothing yet."

She hung up and scribbled some more notes, made a diagram for herself and then looked up at Quent, a strained expression on her face.

"What is it?" he said.

"No more detonators on Ari's end. I'd say it's 100% real. They've got 'em here. Explosives already in place somewhere in the U.S.. Exactly as they claim. God knows what the President can do about it. Luke and I made a terrible mistake. We played right into their hands. Unless we can get the DILR away from Leon, the country is on the verge of some kind of horrific attack."

"Would you mind going over how you came to...?"

Cynthia's embarrassment and frustration got to her and she cut him off. "It goes like this. We made Leon 10 fully functioning detonators. As a test, he detonated two of them. That leaves eight. We equipped them all with GPS laser beacons. Because we thought they were headed for the Middle East, we hired teams of ex Mossad vets, gave them SBNS units and told them to be ready.

"Then Leon played his feint. He sent one of the detonators to the Art Department at Beirut University. It's where his wife used to teach. The SBNS picked up the beacon and Ari's men surrounded the place. But it was just a decoy. Supposed to convince us that rest of the detonators were also on their way to the Middle East. Exactly what Leon wanted us to believe. And we bought it.

"So, that's three, right? Three from 10 leaves seven. Those are the seven tickets to eternity. Bombs planted in our cities. And 'the walls will crush your heroes.' My guess is, that's a reference to Staples Center. They obviously think the bomb at Staples is still functional. Our heroes are the athletes. When the explosion goes off, many of our 'heroes' would certainly be crushed."

"And 'the arts have always been reality's decoy'? What's that about?"

"Ari and his men have got the Arts Department at Beirut U surrounded. But that detonator is only a decoy, said Cynthia.

Quent said, "And there's no way for us to trace the other ones?"

"No."

"Why can't we find them the same way Luke found the one at Staples?"

"The laser beacons only reach a diameter of 60 miles. We'd have to have a grid of SBNS units stretched clear across the United States at 60-mile intervals. That's why Ari's Mossad teams are spread out at 60-mile intervals. They just happen to be in the wrong part of the world. Our driver driving by Staples Center was a complete accident."

They both sat in silence. Each took a drink of coffee. Finally Quent said, "I need to know as much as you can tell me about the Mind's Eye. As simply as you can. What it does. How it works. Luke said he could diffuse the detonators without Leon being aware of it. How does that work? And, what the hell is a DILR?"

Cynthia grabbed a blank yellow pad and began drawing a diagram. She worked at it in silence for several minutes. When she finished, there were four sheets of paper, each filled with hieroglyphics, placed side by side on the table.

She said, "The Mind's Eye has taken us nearly 10 years to develop. Some of the things I'm about to tell you will be hard to believe. Just accept everything I say as fact. It'll make things a lot easier."

"Okay."

She told him all of it: the Lasocular cannons, the lens implants, the 'thought signals' generated within the human brain, the subcutaneous amplifier, the laser message sent through the corneal lens and received by Phyllis (DILR), and the final conversion into mechanical movements.

She told him of Luke's insistence on being the test case. And finally, she told him about the crowning moment; the mind-boggling demonstration at Langley Air Force Base in front of the Top Guns of Central Command's 1st Fighter Wing; the crowning moment when Luke Towne caused an enormous F18 to move its wings – with his mind.

When she had finished, Cynthia sat calmly, allowing Quent as much time as he needed to take it all in. It took him a while. He traced his finger along some of the lines she'd drawn, deep in thought.

Finally he said, "So you were going to wait for confirmation from Ari. He tells you when the detonators have all been installed in the Middle East. Then when Luke and Kathryn de Kennesy are having dinner with the in-laws, Luke stares at the DILR and shuts it all down. End of story. You'd have an army of terrorists surrounded in the Middle East and you'd have the ring leader in handcuffs here at home."

"Yes."

Without another word, Quent punched the scrambler on his cell, hit the speaker phone and got through immediately to Barbara Porter. "Chief...we believe it's 100% real. Doctor Teller confirms it. I agree. The threat of bombs in U.S. cities is real. The worst possible conditions. As many as seven of them."

"I'm in flight to Washington. Can you text me the substance of Doctor Teller's input?"

"Not exactly."

"Pardon me?"

"It's way technical and too complicated for my 7th grade intellect. Doctor Teller is gonna boil it down to a few sentences. I'll need a little more time to make sense of it."

"All right. In the meantime, have you or Doctor Teller come up with anything...hopeful? Any possible solutions? Some way to stop Leon? Something I could report to the Joint Chiefs?"

"Yes. We're working on it now. As soon as we've got all of the details, I'll call."

Cynthia's eyes widened at Quent's statement. But she said nothing.

Chief Porter said, "Take a breath. Hang in there. Tell Doctor Teller to stop beating up on herself. In my book, she and Luke Towne will always be national treasures."

The call ended. Captain Cynthia Teller Towne rose from the table and headed for the bathroom, furtively wiping away the moisture from her eyes. Her shame overwhelming – an added embarrassment in front of this young CIA agent.

Washington D.C. – The White House – Situation Room

In response to Chief Porter's urgent call to the Chairman of the Joint Chiefs, John Lennihan, an emergency meeting was convened at the White House. In attendance were the President, his Chief of Staff Mike Yost, the Secretary of Defense, the Joint Chiefs, the Head of Homeland Security, the Director of National Intelligence, and the Heads of the Senate Armed Forces Committee. The only 'outsider' in the room was General Orin Pierce – attending at President Crowley's request.

Barbara Porter, dressed in a conservative dark blue jacket and matching skirt, sat alone at one end of the long conference table. When Quent's synopsis arrived, she had shared it in private with her long time friend, John Lennihan. Lennihan advised that for reasons not yet clear to him, the Mind's Eye technology had suddenly become non grata at the White House.

On his counsel, Porter skirted the issue, simply stating in her verbal report that Doctor Leon de Kennesy was a legitimate terrorist. She avoided the term DILR, describing it only as the 'button.' In her conclusion, she emphasized that at the moment, Leon had his finger on it.

She set her notes aside, prepared to take questions. But no one in the White House Situation Room uttered a word. The shock had taken everyone by surprise.

"Gentlemen," she said, filling in the silence, "I realize that the sudden emergence of this threat is mind numbing. The discovery of explosives buried at the Staples Center in Los Angeles represents a horrifying breach of our country's security. Even more disturbing is that to my knowledge, none of our law enforcement agencies, homeland security offices, nor anyone in the Military had any awareness of this situation or its escalating developments. It came out of nowhere."

"What about the scientific community?" snarled Orin Pierce.

President Crowley intervened. "Gentlemen, of course you all know General Orin Pierce. I've asked him to sit in because of his unique knowledge of Special Ops and his four decades of experience. Chief Porter, I believe you and the general have met."

"I don't recall ever meeting the woman," said Pierce, maintaining deniability in spite of the President's slip. Pierce glared at her. "But I would appreciate a copy of her report."

"Here it is, Orin," she said calmly. And placed a folder on the table in front of her.

"Very well, General Pierce, please," said the President.

Pierce directed his remarks toward the Joint Chiefs, ignoring Chief Porter. "Gentlemen, months ago the First Lady happened upon an article in a French newspaper. The article connected one of our scientists with a rather infamous Lebanese socialite, Kathryn de Kennesy. She's the stepdaughter of the same Doctor Leon de Kennesy we've just heard about. Our scientists aren't usually mentioned in gossip columns, so President Crowley himself asked us to look into it.

"A background check of this woman showed her to be highly educated, a rising star in Lebanese politics and a favorite of Rafik Hariri himself. As one might expect, from birth she was exposed to the bedrock of Muslim teaching. Upon further investigation we discovered that in her teens, the precocious Miss de Kennesy was often seen in the company of certain Arab businessmen whose political leanings were thought to be anti-American.

"Her profile worsened in her twenties, when she became more than friendly with several young religious extremists, one of whom has now risen to number five on the FBI's list of most wanted terrorists. We judged the woman to be a security risk, especially given the frequency of her appearances on the arm of Doctor Luke Towne."

Pierce cleared his throat and continued. "We called Doctor Towne in and appraised him of the dangers inherent in his relationship with this woman. He became quite angry, rejected our evidence out of hand and suggested that the Government stay out of his private life. At a second such meeting, when presented with evidence of the woman's questionable past, he attacked one of my agents and injured him badly."

"In light of the CIA's report, I would say the bottom line here is this. Doctor Luke Towne became a traitor or at least became an unwitting collaborator with these terrorists. It was undoubtedly Kathryn de Kennesy that turned him.

"I would add that there's a human element that shouldn't be overlooked here. In spite of his credentials as a scientist, Doctor Towne has been divorced for many years. For that reason, he may have been exquisitely vulnerable to such an experienced spy as this woman."

Pierce affected his most somber escutcheon. "Because of Doctor Towne's untimely death, we'll never know all of the details." He paused, once again feigning sorrow at the loss of a comrade in arms.

"My guess would be that after he delivered the detonators, her interest abated somewhat, and Doctor Towne developed a dangerous case of remorse. So they killed him."

The President said, "Thank you General Pierce. What you've described is a very unfortunate ending to a long career of service. Shall we move on?"

John Lennihan, Chairman of the Joint Chiefs of Staff, had championed the Mind's Eye System and its creators from day one. At 62, Lennihan was 6'3" and weighed a robust 205 pounds. When he cleared his throat, it drew the attention of everyone at the table. "Gentlemen, and Chief Porter, my experience of Luke Towne, the scientist, parallels my experience with Luke Towne, the soldier. He was the second most decorated veteran in the history of our Special Forces. I would remind you all that the so-called smart bombs which we lord above our terrorist enemies were invented by the same Luke Towne."

When Pierce started to interject, Lennihan raised his voice, preempting interruption. His icy riposte was clearly directed toward Orin Pierce. "HOWEVER... a tragic accident has taken his life. His guilt remains unsubstantiated. I will not condone throwing dirt on his reputation before his body has even been found and laid to rest. Furthermore, the man's social life is immaterial at this point.

"I suggest it would bear more fruit if we focused on the emergency conditions that brought us together in this room. The damage from this thing has a potential of terrifying proportions. In my view, we have two relevant questions to answer: one, how do we deal with the terrorist threats; and two, can we trust anything this Doctor de Kennesy says?

Lennihan turned to face Pierce. "So, General Pierce, we've heard your in-depth research on the daughter. What have you got on the father? And why wasn't this information shared with us and the other agencies – as ordered by President Crowley's mandate of December 26, 2004?"

Pierce was accustomed to delivering vitriolic outbursts at his subordinates. He was not accustomed to being on the receiving end. Lennihan would soon feel the snake bite. Mentally he vowed to launch a full-court Basement surveillance on the *smart-ass* as soon as he returned to his lair.

But Pierce was prepared. He had known the question was bound to surface. He had thought long and hard about it. The altering of Towne's bio, the stolen Kalashnikovs, the phone records. It went on and on. There was a mountain of evidence to be squelched. Even the slightest hint of The Basement's role in the de Kennesy affair, and he would undoubtedly be blamed for whatever the terrorists were about to do.

By definition, The Basement's activities were permanently off the books. No papers, no records, no responsibility. Pierce had always enjoyed total immunity. He had assumed that by ordering the murder of Luke Towne, the trail would end.

When the President suddenly demanded his presence at this emergency meeting, he knew how the questions would go.

He had survived four decades of witch hunts and pointed fingers. This would be no different. As he had done many times before, he would simply indemnify himself – totally, completely and forcefully.

"Gentlemen," he said, "We have spent months of work and thousands and thousands of tax dollars investigating Doctor Leon de Kennesy. His credentials are immaculate. The man simply has no prior terrorist connections. That's why there was nothing to pass along to anyone. If Chief Porter's information is accurate and the doctor does have his finger on some kind of a button, then he's blindsided all of us."

End of Orin Pierce's problem.

It appeared that everyone in the room accepted Pierce's explanation without question. *This man is the President's personal confidante. All of us are on the same side here; let's move on. Let's start working on the problem.*

Two of those in attendance had a different response. The momentary eye contact between Barbara Porter and John Lennihan went unnoticed by the others.

President Crowley moved on. "Chief Porter, would you describe in more detail exactly what we learned from the Staples Center?"

When Porter finished describing the potential loss of life the terrorists might have caused by detonating the massive installation of C4 at Staples Center, the President called for a show of hands. The decision was unanimous; the terrorist threat was real. The U.S. was suddenly faced with...a potential massacre. *What course of action should be taken?*

At their disposal was the U.S. Government's complete arsenal of attack forces: Navy SEALs, Rangers, short and long range delivery systems, heat seekers, motion sensors, supersonic delivery systems, smart bombs, unmanned aircraft, missiles – the list was endless.

None of it seemed applicable.

Hours of discussion ensued. No resolution. Finally, after almost four hours, Chief of Staff Mike Yost voiced a new suggestion. "Since none of us has come with a way of stopping this bastard, why don't we start working on delivering some of their demands? Let them know we're taking them seriously. Perhaps it could buy us some extra time. Maybe launch a negotiation of some kind."

President Crowley weighed in. "I think Mike is on the right track. If we can get these people involved in a dialogue, we might be able to get close enough to take them down. Let's split up the demands and work on them individually. We'll reconvene in the Oval Office at, say, 10 tomorrow?

"In the meantime, of course, this has to be kept among us. The public must be protected at all costs. Even the slightest hint of explosives waiting to go off, and the whole country would grind to a halt."

Everyone in the room knew that secrecy was paramount. Everyone also realized the President's true concern. One more terrorist threat and the Crowley Presidency would never recover.

61

64 Sunshine Terrace – Topanga Canyon

Quent and Cynthia Teller had been at it for seven hours. Her kitchen floor was covered with crumpled yellow pages. When the scrambler on Quent's phone beeped, it startled them both.

It was Chief Porter. "Quent, tell me you two have made some progress."

"I don't know about progress, but we do have some thoughts."

"That's more than I can say for this end. Go ahead."

"We started with an obvious question. Leon's got the C4, he's got the detonators, and he's got Phyllis to set them off. More important, he knows that we know all of that.

"So why would he concoct such an elaborate story for the press? The terrorist letter. The bloodstains. His wife gutted. Threats on his family."

Chief Porter said, "Whoa, no one up here's even thought to ask the question."

Quent said, "I think Ari Shine gave us the answer. If the U.S. Government doesn't respond to Leon's satisfaction, he'll threaten to go public. He knows that would send the whole country into widespread panic. It would bring the U.S. economy to its knees instantly without a single detonation. And that in itself would be a major strategic victory for terrorism worldwide.

"It's a twist on classic Sun Zi theory. As he said the most effective way to win a war is to not fight it. If you can immobilize your enemy at his core and not have to engage his overpowering military strength, you win. Over time, your enemy will self-destruct internally. And you win by merely surviving."

Silence from Barbara Porter. Her young assistant, Chief Hawk, was turning into a first rate socio-political strategist. His explanation was both insightful and terrifying. Finally Porter said, "So who's Ari Shine?"

"Damn. I never mentioned him?"

"No Chief Hawk, you never mentioned him."

"Okay, ah...first off, I'm sorry. I just heard his name for the first time a couple of hours ago. And second (Quent struggled to be concise) ...here's the short answer. The guy's really smart, former Head of Mossad Demolitions. So Luke Towne sent him over to Lebanon to establish a back-up response. That's in case something went wrong over here and he lost control of Leon."

"You mean we have a back up response?"

"Potentially. Let me put Doctor Teller on with you. She can explain this part of it better than I can." He punched the speaker phone on his cell and set it on the table in front of her.

Cynthia said, "Hello Chief Porter. I'll cut to the chase if that's acceptable."

"Perfect."

"The detonators have a three-way switch: 'On, off, and other.' All of which can be triggered with the Mind's Eye technology. Quentin told me he had explained that part to you in his summary."

"Yes, I think I get it."

"Okay, the detonators have a three-way switch. The first two are self explanatory, on and off. The 'other' position is actually a remote trigger. Presently, it's connected to four of our most devastating weapons; the Lasocular Cannons. The L Cannon is a magnified laser system developed by us at The Facility. It's now considered the Pentagon's most destructive weapon. It's never been used.

"Colonel Ari Shine and his team have mounted four of these cannons in strategic positions in the Middle East. They're pointed at specific targets which were chosen to achieve maximum impact against the extremist world; that is to say, strongholds, training centers, and locations of extremist Islam militancy. The fourth one is pointed at an important Mosque in Tehran that was once run by Ayatollah Jalali-Khomeini. It was chosen for its psychological effect.

"We got the info on terrorist strongholds and training centers from Mossad. The extent of damages resulting from a single Lasocular blast would be unparalleled in modern warfare. Our scientists at The Facility liken it to complete vaporization."

When Cynthia finished speaking, a stunned Barbara Porter said, "You and Doctor Towne created all of this without informing your boss, Morton Ramsey. Our Secretary of Defense?"

A silence from Cynthia Teller. Then, "Yes."

"Doctor Teller, I don't presume to understand the path you took. I've been in the counterterrorism business for many years. I'm sure there is a good deal more to that story. I look forward to meeting you one of these days."

Another pause from Cynthia. "...Thank you Chief Porter. Thank you for that. And I certainly look forward to meeting you. Can I answer any immediate questions for you?"

"Yes, just let me restate, make sure I've got it all. The original plan was for Doctor Towne to be able to control all possible outcomes by visually communicating with the DILR, 'the Phyllis.' He could set it to 'off' and render the terrorist's bombs useless, no matter where they were hidden. Or, he could switch it to 'other' and cause the terrorists to. . .to self destruct strategic areas of their own homeland."

"Yes."

"All right, last question. There's something curious going on at the White House. I felt it in our meeting and so did the Head of the Joint Chiefs. It was like the White House actually knew about this operation beforehand and something went wrong. And now they don't want any part of it. Can you tell me what happened, Doctor Teller?"

Cynthia Teller hesitated. "Orin Pierce. That's what happened. The President appointed Brigadier General Orin Pierce as Luke's control. It went wrong from the first day. They brought Luke in and told him that Kathryn...that his fiancée, Kathryn de Kennesy, was a spy. Luke refused to believe it. He asked to see proof. Pierce refused to show proof, claiming it was classified information. Luke Towne is the Pentagon's Director of Weapons development. No one has a higher clearance than he does. Pierce's answer was ridiculous.

"Pierce is some kind of a megalomaniac. You can't treat a man with Luke's credentials like an idiot. Luke refused to participate. Pierce threatened to arrest him for dereliction of duty. Then he called Kathryn a high class hooker. Luke's a Military hero for Christ sake. No way a man like Luke could tolerate that kind of treatment. No one has put more heart into this country than Luke Towne. But his heart..."

Cynthia's voice broke for a moment, then she continued. "Luke...just had to take matters into his own hands."

"Thank you Doctor Teller. Say no more. I know this is painful. And I understand. I get it. I appreciate your openness. By the way, I also have some experience with Orin Pierce. I'd say your analysis of the man is quite consistent with mine.

"That being said, I hate to be callous, but we've got a crisis on our hands. So I have an additional question for Chief Hawk. Quent, you said something earlier about working on a solution?"

Porter's question hung in the air. Quent finally said, "Is there any way the President or whoever gets the job of communicating with Leon... is there any way of getting a face to face with Leon? Like a negotiation meeting?"

"Mike Yost has already suggested that. And the President ordered us to start working on the terrorist's demands. Yost's thought was to buy time. You have something in mind about that. About a negotiation?"

"I need to confer with Doctor Teller about it. She'll have to walk me through the process a few more times before I know what I'm talking about. Can we work on it and call you tomorrow?"

"Nothing but faith in both of you. Have at it."

When Chief Porter disconnected the call, Quent and Cynthia shared a look of exhaustion. "How 'bout I get you some sheets and blankets? This couch folds out into a bed. We'll start over in the morning."

"Forget the sheets," said Quent. "One blanket's all I need."

Cynthia returned with a pillow and blankets and sat down next to him. "Quentin, I want to apologize to you for all of this. For everything that's happened. I caused this...and I have no valid...I have no excuse to offer."

"Yeah, like I never screwed anything up on my watch."

"Nothing this big."

"Well you don't have to apologize to me. You're the Navy's leading eye surgeon. The way I read it, this whole thing sounds a lot more like a Special Forces Op than eye surgery. You're just too damn noble to put the blame where it belongs."

A deep sigh was all that Cynthia could muster. Slowly she pushed herself up from the couch and walked toward the hallway. When she reached her bedroom door, she just said, "Good night."

She didn't bother to pull back the covers; she just rolled up in the comforter and closed her eyes. Ten seconds later she was asleep.

At four in the morning, Cynthia's cell phone began playing Clair de Lune. She sat bolt upright, shocked out of a nightmare. Still disoriented she flipped open her phone. "Yes?"

For a moment she listened quietly, then snapped, "Who is this? How did you get this number?"

She was silent for a much longer period. Her jaw clenched tightly. She listened and listened. She drew in a long breath and very quietly said, "I promise." Then she turned on the bedside light and began scribbling on a notepad.

When she reached the living room, Quent was already awake. He could see she was shaking. "Who was that?" he said.

"Kathryn."

"Who?"

"Luke's fiancée. Kathryn de Kennesy."

Quent jumped up from the couch and took her by the shoulders. Her body was quaking. The pupils in her eyes had grown dark and enormous. "What is it?"

"He's alive. They found Luke. He's alive."

"Where? How?"

"She said he has a lot of broken bones. His head is distended. He's got a concussion. He's not responding. He's in a coma. She made me promise to come alone. It's at the old Sand Castle Cottages on Pacific Coast Highway."

"The paramedics..."

"No. They can't. With a Grade 3, they can't move him. He could hemorrhage in seconds."

"What are we supposed to do?"

"They're going to operate."

"Who is...?"

"Leon de Kennesy. He's on his way there now." Cynthia walked to the door and reached for her coat. "I'm going to see if I can help."

62

Pacific Coast Highway, California

The Sand Castle Cottages were condemned and abandoned in the 1980s. A Palisades landslide had forever put an end to the 12 little wood cabins that once were a popular overnight spot for lovers. Over time it was swallowed in sections by thick Manzanita bushes and untended brush. By the 90s, it had disappeared completely behind the Coppertone billboards that parallel Pacific Coast Highway.

Gone from sight and gone from memory.

In her haste, Cynthia had missed it completely on her first pass. But on the way back she caught a glimpse of an old blue roof hidden behind the trees and she quickly whipped across the double yellow lines onto the dirt shoulder. She nosed her car as far off the road as the brush would allow and got out.

Using a small flashlight, she pushed through the layers of overhang and brambled kudzu until she finally emerged on a potholed strand of dirt-covered black top. Three old cottages stood side by side, leaning into each other for support. Two cars and a hospital truck were pulled in close at Cabin #3.

As she approached the cabin, its door opened quickly and a woman stepped out onto the slanted porch. She wore tennis shoes, her skirt was wrinkled and there was blood on her blouse; but even in the darkness, her beauty was striking. She stepped down from the porch and extended her hand. "I'm Kathryn de Kennesy. You must be Cynthia. Thank you for coming."

It was hard to know what to say. After letting go of Kathryn's hand, Cynthia said, "Why did you take him here?"

"You're a doctor. You can help him more than I can. Please come and look at him."

"Why did you bring him here?"

"We didn't. We found him here. It's a long story. Please..."

As she lead Cynthia up the steps, Kathryn pointed to a fractured plank on the porch. "Be careful of this hole."

Luke was laid out on a wooden pallet, his body covered with blood and purple contusions. The left side of his forehead was pushed out a full three inches. His skull was obviously swollen. Two bags of fluid were plugged into his left arm.

Adjacent the bed, two women, dressed in green scrubs, crossed back and forth setting up lights and equipment.

"These are surgical nurses from Children's. They're here to assist. Leon should be here any minute now."

Cynthia moved forward and carefully touched Luke's hands, his feet, and then his cheek. He remained unresponsive. Lifting his eyelids, she peered into each eye using her little flashlight. Then she asked one of the nurses for a stethoscope. After checking the vital signs, she stepped away from the bed and spoke to Kathryn. "He's barely alive."

Kathryn closed her eyes in despair and sat down on one of the equipment cases. "Leon should be here any minute. I pray to God he can do something."

"What is wrong with you people? You staged all of this! Leon is a terrorist for God sakes. He's about to murder thousands of us."

Kathryn stood up defiantly. "Listen, Mrs. Doctor Teller, my stepfather is coming here to save my future husband's life because I asked him to come. If you can help in any way, that's why you're here. If you're not, then get out."

The door opened suddenly and Leon rushed in. Dropping his coat on the floor, he walked straight to the bed and repeated the same procedure that Cynthia had just completed.

"Hang two more bags of plasma," he said to one of the nurses. Then he turned toward Cynthia. "You the ex-wife?"

"Yes."

"I need permission to cut."

Cynthia said nothing; staring at Leon, her brow furrowed. *This monster is also a prominent brain surgeon.* She struggled a moment longer, then made the decision. "Granted."

"You're the Navy's ocular surgeon?"

"Yes."

"Could you intubate?"

"I can do the anesthesia as well."

"Relieve the cranial pressure or he'll never make it. You agree?"

"Yes."

"If we get him stabilized, I've got an ambulance outside. We'll take him to St. John's. I can get some scans and we'll see what we've really got here. Agree?"

"Yes."

"Let's do it."

From that point on, Doctor Leon de Kennesy and Doctor Cynthia Teller merged into a surgical team. So high was the level of shared skill and experience that most of the initial procedures were accomplished without need of verbal communication. There was an instant rhythm of motion and purpose. It was as if the they had spent years perfecting a most delicate precision.

When it was time for Leon to begin drilling, the two of them locked eyes in a shared moment of prayerful entreaty: hers to Christ, his presumably to Allah. And he began.

Six hours later, Luke Towne was resting in the Intensive Care Unit at St. John's Hospital in Santa Monica. He was registered as 'Mr. Luke Phoenix.' His coma was still profound, but his vital signs had climbed remarkably.

The hospital pager called for Doctor de Kennesy and he quickly left for the consultation room to study the initial MRI results. Cynthia and Kathryn were left alone, sitting across from each other at a small side table.

Kathryn broke the silence. "Doctor Teller, do you think Luke will regain...do you think he'll ever...I'm sorry Doctor please...would you share your thoughts?"

"Kathryn, I've been a surgeon in the U.S. Navy for 23 years. Your father is by far the most brilliant and facile surgeon I've ever ever experienced. I would put my own life in his hands without reservation."

"Thank you."

"I will tell you also that I know something about the physical stamina that lives within Luke Towne's body. And it's a remarkable gift. If you had told me that he'd walked away from the crash, I wouldn't have been surprised. I also know something about his will to survive. Rangers are made out of some other kind of material than the rest of us. Hardened steel. We couldn't have two more skilled male humans working together on fixing this problem.

"As far as recovery goes, a lot of it will depend on how much oxygen deprivation his brain experienced. And your father is an authority on the treatment of intracranial hematoma and cerebral hypoxia."

Cynthia fished her keys out of her purse, tucked her coat under her arm and stood. "Miss de Kennesy, Luke told me about you. At the time, I assumed his emotions were probably exaggerated by passion. I still don't understand the strange pride that older men get from the affection of a younger woman. But you should know something, he never said a word about your accomplishments, your fame or the way you look. Not a word. What he said was, you were golden – inside.

"I don't understand the conflict that our two countries are locked in. But I'm sorry for the things I said about your father."

Cynthia walked to the door and stopped. "One more thing, Miss de Kennesy. I can see the gold."

63

Washington D.C. – The Basement

After the conclusion of the White House emergency meeting, Orin Pierce saluted his Commander in Chief and retired to his Basement lair. Immediately he called an urgent meeting with select members of his staff. "I want a Class I on John Lennihan. I want to know everything the son-of-a bitch had for breakfast since he was two. Is that clear?"

To his subordinates, sitting stiffly before him, the meaning of a Class I investigation was abundantly clear. The senior agents had an expression for it: 'Find the dirt or lose your shirt.' Many an experienced agent had been demoted for a failure to uncover what Pierce *guaranteed* was buried somewhere in the evidence.

Pierce's next objective was accomplished with a 60-second phone call to President Crowley. "Mr. President, I recommend you appoint Barbara Porter as official liaison between de Kennesy and the CIA. All negotiations should be handled through her."

"Why on earth would you suggest that, Orin? You can't stand the woman."

"Mr. President, I'll guarantee there's going to be some civilian casualties before this thing is over. Staples was just a warning shot. No doubt about it. Hang the job on Porter and you transfer the responsibility away from the White House. Lay it on the CIA. The sooner you can distance yourself from this, the cleaner you'll be when the shit hits. And undoubtedly, sir, it will. You see what I'm saying?"

"Thank you very much, Orin. I'm going to hang up and order it done immediately."

#10 Colonial Road – Bel Air, California

Leon de Kennesy stood in his library admiring the small Gauguin sketch – a study done in 1882 for Gauguin's future masterwork 'Still Life with Fruit and Lemons.' Leon hinged the painting to the left and began working the tumblers on the wall safe set into the cherry wood paneling. "Nana dear, I need to show you how to work this thing one more time in case something happens to me." He removed Luke's DILR from the safe and sat down on the couch.

Nana came into the library carrying a tray of coffee and lemon tarts. "What are you talking about, Leon? Nothing's going to happen to you. You're just the messenger. You don't shoot the messenger, dear. Remember your Shakespeare. You're the conduit. The mediator."

"Yes my scholarly nymph. But there's an older text. Sophocles. 'No one loves the messenger who brings bad news.' They may not shoot me, but I'm not going to win a popularity contest either. It doesn't matter. Just in case of emergency, I want you to know how to trigger this thing."

"All right. All right, but I don't know what you're worried about. You just saved a man's life. Our son-in-law scientist. The famous soldier. When the press finally gets hold of that one, they'll canonize you."

"Yes, but our son-in-law is a traitor, Nan. What happens if they find out?"

"Who's going to tell them? Certainly not his partner. If the woman talks, she goes to prison with him."

"You know me, it's always about contingencies. It suddenly dawned on me that it might be a good idea to try and keep the son-of-a-bitch alive. Who knows, some day in the future, he gets stressed enough, I might get him to steal us a nuke. One never knows. Anyway, will you please just go over this one more time with me, to make sure?"

Holding the DILR aloft in front of Nana, Leon reviewed the sequence of button pushes necessary to trigger the detonators.

She said, "So, it's the exact same sequence you used to test the first two detonators. Right?"

"Correct."

"I got it, okay? I memorized it the first time. So, now let's have some coffee. Let's talk about 4th of July fireworks."

"I'm afraid we've blown that one. More likely it's gonna be the 5th."

"Because...?"

"Because of the goddamn idiots in Houston." Leon began angrily ticking off the names of the target sites on his fingers. "Staples, the Mormons, the Mall, 1st Tennessee, all of them done without a hitch. All primed and ready. But the goddamn Texas bunglers screwed it up."

"I thought you said a child could do it?"

"Well, apparently they sent a child to do it. One of the youngest ones goes into Chase Tower. He's got the key to the storage unit with him. He gets in the elevator and when he steps out in the basement, there's a bunch of Brinks delivery guys in uniform, all carrying guns. The kid panics and jumps back in the elevator. When he gets out of the building, he runs for the parking lot. Then he sticks the detonator in the dirt behind a bush, throws the key in with it, and walks home."

Nana chuckled. "Not to worry, dear. It could have been worse. We've come a long way. A very long way. One more day isn't going to ruin anything. Forget about the 4th of July. Five bangs will be just as loud on the 5th. Here, eat a tart."

Leon took one huge bite of Nana's meringue tart and followed it with a swig of coffee. She could sense his mood lightening.

"Speaking of tarts, darling, what happened with the lovely Barbara Porter this morning?"

When Leon's laugh had ebbed, he found himself gazing at his wife in profound appreciation. "You know it's been a lot of years, Nan. Mullah Rockmani has been magnificent. We've got help from Omar himself, but I could never have gotten anywhere without you. You're a diamond."

"Thank you, my darling. But the credit belongs to you. A weaker man would have given it up long ago. I'll tell you a secret, all my strength comes from you."

The two conspirators embraced for a moment. Then Leon reached for the rest of the tart and swallowed it down before answering her question.

"Porter. Yes. The Queen bitch. She put me on speaker phone this morning. I think there must have been a bunch of government big shots sitting with her. She said she was confident that most of our demands could be accomplished. They were working 'round the clock on it. But they needed another week to arrange the finances.

"Truth is, we needed an extra day to get Houston ready, so I screamed into the phone, 'One more day. And that's it. I'll give you one more day. Otherwise, I go public about the explosives. Is that what you want Porter?'"

Nana quoted Sayyid Qutb. "'So comes the day of reckoning. The sky shall rain fire. The sea shall boil. And Satan's dogs shall be cast into the depths of hell.'"

The Lumber Yard – Two days until detonation

Secretary of Defense Morton Ramsey sat in Chief Porter's office, smoking a cigar, twitching his brows nervously, agitated by the lack of progress. President Crowley had sent him down to L.A. to 'manage this crisis.'

He had initiated the proceedings by presenting Joseph Quentin Hawk with a Presidential letter of commendation for his handling of the Staples Center crisis. "The President and I both feel that you personally thwarted what might have been the most horrific terrorist attack this country has ever experienced."

Quent took the envelop from Ramsey's hands, but didn't open it. "Thank you Mr. Secretary, I am honored to receive this commendation just as I am honored to serve. But in all seriousness, I feel there is still a lot more to do before this threat has been thwarted. As to the Staples part of it, if it weren't for Colonel Luke Towne's performance under fire, and his directions, I would have been just a bystander."

"Thank you Agent Hawk," said Ramsey, dismissively, looking at his watch. "Now, isn't it time for this video conference to get underway?"

A 62" plasma screen and two large dry-marker boards had been set up in front of Barbara Porter's desk. She, Ramsey and Quentin Hawk were about to enter a massive video conference with representatives from the Pentagon; Langley; the House Subcommittee on Terrorism, Human Intelligence, Analysis and Counterintelligence; the Senate Finance Committee; the Office of Homeland Security; and the NSA.

Everyone involved, save Porter and Hawk, had some kind of an introductory statement to make, acknowledging the crisis. The Staples Center incident represented a horrendous breach of national security. A powerful Jihad had somehow walked through our defenses as if we had none. No one could even put a name to them. Complex security measures had been implemented by all law enforcement agencies. The Homeland Security Department itself utilized 22 separate agencies and employed a staff of 200,000.

Yet no one seemed prepared for a threat of such magnitude.

As the exchanges began, there seemed to be no obvious culprit, no single agency to blame. As a result, everyone in the loop feared his agency would inherit the guilt. Their verbal exchanges were shot through with tension. Interagency frictions surfaced over the smallest details. President Crowley's ill-advised order to merge the Intel community was once again transforming problem solving efforts into a witless power struggle.

At the end of the third hour, all they could agree on was that Leon de Kennesy had to be taken out. That left only two possibilities: bring in the sharpshooters and attempt a kill immediately, or incinerate the de Kennesy house with the doctor in it.

Barbara Porter was quick to point out that neither option was foolproof. Neither could guarantee that Leon or his wife or an accomplice would not survive long enough to push the button.

"What if the 'button' isn't inside the de Kennesy house when the action is taken?" asked Porter. "At any given time, the device might be in the doctor's pocket or in his hand, or somewhere else, miles away from the scene."

By the end of the fourth hour, there was still no practical solution. No tactical suggestions. No real consensus. And time was running out.

A frustrated Chief Barbara Porter waited for a moment of quiet amidst the furor. Her voice was calm. "Gentlemen, what say we go to our separate corners, contemplate the alternatives we've developed thus far and reconvene at 7 a.m. Pacific Time?" So high was the level of mutual frustration that all parties agreed readily, and the conference was terminated.

Quentin waited until the plasma screen had gone dark. "Unbelievable," he shouted. "What a pile of pussies."

Secretary of Defense Ramsey whipped his body around to face Quent. "Listen Hawk, just because you got a medal to pin on your shorts doesn't mean you're anything more than a goddamn CIA spook. If I don't see a major change of attitude, I'll see to it that you're out of a job by Monday."

Chief Porter remained calm, her voice articulate, her tone warm. "With all due respect, Mr. Secretary, you do not have the authority to terminate anyone in this agency. These are my people, and termination is my responsibility.

"Morton, I'm aware that you are under severe pressure here. All of us are. We have a grave situation on our hands. And this *intelligence* effort is supposed to be a collaboration. I'm sure you remember? Back in December? The 'albatross' mandated by your administration?"

Her voice intensified. "Having said that, I won't permit threats to my agents, nor insults to my career. Mr. Secretary, you and 25 of your kind of people just wasted four hours of my time. Not one useful idea emerged! From you or the uniforms who get paid to kiss your ass. So until that changes, you might consider staying the hell out of the goddamn spook business – as you so delicately put it."

Chief Porter pushed back her chair and stood. "Now unless you have something of value to contribute, I've got a terrorist threat to deal with. So why don't you let us get on with it and tomorrow we can start over with a clean slate."

Ramsey stood up angrily. "Very well, Chief Porter, it's clear that you don't want my help. Or at least you don't think you need it. So I'll just step aside and let you handle it all. I'll inform the President that you've got this one under control and our help is not needed. There's no need for me to waste my time at your meeting tomorrow. I'll be returning to Washington tonight."

With that, Ramsey left the CLOPS office (still unaware that CLOPS existed) and ordered his driver to take him to the north runway at LAX.

The door closed behind Ramsey, and after a moment of silence, Chief Porter said, "Well, congratulations, Quent."

"I'm sorry, Chief Porter. I don't know what to say. I just kind of forgot he was here."

"I'm talking about the Presidential commendation."

"Oh...yeah that. Well, it was all Luke anyway. Not me."

Porter continued. "And thanks for the set-up. I met Ramsey when he was a lowly speechwriter. He sucked at that job too. I've been waiting 10 years for the right moment to tell that pompous son of a bitch to bite it."

"So it wasn't a screw-up?"

"Oh God yes. It was a major screw-up. As your CIA superior, I'm required to write you a reprimand. And you'll get one. As your CLOPS supervisor, I'm telling you to throw it in the garbage."

"So you agree? They were a bunch of pussies."

"That's one way of describing the finest minds in our government's Intelligence community."

"Then you don't agree?"

The corners of Porter's mouth turned down. "Well..."

Neither of them spoke for a moment.

Finally Quent said, "You know, it's a little easier now to understand why one would consider pulling 'a rogue operation.'"

Porter knew where he was headed. “We talking about Luke Towne or us?”

Quent answered, “Somebody’s gotta call a play here pretty soon, don’t you think, Chief?”

Part III

64

The Rogue Op - Bel Air, California

Two hours later, the CLOPS brain trust, aided by technical input from Dr. Cynthia Teller, had formulated a plan. Their own rogue operation. By 7 p.m. it was in play.

Direct routes from the Santa Monica Airport to Bel Air were laid out, their traffic lights coordinated, and cross streets blocked off where necessary. Time was of the essence; none of the key players could afford to be delayed by traffic conditions.

As CIA's Counterterrorism Director, Barbara Porter closed down the Hotel Angeleno Joie De Vivre and converted it into a command center. The old, circular-shaped landmark hotel (formerly a Holliday Inn) was located at the intersection of Sunset and the 405 Freeway – a four-minute drive to Bel Air's West Gate. An additional minute's drive to the de Kennesy mansion.

After dark, Special Forces teams began landing at the Santa Monica Airport and were hastily bivouacked at the Angeleno Hotel. Racks of specialized equipment were ferried into the otherwise quiet little airstrip and loaded on to Military trucks borrowed from Westwood's Holderman Army Reserve Center.

The fifth floor of the Angeleno Hotel was reserved for a cross–section of government and Special Ops personnel. The diversified group included Charles Wolfe, Head of the Senate Finance Committee; a team of communication specialists from Langley; two U.S. Navy SEAL tactical advisors from Coronado; the directors of L.A's Water & Power and Pacific Gas & Electric companies; a CIA video crew; the LAPD Bomb Squad; and a team of costume consultants and makeup artists.

At 1 a.m., after consulting with the SEAL advisors, Quentin Hawk addressed two SEAL DA (direct action) teams. He would order them to move into the Bel Air neighborhood covertly, choose strategic positions around the de Kennesy mansion, and set up their sharpshooters.

He began by passing a duplicate of Leon's silver Blackberry among the SEALs. "Gentlemen, this is the device he'll use to detonate the bombs. He'll probably be holding on to it at all times as a security blanket."

Each of the SEALs held the Blackberry for a moment, then passed it on.

"Critical parameters, one more time. If the target is holding the silver Blackberry in hand, a clean shot to the head still won't guarantee us success. Detonation requires that four buttons be pushed in sequence. We have no way of knowing if the first three buttons have already been pushed leaving only the final button. A perfect hit could cause the target to fall on the Blackberry and inadvertently activate the last button. Or the Blackberry itself could fall to the ground and discharge the final button. A direct hit to the silver Blackberry could cause immediate detonation no matter what buttons have been pushed.

"So... any order to fire will most likely be a last resort. I will be in constant contact with your team leaders. No shot will be fired without my direct order. No matter what appears to be going on, no shot fired without my command. Clear?"

The SEALs answered as one voice. "Clear."

"As far as we know at the moment, there will be three targets. If possible, depending on your vantage points, I'd like to have permanent crosshairs on all three. We'll identify Leon de Kennesy as #1. His wife Nanette, as #2. And their lawyer, as #3. I realize that none of this is may be possible given your positioning. But this would be optimal.

"On your way into the target area, a CIA video crew will be trailing you from a distance. Their orders are to blanket the mansion's entrance and exits with their closed circuit cameras. You've got first priority in all field ops. They'll stay out of your way.

"One last caution. Leon de Kennesy is an extremely dangerous individual. His motives are still unclear. His responses are unpredictable. Should he or his guards see anything out of the ordinary, he could easily push the button. It's absolutely critical that you not be seen. If you need to inform a property owner that you're taking a position in his backyard or nearby, we've prepared these handouts."

Agent Dumont distributed the one-page documents to the SEALs.

"These will identify you, verify your authority and give the individual or family a number to call if they need further explanation. Good luck. And stay out of sight."

CLOPS Command Center – Joie De Vivre – Los Angeles

When Quent returned to the command center, Chief Porter was reviewing reports from LAPD officers positioned at each of the Bel Air gates. She rang off and motioned Quent to join her at her desk. She had spoken with Leon earlier in the day but had not had time to bring Quent up to speed.

"You were right, Leon was open to negotiate."

"How did it go?" asked Quent.

"It bought us an extra day."

"Great."

"What do I hear in your voice?"

"Nothing Chief."

"You've got a different idea?"

Quent said nothing.

Porter persisted. "Something weird, am I right?"

"Weird?"

"Quent, that's the reason I gave you the damn job."

"Weirdness??"

Porter was all business. "Chief Hawk, let's hear it."

Reluctantly Quent said, "Well...I think Leon's going to push the button no matter what you negotiate. I think all of this is just a way of getting international attention. Ari Shine agrees. When Leon's garnered enough press for his Jihad, I think he'll just push the button."

"The same Dr. Leon who just saved Luke Towne's life?"

"Yes."

"And your reasoning?"

"Two reasons. First, Leon's people didn't pack C4 under buildings all over the U.S. just to let themselves get negotiated out of the chance to kill thousands of us. Second, they've been telling us that's what they want to do for decades. Khamenei said it clearly in 1993: 'Death to America.'"

"So... what are you suggesting?"

Chief Porter's assistant, Ruthie Bender, was working at a desk nearby. Before Quent could answer Porter's question, Ruthie slammed down her phone and moved quickly toward her boss. "Excuse me Chief, you need to have a look at this."

Ruthie pointed the remote control at the bank of closed circuit monitors. Monitor A switched to a close-up of the de Kennesy home. Thick black graffiti had been sprayed across Leon's front gate. The words were large and ugly.

Arab pig must die
Kill all Muslims

Quent riffled through his stack of notes. "I've got something on that, Chief. Here it is. You remember on the first day we managed to get two of our guys on staff, posing as guards."

"Yes."

"Well, two hours ago they both got fired. Mrs. de Kennesy apparently saw one of them on his cell phone and that was it. But he managed to get a text out to us anyway. Hard one to figure. The text says Leon hired the graffiti painters himself. And he told 'em what to write. Gave them the exact wording."

In the stunned silence that followed, Ruthie whispered, "What the hell..?"

"Leon has his own gate graffitied?" said Porter. "And he writes the words himself? What kind 'a game is this?"

"No idea," said Quent.

An hour later, they found out.

Porter had established a discrete line into the hotel for Leon to use during their negotiations. Suddenly, at 3:30 in the morning, Leon's line rang. She answered and switched to speaker phone. "This is Chief Porter."

"Have you seen the front of my house?" Leon shouted.

"I'm not at your house, Doctor de Kennesy."

"I'm being threatened. There's graffiti all over the front of my house. Death threats. Our lives are being threatened. My wife is terrified. I'm terrified. All I'm doing here is trying to help out, and now they want to kill me.

"So you listen, when tomorrow's meeting is over, I want a jet waiting at Santa Monica Airport. A military jet to take my wife and me to safety. This is not negotiable. We want to go back home to Lebanon. My only hope is to go public. The only way to protect myself is to do it in front of the American people. And this is not negotiable either. You get Mark

Hernandez with his FOX camera crew here at my house tomorrow. I want them to broadcast the whole thing – live."

Porter said, "We don't broadcast terrorist negotiations to the public, Doctor."

"Well, you're going to tomorrow. I want the world to see the pressure I'm under and what the American government is going to do about it."

Porter said nothing.

"Did you get that, Porter?"

She could see that Quent was aching to respond. She nodded her permission.

Quent said, "Fox News Live. Presenting Leon's very own reality show. American Idol on steroids. Helicopter shot of Leon speeding down the 405 to the airport. Fade into the sunset as our hero jets home to Lebanon. That's a good one, Doc."

"Who said that?"

"I'm one of the guys assigned to protect you and your fat-ass wife, Jocko."

"Don't you get smart with me, mister. Whoever you are. You listen. I'm doing America a service here. I'm trying to mediate this situation for you. Save American lives."

"You honestly think we're buying that crap?"

"I honestly don't give a damn what you think, sonny. You'll do it. Or you'll all drown in blood."

Leon smashed down the phone.

Dead silence in the command center. Fifteen agents and their assistants had overheard Quent's assault on Doctor de Kennesy. All of them were thinking the same thoughts.

Chief Porter's eyebrows knit together. "Quent, let's you and I take a walk."

Once they were out of the suite and into the hallway, she stopped walking. "You gambled he wouldn't push the button?"

"Not really."

"Not really what?"

"It wasn't a gamble. I knew what the result would be. So I wasn't gambling."

"Explain please."

"It's unbelievable. At the moment, he's got us participating in his charade. Pretending we don't know that he's the one with the button. It's not about some mysterious terrorist Jihad. It's about Leon. He's the one controlling the Jihad. He's the one driving all of this shit. The graffiti thing was the final proof. Tomorrow when the cameras are rolling, he'll offer to turn over his Phyllis, but only after he's safely on a plane. Poor threatened Leon. He's so scared. The TV watchers will be all over it. 'How can we deny this innocent man safe passage back to his homeland? He's a saint. God yes, fly him home.

"He'll promise to contact the terrorists when he's safely on the plane. Once he's in the air, he'll give us the finger, fly off to Lebanon and push the button on the way.

"The American people are his insurance policy. That's what the TV cameras are for. To protect him. He said as much. It's the way he plans to get himself and Nana to the airport. It's his getaway."

As Porter thought it over, the knot in her forehead began to loosen. "You figure the minute we let the TV cameras in there, he's got us over a barrel."

"Unless we come up with some kind of workaround."

"You have something in mind. I can tell."

Quent began outlining one of several plans for dealing with the TV broadcast. But in the middle of his explanation, he was notified that Cynthia Teller had arrived downstairs and was waiting to drive them to St. John's Hospital.

Chief Porter squinted, trying not to second guess her Assistant Chief, but unable to restrain her own curiosity. "I can't help wondering about...uh, isn't this rather unusual timing for a hospital visit? Is there something you haven't told me about Doctor Towne?"

"No. Not exactly. But I thought if he could tell us something about the Mind's Eye process that we don't know, maybe it could help us turn the damn thing off."

"I thought he wasn't able to speak yet."

"He isn't."

Nothing else needed to be said. The desperation implied in Quent's answer was dramatic enough. Chief Porter simply nodded, wished him "Good Luck" and went back to work.

Quent took the elevator down to the lobby and climbed into the passenger seat of Cynthia's car. "Hi Quent," was all she said. Without another word, she squealed out on to the 405 and raced toward St. John's Hospital.

St. John's Hospital – Santa Monica

In the elevator, Cynthia explained, "Luke's registered under the name Luke Phoenix. It was Kathryn's idea. She wanted his name kept confidential. Said she didn't want the murderer to know he'd failed."

Quent said, "This Kathryn woman is really something. First she tries to have him killed. Then she calls a murderer to operate on him. Then she checks him into a hospital under a fake name to make sure he's protected."

Before Cynthia could respond, a large man wearing a baseball cap stepped out of Luke's hospital room. "Good evening Chief Hawk. Ah...Sir, my partner is down the hall going to the little boy's room."

"Hi, Duke," said Quent. "Don't worry, I know you guys are on it. Duke Furillo, this is Doctor Cynthia Teller, Luke's partner...and former wife. Doctor Teller, Duke is one of our best."

"Glad to meet you, Duke. And very glad you're here."

"My pleasure, Doctor Teller."

Turning toward Quent, Duke said, "Sir, a Miss Kathryn de Kennesy was here most of the night. She left this morning when we came on. Said she'd be back this afternoon."

"Any change in his condition?" asked Quent.

"Miss de Kennesy said he woke up a second time. And he blinked his eyes in response to a question she asked him."

Cynthia said, "That's very good news. Doctor de Kennesy has put him on Dilaudid for pain. So many broken bones in his upper torso. Dilaudid's five times stronger than morphine. When Kathryn called me last night, she said that Luke woke up another time and said her name."

As Head of Ocular Surgery for the U.S. Navy, Doctor Cynthia then reverted to form. "If he actually recognized her, that would be a fantastic sign. But sometimes comatose patients make physical movements, and loved ones mistake them for recognition. Often they're just involuntary muscular contractions and they don't indicate conscious awareness. But speaking is potentially a wonderful sign."

When they entered his room, Luke was barely recognizable. There was an oxygen tube taped beneath his nose. His upper torso was completely covered in a plaster cast as were both of his arms from shoulder to wrist. Bags of fluid were draining medicine into the veins of both of his hands. His head was entombed in gauze except for small openings for his eyes, nose and mouth.

Cynthia immediately opened the chart that was clipped to the foot of his bed. After paging through the report she said, "He's made remarkable progress; but it's still too early to know the extent of damage to the brain."

"So, is it safe to wake him?"

"We can try; but we can't force it. If he doesn't respond to verbal stimuli or to gentle touch, he's not ready. And it's best to leave him alone. Usually, it's a wait and see proposition."

Luke did not respond to anything.

65

Bel Air – West Gate – California

LAPD officers had been stationed at the Bel Air gates around the clock for the last 48 hours. Their job was to turn away anyone who was not a resident. Their presence was explained to locals was as routine preparation for a Presidential visit to an unnamed family living *behind the Bel Air gates.*

Anchorman Frank Hernandez and the Fox News team arrived at the West Bel Air gate 1½ hours before they were scheduled to be admitted. Hernandez became enraged when he was refused immediate entry.

As the agent currently in charge at command central, Angie Dumont took an angry call from Fox station manager Fredrick Landau. "You must be new to the LAPD, Officer Dumont. The President is a public figure. You can't shield him from our news team. It's part of the Constitution. Freedom of the press."

"Listen closely Mr. Fair and Balanced," said Angie, "I don't work for the LAPD. I work for Homeland Security. And the President isn't coming to visit. That was just the cover story disseminated by the LAPD to the local populace. We called Mr. Hernandez yesterday and explained that to him, informed him of the real circumstances, and offered him an exclusive to cover it. You might want to ask your own people what story they're covering before you demonstrate your ignorance any further."

"You can't use that tone with me, lady..."

She cut him off. "One more thing; impeding an action by the Department of Homeland Security carries some heavy jail time. In that regard, you might inform Hernandez that he's here as our guest and he will be admitted exactly when he was told to be here. And last of all, Fred, you're milliseconds away from being arrested for obstruction. So it's your call. Would you like to waste any more of my time?"

The line went dead.

Angie Dumont smiled to herself. She was already learning a lot from Chief J. Quentin Hawk.

#10 Colonial Road – Bel Air, California

The de Kennesy mansion sat on a beautifully landscaped knoll. A flight of 76 concrete stairs was sculpted into a gentle slope leading to its lower terrace. At the bottom of the stairs, placed dramatically in the center of a eucalyptus grove, were a slate-bottomed swimming pool and a red clay tennis court. On the eastern side of the property, overlooking the tennis court, was a long rectangular structure known as 'the pool house.'

Renowned designer Kelly Wearstler had been hired to do the de Kennesy pool house in exactly the same style as the cabanas she had done at the Miramar Hotel in Santa Monica. Nana de Kennesy had spent a week at the Miramar, waiting for some final remodeling touches to be completed at the Bel Air mansion. While there she had fallen in love with the hotel's cabana décor.

The spectacular pool house cost Leon $350,000 (plus construction and plumbing) and was featured on the cover of Architectural Digest. The interior was done in two-toned sand-colored sisal flooring, rich chocolate-colored canvas furniture and white canvas curtains which separated the long space into a series of semi-private cabana sections. Depending on the number of guests, the curtains could be pushed aside to incorporate any number of guests.

Visitors reached the de Kennesy pool house by walking down the concrete steps, traversing the lush tropical plantings of the lower terrace, crossing a stone bridge and following the path to the pool house's opaque glass doors.

Family members simply took the elevator to the interior tunnel that ran beneath the tennis court.

Detonation – July 5th 2005 – The Pool House

Nana de Kennesy, acting as Leon's behind-the-scenes Svengali, had arranged the interior of the pool house to look like a congressional hearing; one long dais for the U.S. Government was set opposite a much smaller table for the de Kennesys and their lawyer.

American Goliaths versus Little David.

During their security inspection of the pool house, Chief Porter's team had been allowed to set placards on the dais to indicate the seating arrangements. Seating was a critical element in the elaborate CLOPS masquerade that was about to get underway.

From left to right, the placards read: John Thomas, L.A. Architect; Charles Wolfe, Head of the Senate Finance Committee; Barbara Porter, CIA Counterterrorism Chief; Binyamin Eitam, Israel's Minister of Finance; Quentin Hawk, Advisor; Cynthia Teller, Senate Select Intelligence Committee; and Martin Crowl, Assistant U.S. Attorney General.

Only two of the officials at the dais were genuine. The Finance Committee's Charles Wolfe, a familiar face in Washington and frequent guest on 'Meet the Press;' and Chief Barbara Porter, CIA Counterterrorism, the official in charge.

The other five were players - part of a perilous deception.

All of the imposters hoped that the makeup and wardrobe experts had done an adequate job of aging, disguising and dignifying their fake identities.

The Fox News team was allotted two camera set-ups, one behind the main dais, and one behind the de Kennesys. Before he was allowed to set up, Anchorman Frank Hernandez was given a list of restrictions. No cell phones were allowed inside the pool house. Questions would not be permitted. Whispered commentary was permissible so long as it could not be heard by the meeting's participants. Once the meeting began, there would be no communication between the camera crews and the broadcast truck.

Attempting to sound like a peacemaker, Leon had insisted, "Negotiations cannot and will not be conducted with guns present." To that end, Leon's bodyguards stood at the top of the exterior stairs and thoroughly patted down every person before allowing anyone to descend to the lower terrace.

The only weapon in the room would be Leon's DILR.

Chief Porter opened the meeting by addressing the TV audience. "Ladies and gentlemen, you are about to witness something unprecedented in the history of U.S. security efforts. This is a live broadcast of our government's efforts to come to terms with a major terrorist threat against our citizenry.

"We are at the Bel Air home of Doctor Leon de Kennesy, the Head of Brain Stem Research at Children's Hospital in Los Angeles. The doctor has been contacted by a nameless group of terrorists. They threatened to murder his family if he refused to communicate their demands to the U.S. Government. After verifying the authenticity of the terrorists' claims, your government has agreed to open a dialogue and consider their demands.

"At Doctor de Kennesy's urging, the officials on this dais have come here to interact with the terrorists. In a moment, President Crowley will explain this decision in more detail."

Standing behind his camera team, Fox newsman Frank Hernandez whispered to his team, "Push in close on Chief Porter's face." His audio and video feeds were being sent directly to the Fox News mobile truck parked at the curb in front of the de Kennesys' house.

But the Fox News truck was empty.

Ten minutes before the meeting was to begin, Homeland Security Agents, acting in the interests of national security, had removed the Fox technicians from their positions. The Fox team was moved to a windowless bus (aka holding tank) parked two blocks away from the de Kennesy home. As an extra security measure, CIA agents had then taken possession of the mobile news truck and rendered it inoperable.

Unaware that the feed had been pulled, the colorful Hernandez whispered his running commentary into his microphone. "The woman speaking is Barbara Porter, our country's Chief of Counterterrorism. This is one tough lady with 20 years' experience as a CIA operative."

Chief Porter continued, "Doctor de Kennesy is operating under extreme pressure and has expressed his desire to simply facilitate this communication, and then be allowed to return with his family to the safety of his home in Lebanon. As soon as this meeting is over, we will provide safe escort for the doctor and his wife to the airport.

"And now, President Rundle Crowley wishes to express his personal gratitude to this courageous individual."

At that moment, the DILR concealed in Leon's breast pocket began to ring. The startled de Kennesy pressed the cell phone to his ear. "Yes."

"Doctor de Kennesy, this is a call from the President of the United States. Perhaps you would put him on speaker phone so our viewers might hear President Crowley's words of gratitude."

Although Leon had not been told about the President's call, he instantly he realized the power of the moment. It would be seen as a momentous accomplishment by his extremist financiers. And by terrorist interests globally. Most important, it would be undeniable certification of success of his Silent Jihad.

Leon quickly pushed the speaker button and set *Phyllis* carefully on the table in front of him. Then he leaned forward and placed his forearms on either side of the PDA like a protective sphinx, sheltering the device with his with his body, vigilant, ever aware of its potential.

The moment of truth for Quentin Hawk had arrived.

On the far left of the dais, seated behind a faux name placard that read 'Architect John Thomas,' was Captain Mo Morris, Squadron Leader of the 1st Fighter Wing U.S. Central Command. And on the far right of the dais, masquerading as Attorney General Martin Crowl was another Top Gun, Captain Dink Moran Jr. In the center, posing as Israel's Minister of Finance, was ex Mossad Colonel Ari Shine. All three of the ersatz 'government officials' had been trained by Cynthia Teller to communicate visually with Phyllis.

It was now a question of sight lines and timing.

There was a planned pause before the President began speaking. The pause and the spurious praise that would follow were a subterfuge. All of it choreographed to buy time for the imposters to make a visual connection with Phyllis. The three of them had been positioned to cover 180 degrees of Phyllis's DILR lens directional potential.

Unfortunately, Leon set Phyllis down so that her lens was pointing directly at Ari Shine. Ari's rate of contact (25 seconds) was markedly slower than the Top Guns whose weeks of practice had honed their times to a mere 9 seconds.

Instantly Ari's face went blank as he began the cycle of thought cues he had learned at the Hangar. His ability to focus was legendary. But the pattern of thought cues he had memorized so many weeks ago were difficult to summon. He had to reboot the mental process several times.

"This is the President of the United States. Doctor de Kennesy, I wish to thank you publically for your service to this country. Under these most dire of circumstances, you have put your family's safety at risk. And you have unselfishly come to our aid. I want our citizens to know how important this contribution is to our national security. I know I speak for all of them when I assure you that we will not forget your name nor your courage."

From the dais, five pairs of eyes were riveted on Phyllis's faceplate, waiting for double green lights to flash indicating that a successful contact had been established.

The President's remarks lasted almost 45 seconds. No green lights appeared.

Unlike most cell phones which have a speaker on the back and a mic on the front, The Facility's techies had moved Phyllis's speaker to the front of the device. Consequently, there was never a need to flip it over to hear the speakerphone more clearly.

In the midst of the President's remarks, Leon realized that the sound of the President's voice was aimed in his direction. *The Muslim world must hear every word of this.* Quickly, he spun Phyllis around, leaving her lens angled slightly to the left.

Ari's sight line was compromised.

As the President started to sign off, Cynthia interrupted him. "Mr. President, this is Doctor Cynthia Teller. Doctor Leon de Kennesy, this remarkable man, has given us another very special gift that even you are not aware of. One that has gone unnoticed. One that the doctor has never mentioned." Her eyes flicked momentarily to the right, toward Captain Mo Morris, her star pupil.

She slowed her voice dramatically, attempting to buy as much time as possible. "Two nights ago, in the midst of death threats to his own family, Doctor de Kennesy raced across town to perform an emergency operation that few surgeons are even capable of. I was there to act as his assistant. Doctor de Kennesy literally saved the life of one of our country's premier scientists. A man whom you have personally honored with a medal of courage, Doctor Lukas Towne."

Phyllis's tiny green lights suddenly blinked twice and went dark. Captain Mo Morris had done his job. Cynthia simply stopped talking, slumped forward and cradled her head on her arms. With an exhausted sigh, she whispered to Quent, "You're on."

Quent looked toward Barbara Porter and they shared a moment of satisfaction. In the odd silence of the moment, Leon sensed that something had changed. He snatched Phyllis and slipped her back into the safety of his pocket.

Quent stood and began walking along the back of the dais. When he spoke, his words held an edge of confidence that can only come from powerful certainty. An edge that Leon, victor of a thousand battles, would surely recognize.

"Doesn't matter where you put it now, Leon. The game's over. You just don't know it yet."

Leon kicked back his chair and rose to his full stature; renowned surgeon, millionaire inventor, 40 years in the trenches, 6'3", 195 pounds of extremist bile rumbling behind his beard. He shouted into the cameras, "Citizens of America, you are my witness. Is this the way you Americans speak to your allies? Your friends? Your healers? Am I to believe the words of your President or this mercenary puke of a soldier?"

"They can't hear you, Leon. We pulled the feed. There's no video. It's dead air. The dais, the cameras. It's all bullshit – just like your terrorist threats."

Leon reached into his breast pocket and withdrew Phyllis. "Oh really! Why don't you ask the scientist bitch there next to you? Ask her about the thousand pounds of C4. I've already pushed three of the buttons. Ask her what happens when I push the last one."

Leon waved Phyllis high above his head, his large fingers wrapped securely around the faceplate. At the same instant, the voice of a SEAL team leader spoke into Quent's earpiece. "Crosshairs on target #1. At your command."

Quent pressed his finger against his ear. His words were audible to everyone in the pool house. "Do not fire. Repeat. Do not fire."

Then he spoke to Leon. "I don't want them to kill you yet, Leon. I have more to say first."

Leon laughed. "You idiot. They would have killed me by now if you weren't afraid I'd push the button."

Quent sat back on the edge of the dais, locker room style, comfortable. "Well, there's a bit more to it than that." Quent's confident attitude was having its effect on Leon. He moved to stand behind his wife. He put his left hand on her shoulder.

"Nana's not going to get you out of this one, dickhead."

"You think I'm afraid to die for my faith? You think that soldiers of Allah should fear the power of Satan? The devil you serve.?"

"Here's the deal, big shot. Luke didn't tell you the whole story. He tricked you. I guess he tricked Allah too. You push the last button on that faceplate and half of the Middle East goes up in smoke."

Leon crossed his arms in front of his chest, protecting Phyllis in the fold of his forearms. "Let me tell you a story, you pig American. When I designed the trigger that blew a hole in the side of Flight 209...you remember Lockerbie, don't you? Before I killed 259 of you pigs, they told me the same thing."

Someone gasped. There was a commotion somewhere behind the dark canvas curtains. Leon continued, his venom overflowing, spitting out the words. "Oh, it'll never work, Leon. It'll never work. That's what they said. The plane is bomb proof. You can't sneak anything big enough on an airplane.

"You're insane, Leon. You can't bring down the mighty American airliner. Well, count 'em asshole. Read your history. Count the dead ones strewn all over. . .Lockerb..."

The sound of the pop was insignificant. But the result was devastating. The front of Leon's face exploded in a blob of red goo sliding down onto the back of Nana's neck. His body fell forward on top of her, his weight forcing them both underneath the table.

Poking out of the canvas behind Leon's table was the square black barrel of a Glock 27 – still pointed where Leon's head had been. The gun wavered. Then dropped to the floor. The shooter's body fell awkwardly through the canvas and collapsed on the floor next to the weapon.

It was Kathryn de Kennesy.

In the madness of the scramble that ensued, Nana de Kennesy pulled Phyllis out of her dead husband's hand, hesitated a moment, then slowly raised herself up behind the table.

From the dais came a deep-voiced scream. "In the name of Allah, don't do it!" The words were in Farsi. The voice belonged to Ari Shine. "Nana. It's true what he said. I put the weapons there myself. Inside Beirut and Beit Lahia. Where your fighters were born. Where their families are. You'd be killing your own people. Mrs. de Kennesy, for God's sake, don't do it. These weapons were never supposed to be used. It was supposed to be a stalemate."

Nana shrieked, "We are Shaheed (martyrs of Islam). The Caliphate is our destiny. You will not defeat us with threats." She raised the DILR above her head.

Quent had raced from the dais and was now standing directly in front of the blood-spattered, wild-eyed Nana de Kennesy. He shouted into her face, "Go ahead, Nana. Do it! Do it! Kill your own people. It's what we want."

On Nana's face – a sudden confusion. A moment of uncertainty – her expression clouding. In that instant, Quent launched himself over the table, arms extended, pronating like an airborne linebacker, reaching toward the DILR in her raised hand.

At impact, her small body was no match for his 217 pounds. As they fell backwards, he was able to wrap both of his hands around the DILR. And just before they hit the ground, her grip relaxed. It was a simple task for him to pry the little PDA away from her.

Before Quent could get to his feet, two of his agents had their hands on the hysterical woman, dragging her away from the commotion. Quent stood and shouted into his mic, "Stand down. Stand down."

A SEAL sharpshooter, braced firmly in an adjacent eucalyptus tree, lifted the barrel of his Bushmaster A3 BBL rifle and removed his crosshairs from Nana de Kennesy's left temple.

Inside the pool house, Quent saw Cynthia moving along behind the dais looking expectantly in his direction. He held up the DILR and ran back to the dais.

Hunched over Phyllis's bloody silver faceplate, hands shaking, Cynthia carefully entered the failsafe code as a final precaution.

EPILOGUE

Chief Barbara Porter convened an immediate debriefing session at her headquarters at the Angeleno Hotel.

In attendance were Charles Wolfe, Head of the Senate Finance Committee; Dan Horgan, the SEALs advisor; Watch Commander Mike Panser of the L.A. Police Department; Cynthia Teller; Quentin Hawk; and Ari Shine.

Each participating member was to make a formal statement from which a summary document would be prepared. At the request of John Lennihan, Chairman of the Joint Chiefs, Chief Porter was to submit two documents; one, the all-inclusive document for the Murder Book, and the other, a 'coverage' document to be used by the Crowley Administration.

One by one, each participant gave a description of his knowledge, participation, and/or his observations of the relevant events.

In his statement, Quentin Hawk explained that, given his limited knowledge of the DILR's functions, he feared Nanette de Kennesy might have had time to somehow reactivate the device, and so, he had Dr. Teller enter the fail safe code.

Suddenly, in the midst of Quent's statement, every TV monitor in the room began to flash. The cable news media was about to go 'live' to present 'breaking news.' But the audio feeds in the Hotel's conference room had been turned off in preparation for the debriefing session.

When the monitors finally held picture, there was no sound. As a result, the otherworldly scene that splayed across the multiple screens was presented in a kind of eerie silence.

The images were dark and hard to distinguish. It was obvious, however, that all of them were aerial views. They showed a 2½ square mile section of charred desert sand. But the devastation below was so complete that nothing was recognizable; no familiar forms or structures, just a few burning hot spots. Whatever had been there before had somehow been vaporized.

The surrounding air space which was blackened by a thick plume of powdery dust, as if a volcano had spewed its innards 3000 feet into the atmosphere.

The volume in the conference room was suddenly restored in time to hear the commentator say, "Experts are not sure how this happened. The devastation covers about two to three square miles. But there was no aircraft within 50 miles of the scene. Experts are telling us that no known missile could have caused this unusual pattern of demolition. Whatever it was that caused this destruction – no one has yet taken credit for."

Quent's face was knotted in disbelief. "But we deactivated the DILR."

Ari Shine spoke up. "Yes, we did. But I can explain what happened."

All eyes on Ari Shine.

"The Mind's Eye visual command was supposed to shut down the DILR. It did. But apparently Nana was able to reactivate the device by reentering the code. And I think before Quent got to her, she pushed the final button."

Ari looked toward Cynthia Teller whose face had turned ashen. She affirmed the possibility with a nod of her head.

Ari continued, "But in case something went wrong, there was one additional failsafe measure. Colonel Towne created it. He called it a double down. It was to be both 'a proof of concept,' and 'an international terrorist wake-up call.'

"He had us install each of the four Lasocular Cannons in different strategic locations in the Middle East, all according to plan. But he instructed me to activate only one of them – the one in the desert. What you are witnessing at the moment is the total annihilation of a Hamas training camp in the southern desert of Waziristan."

St. John's Hospital – Santa Monica

Kathryn de Kennesy was taken by ambulance from the de Kennesy home to St. John's Hospital where she was placed on the 8th Floor Psychiatric Ward for observation. EMTs at the scene reported that she was mute, that all muscle and motor activity had ceased, that her limbs had become rigid, and that she was unable to maintain eye contact.

After enumerable tests including Magnetic Resonance Imaging, Magneto Encephalography and Positron Emission Tomography, specialists at St. John's Hospital reported that Kathryn's brain structure and function had been altered. They listed the cause of her condition as intense physical and emotional trauma.

Their diagnosis was advanced catatonia.

Prognosis

Catatonia normally responds quickly to medication. Renowned psychiatrist Doctor A. Pack was brought in to administer psychopharmacological drugs; but after several days of treatment, he reported that he had been unable to elicit any response.

Ten days had passed. Kathryn de Kennesy remained speechless, immobile and unresponsive.

In Room 901, one floor above Kathryn, Luke Towne was making slow progress. Chief of Staff Doctor Arlen Woods was guarded in reporting his prognosis. "As long as there's an improvement each day, even a small one, he's headed in the right direction. And his prospects for recovery are good."

Electroconvulsive therapy was suggested as the next step in treating Kathryn's condition. When consulted, Doctor Cynthia Teller refused to allow shock therapy and requested instead that Kathryn de Kennesy be moved upstairs into the same room with Luke.

Six days later, Kathryn de Kennesy called down to the hospital kitchen to order a special breakfast on behalf of patient Luke Phoenix. Three weeks later, the couple left St. John's Hospital; Luke, seated comfortably in a wheelchair pushed by his fiancée, Kathryn. They were flown to a private mountain retreat to continue the lengthy process of healing.

Togetherness proving to be the most powerful recuperent.

Blood from Luke's body was found high in the trees of Topanga Canyon by ex-Basement mercenary Ollie Jordan. It was Ollie who tracked the semi-conscious Colonel to the Sand Castle Cottages and notified his fiancée. The remarkable tracking skills he inherited from his Nez Perce ancestors will not soon be forgotten by Colonel Luke Towne, nor by Quentin Hawk. In the future, Ollie might well become a valuable asset.

The Manuscript

A Quentin Hawk novel

Brian Neary

Turn the page for a preview of

The Manuscript

1962 – Cu Hong – Dien Bien province, Vietnam

Major Orin Pierce was famous for his generosity. As the chief scheduling officer for the U.S. Military Hospital in Vietnam, he had arranged for many critically injured Vietnamese to be treated in a facility otherwise reserved for American casualties. Among the provinces along the South China Sea, Pierce had earned the very reverent nickname of "Saint Orin."

But the Major's special assistant, Sin Lee, has remained a mysterious addendum to the Major's noble life in Southeast Asia. To all who knew him, Pierce was a kind-hearted, efficient, and generous military officer. By contrast, his right-hand man, Sin Lee, was known to be an evil, cold blooded, manipulative psychopath.

It was a strange liaison; a counterbalance of good and evil. And it raises questions about the much-vaunted Major Pierce; the same Pierce who now holds the title 'Brigadier General' and who for many years has served as Head of Presidential Black Ops. The once generous "Saint Orin" has somehow become the most feared presence in the White House; a moniker he has enjoyed for three decades.

It began more than four decades ago.

The Cu Hong – Vietnam – 1962

The Cu Hong (*gorge*) settlement was five square miles of distressed humanity – crushed together like cans of compacted garbage – left to rot in the blistering sun of Southeast Asia.

The Cu Hong is home to the White Hmong, a tribe of ethnic refugees, descended from the mountains of southern China in the 18th century.

Known as 'mountain people,' the White Hmongs have been outcasts for two centuries – a tribe without a nation, shunned by the mainland Chinese, impoverished by decades of war, and paralyzed by their country's neglect.

Their *town* was a slaughter of hovels and lean-to shacks roofed with flattened beer cans and tinfoil. Their wealth was reckoned in bamboo poles and discarded pieces of plywood. Their privacy was marked with sections of chain link fence. Their meals were fried and boiled and eaten on dirt floors.

The way in to Cu Hong was not listed on any map. It wasn't a road, but rather a downhill tangle of cracked cement and yellowed vegetation.

At 3 p.m., on a blistering July afternoon, an old Mercedes slowly navigated the declivity of the potholes and gravel leading to the Hong's one entrance. The edifice was marked only by where the concrete ended and the dirt and garbage began.

The car had no license, no chrome, no markings to distinguish it from a hundred others mired in the gridlock of Southeast Asia; yet everyone in the Cu Hong knew exactly whose car it was.

The Mercedes stopped in the dirt. Its driver, Sin Lee, unfolded from the front seat, stood upright in the road and brushed the dust from his bent frame. He was dressed in ragged peasant clothing; a wrinkled, sand-colored hip-length shirt and loose-fitting black pants. His wide-brimmed felt hat was pulled low to cover his embarrassment – Sin Lee's face had been terribly scarred by fire.

His gate was awkward, his shoulders stooped, yet there was one glaring exception to his disheveled pretense. Sin Lee was never seen without his briefcase – a black Cartier of highly polished alligator skin with gold clasps and ornate gold handle grips.

The sight was as much a contradiction as the man.

Hundreds of dark eyes watched him from the shadows as he walked purposefully into the heart of the Cu Hong. He was the only outsider who entered the place without fear.

Three minutes into the labyrinth of alleys and crawl holes Sin Lee arrived at the dwelling of Pham Po Anh. The pathetic patch of dirt was only distinguishable from the rest of the hovels because of its front door – a frayed piece of dull red carpet stretched between rusted tent poles.

Sin Lee was expected. The instant he arrived, a hand reached out from inside and pulled the remnant aside. Sin Lee stepped through. And there, in the humid darkness, the Anh family stood at attention. The little space was charged with their anxiety. They had prayed this day would come.

Sin Lee spoke softly. "My friends, your wish has been granted. Bring the boy to the Hospital at 2 p.m. tomorrow. The surgeons will operate tomorrow morning. And when they are finished, his face will be normal."

He pulled a sheaf of papers from his briefcase and handed them to the father. Then he hoisted one of the couple's twin children into his arms. There was a horribly disfiguring gap in the center of the child's upper lip. Pham Junior had been born with a cleft palate.

"Your son will be handsome. I guarantee it."

The mother came forward, tears streaming from her eyes. "We have no money. How we deserve this? We cannot pay. Is this true? Can this be true?"

"Yes, this is true. I promise."

Mrs. Anh bowed her head, took hold of Sin Lee's hand and pressed it to her face. "You are great man, Sin Lee. From God. A holy man." Tears poured down her pale yellowed cheeks.

Sin Lee gently drew back his hand and lifted her face. "No mother, not I. It is Major Pierce. He pays for everything. He is the great one. I just deliver the papers for him."

He set the little boy down and watched him scurry back behind his mother's skirt. He spoke again, his voice even softer than before. "Major Pierce is a very great and generous man. He asks that no one mention his name. He asks only for your prayers and your silence. Nothing more."

"Every day of my life, I will pray for him," she replied. "I will ask the holy Duc Chi Ton to bless him always."

"Good," answered Sin Lee.

The father's eyes flicked toward his wife then back to Sin Lee. There was an awkward silence. Mrs. Anh hastily pushed the two little boys ahead of her and disappeared behind a frayed gray sheet that walled off the family bedroom.

The two men stood facing each other in the dank silence. Sin Lee, his scared face twitching in the heat, Pham Po Anh, his thin body trembling in fear.

"Well. Where is she?" said Sin Lee impatiently.

"My daughter is very beautiful. Perhaps the Major Pierce might pay me something for her?"

"That was not part of the agreement. Bring her now!" The voice had lost its kindness.

"But the Major Pierce...he is such a kind..."

"He isn't in this!" roared Sin Lee. "This part is mine! Between you and me! You knew that. Pierce doesn't know. He can never know. If I ever hear one word from anyone about our arrangement, you and your sniveling wife will be dead before the sun goes down on this shithole you live in! Do you understand me?"

"I get nothing at all for her?" whined the little Hmong.

"She's worthless. You should pay me to take her, you greedy little roach."

Pham knew it was true. In Hmong society, girl children were considered a curse, an unwanted mouth to feed. The streets of Vietnam were filled with urchins, most of them girls cast out by their fathers.

Feral children. Generations of them.

Pham Po Anh tried again. "But... "

Sin Lee flew across the room, driving his large body into Pham's 90-pound frame, smashing the little Hmong into the chain link wall of the shack. Like some giant human forklift, he drove his pointed fingernails into Pham's throat. Harder. Deeper; closing the airway.

The skinny arms began working up and down like a helpless wire puppet. But it was hopeless. In seconds Pham's tapered eyes began to bulge.

Sin Lee watched impassively. The face began turning red. Then blue. And just as Pham was about to lose consciousness, Sin Lee released his grip a fraction.

"Stay with me now. Stay awake. Take a breath. We're not finished yet. Let me help you." Sin Lee pushed his scared face close to Pham's ear and bit down hard on the wrinkled ear lobe.

Pham screamed out in pain. The scream gradually deteriorated into a quiet blubbering.

"That's better, you piece of shit. Now, where is she? Her name is...?"

Pham didn't understand he was being asked a question. He made no reply.

"Her NAME, you ignorant toad. What's her name!"

"May May," croaked Pham.

"Yes, that's it, May May. May May's going to Arizona, Mr. Anh. She's being adopted. By an American couple. They've seen her picture. I gave them my word."

Pham Po Anh stared at the ground, overcome with his own disappointment.

"So here's the agreement. I take the girl now. You say nothing. Not one word EVER. Or there's no operation. No Major Pierce. You understand? No operation. Your ugly kid will go through life with a sinkhole for a face! And I'll see to it that the other one gets an inch cut out of his upper lip too, so they'll still match."

Sin Lee pushed the terrorized little Hmong down on his knees in the dirt. "Now, where is she?"

"Waiting by your car, Sin Lee."

Sin Lee drove off with little May May sitting on the seat next to him. There was no couple in Arizona waiting to adopt. Little nine-year-old May May was never seen again. She simply vanished – on the same day that Sin Lee did. The same day that Major Orin Pierce was called to Washington to assume his new job.

BRIAN NEARY began his literary career in Los Angeles as an English teacher. When he was fired for utilizing tape recorders and video technology as part of his curriculum, he launched an exciting career touching all parts of the entertainment industry.

As a TV writer...numerous comedic and dramatic writing credits, among them SNL, General Hospital, Owen Marshal, Hawaii 50 and Late Night.
As a journalist...staff writer for Lifestyle Magazine, contributor to LA Times, R&R and People.
As a cable exec...cofounder of the cable network E! Entertainment; the channel's first VP of Production
As a composer...writer/producer of two #1 Billboard hits, numerous gold records, named to Rolling Stone's Hot 100 producers. Created more than 80 single recordings by a wide range of artists including Kenny Rogers, Olivia Newton John, Quincy Jones, Eric Clapton and Dionne Warwick.
As a live show producer...the road show of The Wiz; producer/director of The Funny You Should Ask comedy show for HBO.
As a video game designer...created "Slammin" a multi player Sony PlayStation game.
As a screenwriter...recently honored with the prestigious Hollywood Screenplay Award for the feature screenplay 'Legend.' A Member of WGAw, ASCAP, BMI.
As a nerd...a degree in English from Loyola University and an MBA from USC.

Brian lives with his wife Karen in Carlsbad, California where he's working on the next Quentin Hawk adventure. Visit his website at bneary.com.